Dr Duncan Graham is a writer, senior counsel at the New South Wales Bar and medical doctor. He is the co-author of *Why Patients Sue Doctors* (Elsevier, now in its second edition).

For well over a decade, Duncan acted almost exclusively in cases involving men and women suffering from asbestos-related diseases. He has litigated numerous test cases for defendants, cross-examined many people dying from mesothelioma, and read thousands of medical articles on the subject. He was also responsible for developing legal strategies, especially in the handling of scientific evidence, to address the asbestos diseases epidemic. Duncan's knowledge of the history of the asbestos industry, the medical issues concerning asbestos, the role of governments and big business over the years, and the key issues in asbestos litigation is unparalleled.

His practice now focuses on medical negligence and medical law. He has represented hundreds of people injured through the negligence of hospitals and doctors. Duncan has also specialised in class actions involving pharmaceuticals and medical devices. He recently acted for patients injured by faulty orthopaedic implants, and for thousands of women injured by manufacturers of vaginal mesh like Ethicon. He has a reputation for taking on challenging cases, particularly those raising complex medical issues.

Duncan lives in Sydney.

Also by Dr Duncan Graham,
co-authored with Bernard Kelly, AM and David A. Richards, OAM

Why Patients Sue Doctors

Where the Dust Settles

Duncan Ewing Graham

First published in Australia in 2025 by Dr Duncan Graham
d.graham@mauricebyers.com

A catalogue record for this work is available from the National Library of Australia

ISBN: 978-1-7638250-3-1 (paperback)
ISBN: 978-1-7638250-2-4 (ebook)

Produced by Broadcast Books, www.broadcastbooks.com.au
Edited by Amanda O'Connell
Proofread by Puddingburn Publishing Services
Cover design by Christa Moffitt, Christabella Design
Cover photograph: Rose Marinelli/Shutterstock
Typeset in Times New Roman 11.5/18pt by Matthew Oswald, Like Design
Printed by IngramSpark

Where the Dust Settles is a work of historical and legal fiction. It is based in part on well-known actual events, participants in those events, publications, researchers, places, legal cases and matters of public record. All names, characters, conversations and the places and events in which the story unfolds are, however, products of the author's imagination. Any resemblance to living or deceased persons is entirely coincidental.

To KEG, for all my reading and writing

Prelude

i. 1932

Harry Langlands was an ugly bastard. He wandered the northwest of Australia as a prospector, looking for the wealth of minerals he was convinced lay underground.

His wants were simple and easily satisfied under the big blue canopy of the sky. He spoke very little. He did not need to. Out in the dusty hills, amid darting geckos and spindly, sharp bushes, there was plenty of room to roam without coming into human contact. He liked it that way.

Harry knew the rough red mountains of northwest Australia better than most. Yet every twist of a honeycombed gorge revealed secrets he could never have imagined. He found iron ore down one gorge and staked a claim. More discoveries in the mighty Hamersley Range followed. Money came in, but Harry kept searching.

It was while traipsing through the heat and dust of Disaster Gorge, a narrow slit between terraced walls of rock, perpendicular to the spine of the Hamersley Range, that Harry noticed a steel-blue sheen in an escarpment, the like of which he had never seen. Venturing to the floor of the canyon below, he found chunks of red crusted rock with a core of blue grey. He picked up a fist-sized piece and noticed the straight-fibred blue material beneath the red-brown shell. The fibres lay in perfect parallel lines like miniature organ pipes. Harry plucked at them and the fibrous strands expanded, breaking up into sharp blue needles as he teased the strands further.

It was magical stuff.

He looked up at the cliffs and the blue mineral that ran all through the narrow gorge. Whatever it was, Harry figured it must be valuable. He collected some samples and set off for the nearest town to lodge a claim.

Harry's hunch proved correct. It was special stuff. Very special. He had discovered blue asbestos. And companies wanted it because of its amazing properties. It was a fire retardant, a good insulator. It could be added to cement and sand to make building sheets or pipes that were light and strong. It was indestructible, resistant to acid, heat, the weather. Harry had no difficulty selling it.

But the money that rolled in didn't make him happy. The fortunes others made from asbestos didn't make them happy either. In the end, many wished Harry had left the stuff lying on the ground in Disaster Gorge.

ii. 1946

The chairman was a mammoth of a man, well over six feet and approaching twenty stone in weight. He had a voracious appetite for food, money and acquisitions. He was nicknamed 'the Big Ship', although nobody had the courage to say it to his face. 'Let's just say that there's a great deal of money to be made,' he rumbled.

'Yes, but the stuff's apparently dangerous,' objected his chief executive, who looked more like a watchmaker than the manager of a national conglomerate.

'Nonsense!' the chairman thundered. 'The report from the government medical officer says that asbestos is … here, I'll quote it to you … "only dangerous in the asbestos textile industry at doses in excess of five million particles per cubic foot".' The chairman glared at his chief executive officer, beads of perspiration forming between the thin grey wisps of hair slicked back over his scalp. 'Now, last time I checked, we were planning to mine this blue asbestos, not make clothing out of it! So, what's the problem, Fergus?'

Fergus Hamilton sighed. He had little knowledge of mining, engineering or medical science. What he knew was how to avoid unnecessary expenditure and rein in a spendthrift board. A slight Scottish number-cruncher who had worked for V&L Ltd for two decades, he was tough and stubborn despite his frame. He could smell a risk as soon as anyone in business. Hamilton also knew a crank when he saw one. Sir Llewellyn Williams was definitely that. He had to find a way to turn the big man away from his lunatic views.

'Llew, that sounds more like sophistry than sound advice. We have no idea whether conditions in a textile factory will be similar to the exposure conditions in our mine and mill. Shouldn't we first find that out?'

'Sophist-bloody-what? Look, we asked the government and they gave us an answer. End of bloody story as far as I'm concerned.' If he'd been on the savannah, Fergus would have run for cover, fearing a charge from a bull elephant. Instead, he had to sit and listen to the outraged trumpet of the chairman's voice. 'Fergus, it's 1946, in case you've forgotten. We bought the mine from Langlands more than ten bloody years ago, and nothing's happened! Not a thing – unless you call the dribble of asbestos we currently get out of it something. And I don't for one. It's about time we got cracking. The war's over. We're dragging the chain. Now, I want this Disaster Blue mine developed!'

'But –'

'There are no buts about it, Fergus. The Yanks were pouring the stuff into their warships during the bloody war! We should have been in on it then. Now that the war's over, there's a lot of power stations, factories and houses to build. And this asbestos is a miracle fibre. It can be used in everything. Our blue crocidolite is the best there is. That's what the geologists told us when we were investigating whether to buy the rights. They should know. They know all about rocks and dirt and that sort of thing. They weren't making it up, were they? I don't like the idea of paying all that money to Langlands and not bloody well making a go of it. Our scientists, engineers, metallurgists and what have you have been fiddling around for too bloody long. It's a joke. I want action! Goddammit, Fergus, we've got to get into it, and quick smart! Before somebody discovers a mother lode of asbestos someplace else.'

Fergus regarded his chairman phlegmatically. Sir Llew wasn't used to opposition. He'd rarely had any. He'd risen through the ranks of the business world by bluster, bullying and deceit. He had a highly developed rat cunning. He knew a good deal when it presented itself. For him, the essential step in any venture was to get in early and clinch a deal. Difficulties could be sorted out later – by others. Fergus Hamilton was always one of the others who attended to the detail. He wasn't always successful in steering the Big Ship into safer waters. Sir Llew didn't like to lose at anything.

'Llew, the government medical officer told us to make an independent assessment of the health risks of asbestos mining. He suggested we visit the blue asbestos mine in the North West Cape of South Africa. It's been going for years and may be able to provide us with important information. We should at least call them.'

'You've got to be joking! They're a competitor. As soon as our mine at Disaster Gorge starts producing to its capacity, we'll be fighting them tooth and nail for market share. No, let's get on with it now. I'll be sounding out the rest of the board this afternoon. I'm sure they'll agree to forge ahead. So, get used to it, Fergus, and start assembling some figures for us to work out what it'll cost to have Disaster Gorge developed.'

Hamilton could see the risks, the craziness of trying to exploit a small deposit in a remote part of the country. The South Africans and Canadians had huge reserves. How could V&L possibly compete? It was a dirty industry as well. The mining men he'd spoken to had assured him of that. It didn't make sense. Sir Llew must have some other angle. Fergus could not see what that angle was.

'We've already analysed the cost of developing the mine further. It's prohibitive. The company can't afford it. We'd need to build a town with appropriate infrastructure and construct a road and rail service to the nearest port to ship bags of the fibre to the eastern states for manufacture. And then there are the workers.'

'Fergus, you worry too much.' The big man smiled like an indulgent father. 'Do you think I'm going to let V&L, a company in which I hold a significant number of shares, pay for all that on its own? Not on your nelly.' Fergus saw the amusement in Sir Llew's eyes. 'No, Fergus, this job will require some help from our friends. Once it's properly explained to them, I'm sure they'll also see the value in Disaster Blue becoming a vital national commodity.'

◆

By all reputes, Disaster Gorge was hell. It was virtually uninhabitable. If V&L and its major shareholders – Sir Llew and his family – were going to earn a tidy profit from the exploitation of Harry Langlands' rights, Sir Llew knew he would first need to speak to one of his good friends in politics.

Where better to start than the Shadow Minister for Industry, Supply and Development, Sir Archibald Hughes.

Sir Archibald had been in federal politics for thirty years. He had known the V&L chairman for thirty-five years, since they'd been at university together. They had trod similar paths to power: both came from wealthy pastoralist families, both boarded at top-notch schools – Scotch College for Llewellyn, Melbourne Grammar for Archibald. Both were at Ormond at Melbourne University, and both turned out to be less than auspicious graduates – apart from their unquestionable success in networking.

Sir Archibald had had little cause to regret his inattention to the arts and law subjects he'd been enrolled in, because shortly after his graduation his networking skills paid dividends when he was invited to contest pre-selection for the safe conservative seat of Kowmung. It was a seat for the establishment and a sinecure for life, serving the similarly minded constituents of Toorak, Armadale, South Yarra and Malvern.

Thanks to his cronies, the pre-selection proved a non-contest. Archie's network put paid to any opposition. Within six months of becoming the Liberal member for Kowmung, he married a local heiress and moved into a substantial dwelling in his electorate. He had never looked back, or did so only occasionally.

When the Liberal government of Sir Ian Irons won its first term in office, Archibald was gratified to find himself in Cabinet as the Minister for Supply and Development. This required him to be seen at important events, to look impressive, and to sport an assortment of silk handkerchiefs in the breast pockets of his suit coats. Archibald performed these duties diligently. He was noticed. In fact, he was so impressively noticeable that he found himself Sir Archibald at the end of Irons's first term, before the Labor Party was miraculously swept into power. When he was assigned a second portfolio as Shadow Minister for Industry, while retaining his position as the Shadow Minister for Supply and Development, Archie knew he had reached the inner sanctum. Once the conservatives were re-elected, he believed his position would be pivotal in the reconstruction of Australia after the war. There would undoubtedly be numerous 'opportunities' for a careful minister responsible for industrial expansion and national development.

Sir Archibald enjoyed meeting up with old mates. But you had to be wary. Not all could be trusted to play it by the book. When he heard Sir Llewellyn was on his way south to see him on 'business' at his home in leafy Toorak, he winkled a few details from Sir Llew's chief executive the day before the meeting – friend or no friend, he had to be sure of his facts. The war was barely over, yet everyone, bar the Labor hacks in government, seemed to have an idea about how to rebuild the country.

When Sir Llew and Fergus arrived, Sir Archibald was seated on a capacious cane couch on the verandah of his stately home, smoking a cigar and gazing wistfully at the maid's bosom as she attended to her duties. He ushered the two visitors into his library to discuss business. There, with refreshments in hand, Sir Llew got straight to the point.

'Listen here, Archie, I need a favour.'

Archibald screwed up the furrows of his face. 'Yes?' he drawled. 'What is it you want from me this time, Llew?'

Sir Llew snorted in feigned indignation. 'Come on, Archie, when do I ever ask you for anything? This is about a proposal where we all benefit. Even the country, this time! Hah! Hah! Hah!'

'Well, Llew, tell me how that is. You've an asbestos mine in some God-awful hole in Woop Woop, Western Australia that you want to develop. It sounds terribly unnecessary to me, Llew. There's plenty of iron ore up there, and that's doing very well. What do we need this asbestos stuff for? And how can I possibly help,' – or benefit, he thought – 'with this plan?'

'Don't worry, Archie. This thing's a sure-fire winner. Listen to what Fergus has to say first. He might not have told you all the salient facts when you spoke yesterday.' Sir Llew turned his head to the officious Scotsman and nodded. Hamilton launched into his spiel. He had worked out Sir Llew's 'angle'.

'As I've already suggested to you, Sir Archibald, asbestos is a miracle fibre. We have it here in this country and it has the potential to make us all very, very rich. The problem is getting it from outback Western Australia to the eastern states where asbestos cement sheets are made. We think this is urgent. We believe the fibre should be exploited as soon as possible before overseas companies get too much of a stranglehold on our local market. All the fibre used in Australia currently comes from Canada and South Africa at great cost. I expect you know asbestos is used in brake linings, insulation for power stations and the manufacturing industry. Everybody's using it.'

'I'm listening. Go on,' said Archie.

'Asbestos cement sheets are being used in increasing quantities in the housing sector. Just look at how well Henry King Industries is doing. It's fast replacing timber and brick as the favoured material for house construction. The asbestos cement companies are producing more and more sheets every day. All our research and marketing people are saying the same thing. There's a housing construction boom, Sir Archibald; this nation needs rebuilding after the war years. And we're right in the middle of it.'

'I'm aware of all this, Fergus. It is, you know, something of interest to us on the conservative side of politics. I'm not sure the Labor minister will be as interested.'

'Of course, Sir Archibald. He won't be there forever, as you know, nor will his Labor mates. You'd also know that asbestos has been used in the United Kingdom and America for years. We've been using a bit of it here in Australia but nothing like over there. Fibre is the problem. We're isolated here. The industry depends on overseas fibre. If we're to become self-sufficient, we need to produce our own fibre, and stop importing this African and North American stuff. This mine at Disaster Gorge will give us everything we need.'

'How's that?'

'Well, blue asbestos is the superior type of fibre. Its scientific name is crocidolite. It's a very straight, tough fibre that has filtration and tensile properties perfect for the manufacture of asbestos cement sheets, corrugated roofing and water pipes. The manufacturers are using a lot of white and brown fibre, but our Disaster Blue is far superior.'

'I get the picture. So what do you want from me?'

'We need government assistance to obtain a suitable workforce to live up at the gorge to run the mine. We need help with infrastructure, such as road and rail services, but most importantly we need to have a tariff structure in place that virtually compels the asbestos cement manufacturers to buy our asbestos rather than the African or North American fibre. We believe that they can, with the right … shall we say commercial imperatives, be persuaded to buy our blue.'

'Anything else you two want?' Archie asked sarcastically. 'Your own country, for example, or a modest principality in Europe?'

'Come on, Archie, settle down. Don't be ridiculous. This asbestos thing makes a great deal of sense and you know it,' Sir Llew said, trying to placate his old friend.

'It may do. But we're not yet in power, and even when we are – and surely that can't be too far off – I'm the one who'll have to get it through the government, you know. Right now, I'm the one who'll have to lobby hard with the few Labor mates I have. All I can do is get the thing moving in the right direction. Set the wheels in motion, so to speak. With a few whispers in the right ears, I might be able to do something. But these fellows are not on our side, you know. And the whole thing is entirely impossible without the backing of the West Australian government. In case you forgot, there's a Labor government out there as well. It'll be a tough ask getting those Commie bastards onside. It's like a different country over there. Luckily they won't be there for much longer if our number-crunchers are correct. But right now they are, and I can't do too much. And what's more, I haven't heard a thing about how this is going to be good for me.'

'Well, Archie, let me at least allay your fears on that side of things.'

◆

Later that year, when Archie Hughes sat back comfortably in the new wing of his clifftop Portsea mansion, reviewing his share portfolio, he reflected on how right Llew Williams had been. The Disaster Blue mine was good for the country. It created jobs, populated the northwest, played a key role in building houses. The mine was a real boon and exactly what was needed after the war. He was sure an Irons government would see it the same way when it inevitably was re-elected. He was hopeful the Western Australian government would also be impressed. Archie looked down again at the pages on his lap. It had been an excellent year for V&L shareholders, like himself.

iii.

Sir Archibald's Labor contacts saw development at Disaster Gorge in a similarly enlightened way once the benefits were properly explained to them. They nonetheless stressed the importance of a personal approach to the West Australians. And so, Sir Archibald, Sir Llewellyn and Fergus Hamilton travelled west.

They didn't know what to expect. Kevin Grubb and his Labor team had come to office during the war on the back of the party's federal success. According to Sir Archibald's intelligence, many within the government were staunch union men. Some reputedly wanted to secede from the Commonwealth. Others, like the Minister of Mines, Dick Spooner, were supposedly left-wing zealots.

They needn't have worried.

Premier Grubb was a moderate. He governed a huge underdeveloped state inhabited by pitifully few people. When the three flew out of Perth after their audience with Grubb, they knew they had their man.

Kevin Grubb also had his man. Indeed, the perfect man for the job.

The following day, Dick Spooner walked up the flight of stairs and along the dark corridor to Kevin Grubb's chambers. He knocked.

'Yep!' bellowed a voice from within. Spooner opened the door and entered. Without looking up, Grubb motioned for him to be seated.

'Premier?' Spooner inquired.

'Hold on, Spooner, will be with you in a minute.'

Dick Spooner waited an eternity before the premier finally put his fountain pen down, took off his spectacles and rested back in his soft leather chair, looking at his minister. He held his gaze until Spooner looked away, down at his twiddling thumbs.

Grubb knew Dick Spooner was unpopular with his colleagues, who considered him at best a narrow-minded dunce. His obvious lack of sophistication irked many in the Labor Party. But his particular brand of brainlessness was precisely what the premier needed for post-war Western Australia. Jobs had to be done; tough calls had to be made. There was no room for radicals, secessionists or other eccentrics. Grubb wanted someone who was blindly loyal to the cause – that is, Kevin Grubb's cause. Dick Spooner was the man.

'Dick, I've called you in to discuss some very important issues that have come to my attention following a meeting yesterday with the federal Shadow Minister for Industry, Supply and Development, Sir Archibald Hughes, and some gentlemen from V&L Ltd.' The skin of the premier's face was thick and leathery, as if he had spent his life outdoors. It gave him a hard-man image, which he liked.

'Yes sir, I heard you met with them. No doubt they have a scheme in mind to once again exploit West Australian workers.'

Inside, the premier winced. He fixed Dick with his unnerving green eyes. Waiting, watching the man squirm. 'Now Dick, I don't think we should be too hasty. Party politics isn't everything. You have to weigh up the benefits to this great state before dismissing the proposal altogether. You see, Dick, there's a great empty tract of land up north in this state. And while it's empty, we remain vulnerable to invasion. Just look how close those blasted Japs got during the war. They bombed Broome and Wyndham. We can't simply leave the area free to be claimed by any invading force. We need people up there. We need towns, ports, roads, railways. We have to populate or perish, Dick. That's the simple fact of the matter. You understand that, don't you?'

Spooner nodded. He listened as the premier outlined the proposal to develop the Disaster Gorge asbestos mine.

'Dick, sometimes it suits us to make deals with the other side of politics and with big business. If they have something we need, then I see no problem in helping them. It will be in the national interest. In the state's interest. Look at the jobs that'll be created, the revenue we'll receive from the use of our railways, ports, freight. And from the asbestos itself. Look what's happened with iron ore. This will be no different. We owe it to the workers and working-class families of this state to press ahead with the mine. We may not win the next election, Dick. Politics is a risky business. Don't you want to leave a lasting legacy of our years in government? To leave our mark on this great state?'

He knew Spooner was easily swayed by rhetoric, particularly if it fell from his own lips as premier. He had been cultivating the man ever since Spooner first entered state politics. It was time his mentorship bore fruit.

'Well, now that you say it like that, I can see how it could be a good idea – I mean it is a good idea. A very good idea. What can I do to help?' Spooner asked.

'Well, Dick, I want you to join a committee being set up to oversee the development of the northwest of the state. The committee will have members from the federal government, private enterprise and our own government. I want you on that committee as my right-hand man. You'll be directly answerable to me and no one else. You will do as I would. I'll naturally expect you to keep on serving as Minister of Mines. You'll be taking on a very great responsibility. Do you understand me?'

Grubb looked hard at the minister until Spooner shifted his gaze and his bowels gurgled audibly. He nodded.

'My secretary will fill you in with all the details.'

The meeting was over.

At the door, the premier pointedly penetrated Spooner's personal space. He didn't care that the man's breath smelled of tobacco, coffee and dental decay. He firmly clasped Spooner's limp fingers with his right hand while he planted his left hand solidly on the minister's right shoulder.

'Dick, I know I can trust you with this. I don't want any stuff-ups, any delays. You give those men from V&L everything they want. Everything. They are our friends, Dick. Have I made myself clear?'

Spooner nodded.

Grubb smiled. He patted Spooner vigorously on the back.

'Good man. Now, go and speak with my secretary about the fine print.'

◆

Within a month of his meeting with the premier, Dick Spooner found himself chairman of the newly established Northwest Development Committee. He took the role very seriously. By the end of his third year at the helm, all of V&L's wishes had been met, the Disaster Gorge township had been built and production at the blue asbestos mine had increased exponentially. Spooner made sure V&L got everything it needed. He saw it as his duty. He even learned to enjoy the committee meetings with Sir Llewellyn Williams, Fergus Hamilton and, from the end of 1949 when the Liberals regained control of federal parliament, Sir Archibald Hughes. Perhaps he had earlier been, as Grubb suggested, too hasty. These men were very friendly. They were always smiling at him, slapping him on the back, nodding enthusiastically at his suggestions. Decent fellows after all.

◆

Kevin Grubb was most obliged with Spooner's dedication to the job. He was also very pleased with various substantial additions to his bank account over the next decade. They supplemented nicely the pension he received for his years of loyal service to the people of Western Australia.

PART I

Chapter 1

1958

James Henderson's sentence was over. He sat smiling to himself as the train shook and rumbled south towards Perth. All he could think of was Jenny Jenkins and, as he did so, the horror of the past two years ebbed out of him. It was already a lifetime away.

But was it? He hoped Jenny would be there for him. She had to be. The thought of her had given him the strength to get through the ordeal of Disaster Gorge. The letters she'd sent had kept her alive in his mind. He thought he knew his own feelings. But had he wrongly interpreted her feelings towards him? Why would she bother writing if she didn't feel something towards him? They had promised that they would wait for each other, but that could easily have been the fear speaking – the fear of being alone in this new country. He tried to push the anxiety aside.

But it had been two years. While he was up in the dust, she was in the city – a formidable challenge for any relationship, let alone two people who had only met for a short time. And then there was the question of the English doctor. James didn't know what to make of him. Jenny had mentioned him briefly in one of her letters and afterwards revealed so little about the connection that James's imagination ran wild. Jenny had come when this man had summoned her. She had crossed an ocean for him from England to Australia. Despite what she told him in her letters,

James could imagine the lure of the clever young doctor. Why on earth would she wait for a Scottish nobody called James Henderson?

As his head rocked to the rhythmic bumps of the train, he closed his eyes, thinking of Jenny. He sat slumped on the bench seat in an endless torment: one moment in a reverie dreaming of her, imagining her in his arms, reliving their first days together; the next jolted awake by the scars of the Hamersley and the fear of losing her. He opened his eyes and turned to gaze out the window at the staggering vastness washing away in a blur of colour. It seemed as though he'd been travelling for years. Searching for something never quite within reach. Was Jenny Jenkins another illusion?

Chapter 2

The train trip took three days. There'd be plenty of time for James to torment himself with his fluctuating emotions if he didn't make an effort to rein them in. He wasn't negative by nature, even though the past two years had tested his belief on that score. If he were, James knew he would never have made the effort to leave Scotland. He'd still be in the dismal family home in Paisley thinking bleak thoughts and aspiring to nothing. As he settled into the bounce and shake of the train, it didn't take long before he could once again picture Jenny in his mind's eye and remember how he had got to this point in his life.

He'd had Jenny largely to himself for the voyage from England to Australia. He hoped he could now have her to himself once again as he travelled with his memories to Perth.

During the long passage on the *Neptune,* there'd been very little to do. James wasn't much of a reader and wasn't interested in quoits or the other pastimes offered to passengers. He certainly didn't like the idea of spending most of the day in the minuscule cabin he shared with a Welshman and two English brothers. He thus spent many hours walking the decks of the yawing liner.

As his feet steadied and his sea legs grew, James was able to make rapid progress along the length and breadth of the ship. He familiarised himself with each level and section. He came to recognise many of the passengers from his regular rounds, and they him. There were warm 'Hellos!' as he passed at a brisk walk or nimbly descended a ladder, one hand aloft in both greeting and farewell, disappearing as if drowning under the deck. Sometimes, he stopped to talk.

The passengers tended to stick to their own groups. Many came from the same town or region. Married couples congregated together. They were berthed on decks above the single males like James. Single women, a rarity, were two decks higher.

He wasn't a garrulous man and didn't need to belong to a group to feel secure. But he wasn't shy or lacking in self-confidence. He knew his limitations and was comfortable with them. He'd learned to operate within those restrictions and not to rail against what nature and nurture had given him. This self-acceptance or self-containment made James generally feel at ease around others. And they seemed to find his aura of calmness alluring. He was often puzzled by the reaction. It was only later that he discovered that his honesty and direct speech were real gifts. Although he heard many jibes as he skipped along on his walks, very few passengers showed him disrespect.

He first noticed Jenny on the third morning of the third week when he stopped to chat with four of the single women on the leeward side of deck C, midway between the bow and the stern. He had been pausing to talk to the women for a week. It was the first time Jenny had joined the group. She had, until then, been 'indisposed', as she later explained to James. As a result, she stood out from the others. James, however, thought Jenny would have shone like a beacon in any crowd. She again shone brightly in his mind as he sat watching a deserted country railway station recede over his left shoulder.

Jenny Jenkins was a neat, compact beauty. She had blonde shoulder-length hair, opalescent eyes and high cheekbones. Her lips were full and inviting; her chin determined. Although slight, with gentle curves, she moved with purpose and vigour.

'I don't believe we've met. I'm James Henderson,' he said.

'Hello, Mr Henderson. I'm Jenny Jenkins. Pleased to meet you.' She spoke softly but clearly, with a southern English accent.

'Please, it's James.'

'Jenny.'

'Hello, Jenny. Glad to meet you, too.' He bowed slightly and somewhat self-consciously, his face blooming with a wide grin. They each held the other's gaze a fraction longer than would normally be considered decorous. It was the type of little linger that caused others to notice, to smile in recognition of its significance and, afterwards, to prompt knowing nods and playful prods.

'It's a fine day for a walk, James,' one of Jenny's colleagues said.

'It certainly is, Annie. After last week's weather, it should be smooth sailing from here on. That's what one of the lads in my cabin is predicting. He claims to have got it straight from one of the officers. I hope it's true. This good weather brings out the best of us, you know,' he added, with an almost imperceptible wink at Jenny. The group giggled but Jenny's face was slow to light up, and when it did it was with a subdued glow.

Why such a lukewarm response? he asked himself. He must have said the wrong thing. His face reddened. 'Well, I must be on my way. Nice talking to you, ladies. Nice meeting you, Jenny.'

'Don't you go, James. There's a whole day to do your walking. Stay and keep us girls company,' Annie pleaded.

'No, not right now. I've got to keep moving. Warm up a wee bit. I'll see you again for sure.'

He sped off down the deck and disappeared behind a lifeboat.

He was in a quandary. He neither felt like walking nor going back to his cabin. He found a quiet spot near the bow and stared out to sea, ruminating about the encounter with Jenny for the rest of the day. He thought there had been a spark between them. What had he said that had ruined things? He was only trying to be pleasant. Was he too obvious, not nearly as witty as he thought, not respectful enough? Did he really know anything about other people at all?

Eventually, when he returned to his cabin, the Welshman's incessant whining about his health and the Englishmen's harmless chatter distracted him from his own doubts. He resolved to make amends the next day.

◆

Shortly after breakfast, James set off around the decks of the liner. He was beginning to despair when, after his second circuit of the decks, there had been no sign of Jenny. On his third trip around deck C, he finally spotted her with another woman. As he approached, they turned to greet him. Both smiled. 'Hello, Mary. Hello, Jenny,' he said with enthusiasm.

'Hello, James. It's good to see you out and about again today. We didn't see you yesterday afternoon. We were worried you might have fallen sick or even gone overboard.'

'Not a chance, Mary. I was out on the decks. You must have missed me, that's all. Anyway, it's good to see you both today. I hope you're feeling well and enjoying the weather. It's another fine day for a stroll around a ship in the middle of nowhere.'

'It is indeed. And yes, we're well. Jenny was just telling me exactly that.'

'That's good. Would the two of you like to walk with me for a bit?'

'Of course.'

James couldn't sense any reticence on Jenny's part. He briefly looked into her eyes and felt he could see some emotion within their blue-green depths. He turned and guided the women along the deck as the ship ploughed through the calm ocean.

After a while, he nervously broached the matter that had been preoccupying him. 'I think I might have said something to offend you yesterday. I'm sorry if I did.'

'Don't be ridiculous,' Mary answered with a smile. 'I can't even remember what you said yesterday.'

James, however, was looking at Jenny. 'You didn't offend me or anyone, James,' she said. 'In fact, it was the complete opposite.'

'Then, why…' He stopped talking as she lightly touched his hand. He glimpsed a smile. His tensions eased. And as Mary had witnessed it all, the next day everyone in Jenny's group was thinking romance.

James did nothing to dispel the rumours. Each day, or twice a day, and sometimes three or four times a day, James came calling on the women on deck C for a conversation with Jenny and her friends. There was, however, no mistaking who held the centre of his attention. Jenny's friends often stepped back to allow the couple to talk in private. He could sometimes hear them teasing her with lascivious predictions. Happily, he heard nothing but feeble objections from Jenny. Eventually, the women left the two of them to themselves.

At the end of the fourth week, James was emboldened to ask Jenny to walk with him to the upper decks. While she agreed, he felt she wasn't quite sure of herself, as if this was taking a step too far. It didn't help when his invitation set off a loud round of laughter from her friends.

James went up the laddered chute first. He waited, ready to help, watching Jenny ascend. As she neared the top, she looked up at him, her cheeks flushed and a smile on her lips. James felt a warmth suffusing his heart. He realised it had never been there before. It thawed the ice that had been piling up inside him ever since he could remember. As he took her hand and helped her onto the deck, he smiled as well. He felt as though he was on the verge of great happiness.

But if you let go of yourself, something bad might happen, he reminded himself sternly. You could lose your father or your mother or worse. He had to control himself. He didn't want to ruin things by letting his bursting heart take over.

Safely on the upper deck, Jenny let her hand remain in James's. His grasp was tight, but he hoped not desperate. She gave his hand a fleeting squeeze. The train in his chest slowed. He looked at the golden hair swept back from her cheeks. Her bright eyes. He softly and briefly touched her face with the back of his fingers.

As they set off on their promenade into the salty wind gusting around the lifeboats, halyards and metal skeleton of the ship, James felt his misgivings subside. He sensed an understanding between them. A bond that avoided the need for idle talk. An intangible thing embracing them like the heat from a fire when you come into a room from the cold.

Chapter 3

James and Jenny walked the upper deck in silence, James worrying how to begin what he imagined would be the first real conversation of many they might have for the rest of their lives. To his relief, Jenny was keen to know all about him. And once she started quizzing him, he couldn't stop his own flurry of questions of her. He quickly found out that she was a midwife, and had come from Sussex in the south of England. He was about to explore her family background, when she interrupted and pressed him for more information about himself. This wasn't something he was usually comfortable talking about. Family was something that was your own. Who would be interested in his life anyway? But the way she looked at his face, at his straight fair hair neatly parted, into his vivid blue eyes – he felt safe, safe enough to open up about himself.

'Well, you know, there isn't much to tell. Or not much of interest. I'm a pretty dull fellow if you want to know the truth.'

'Oh, I'm sure that's nonsense, James. You can't be that dull if you've decided to travel to a far-off country like Australia. That takes something special.'

'Daft, perhaps.'

'No, it's brave. To do it on your own without anyone there for you at the other end. That's terribly brave.'

'You're doing the same thing. Do you think you're brave too, Jenny?'

She paused, as if thinking what to say. 'A little, but you see I have a brother in Perth that I haven't told you about. Hugh. He's a doctor. He left England four years ago when he'd had enough of treating tuberculosis patients in our home town of Midhurst. Sorry, I know you don't know where that is. It was incredibly depressing. Anyway, Hugh says it's wonderful in Australia. Now he wants the whole family to come over and I guess I'm the first of the rest of us to give it a go.' She stopped and looked at him and then back out at the rippling sea. She went on hesitantly. 'So, you see, James, I won't be alone, like you. I'm not very brave at all, really.'

'I don't believe that for a minute.'

She smiled. 'James, that's enough about me. I thought we were talking about you. That's what I want to hear more about.'

'If that's what you want.'

'It is.'

He looked at her, trying to work out why she was reluctant to tell her own story. James imagined she was feeling a pang of loneliness about leaving her home. God knew, he occasionally had such fears no matter how much he had disliked the future that lay ahead of him in Scotland. Maybe she needed to hear someone else's story to take her out of herself and her thoughts.

'As I was saying, it's a very dull tale. I'm a nobody, Jenny. A poor wee Glaswegian. Born on 20 May 1935 in the Vale of Leven Hospital on the shores of Loch Lomond. A beautiful spot, for sure, but always cold and wet. My dad, John, was a butcher in nearby Paisley. My ma, Fran, was a midwife at the hospital. I'm the runt of the litter. I have two big sisters, Rosemary and Kate. They're nurses like my ma, and like you as well, Jenny. They're both married and I'm certain they won't be following me out to Australia. That's about it.'

'Come on, that's simply not good enough. I'm not going to let you off so easily. Tell me more about where you lived and more about your family. I want to know.'

Of course, there was more. But James wasn't sure he wanted to dwell too long on the past, let all of that bleakness out of the bag. Slowly, with Jenny's coaxing, he opened up to her and told her about his life, about his family, his home, how he got to where he was by her side. It wasn't a great story, nor a particularly uncommon one.

His family lived in a clean but cramped terrace, two hundred metres from the entrance to the Vale of Leven Hospital where he was born. The local pub was just around the corner. As his mother tearfully recounted to him years later, it was there that John Henderson celebrated the birth of his only son. For the first and last time in his life, his father sat till closing at the smoky front bar, downing pints of Younger's Tartan Special with whiskey chasers, rambling on in high spirits about the future for his boy. A quiet, hard-working man, it must have been one of the few times he permitted himself the freedom to enjoy a special occasion and to venture an opinion about the future. He had been too young to fight in the First World War, but was just the right age to have his head blown off by a howitzer in France during World War II.

Although he was only young, James could recall how tough it was after the war. James's mother wanted him and his sisters out of school and working as early as possible so that food could be put on the table. His sisters started work at the district hospital and at the age of sixteen in 1951, James went off to the massive ship-building works on the Clyde as an apprentice fitter and turner. It was filthy, demoralising work, but James never complained. He imagined he had the same capacity for self-sacrifice to better the lot of his family as his father. James would have liked to have stayed at school. He was no great scholar, but could see the advantage in trying to better himself. He believed that each generation should try to go one step higher than the one before, if only out of respect for what had been done to create new opportunities.

The Hendersons survived. A simple, toiling, dourly content unit.

Eventually, Rosemary and Kate married local men who also worked on the docks. They moved into small, depressingly dark houses, and gave birth to many wiry children, destined to keep the cycle on the Clyde turning. James wanted more, but he had to think of his mother. She was on her own and needed someone to be with her.

He finished his apprenticeship. Got good work. James knew he was only a light-framed, stringy man, who wouldn't have been out of place in the featherweight boxing ranks. At the same time, he was confident in his body and how he appeared. He was aware of the surreptitious glances of the girls around town when he was soaped and scrubbed after work. His forearms were sinewy and strong, his legs sure and agile. He also knew he was well regarded by his employer as a skilful, reliable tradesman. By the age of twenty, he worked side by side with a team of welders, fitters, turners and boilermakers, building the clunking innards of big steel ships. He worked in dark, confined spaces. The air was always putrid. It stank of oil, grease, the sweat of labouring bodies and stale, panting breath.

That was on the good days. On the bad days, battalions of laggers swarmed into the hulls, spraying some type of feathery fibrous material on the bulkheads and turbines. Half-cylinders of pre-formed insulation were placed around steam pipes and cemented together to form tubes. A loose, crumbly, coarsely fibrous composition was mixed with water in ten-gallon drums to form a slurry, which was then slapped onto the boilers and pipes around the tricky bends and switchbacks where the pre-formed cylinders did not fit. The air became an impenetrable soup. The dust stuck in his hair, his clothes. It irritated his skin, creating a prickly, itchy rash. On days like that, James longed for the end of the shift, and relished the first deep breath he took above deck of the fishy, muddy stench of the Clyde.

The year James turned twenty-one, his mother died of lung cancer. She had smoked cigarettes since she was a girl of thirteen. Everyone did.

And so in 1956, James found himself the sole resident of the house he had grown up in. It was a bleak, drab place. How had he felt such joy in it before? He remembered sitting at the small kitchen table after work one evening, wondering what it was all about. He had worked five years in the filthy darkness of the docks. Both his parents were dead. His sisters were married with their own families. He had nothing but this plastered-brick home and a host of depressing memories. The cold fog of Glasgow crawled up the valley, threatening to render his wintry life permanent. He smoothed the etched wooden tabletop with the flats of his hands. Specks of food were imprisoned in the cracks, ink and pencil marks from homework fading into the tan surface. He stretched his feet out on the linoleum floor, his thick-soled work boots disproportionately large for his thin legs. He stared down at his feet, the patterned floor. Then he slowly gazed up and around the room. A demoralising little space. Despite the noisy family conversations, the spit and splutter of bacon and eggs, the bubbling hiss and whistle for tea, it had always been a cold house, he thought. A miserable place, full of death. And it could be his mausoleum too. He could feel even then the faint, but definite, pull into darkness.

James had never spoken for so long or shared so many of his most intimate thoughts. He trembled with the recollections, even though he and Jenny stood at the rails with a warm wind blowing across their faces. As he'd been speaking, he'd largely gazed into the distance, focusing on nothing but his memories. When he turned, he saw Jenny's concerned, kind, beautiful face. It was almost enough to bring him to tears.

'I knew at that moment that I no longer wanted to stay where I was. It was too dark and gloomy, too cold, too depressing. I couldn't stand it any longer. But I had no idea what I could do about it. I only knew how to work at the shipyards. I couldn't immediately picture anything else. Where would I go? Glasgow was all I knew, no matter how bad it was.

'Some time after that, I'm not sure how long, I read a notice on the information board in the canteen at work. I'll never forget it. It said something like:

The Australian government wants you! Come and live in the jewel of the Commonwealth crown. The Australian government will assist suitable applicants to migrate to Australia. It will pay your fare, living allowances and find you employment. Do not be disappointed, apply now. Men and women with trade skills will be looked on favourably. Please contact...

'For some reason I started feeling a wee bit dizzy. It was very strange. My head was pounding, and my heart seemed to skip a few beats. I felt like my world was spinning.

'I steadied myself and walked over to a table with my tea and sandwich. I sat on my own, thinking, trying to work out why I felt so funny. I'm a pretty simple man, Jenny. I was either about to die from some terrible illness or someone was trying to tell me something. I figured I was in good shape so that it must be some kind of message.'

He checked that Jenny wasn't laughing at him. As he already knew would be the case, she wasn't. 'I just sat there sipping my tea, and eating my sandwich, chewing slowly over where my life was going. I knew for certain I wanted change, and after work and over the next few days, I let the idea wash around inside me, if you know what I mean. Was it a sign to get out – to go to Australia? God, telling you this is so embarrassing.'

'Why? It's normal to want to get away from something bad. Why do you think I'm here? We have to try.'

'I guess that's right, but I still feel daft telling you this.'

'Please don't.'

James recalled precisely how he felt at the time. He knew for certain that he no longer wished to feel marooned, alone, sad. He needed to escape, to get out into the world, to be part of it. He had to find a way out of the oppressive tunnels and holes of the dockyards. Otherwise, they would kill him.

Slowly, tentatively, a picture took shape and gained clarity.

'You see, Jenny, I believed of all the workers at the docks that day, the notice was directed at me alone. It was a direct, personal call to me. It came to me when I was already wrestling with thoughts of escape. I needed to respond. This was the opportunity I'd hoped for and I needed to take it. I could work that much out.

'So, after work one day, I went to the office identified in the notice. I was given some forms by a friendly woman, who asked me to bring them back when I'd filled them in. Four weeks later, I attended an interview in the city. Six months after that, I farewelled my sisters, brothers-in-law, nephews and nieces, and left on a train for London. All I have is my savings, a few family photographs, Dad's medals, and a third of what we got from the sale of Ma's house. It's not much. I don't really need much.

'And now I'm on a ship to Australia and I've found you! I know it's not much of a story. Probably everyone on this ship could tell you something similar – there's no other reason to be making this trip to the other side of the world. We're all searching for something. I know I was.'

When he turned again to look at Jenny, he felt an immediate desire to be with her forever. Her face was awash with feeling, wisps of her blonde hair fluttering in the breeze. She put her hands on his as they gripped the railing, the smoothness of her skin resting against his bony knuckles. Sharing his private thoughts had been cathartic, even exhilarating. He didn't know what she would make of them, but he felt that he could trust her with his emotions. He had to. He had given them to her and now he couldn't take them back.

As he sat pondering events in the carriage from Port Hedland, he wondered whether he could be as certain as he then was. Were his emotions still safe? Would she be there?

Chapter 4

'Why Perth? Why not Sydney or Melbourne? I've told you why I'm going to Perth, my brother arranged it and he's organised a job for me at the hospital. But why are you going there? Are you going to work in Perth?' Jenny asked James.

'No, when I signed up, I didn't care where I was sent to. By all accounts, Western Australia's warm and sunny, which is exactly what I need. So, when I was given the option of working there, I thought, when can I start? The Australian government's fixed me up with a job as a fitter and turner at a mine up in the north – it's called Disaster Gorge. I'm disembarking at Fremantle, then I'll be travelling up there by train. The mine owner's a well-respected company called V&L Ltd. I should be well looked after.' He paused, then added, 'I just wish I'd known about you before I was in such a hurry to accept the first job I was offered. It doesn't look as enticing without you there.'

Jenny blushed, and pushed on quickly with further questions. 'How far away from Perth is the mine?'

'Quite a way, I gather, but I don't really know. Australia's so much bigger than back home. I have to work there for at least two years as part of the agreement with the Australian government. I'm sure the time will fly by. The weather will be fine. As far as I know, it doesn't rain much up there. Sunshine all the time. Can you believe that, Jenny? A place where there'll be light. A place where you don't have to shiver all the time because of the cold.'

'It sounds almost too good to be true. I'm looking forward to Perth as well. People tell me it's a beautiful town. Near the ocean. Plenty of sunshine.' At the time, James thought she sounded far from convincing. Did he now know the reason why?

'I'm sure we're both going to enjoy it,' he replied. 'It'll be an adventure, don't you think?'

James gave Jenny's hand a reassuring squeeze. She moved into his body a fraction more, as they continued their walk. She smelled clean and comforting.

'I guess I don't really know where I'll go after the mine,' he ventured. 'I might fall in love with it up there and stay. You never know.'

She frowned. 'Don't say that.'

'Would that be something bad, Jenny?'

'Well, it could be. I mean, I wouldn't want you to miss out on seeing Perth ... Or you, maybe?'

She blushed.

'I'll be lonely in Perth. I don't know anybody there except my brother.'

'What about Annie or Mary? And your brother? He'll probably introduce you to many handsome doctors. I bet he's already earmarked one for you, Jenny.'

'Don't say that, James. I don't need a matchmaker, thank you very much.'

He felt rebuffed. There was some touchy issue under the surface that he felt he should avoid exploring. It was the second time he had irked her in some way. He was truly hopeless at reading people and situations, he thought.

They continued silently along the deck.

◆

The next day, Jenny was waiting for him with Annie and Mary. As he approached, she left the other two women to accompany him. They didn't seem to mind. Jenny was in good spirits, the previous day's uncomfortable moment apparently forgotten. James reached for her hand as they walked around the rim of the *Neptune* together. His confidence in what he perceived to be their affection for each other returned, but his attempts at extracting fragments of her life story foundered for most of the day.

'I've talked myself dry about my boring life. What about you? Jenny, I'd love to hear more about your life. I've not much to go on so far.'

'There's not much more to tell.'

'I'm not buying that for a second, Jenny. I want to know all I can about you.'

Jenny smiled briefly. 'All right. What do you want to know?'

'Like I said, everything.'

As Jenny's expression became serious, James started having second thoughts. He shouldn't have pestered her. He really was an idiot at times.

'Well, first of all, my family is very ordinary,' Jenny began quietly. 'We've lived in the same area for generations. A long line of Jenkinses and Briggses – my mum's family name is Briggs. I was born at the local hospital on 14 August 1935, the same year as you, James.

'Dad was a gardener at the Cowdray estate on the outskirts of town. His family had worked on the estate probably for centuries. Mum was a nurse, who worked mostly at the hospital where I was born. I don't know how she juggled her work and raising the five of us. She was the kindest, strongest person I've known.'

She wavered slightly before resuming. 'James, they're both dead, killed in a bomb raid during the war. I don't know how the rest of us were spared. I can remember sirens going off regularly as the German planes flew towards London, but sometimes bombs fell around the local villages, and one hit our house. My younger brother, Cyril, was also killed. It's all a great blur for me now. Everyone walking around as if in a nightmare.

'My sisters and my brother, Hugh, and I lived with our uncle and aunt until the war was over. My eldest sister, Patty, lives at the old family house now with her husband and children. She's a teacher and so is my other sister, Robyn, who lives in nearby Petworth with her family. Because Hugh was clever, and went on to study medicine in London, there are no more Jenkinses working on the Cowdray estate. The old castle is in ruins anyway. The town's tiny and very quiet—'

'I'm so sorry, Jenny, that's terrible. Your poor family.'

'It's okay, James, it was a dreadful time for everyone, including your family too. There was a lot of suffering. I don't want to look back on those things anymore. I don't want to think about them. We have to move forwards. Always move forwards.'

'You're right Jenny, but it's hard to get over those things, if you ever do. Sometimes the past comes back to hurt you.'

They hugged each other, weeping. 'It's going to be all right, Jenny,' James whispered in her ear.

'I hope so, James. I hope it will be.'

Chapter 5

By the sixth week of the voyage, James could feel the increase in the temperature. The sky was forever blue. Jenny forsook her shawl, and James his coat, for their walks around the ship. A sense of anticipation percolated through the cabins. They would soon reach Australia. Their lives would change for good.

James tried to spend most of the time with Jenny. It wasn't always possible as preparations for arrival meant that the ship was bustling with crew, and passengers had to attend to their own affairs. While James's meagre possessions were quickly packed in a single suitcase, Jenny required more time. Her friends also demanded her attention as they were all going on to Perth together. In the final few days, they were seldom alone. The times he managed to share with Jenny were, however, the happiest James could recall in his life.

When land was sighted one afternoon, a buzz of excitement spread through the ship. James began to grieve his imminent loss. He felt the keen conflict between uncertainty and excitement as the journey's end approached. For him, arrival in Australia had different connotations from the majority of the passengers. He was sure it was also different for Jenny. It meant that their time together was drawing to a close. He could sense the turmoil in her. Could she apprehend his own melancholy and anxiety? Was it suffocating her, pushing her away?

Perhaps it was the fear of losing something good that drove James to embrace Jenny one evening. He may have been prompted by the glow of the sunset gleaming above the placid deep-green waters on the horizon. He put his thin, strong arms around her, drew her to him, and kissed her. He loved her, and he believed that she felt the same way about him. They held each other close as the light faded, and the first stars twinkled low in the twilight.

'I don't want to lose you, Jenny. I don't want to go to Disaster Gorge. I want to be with you. I know I have to do it, but God I don't want to.'

'James, I don't want to lose you either, but I'm scared I will. I'm scared that this is just a dream and we'll have to bring ourselves back to reality and go on with the lives we planned before we even walked onto this ship. It would've been better if we'd never met. It would be so much easier.'

'Don't say that, Jenny. This is the best thing that's ever happened to me, even if it ends up being only these few weeks. I'll remember it always.'

'I'm sorry I said that. I don't want you to go to Disaster Gorge. I know nothing about it, but it sounds like a bad place. How can anything good come out of a place with that name?'

James felt her shaking in his arms. 'Don't worry, Jenny. I'll be fine. I have to go. You know that. I have an agreement with the Australian government. It won't be forever. It's only two years.' He couldn't believe he was trying to reassure her; to him it felt like a life sentence.

'Maybe you can come up and visit me. I may be able to take time off to come down to Perth to see you. We could meet halfway, I don't know. I'm not great with words, but I'll write. I hope you'll send me a few letters too.'

'Of course I will. I love you, don't you know? I'll write to you every free moment I have.'

There, he wasn't dreaming! He knew now for certain. It was as if all his past life had been wrested from him, leaving him here with this beautiful woman, at the edge of a new adventure.

'I can't believe this has happened. I'm so happy, Jenny. I love you so much. I don't know what to do, what to say. I don't want this to stop – ever.'

'There's nothing to do or say, James. We can't change what's about to happen. But I'll be waiting for you.'

'I know, I know it has to happen. As soon as I've finished at Disaster Gorge, I'll come and get you, Jenny, I promise.' He hoped he didn't sound too anxious.

They held each other until all light was gone. The night was balmy. The usual evening chill had been warned off by the approaching continent. Even so, Jenny was shivering. He kissed her and kissed her again. Staring into her eyes, he saw a world opening up before him. They were both in it.

He remembered that moment clearly. Had he failed to see something else in her eyes? Had he refused to see the doubts that almost certainly were there?

Chapter 6

James opened his cabin door, still flushed with emotion, lost in romantic thought.

'The tea was cold and the meat was off. I've had better meals in boarding school,' the Welshman moaned. He let rip with a thunderous fart from the depths of his sizeable arse. 'See what I mean. It's gone right through me like a dose of salts. Awful stuff, Henderson, awful bloody stuff. I hope there's better food on land tomorrow. I've personally had enough.'

James sat down on his bunk in sudden despair.

'Cheer up, old boy,' one of the Englishmen said, stuffing a singlet into his too-small bag. 'We'll be free of this barge tomorrow.'

James nodded at him sombrely. It wasn't the sort of freedom he wanted.

The next morning, the passengers woke to a still ship. The *Neptune* was berthed in the port of Fremantle. The ship's officers went about broadcasting the news and advising that all persons must be ready for disembarkation later that morning. James checked he'd packed everything for the fourth time and sat waiting on the edge of his bunk for the call,, his compact cardboard suitcase resting on his knees.

He lost himself in a well of thoughts about Jenny, occasionally looking up through the porthole at a patch of vibrant blue sky. He was oblivious to the noise of the men in his cabin. They soon gave up on the idea of engaging James in their conversation. They left him staring into space, immersed in his awful longing.

Finally, at 11.00am, there was a rap on the wall outside the cabin and an officer told them to file out and onto the deck. James was first up and out. He desperately hoped he'd be able to see Jenny and say goodbye.

The hallway was thrumming with passengers edging their way forward and out into the sun. When James emerged into the light, he felt disoriented. With the other single men he was being herded along the deck towards a walkway to the quay. A crowd of hatted heads waited on the dock. Behind it, buses and trucks trembled as their engines idled. James could see a similar walkway forward of the one he was moving towards. There was a third towards the ship's stern.

James turned anxiously left and right, searching for Jenny. He couldn't see her. Had the single women already gone?

Swept along in the throng, James at last stepped onto Australian soil, or bitumen, at least. He swayed a little as his inner ears adjusted to motionless earth. He looked around cautiously. Faces burnished by a fierce, southern sun stared at him. He walked on behind the line of men. He could see they were being directed into a large timber building.

James lifted himself onto his tiptoes, peering out through the crowd. 'Come on, Henderson, get a wriggle on,' he heard a Welsh voice behind him. 'I've had a gutful of this crowd. If I'd known that—'

Then he saw her. A blonde cascade of hair falling from under a summer straw hat. Her head was moving from side to side, as if searching for something. He could almost see her anxious expression. He edged his way towards her, hoping for contact. 'Jenny!' he yelled. There were too many people. Too much noise. He couldn't get to her. He was being jostled towards the door. He would never see her again. He was pushed from behind. 'Come on, Henderson, move along.'

And then she saw him. Her green-blue eyes locked onto his. They stood transfixed, the union of their gaze deadening the noise of the world around them. Time stopped. She smiled at him, tremulously. He smiled back. He hoped his face expressed the comfort he wished to give her. She lifted her gloved hand. Not high, but about as high as her cheek. She gave a brisk, earnest wave. Her smile broadened. James raised his own arm, just as he was swept into the building He watched from within as her smile melted from her face. Her hand remained up, the fingers curling downwards to the palm, holding vainly onto the warm Australian air for support. The chugging roar of engines returned.

Chapter 7

After he passed through Customs, James found himself with a host of other British migrants on a bus and then a train to Perth. On arrival, he was shunted onto a train back to Fremantle, and then onto a freighter to Port Hedland. Finally, he rode in a rattling, dirty train to Disaster Gorge.

He had lost his bearings in Perth – a glorious, bright town for sure – but he was used to a river being on his right and not on his left when he entered a city. He thought the coast should also be in the opposite direction. He knew Jenny would be happy in Perth even from the abbreviated view he'd had of the place from various railway sidings. She had her brother and her friends from the *Neptune* to look after her. He only had himself.

He got little sleep. Emotions of loss, despair, anger, frustration and wonder blurred and ran together like paint. And as he stared out the train's window on the last part of the tedious journey, he could only see endless miles of red dirt and rock. There was some breeze through the windows, but James could nevertheless feel the heat. This was a hostile, unwelcoming land.

He thought of Jenny. They had been less than forty-eight hours apart, yet their time together could have happened in a different lifetime to different people. But he had clearly heard her say that she would wait for him. She had said that she loved him. These things had happened. He wasn't making it up.

When he finally arrived at the township of Disaster, he was close to collapse. The nervous energy rioting in his brain was the only thing keeping him going.

And now two years later, he was back on a train, and those visions were again playing themselves out in his head. When he'd been with Jenny, he'd thought they were embarking on what would be an adventure together. Like him, she was leaving the United Kingdom to start what she hoped was a happy new life, far from the claustrophobic skies and stuffy, gloomy world of the past. But he now knew that, unlike his, her adventure was not necessarily a solo affair. There was her brother's friend, a doctor she'd known in England. He'd learned this secret later, toiling in the heat and dust of Disaster Gorge. It had torn him up then and he was still riddled with doubts as he hurtled towards her on the train.

Perhaps he should have succumbed, like everyone else, to the wretchedness of north-western Australia and not kept her as a shining light in his heart. Had he been a fool? Was he still a fool? When he remembered what he'd been through in the past two years, he felt he could be a wee bit kinder to himself. It wasn't his fault that he'd needed her there in his mind's eye. It had been survival. Nothing else but thoughts of her would have sufficed.

♦

Set in the middle of a spectacular wonderland of red escarpments, wild ancient mountains and deep, serene gorges, Disaster was a dump of a town.

James arrived late in the afternoon with nine other men. All were immigrants. They were driven by a company foreman in the back of a truck to a corrugated-iron house. 'This is it, fellas,' he said, and showed them in. 'Make yourselves at home. Take whichever bed you like. Get a good night's sleep. Work starts tomorrow. Somebody'll be by in the morning to pick you up. See you later.'

James looked around. For a moment he was homesick, felt a faint desire for the cold, dark squalor of Scotland. He forced those thoughts from his head. The structure he stood in was more of a dormitory than a house. It had three rooms. The first room was a new but basic kitchen. The second was a bathroom with an astonishing blue swirly-patterned sheeting on its walls. The final room was the bedroom. It had five narrow beds lined up on either side. They had an unhappy sagging quality about them.

Despite its uninviting appearance, James was so exhausted that he lay down on the nearest bed and soon drifted off to sleep. Most of the others did too. It had been a long, draining journey from the other side of the world to get to this place.

When he awoke, it was early morning, and still dark. The other nine men were sleeping, their gurgling and swallowing the only sounds in the peaceful room. James glanced out of the one curtainless window. A tree with twig fingers moved almost imperceptibly in the moonlight. It made an eerie squeaking sound as it scraped against the iron roof. James thought of Jenny and wondered if she was thinking of him. He hoped her hospital accommodation was better than what he had here in Disaster. It probably was. Anything was better than this. He played her words of love to himself. Very soon it would all be over. He drifted back to sleep.

Two hours later, James was awakened by coughing, snorting, the unzipping of bags, the spring of clasps being released. One of the Italians was naked next to him, bending over to pick up something on his bed, his heavily carpeted backside destroying all traces of the pleasant dream James had been in.

'Don't mind old Giuseppe there, Henderson, that thing of his won't bite,' one of the Irishmen said with a smirk. 'Better get up, boy, we'll be off to the mine soon.'

James got up and went to the bathroom. The door was closed. He went outside to what someone had called 'the dunny'. It too was occupied. He pissed on the ground. Light was just starting to roll over the hills to the east. Back to the west, a wedge of sunlight cut into the mouth of Disaster

Gorge, opening up its red mucosa, displaying the tongue of water at the base.

There was nothing to eat for breakfast. There was no food in the house. Provisions would be bought later from what was left over after nights at the pub.

James put on some clothes for work. These had been allocated to him at Port Hedland. He had a white singlet, a khaki button-up shirt and khaki-brown cotton trousers. He had tough leather work boots. Once dressed, James shared a pot of black tea with the other men. The tannin puckered his mouth, making him feel dry.

The day was going to be hot. The sun had risen above the hills; its rays were already potent. James went outside and sat with two of the Italians on the front porch. They nodded to him as they smoked their roll-your-own cigarettes. They offered him the pouch of tobacco. He declined. He would be one of the few non-smokers in the town.

Very soon, a beaten-up black truck pulled up before them amid a rising curtain of dust. A big red-faced man leaned out of the window and yelled, 'Come on, you loafers, stop slacking and get your arses into the truck. You've got work to do!' He laughed as the ten newcomers climbed into the open tray of the vehicle.

The men sat on wooden benches, five each side at the back of the truck. James looked out over the opposite heads at the surroundings. The town was cheerless and repetitive. The streets were dotted with corrugated-iron dwellings similar to the one he'd slept in. Dirty-clothed, dirty men were hopping into trucks and cars and heading along the roads in the same direction. A huge billow of red dust spiralled into the air behind them. In front, lay the russet walls of Disaster Gorge.

The gorge had an undeniable grandeur. As the bouncing truck drove into its heart, it was impossible not to feel the antiquity of the place, or to marvel at its rugged beauty. It had an ageless, haunting, menacing life force all of its own. This was a dangerous place, James thought. A place you had to respect and treat with caution.

Up close, the cliffs were made up of thousands of red, brown, orange and yellow pancakes of rock piled one on top of the other, cut through with occasional thin streaks of bluish grey. Parts of the cliffs were broken, with the scree fanning out from the sheer rock face like an apron. The sides and tops were sparsely covered by scrubby brush and dwarf trees. An obsidian pool lined with eucalypts lay at the centre.

The truck lurched to a halt at the base of a scree slope. At the top of the scree, the escarpment stood perpendicular, capped by a red-brown and yellow layer of earth. The surrounding slopes were blue-grey from the tailings. The mine itself was dug into a craggy-faced, blue-stained mesa.

The workers' vehicles were parked higgledy-piggledy in the dust at the base of the mine. There were also some trucks at the top of the mine where a switchback road was carved into the contour of the slope. Looking up, James could see a long building just beneath the top of the escarpment. Below this, other buildings had been erected in a stepped fashion. Half way up, a corrugated-iron shed jutted out from the other buildings hugging the steep slope, its head buried deep into the rock, its tail projected almost into thin air before turning at right angles to form a chute into a large corrugated cave of a building near the bottom of the cliff and the carpark. This must be the mill, James thought. It was evident that the asbestos was mined in stopes high up the slope and moved by conveyor belt down to the mill. In time, James would learn all about the operations of the mine and mill. For now, he simply had a crude idea of its machinations.

'Okay, you new boys, over here!' shouted the foreman from the night before. 'I hope you all had a good night's sleep like I told you. After I've shown you the ropes, you'll be doing a hard day's work. For some of you blokes, this'll be the first time.' He laughed, eyeballing the Italians.

The foreman was dressed in shorts and a blue singlet covered with streaks of salty crystals from his sweat. There were heavy work boots on his feet, with red woollen socks poking over the edges. He had a grimy hard hat on his tanned, ruddy head. It was obvious to James that he and his new mates were seriously over-dressed.

It was only 8.00am, but already the gorge was like an oven. The heat was so bad James could almost smell it. A dry searing heat that made breathing difficult.

'Righto, come on, over here. My name is Bert Bertwhistle. I'm the mine foreman. You got any problems, you come and see me. Let's get cracking.'

Bertwhistle marched the men up a well-worn path to the first of the mill buildings, which housed a large loading dock. Bulging brown hessian sacks were stacked almost up to the roof. Each bag had 'DISASTER BLUE ASBESTOS' stencilled in black lettering on its front. A few workers, wearing only shorts and boots, were shifting some of the bags onto the tray of a truck. They grinned at the new workers as they lugged the big sacks about. Some of the bags were torn or poorly stitched at the top. With each movement, plumes of blue-grey dust lifted into the air. A faint blue haze tinted the air of the shed.

'This is the loading area, as you can see. The bags of Disaster Blue are loaded onto the trucks and taken to the railway where they'll be freighted up to Port Hedland and shipped around the country,' Bertwhistle explained. 'You mightn't believe it, but you boys are looking at the biggest asbestos mine in the country and the source of a booming asbestos products industry over in the eastern states. Let's take a look at the mill and see where these bags come from.' James felt like a schoolboy on an excursion.

The men walked further into the sawtooth-roofed mill. The first thing that struck James was the dust. A blizzard of blue filled the space. Filtered light sparkled and dodged its way through the cloudy interior. Men were shovelling piles of asbestos into bags. Through an opening in the roof, chunks of blue-grey rock were emptied into a whirling machine. Its paddles revolved in raucous cycles, crushing and teasing a blue-grey fibrous material from its mother ore.

They walked over to the machine. Bertwhistle stooped and picked up a fist-sized hunk of the stuff. He handed it to James, shouting, 'This is what this is all about! Crocidolite! Blue asbestos!'

James was amazed at its other-worldly appearance. The rock was steel-blue in colour, with a sheen like slate. It consisted of vertical fibrous tendrils. James pulled a band of the fibres out and they divided into thinner and thinner needles. Some parts of the rock had been teased out already, and had the appearance of strands of matted blue-rinsed hair. It was spellbinding. James had to be nudged by Bertwhistle to pass it on.

They were then led up a ladder to the chute. It was at the end of a long conveyor belt along which a stream of blue ore jiggled and jostled its way to the drop to the mill.

Up they went, heading towards the mine. They donned headlamps and crabbed their way behind Bertwhistle into the stopes. Miners chiselled and picked at the veins of crocidolite deep in the heart of the cliff. There was little air in the dark, cramped tunnels. And what there was contained a suspension of blue-grey dust, occasionally glittering when struck by a beam of light from a headlamp. James was glad that he didn't have to work in these dirty holes. He pitied the Italians, who, Bertwhistle said, were going to work in the mines. He was relieved when he returned to the mill, met his leading hand and began work on the various machines. He had a maintenance role. As it turned out, there was a lot to do to keep the mill operating. Fortunately, the machines were not much different from those he'd maintained in Glasgow. As he got into his day, James recognised that Bertwhistle had been right about one thing: it was hard work. Hot, dirty, physical work.

◆

It took two weeks before James settled into a routine and had the energy to write to Jenny. He'd been formulating sentences in his head for days, but when he sat outside under a tree with a wad of paper on his lap, he was lost for words. Naturally, he wanted to say how much he loved her, but the ugly environment proved an impediment. After several scratchy starts, he managed to complete his first letter.

Dear Jenny,

I'm sorry I haven't written sooner. It's been so busy and tiring, I've found it hard to start. I'll do better from now on.

You wouldn't believe this place. It's the hottest place in the world and everything is red and dusty. I'm dirty and I stink and so does everyone else. I'm glad you can't see me like this as I'm sure you'd want to run a mile in the other direction.

The work's hard, but I can handle it. All we do is work, eat and sleep. At least the time goes by very fast. I'll be back with you before you know it.

The houses in Disaster are all made from corrugated iron or from cement sheets. They're not very nice. The roads are covered with the tailings from the asbestos mine and are blue, which looks quite amazing when everything else is red.

There are two schools, five pubs, a grocery store, two churches, a playing field, a small hospital and a cinema. The population is only about twelve hundred. The streets are all simply named, like First Avenue, Second Avenue, Third Avenue, First Road etc. I live on Fifth Road. It looks like all the others.

I don't think you'd like to visit here, Jenny. It's pretty rough. Most of the people are men. There are very few married men. You might cause a riot if you came here, especially after the boys had been to the pub!

I live with nine other men – two Irishmen, one Englishman and six Italians. They're a friendly group, although it's hard to understand the Italians and they all seem to like getting drunk whenever they can. I work in the mill, not the mine. I'm part of a gang of fitters, turners and machinists who keep the plant going. Sometimes, I help out shovelling the asbestos into bags for shipping off to factories around Australia.

It's definitely dusty, dirty work, but nothing I haven't done before in the shipyards at home. I'm told by the foreman that asbestos is a very valuable mineral and that they need it to build houses throughout the country. I suppose someone needs to do it and I'm not going to step back from a hard day's work if that's what they need. I don't have to do it for ever either. Just long enough to get some more money together to start a new life in Australia. With you.

How are you going, Jenny? How's the hospital? I bet your brother was happy to see you. Have you caught up with Annie or Mary or any of the other girls from the ship?

I'd love to hear from you, Jenny. No hurry. You'll be busy delivering babies and looking after new mothers or seeing the sights of Perth. If you want to write, I live at 3 Fifth Road, although I think if you send a letter addressed to me at Disaster, it'll find me.

I miss you, Jenny.

Love you always,

James.

Once he'd sent it, James couldn't think of anything but a letter waiting for him when he returned from the mill. The days became longer rather than shorter. He wished he could focus on work, but that was horrible.

Early in the fourth week, the leading hand showed James and the other mill workers where they could find masks if they were bothered by the dust. They were flimsy paper things that fitted poorly, particularly for the men who had beards or moustaches. It was impossible to breathe with them on. The majority of the workers, like James, discarded them, wore them dangling by elastic straps around their necks, or used handkerchiefs on the bad days.

The dust was a perpetual nuisance. It was difficult to ignore and would often get on James's nerves. And the sharp spikes of the crocidolite gave him and the other men a rash as it moved across their sweaty skin. The spicules got into their eyes, making them bloodshot and itchy. The men's work clothes were covered with particles by the end of the day, giving them the look of big, blue, spiky anteaters.

At their house, James noticed that everyone coughed. It couldn't have been just the smoking. James didn't smoke, and he was coughing as much as the others. There was something always catching in his throat. It was the dust, of course. He kept on telling himself that it wouldn't be forever.

On the day he learned about the masks, James received his first letter from Jenny. It was in a pile of post on the kitchen table when he got back from work. He'd never seen Jenny's handwriting before and he could picture her just by looking at the neat blue script on the envelope. While he desperately wanted to read the letter straightaway, he resisted the urge until he'd scrubbed the grime from his body. He went outside under his favourite tree and delicately prised the envelope open.

My dear James,

I was so happy to hear from you and find out that you're well and thinking of me. I'm thinking of you too. I miss you too. There's so much time to go.

From what you've told me, Disaster Gorge sounds a most vile place, but I know you'll be strong enough to see it through. Please take care of yourself. I would love to see you, but I too am very busy and I don't think it will be possible to travel that far north, especially as you say, it's not really a place I'd enjoy. I doubt there'd be any riots even if I did come!

Perth is a beautiful city and all the people are very friendly. I'm planning to stay in the nurses' quarters for at least a year because I need to save money. Hugh lives in a little house in a suburb called Subiaco. He walks to work at the hospital. He's been very kind in introducing me to his friends and including me when he goes exploring around the city. We've been to Kings Park which has a lovely view of the Swan River and we've also gone to some of the beaches. They're really nice. The sand's so white it almost blinds you. The water is clear and warm, although I've only tipped my toes in so far. I haven't yet bought a bathing suit. Hugh and his friends go out quite a long way. The waves look big and scary out there. I'm not used to surf like that.

Annie has moved to Melbourne, but Mary's still in Perth. I see her occasionally. She works in the city in a big department store. She asked me to say hello when I write to you, so, 'Hello' from Mary.

I don't know if you remember Alice, one of the other girls on the ship. She's also working at the hospital and has been seeing one of the doctors on the ward who's training to be an obstetrician. She's very lucky as he's a very caring person and quite handsome as well.

A lot of women seem to be having babies here. It's always very busy. I work at all times of the day, sometimes several nights in a row. We even had two sets of twins last week. Unfortunately, one of the babies died soon after birth, which was very upsetting. It sometimes happens and it's part of the job I don't like. Otherwise it's such a happy and exciting time for the parents. I can't help but feel their excitement too.

That's all the news I have at the moment. There's not much to tell.

I miss you so much, James. I try not to feel lonely, but it's hard not to. Please write soon.

Your loving Jenny.

James read and re-read the letter. He wished he could see Jenny and feel her in his arms. How was he going to survive the months ahead? It was a challenge.

◆

The men worked five days per week, eight hours per day. When they unloaded themselves from a company truck at the end of a shift, they showered or hosed themselves, then sat about wondering what to do. Boredom hit them flush on the jaw, knocking them senseless, compelling them into the town's pubs. There, James watched them guzzle beer until the emptiness was drowned, and the pain of the long, hot, filthy days was numbed. James considered himself a temperate man, but the harsh life regularly tempted him to turn to the drink with the same commitment as his colleagues. Instead, he'd go along with them to the pub and sit on a beer or two until closing time. Around him whirled a desperate tumult.

Starved of female company, other than the buxom old matron at the hospital who administered first aid as required and the poxy hookers who drifted into town from time to time, there was no respite, no softening of the edges. With so much frustration in the brutalising environment, fights were inevitable. The fiery Italians had little understanding of English idiom and, when drunk, interpreted everything as an insult. The Irish, on the other hand, were perpetually searching for an insult so that they could start a fight. They were all rough, dirty men, swinging big haymakers; stumbling, falling; punches hitting temples; glasses smashed and thrust angrily forward; faces cut. James knew that they weren't bad men. They were men like himself. They may have been simple, uncomplicated, but they were fundamentally good. Even the strongest found it difficult to survive in that place unscathed.

James looked for peace and comfort at church, but the Sunday ministrations were hopeless. He attended for a few weeks before giving up. Some of the priests drank as avidly as their wayward parishioners. They couldn't stop the ceaseless degradation of the lonely men. James struggled not to go under.

Chapter 8

Nothing exciting ever happened at Disaster Gorge. The listlessness was contagious. Occasionally, there was an accident at the mine or mill or someone got badly injured in a fight, but it was generally routine. That's why James remembered clearly the day when he heard the humming of an engine in the sky.

He looked up from the hessian bag he was feeding asbestos into. A little twin-prop plane was yo-yoing its way through a swirling orange haze towards the microscopic runway near the town. It was a blustery, dusty day. James thought he wouldn't like to be up there in the wind. He'd never flown, but it didn't look like ideal flying conditions to him. From his elevated position at the entry to the mill, he could see the aircraft rolling and bouncing to a halt. He thought that there must be some very important people in the plane as he knew that only management flew in and out of the area in the company aircraft.

When James had arrived for work that morning, the mill was quiet. The leading hands told the men that Bert Bertwhistle had instructed them the previous evening to turn all the machines off until further notice. James had assumed it was for maintenance purposes. Strangely, nobody was asked to attend to the machines, but instead the men were directed to do other chores, like filling bags with fibre. Shortly after the plane landed, James and the others doing the shovelling were told to finish up and stack the bags neatly against the wall of the loading dock.

Later, towards lunch time, James heard a car engine and looked up to see Bertwhistle's ute crawling along the floor of the gorge with another, gleaming, car behind it. Bertwhistle never drove at a snail's pace so this also seemed odd.

He was close enough to the car park to hear the conversation when the vehicles pulled up. 'Well, here we are,' announced a man with a deep voice. He wore clean trousers, a white shirt, and shiny black shoes. 'The Disaster Gorge mine and mill.' Two other men climbed out of the car. They too were neatly dressed, but sported obviously borrowed work boots. The first man directed them to don the hard hats they were carrying. 'We take safety very seriously here. You can never be too careful.' James smirked at what he thought was a joke.

Bertwhistle and two other men emerged from his ute. James had never seen them before either. He noticed that Bertwhistle had spruced himself up by donning a blue short-sleeved shirt over his customary singlet.

'Come on, gents, this way,' he instructed. 'If you would follow me, we'll start the tour.'

'Actually, Mr Bertwhistle, we're here to inspect the mine, not go on a tour,' corrected one of the men from the car.

'Sorry, Dr Smith, yes, let's start the inspection.'

Birtwhistle ushered the group past the transport bay into the mill. They walked past James and the bags of asbestos he'd helped fill and stack. No loading was taking place. The other man from the car carried a camera and took a photograph of the loading dock with James in it.

'Henderson, will you please grab a few face masks for our visitors? And get one for yourself as well. You can come with us,' Bertwhistle said.

James ducked into an office near the entrance to the mill and returned with six masks. He put one on himself. He knew enough not to ask questions about why he'd been instructed to do so.

Inside the mill, there was very little activity. Even so, a thin cloud of grey-blue dust hung in the air. All the workers were wearing masks, which James knew never occurred even when the top company brass visited the mine and mill.

'I see the men are wearing masks, Mr Stephenson,' the man called Dr Smith said to the deep-voiced man. James deduced that he must be Fred Stephenson, the mine manager. He'd never seen him before, but some of the men who had said he was a bullshitter.

'Yes, they are. As I said, we take safety very seriously here.'

'Of course, Dr Smith, we consider the dust to be harmless, other than as a general irritant. It's always good practice to keep dust down. We encourage our men to use the masks for that very reason,' explained one of the other men. He spoke with a lisp, almost a hiss.

James wasn't usually critical of people, but he couldn't help disliking this man. He seemed slimy.

'Yes, good idea,' said Dr Smith. Turning to the man with the camera, he continued. 'Stanley, would you mind taking a few measurements?'

'Certainly,' replied Stanley.

'Crick, here, will also take some readings,' lisped the slimy man, indicating the person standing next to him. 'So that we may obtain a more accurate assessment of the environment and will be able to compare notes, so to speak.'

'I'm sure that won't be necessary, but if you want to I'm not going to stop you,' said Dr Smith. 'Stanley is a first-rate hygienist.'

'I'm sure he is. Even so, we'll take our own.'

James watched from nearby as Stanley and Crick set up equipment near the conveyor belt and fiberiser.

The machines may have been idle, but the layer of dust on their surfaces was obvious as James saw Dr Smith wiping his finger through a big pile of fibre on the surface of a bench. Smith then looked at the floor and, as James followed his gaze, he too saw a dirty mess interspersed with fragments of crocidolite. Dr Smith held up a sample from the floor, teasing the fibres apart. The sharp needles fell in lumps to the ground. The more he teased them apart, the finer the fibres became. He fanned out a portion like an accordion and held it up to the light. James knew how mesmerising asbestos could be.

After Stanley and Crick had finished with their equipment, Dr Smith asked Bertwhistle to turn the mill on.

'Oh, it's not the right time for that. The conveyor comes on twice a day: it won't be on for another two hours,' explained Bertwhistle.

'Yes, that's correct, I'm afraid,' Fred Stephenson chimed in.

'It will be up and going when we get back from the mine, won't it?' answered Smith.

'I suppose so.' Stephenson sounded evasive.

If asked, James would have told Dr Smith how Bertwhistle had ordered all the machines to be switched off that morning. But Dr Smith, with his keen eyes behind black-rimmed spectacles, didn't look like a man who needed any help in working out what was afoot.

As the visiting party returned to their cars, and wound their way up the zig-zag track to the top of the cliffs, James remained at the mill. He watched as Bertwhistle led them in single file, stooping, into the stopes.

Two hours later, the dignitaries returned down the slope.

Operations in the mill were still suspended.

'I'm afraid there's been a problem with the machinery. I'm told it won't be up and running for a couple of days. Sorry about that, but it's simply out of our hands,' James overheard Stephenson tell Dr Smith. 'We'll try and have it back working tomorrow but there's a chance it won't be before you depart.'

'Very well. That will do for today. We'll come back tomorrow before we fly out and see if we can take some readings while it's operating.'

'Good-oh,' replied Stephenson. 'Let's get back for a drink. I'm parched!'

◆

The next day, the mill was still down. James occupied himself with the other men, filling more bags with asbestos, until he heard a humming roar of engines and saw a plane take off over the orange and blue chiselled cliffs of Disaster Gorge.

'Okay, you bludgers, crank her up! Let's get back to work!' someone yelled.

Chapter 9

The months slipped by. James's image of Jenny became distorted, idealistic. She occupied a blissful space in his mind that he entered to escape the awfulness around him. He started questioning his own perception of their relationship and the accuracy of his memory of their time together. He tried to focus on what he was going to do after his time at Disaster Gorge ended. Eventually, these plans became preoccupations. He kept stewing over them in the heat, a monotonous drone in his head.

He continued to write to Jenny. He tried to sound optimistic, if only to lift his own mood, but he was no wordsmith and the atmosphere of his quarters was hardly conducive to romantic writing. He knew he was becoming obsessive about the future and this made him apprehensive about the effect of his words when he wrote to her. He didn't want to put her off.

Dear Jenny,

Thank you for your last letter. I enjoyed hearing about the maternity ward and your trips around Perth. It sounds so much better than up here in hell. I can't describe it in any nice way. It's a very unpleasant place.

At least I've only got twelve months to go now. I can't believe a year has gone. I miss you as much as ever. Will you still be there for me at the end of it all? I hope I won't have changed too much from being up here. Maybe some of this badness will have rubbed off on me. I hope not. I try to be the same man I was when you knew me on the Neptune.

There's still not much to do up here except work and sleep. A lot of the men go to the pubs at the end of the day and spend all their wages on beer. I've been trying to save some money because I want to make sure my time up here will be worth it. Some of the lads are like me and indentured for one or two years. We often talk to each other of our plans after Disaster. Some of the boys have interesting ideas. I feel sorry for the men who have nowhere else to go and will remain here. I don't know how they'll get out of here if they drink all their money away and don't make an effort to escape.

Jenny, I've heard a lot of things about the eastern states. Many of the lads have family already over in New South Wales or Victoria or Queensland. They tell me the west is no good. Western Australia is a backwater, a great big backwater. All the people live over on the other side of the country. That's where the factories are. That's where all the building and construction happens. More jobs. Some of them are going to head over to Sydney or Melbourne after their time's up in the mine. I think that's where the opportunities are. That's where the work is. I reckon that's where I should give it a go too. I know you have your brother and your work in Perth, but do you think you'd like to see the eastern states and give it a go over there, too? I'd love to be able to travel there with you. I can afford the move. I still have my savings from Scotland and the money from my parents' house. I've some wee savings from up here as well.

I'm sorry if this sounds scary or too pushy on my part. I miss you, that's all, and I can't wait to see you again.

Please write soon.

Love,

James.

After posting this letter, James worried that he'd assumed too much about Jenny's feelings. Twelve months was a long time. Anything could have happened. He felt foolish. This feeling was magnified by the absence of a prompt reply. Jenny was usually diligent with her correspondence. She always assured him she was counting the days until they could be united again. She ended each letter with her love. This always lifted James's spirits. Now, the hiatus was making him wish he'd never sent the stupid letter. When will you ever learn? he asked himself.

About a month later, James received Jenny's response.

My dearest James,

I'm sorry I haven't written sooner, but work has been extremely busy and I've been so very tired.

I read about your plans to go to the eastern states with great interest. It does sound very exciting over there. After travelling all the way from Scotland, I'm sure another long trip won't be too hard for you at all.

I've been agonising over my response to your letter for weeks. I need to tell you something that I should have told you right from the beginning. It's been terribly unfair of me to have hidden it from you. All I can say is that I care about you and haven't wanted to hurt you. Now that you've told me your plans for the future after you finish at Disaster Gorge, and now that I know you want to include me in your plans, I don't think I can keep this from you any longer.

James, when I told you that I was coming out to Australia at my brother's suggestion and to be with him to start a new life out here, I wasn't being totally honest. While it's true that Hugh encouraged me to come to Australia, and organised a lot of things for me, there's someone else who's also been involved with this whole journey. I must now tell you about him.

His name is Trevor Hungerford. He's a doctor and one of Hugh's closest friends. I've known him for three years. Hugh introduced us when I was training to be a nurse in Sussex. He's a few years older than I am. He's training to be an obstetrician and works at the King Edward Memorial Hospital with me. We saw a great deal of each other when I was back home. Indeed, it was his idea that I follow him out to Australia after he and Hugh settled in to working life in Perth. The reason he did this was because we're engaged to be married. James, I'm so sorry I didn't tell you this before. I'm sorry you're hearing this for the first time in a letter rather than face-to-face. I know it's not the right thing to have done. You must surely hate me now that you know I've lied to you about something so important.

I owe you an explanation and I'll do my best now.

I left England unsure about whether I was doing the right thing. Trevor's a lovely man. He's very generous, very attentive. He was talking about marriage about six months after we started seeing each other. Although Hugh had mentioned how much Trevor adored me, it still came as a surprise when the subject of marriage came up. Of course, he's a doctor and terribly clever and handsome in his own way. His family are quite well off too and live in a very nice town in Hampshire not very far from Sussex. The thought of marriage to Trevor has caused me a lot of stress. It's been quite nerve-racking as I'm not sure what to do. I was very young when he started talking about getting married. I still am. I wasn't sure he was right for me.

Trevor was very patient with me in England. He said he didn't want to rush me in any way. Didn't bring the subject up for some time. Hugh, on the other hand, was on at me about what a perfect match I'd be for Trevor and that he'd make me extremely happy. Eventually, I started thinking Hugh was right. Why couldn't I be happy with a man like Trevor? So, when Trevor formally asked me to marry him and to come out to Australia with him, I decided I was mad not to accept. I wanted to get away from the place that had so many terrible memories for me and to start a new life. Here was a man who wanted to help me do just that. And he said he loved me too. So, I said yes. I imagined all would be fine and good and that I'd learn to love him and be happy – except, James, I met you.

I realise you'll find it hard to believe anything I tell you now, but I want you to know that this is the truth. When I first met you, when I first spoke to you, when I first looked into your eyes, when I first kissed you, I knew you were for me. We were meant to be together. It was fate. I love you with all my heart. Can't you see that? I know you can.

I don't want to hurt Trevor and I certainly don't want to hurt you, but I guess I've done both. Trevor keeps on telling me to take my time, to give it time. He's hard to avoid as he works at the same hospital in the same department. And there's the pressure from Hugh. He hasn't been impressed by what he describes as my vacillations. I don't know what that means, but he says I can't keep Trevor guessing. It's not fair. I briefly mentioned to Hugh that I've met someone else – you. I haven't told him much about you, although he knows you're a Scot and that you work in a mine in the far north. To him, it would be a monumental embarrassment not to go through with the marriage, or even for people to know I'm considering going off with a Scottish fitter and turner. He's very angry at times. I assure you, I don't think like that. Not at all.

I'm up for an adventure with you. I truly am. Now that you've heard my secret, however, I understand if you no longer want to have anything to do with me. All I can say is that I love you, James, and that I dearly would love to see you again and to be there to meet you when your time at Disaster Gorge is over. You must believe me.

Please write to me, James. I'll feel empty until I hear that you have forgiven me. I miss you.

Love Jenny.

James was stunned. The folded paper sat on his lap, moving in the breeze, threatening to take off and fly away like all the other rubbish gusting through the town. All the moments of doubt he'd sensed in Jenny now had a name: Trevor Hungerford. He'd misinterpreted her occasional diffidence as the result of something he'd said or done. All along there had been another person standing there between them. How could he have been so stupid? He'd been right all along to have gauged the chance of a girl like Jenny falling for a nobody like him as less than zero. He wondered how on earth he could compete with a smart, handsome doctor. After this dirty job, James had no future but more dirty jobs. He should give up.

And yet he was sure she had said that she loved him. He looked down at the fluttering paper. She'd written it as well. He re-read the letter. She said she would travel east with him. But he couldn't understand why she had failed to say that the engagement was off. If she truly loved him and not Trevor Hungerford, then why hadn't she called the whole thing off? Perhaps she had and had just forgotten to mention it in the letter? That made no sense whatsoever. It was obvious that nothing had happened and that Trevor still thought he was going to marry Jenny Jenkins. She'd asked for forgiveness, but that seemed like a plea to forgive her for choosing Trevor Hungerford – perhaps from pity, perhaps as her duty – and, in consequence, for tearing James apart. His anguish was unbearable.

'Coming to the pub, Jimmy?' one of the Irishmen asked, grinning as men did when picturing the first beer on the bar.

James folded the letter into his pocket.

'Yes,' he answered and got up from under the tree.

He answered yes many times more in the ensuing months. It was far easier than finding the resolve to reply to Jenny's letter.

◆

He sat in the train and closed his eyes so that no one could see his shame. For a time, he had lost his dignity in that northern hell.

He'd been driven to drink like the rest of them. Drunk and tired, he would stagger into bed, and wake in the morning parched, with a massive head, almost too big to lift from his pillow. He'd resolve never to do it again, but as the day worked the poison out of his body, and the lather of sweat cleared his head, he would lose his resolve.

In that perpetual summer, James sometimes couldn't sleep at all. The noise from the brawls could never be quietened. They roared across the still, hot night until, exhausted, the sweaty protagonists fell to the earth and slept. James would then collapse into a type of slumber that never seemed enough. Sometimes, he woke in the early hours of the morning and couldn't return to the oblivion he craved. He'd lie awake, baking under the tin roof, listening to his room mates' hacking coughs and exhausted moans. He ventured inwards and found only self-pity. He hated himself in those moments. He couldn't bear to think of Jenny.

Chapter 10

James stirred in his seat on the train and opened his eyes. He didn't want to think those thoughts again. He'd gone into some very dark spaces, places he hadn't thought were within him, places he thought he had long buried. He watched the greenery now appearing in the landscape, looked at the passengers sleeping peacefully, talking quietly and happily to each other, or reading contentedly. He had got through the worst of it in time, sufficient to halt the self-wrecking drunkenness and to reclaim something of himself. Although it was an ugly time, he obtained a singular satisfaction in manfully gaining control of himself. He started to think less of his own hurt and more and more of Jenny. After months of self-imposed purgatory, he found the courage to write to her.

Dear Jenny,

By now you probably have given up on me and believed I was never going to respond to your letter. Maybe you're already married to Dr Trevor. I know it's been weeks and weeks since you wrote. I wouldn't blame you if you were. It would be my fault for being too weak or too proud. I should have written to you much sooner. I'm sorry I didn't. I've been so daft. I hope you haven't married him. I don't wish him any harm, but I don't want him to have you.

Whatever's happened, I want you to know that there was nothing for me to forgive. You were only trying to protect me. I should be asking you to forgive me for ignoring you. I still love you and want to go on our big adventure together to the east. I miss you, Jenny. I only have a few more weeks left up here and I'm desperate to see you when I come to Perth on the train. Will you be there?

I hope you will be.

He didn't expect a reply. After a week without one, he resigned himself to his loss and tried to focus on work. As he tightened screws or dismantled parts, he chastised himself for being so weak. He refused, however, to turn to the bottle again to blot out his pain. He got by, functioning like one of the machines he maintained in the mill.

With two weeks of his sentence remaining, James returned from work and as usual checked the small pile of mail on the kitchen table. There was again no letter – but there was a telegram. He read the words on the slip of paper:

I will be there. Jenny.

Chapter 11

James was one of the first passengers to disembark. He stepped off the train with his battered cardboard case and looked down the length of the concrete platform. There were very few people waiting. But she was there. She stood twenty yards away: petite, anxious, beautiful. Looking at him inquiringly. Her eyes seemingly questioning his intentions and his heart. Her red lips moved into a tentative fragment of a smile. Her gloved hand rose to greet him, hanging in the air uncertainly as when he'd left her. James smiled. He watched as doubt disappeared and her face lit up. They walked towards each other in pure, liberating joy.

'Jenny!'

'Hello, James.'

They paused for a second, a couple caught within a private, irresistible electricity, as the business of the railway station languidly flowed around them. Then they embraced. They held each other tightly. So tightly the tide of air stilled in their lungs. They kissed. The long months of aching separation and anxiety were released. Jenny wept, then laughed. James turned her face gently away to see her tears. And then he hugged her again.

'I've missed you so much. I can't believe you're here with me. I haven't been able to think of anything else for ages.'

'James, I said I'd be here and so I am. Don't you understand? I love you. I want to be with you.'

'I know. I've been so stupid.' They kissed again. 'I love you, Jenny. I don't know how I got through that up there without you.'

'It's over now. You don't ever have to leave me again. I'm going nowhere other than with you.'

They stood holding each other, whispering affections, until a porter politely asked them to move so that he could push his trolley of luggage along the platform. They moved aside apologetically to let him pass. He shook his head as he trudged by. They laughed, held each other again then walked to the exit, James with one arm around Jenny, the other holding his small suitcase. They emerged into warm sunlight and a gentle sea breeze.

'Where to now?' Jenny asked.

'I've booked a room at the Royal Hotel for a couple of days. I had no idea where to stay and I was worried you wouldn't be here. We could go there so that I can have a bath and get changed. I must smell awful. I've been on that train for three days. We could have a meal, if you don't mind waiting. That is, if you're not working or have other plans.'

Jenny laughed. 'That sounds perfect. I'm not working today. I have no plans but to be with you. Surely, James, you're exhausted after that trip. Three days! You can't have slept. Don't you want to sleep?'

'Nothing could be further from my mind!' he said, as they crossed the road. 'Jenny, I've got so much to talk to you about. Where I want to go – Sydney, I think – what I want to do with the rest of my life. I've had a lot of time to think about these things, but I don't want to—'

He stopped and looked at her. 'Sorry, Jenny, I'm getting ahead of myself. I haven't asked what you want or anything about yourself or what's been happening in your life. I do want you to come with me, though. But if you want to stay here and you'd be happy if I stayed here too, then that's what I'll do. I want to do whatever makes you happy, that's what I'm trying to say.'

She laughed and squeezed his hand. 'James, you are so serious sometimes.'

'I know. I'm sorry. I'm just so excited being with you. I'm getting carried away. Tell me to be quiet and I will.'

'Don't stop. It's one of the things I love about you the most. You're so earnest. So genuine. I wouldn't want you to be any other way, James. Never change.'

James was unsure whether being earnest was good. He wasn't even sure he knew what the word meant. 'I promise I won't. Look! There's the hotel,' he said.

As they entered the lobby and he saw how grand the hotel was, James worried that he was over-reaching. He'd lived for two years in grime and dust. Everybody seemed to be looking at him. What was a mucky little man doing in this magnificent establishment, they must be thinking. He went shamefaced to reception and checked in while Jenny waited in the lobby. The staff were courteous, but he nevertheless felt uncomfortable. He paid for his two nights' accommodation and went upstairs to his room. When he returned, he felt like a new man. Jenny rose from her chair and wrapped her arms around him. 'Now that's the James Henderson I fell in love with,' she said as they made their way into the dining room.

James felt self-doubt creep over him again as he looked at the menu. 'Jenny, I have no idea what to order. I've never eaten a fancy meal in my life. The best food I've ever tasted was my ma's roast lamb, but we didn't get to have it very often.'

'I'm no expert either, James. Back home in Midhurst, the height of fine dining was at the Spread Eagle Hotel, and I only went there once. I can't even remember what I ate. I have to confess though, and I know you won't like this, but Trevor took me out for a meal here and I had the most beautiful fish I've ever eaten. Whiting, I think it was called. We could have that if it's available.'

'Whatever you think best,' he said.

'Come on, James, don't look like that. Don't let Trevor spoil the day. I'm sorry, but you know we have to talk about him at some stage. We can't just let him come between us. It's over. I'm here with you, not him. The reason I went out with him was to tell him that the engagement was off. I think he knew already through Hugh. I never loved him, James; that's the God honest truth. When he proposed, I didn't think I had any choice in the matter. Hugh was so persuasive, telling me that I'd be ruining my life if I didn't take the opportunity. I know Trevor's a good man, but he's not for me. You are. Of course, Trevor didn't like what I had to tell him, but he seemed to accept it. I see him at work from time to time and we remain friendly. But I'm not interested in him. Please believe me, James. I know I should have told you right at the start, but I was confused by my feelings for you and what I'd promised Trevor.'

'No, I'm sorry, Jenny. I shouldn't have reacted like that.'

'It's all right, James. And by the way, I don't want to stay here in Perth. It means nothing to me. It's a lovely city, but I don't see myself living here.'

'Really?'

'Yes. Hugh's practically disowned me and I don't know anyone besides Mary and Alice and some of the other nurses. What you told me about Sydney and Melbourne sounds much more exciting. If Sydney it is for you, then Sydney it will be for me – for both of us.'

'So you do want to come with me to the other side of the country?'

'Yes. What's wrong? You look very serious again, James. What are you thinking?'

Suddenly realising where he was blundering at break-neck speed, James hesitated. What am I doing? he thought. He'd rehearsed a moment like this in his head on the long train trip to Perth, but he hadn't imagined it would happen so quickly. Jenny looked at him, waiting.

He thought a moment longer. 'You see, Jenny, I was hoping … you know … and I wasn't ready to do this so soon, but … you know … I was hoping you would marry me.' He was having trouble reading her reaction. He forged on. 'Jenny, will you marry me? Will you marry me and come with me to the eastern states?'

'Oh James, I thought you'd never ask. Of course, I will! Why else would I be with you right now?' She laughed.

James was overjoyed, although his face felt on fire and he was sure everyone was looking at him.

'Fantastic,' he breathed, and leaned over and kissed her. Everyone was definitely looking at him now, he thought.

The waiter approached. 'Are you ready to order, sir?'

'Whiting for two,' James said.

◆

Later, after lunch, they were sitting on the edge of James's bed. Nobody had appeared to care in the least when Jenny followed James upstairs. They could have been newlyweds already, although that didn't stop them feeling nervous and conspicuous. They were silent for a long time before James reached across to bring her towards him. As they touched, they lost balance and fell backwards onto the mattress in a clumsy, fervent embrace.

The curtains swayed out and in as a breeze eased through the windows. A splatter of light fell across the wallpaper with each movement, illuminating columns of flowers separated by thick golden lines. The bustling sounds of the city entered the room as the afternoon shadows lengthened.

Much later, as they still held each other, the susurration of the curtains felt like the only sound in the world. The light was fading. Their thoughts turned to the future and they held each other more tightly as if by sheer willpower they could forever keep the cares of the world at bay.

'What are you thinking?'

'What we should do next. What about you?'

'The same. We need to have plans, James. We need to work out exactly what we're going to do. I haven't really thought about it, but now we'll have to.'

'I know. I've been bouncing some ideas around in my head for a while now. I figure I have to get over to the east and get us sorted. I don't want to leave you again, Jenny, but I think it would be a good idea for me to sail on ahead to do that before you come east. I know the next ship leaving Fremantle is sailing to Sydney. That's as good a place as any to start our lives together. I've heard a lot about it. It's the biggest city and probably has the most opportunity for us. I think that's where we should go. I'm sure I can easily get a job. And once I'm settled, you could come over. What do you think?'

'James, I don't want to be on my own again. When are we ever going to be together?'

'I promise we will be soon. We've got to do a wee bit of planning now so that it's easier in the future. It won't be long, Jenny. We've done it for two years. We can do this.'

'I don't like it, but I guess it makes sense. I know I can't leave work at such short notice anyway – I mean I can, but it wouldn't be the right thing to do. It'll take me about a month to settle everything here. Given how good everybody at the hospital's been to me, I'd rather not leave them short when there are so many babies that need delivering. I'd also like to patch things up with Hugh if I can. I could find out about jobs in Sydney so that I've got something to go straight into if possible. Somebody will give me an introduction or put in a good word.'

'Of course they will. I don't like this plan I've come up with. But I think it's the right thing to do, Jenny. Besides, we've still got some time together before I go. I'm not running away just yet.'

As it turned out, James only had three days to wait before leaving for Sydney.

Between her shifts, Jenny took him to some of the sights around the city, to places where she'd found the space to think. They strolled along her favourite beaches, feeling the hot sand massaging their pale feet, and sat gazing out at the deep blue swells rolling and crashing apart into a spume of foamy white gems. They were happy, expectant. The country offered them so much hope.

PART II

Chapter 12

James arrived early for his first day at the Henry King Industries factory at Riverwood on the banks of the Georges River. When he'd secured the job, the foreman told him to arrive half an hour before starting time so that he and the other new workers could be shown the ropes. It seemed there were always new men signing on to work for the company.

It was an exciting day.

Although James had found that men with a trade were in short supply in Sydney, at first he'd only been able to obtain a few weeks work here and there at places like the Tooths brewery, the Goodyear tyre factory and the Balmain Power Station. He desperately needed a full-time job so that he and Jenny could have more security. He made contact with a few of the men he'd worked with at Disaster Gorge. One of them suggested he approach Henry King Industries as they were often after men to work in their asbestos cement factory. It turned out to be a good suggestion because he was offered full-time employment on the day he turned up to apply for a job. James hadn't hesitated to accept. He felt very lucky. The foreman told him, 'You're just the sort of bloke we're after, Henderson, a trained fitter and turner with experience working with asbestos.'

It was a warm sunny day as James walked through the gates to the factory. A big sign told him that he was at 'The Home of Genuine KIL Fibrosheet'. He looked around and saw a series of sawtoothed buildings constructed of unpainted, deeply contoured corrugated sheeting. He later found out that they were asbestos cement sheets, the same sheets that had been used to build the Tooth brewery and the other factories at which he'd already worked. They were also the same sheets that he'd seen at the mill at Disaster Gorge. These ones were a dirty grey-brown with splotches of blue lichen, but James didn't care what they looked like. It was a bright Sydney day and he was starting a well-paid permanent job.

He walked into the factory office, a small appendage to the main buildings, where he was warmly greeted by a receptionist. Two other new men were already waiting there. Another three arrived shortly after James. A very tall man came out of a room behind reception.

'Morning. I'm Bill Kruger, the factory manager. I'll be telling you something about the company before Jack Taylor, one of our foremen here, shows you around the factory and takes you to where you'll be working.'

Kruger ushered the men into a brightly lit meeting room and waved his big hand dismissively towards some chairs. He was an imposing, gruff man with incongruous waves of luxuriant silver hair sweeping from one side of his head to the other. He picked up a cup of tea, looked penetratingly at James and the others while taking a sip, then started a spiel he had obviously given many times before.

'Today, you're starting work for a well-respected, highly successful family company, Henry King Industries Limited. I've been working here for fifteen years and can assure you it's a great place to work. You'll be well looked after. I'm sure you'll all enjoy your time here and I trust it will be for many years to come.

'Now, a bit of the history of this place. The company was founded by a Dutch immigrant, Henry Konings, who arrived in Sydney in the 1880s. If you can believe it, he originally started out in embalming and running a funeral parlour in Hunter Street. He soon branched out into fruit preserving, cordials and small goods. He dabbled in leathers, rope, clothing, hardware. A very industrious man was Henry Konings. Always on the lookout for fresh business opportunities. There was nothing he wouldn't consider or do.

'Several years after coming to Australia, he Anglicised his name to Henry King, but he maintained his connections to Europe and travelled there regularly to investigate new products and profitable ideas. While on a business trip after the Great War, Henry was impressed by some new building boards he saw in Belgium. They were made of paper pulp, asbestos fibres, cement and sand. The boards were light and easy to use. Whole walls could be erected in a fraction of the time it took to use timber and bricks. He signed a contract with the Belgian manufacturer to import the boards.

'On his return, he started advertising the new asbestos sheets. There was initially a modest turnover, but as the product gained acceptance he could barely meet the demand. After a decade of importing asbestos cement from Europe, Henry decided to establish his own factory to produce the sheets in Australia. He needed help to do it.

'As I said before, this is a family company. In 1908, Henry married Elise Josephson. They had two sons, Gideon and Gordon. When Henry decided to start a company to manufacture asbestos cement products, Elise's family injected capital into the venture. Gideon and Gordon also entered the business. The new company was called Henry King Industries Limited.

'By 1935, the company had imported modified paper-making machines known as Hatchek machines to start making its own sheets. You'll see those machines later this morning. The company built a factory on the Georges River and started production. And gentlemen, that's where we're sitting right now. The factory Henry King started in 1935.

'The business did very well. The company now owns and runs factories in most Australian states. It employs hundreds of men like you. You'll be working for a company that has a proud tradition in building this great country of ours.

'Unfortunately, old Henry died in 1946. The company continued under his sons, Gideon and Gordon King, and their cousin, Emmanuel Josephson. Now the third generation of Kings and Josephsons has entered the company. So, it's still very much a family concern despite the fact it's now listed on the Stock Exchange. The family are very hands on. You never know, you might be fortunate enough to meet one of these men. You'll like them.'

James was impressed by Kruger's words despite their rather pat delivery. He was keen to belong to and feel part of a family concern.

'Right. Jack should be ready to take you around the factory. Let's go.' Kruger strode out of the room, the men following in his wake. At the factory's entrance, he introduced them to Jack Taylor, who took charge, leading the men into the heart of the factory. In contrast to Bill Kruger, he was a genial, neat man of about forty. He spoke loudly because of the din, gesticulating at pieces of equipment as he went.

Inside, the factory was vast. It stretched from the loading dock, where flat-tray trucks stacked with familiar hessian bags of asbestos fibre were rear-ended into an opening in the walls, down to the Georges River where Taylor pointed to the sand and cement being unloaded from low-slung barges.

'The company gets its asbestos from all around the world and from Australia too. You'll soon learn about the different types of fibre. The white asbestos – chrysotile – comes from Canada, the brown asbestos – amosite – from Africa and the blue asbestos – that's crocidolite – from Western Australia and Africa. The names of the mines are stencilled on the bags, as you can see.'

James looked at the black, red, green and blue lettering: 'Disaster Blue', 'Cape Asbestos', 'Canadian Chrysotile', 'NW Blue'. Some of the sacks were torn or split. This was nothing new. He knew first-hand how hard it was to keep the hessian bags intact. After the bags were unloaded from a truck, the driver swept the loose fibres off the tray and onto the tarmac.

The men were then taken to the blower room and tide mill area. 'You'll be starting here as a fitter and turner, Henderson, along with Guthrie, who'll be in the asbestos gang.'

James watched as the men in the asbestos gang grabbed the bags of raw asbestos and by brute force lifted and emptied them into bins. The hessian sacks leaked their contents over the heads and shoulders of the men as they went about their tasks. After the fibre was emptied into the bins, it was shoved down chutes into what Jack Taylor said was the hammer mill, which pulverised the fibre into fine, feathery particles, which were then blown through ducts into storage hoppers.

'Your job will be to keep the machines working, Henderson. It shouldn't be too difficult as we have top-class engineers in the company to design and make the very best machinery. I'll get one of the leading hands to show you what's what after we've finished the tour. It's dusty, as you can see, but it's critical to the whole process to make sure all the fibre is teased or fluffed out before it's raked into the tide mills over there, where water's added. As you can see, the slurry is mixed together with those beaters before being mixed with sand and cement to make the perfect asbestos cement sheet. It changes now and then, but by and large there's about ten to fifteen percent asbestos in the mix, sometimes of different fibre types depending on what the final product will be. For example, the corrugated asbestos sheets have more blue asbestos in them than the flat sheets.'

Jack Taylor wasn't wrong. It was very dusty. James thought the blower room was not unlike the mill at Disaster Gorge. Looking into the area was like looking through frosted glass. You could only see blurred images, vague apparitions of workers.

After the tide mill, Taylor showed James and the other men the finishing area.

'So, what you see now is the liquid mixture from the tide mill being rolled out onto felt rollers. We put a number of layers of this wet sludge on top of each other to make sheets of a predetermined thickness. It's exactly how paper is made. Once the desired thickness is achieved, the wet sheets are rolled out onto a conveyor belt where they're cut and left to cure. After they've dried out a bit, the sheets are still what we call green. Now, if you come over here, you'll see the green sheets being sanded, trimmed and labelled with the famous black Henry King Industries brand: 'Genuine KIL Fibrosheet'. That's what it's all about, boys. Making these sheets of what everyone calls 'fibro'.'

James noticed that the finishing area was also dusty. The belt sanders were not enclosed. As each sheet travelled under the belt, pale-brown dust belched out the sides.

After the tour, Jack Taylor introduced each man to the leading hands in the areas they would be working before calling smoko and showing them to the canteen. It was a friendly place. James shook a great many hands and had forgotten just as many names by the end of the day. He remained buoyant about the new job and stayed at work later than the others so he could continue familiarising himself with the machines and how they worked.

By the time he arrived home, however, he was exhausted. He hoped it was going to work out. He wanted it to. As he walked through the back door after taking off his shoes and saw his wife in the kitchen, his mood lifted.

'Hello, Jenny. What a day.'

Chapter 13

It had been a whirlwind six months. An emotional six months. James frequently pinched himself to establish that it was real and to prove that he was actually married and living with Jenny in Sydney.

After arriving in the city, he'd lodged in a boarding house in Redfern, finding temporary work at various factories while looking for a place to rent and trying to reset his bearings. Jenny wrote to him regularly to keep him up to date with her progress in tying up loose ends in Perth. It had been much slower than planned. At last, one afternoon after work, Mrs Perkins, the landlady at the boarding house, handed him the long-awaited letter from Jenny, confirming her departure. It had been almost two months since he had seen her.

My dearest James,

I'm missing you like never before, but soon we'll be together! I'll be sailing on Orcades next Wednesday, 21 February 1959. I arrive in Sydney on Sunday, 25 February, weather permitting.

The head midwife has been awfully good to me and has let me keep working for as long as I've needed. She's offered us both her congratulations. She gave me an excellent reference, which I think made it easy for me to get my new job as a midwife at the Crown Street Women's Hospital in Surry Hills. That's not far from Redfern, I'm told.

I've arranged to stay in the nurses' quarters at the hospital – it's the best solution until the wedding. I hope they're as good as the rooms in Perth where I've had a nice view of the river.

Everybody on the ward has been most kind. One couple named their new daughter Jenny and said they hoped she'd turn out to be as lovely as I am, which made me blush but was very nice to hear.

I'm afraid Hugh hasn't been so nice. In fact, he's been horrid. I feel very hurt. He refuses to forgive me for making a fool of him and 'throwing my life away'. I don't understand why he's taking it so personally. After all, it's my life to throw away and not his. And I definitely don't think I'm throwing my life away by marrying you! Not at all. I hope one day he can move on from this, but unfortunately he won't be coming to the wedding. Neither will any of my family from England. I didn't expect that they'd be able to, seeing as how far away we are and how much it would cost, but reading between the lines I think they're all rather disappointed that I won't be marrying Trevor. Of course, they send their hearty congratulations to both of us and apologise for not being able to make it. They would definitely love you as much as I do if they met you, but there's something in the tone of the letters that leaves me a little upset. I can't say what it is, but please don't worry about it, dear.

Trevor actually was very generous with his good wishes when I told him what I was doing. Although he spoke at great length about how he was close to finishing his training, he seemed sad to me. I hope he finds someone soon. He deserves it.

So, the news is, James, that we'll be having a very small wedding, almost the smallest wedding possible. So long as you're there, that's all that matters. I'm happy for you to start arranging it so long as the minister is a nice man.

I look forward to being in your arms,

Your loving, Jenny.

James didn't know much about churches, and his experience at Disaster hadn't given him much confidence in the clergy. He thought it was better to find a house to live in first so that they could become part of a community. He was very concerned about how Jenny was feeling – all alone over there, ostracised, fretting – and he was the reason for all of it. He needed to get moving to put some sort of structure in place for her so that the upheaval of landing in another strange city didn't make her feel worse.

Fortuitously, the day after he received the letter, James found a small pastel-green fibro cottage in Bankstown to rent. It was modest at best, sitting like a matchbox under its unpainted corrugated fibro roof on a dead-flat featureless block. But he liked the fact that it was new and in an area with young families. It was simple, clean and bright. He hoped that Jenny would like it too.

As the day of her arrival approached, James started to panic. Where was the best place to get furniture? Bed linen? Towels and homewares? Mrs Perkins stepped in when she saw him floundering and with her help he very soon thought the little cottage was looking quite comfortable and homely. He was still anxious that Jenny might regret her decision to leave Perth, her brother and Trevor Hungerford to be with him. He was eager to make her happy and to show her that she had made the correct choice.

◆

On the day Jenny arrived in Sydney, James was there to meet her. And as before at Perth Central Station, all the anxieties melted away as soon as he saw her golden face and they embraced.

'I've missed you, Jenny. It's so good to feel you in my arms at last. God, my heart's pounding. Can you feel it? Stop beating like that you stupid thing! It's definitely the last time we do this, Jenny. I'll never leave you on your own ever again. I absolutely promise this time. Even if it's only for my own sake!'

'I promise too, James. These past eight weeks have been terrible.

Everything's been so hard to handle and very distressing. I missed you every day. I felt so alone even though there were so many people around me. It was worse than when you were up at Disaster Gorge.'

She looked up from their embrace. James saw that she was crying. 'What's wrong, Jenny? What's the matter?'

'Nothing. I'm just happy to be here with you and to start our lives together, that's all. They're tears of happiness, James, not sadness.'

He wasn't so sure. The only thing he had the power to do was to hug her, kiss her and be as positive as he could. He thought she might have left part of herself in Perth. Perhaps it would never come back.

'Let's get you organised at the hospital; it's just up that hill over there, and then I'll show you where we'll be living after we get married. That is, if you're up for it.'

'Of course I am, James. I need to keep moving at the moment. Tell me everything you've done. I want to know every detail.'

He leaned away from her to obtain a better look. He gazed at her rosy cheeks and the shifting green and blue of her shining eyes and smiled. He took her bag from her and led the way up the rise. She had given away a different life altogether to be with him. He hoped he could be everything she would ever need. Did he have that within him?

Chapter 14

'That's certainly quite a day, James. You've been gone for a very long time. I won't be happy if they're the hours you'll be working at this new factory. If they are, when will I ever see you?'

'No need to worry, Jenny. I decided to stay late so that I'll know precisely how the machines work and what I'll need to do. I don't want to make any mistakes, and get sacked. This job's very important for both of us.'

'Really, James, sometimes you worry about absolutely nothing. I've no doubt that you're probably the best worker they've ever had there, and they'll find that out within the week. Go and have a shower and then tell me all about it. Dinner's almost ready.'

When he returned, and sat down to Jenny's beef and vegetable stew, James felt invigorated.

'Thanks, Jenny, exactly what I was wanting. How was your day?'

'I did some shopping and cooking. Cleaned up things. Washed the bedclothes. Nothing very interesting. I'm at the hospital for the next five days, so I got everything done today. One day, James, it would be good to own a car. It would make the shopping so much easier.'

'Well, now that I have a full-time job, we may be able to afford one very soon.'

'I do hope it's a nice place to work and that they're going to look after you.'

'Jen, the people are friendly and helpful. I have a good feeling about the place. To be honest, it's a wee bit dirty and dusty, but it's a factory and that's what they're like. It's part of the job. Other than that, it seems good to me.'

'I thought you were never going to work in a place like Disaster Gorge again.'

'It's not the same, I promise. Nothing like it. There's definitely some asbestos dust floating around, but you can't avoid it when you're making asbestos cement products. We were told by the manager this morning how important asbestos cement is to housing in Australia. If the factory didn't make the sheets, houses couldn't be built and we'd get nowhere. It might be a dirty job, but the pay's excellent. It's not like Scotland or Disaster Gorge at all. Here, they recognise that you work in dusty conditions so they pay you more. You get compensated because it's unpleasant. It's a nuisance, Jen, but I'm used to it.'

'James, I don't want to hear you coughing and spluttering at the end of the day.'

'I won't be. Anyway, when all's said and done, if we're careful with the money, I reckon by the end of the year we'll have earned enough to buy our own home. How good will that be? Worth putting up with some dust, I'd say. We'll need my savings and my inheritance and what we can add from our jobs, but things are definitely looking up. I even think we'll be able to buy a car as well.'

'So long as you're sure and you think they know what they're doing, then I'm happy, James. It does sound rather exciting, I agree.'

'Oh, it's good, Jen. I heard all about it today. It's a family company and the family members who run the show come out and visit the factory and make sure everyone's happy. They've got factories all around the country, so they must be doing something right.'

Chapter 15

After what they'd experienced since leaving the United Kingdom, James was glad that he and Jenny quickly settled into a simple routine. They both worked very hard, but as their bank book showed, it was worth every ounce of effort.

He'd been right to leave Western Australia.

Perth had been wide, bright, sandy and slow. Sydney was also ablaze with light, but it was no sleepy country town. You could see industry all around you. Factories, docks and power stations dotted the harbour. What an expanse of water! James thought. It was as if an axe had been used to cut a great jagged chunk from the continent into which had poured the deep green-blue of the ocean. It put the lochs of Scotland to shame. And then there was the bridge spanning it all. Man hadn't simply connected the two sides of the harbour, he had mastered the elements. He had created something of sandstone and steel as solid and enduring as anything in the environment. Sydney was a place in which James thought he and Jenny could also take hold, put down roots, prosper, build a family.

The Henry King factory gave James that opportunity.

◆

'Hey, Henderson, see Kruger over there with that old man,' his foreman, Geoff Blaxland, said, pointing towards the factory entrance. 'That's Mr

Gideon King, one of the directors. Henry King's son. His sons, Andrew and Phillip, are the ones really in charge now, but he still comes into the factory to check on things.'

James watched the portly man walking beside the towering Kruger. He stopped and chatted with some of the workers.

'Look busy, he's coming this way.'

James felt Gideon King and Bill Kruger's presence rather than seeing them nearby. Then he heard Blaxland's voice.

'Good afternoon, Mr King, very glad to see you again.'

'Thank you, Mr Blaxland. Who is this young man working with you?'

James looked up. Gideon King was markedly taller than him, a wee bit taller than Blaxland, but nowhere near Kruger's summit.

'James Henderson, Mr King. He's been with us a few months now. He's one of our very best fitters and turners.'

'Is that so? Well, Mr Henderson, what do you say to that?' Gideon asked.

'I wouldn't know, sir, but I do my best.'

'Is that a Scottish accent I hear? And if my memory still serves me, a Glaswegian accent. Am I right, Mr Henderson?'

'You are indeed, sir. I'm from a wee place on the outskirts called Paisley. Learned my trade on the Clyde dockyards.'

'First-rate training, I'll bet. Welcome aboard, Mr Henderson. I hope you enjoy it here. We try to make everyone feel part of the family. I trust Mr Kruger and Mr Blaxland have been doing just that.'

'Yes, they have. I'm very grateful for the opportunity.'

James wouldn't have described Kruger as warm or friendly, but Blaxland had taken him under his wing and seemed to be always looking out for him. He was the foreman responsible for the asbestos gang, unloading materials, the tide mill and the blower room.

'Very good to hear, Mr Henderson. How have you found the work? Are all the machines working properly?'

'Generally they do, sir, but I'm kept fairly busy making sure the tide mill's running as it should.'

'You make sure you tell Mr Blaxland or Mr Kruger about any problems. We have some very good engineers in the company, who are always up for a challenge to improve things or make new equipment to solve any problems. Far better that we do these sorts of things in house rather than relying on others.'

'I will, sir.'

'Good to meet you, Mr Henderson. I trust we shall meet again.'

'Goodbye, sir.'

James thought he was an agreeable old man. It was impossible to guess his age. Although he had a stoop and moved slowly, his smooth face had a healthy tan and his eyes were lively and intelligent.

'Not a bad old boy, is he?' said Blaxland.

'Very friendly. I like him.'

'Okay, now what was the problem with the tide mill you were talking about? It looks good to me.'

'Geoff, after I fixed the mixer last week, it doesn't seem to be producing an even slurry. Can we stop it for a while so I can check on something I think could be the problem?'

'Okay, just wait for the old boy to leave with Kruger. I don't like him seeing the factory down.'

If he'd been completely honest, James would have told Gideon King that the tide mills were always breaking down and he was kept busy bringing the paddle-wheeled contraption back to life. Hands on hips, proud of his handiwork, he would watch the tornado of fibres spin into the air, the white curly fibres of chrysotile 'holding hands' together and falling to the floor; the dart-like amosite and crocidolite gliding through the air for hours like tiny paper planes.

As the tide mills were not separated physically from the rest of the factory, the clouds of dust generated by the process were free to float through the entire atmosphere. James had been there long enough to experience the westerlies sweeping through the open factory doors, whipping up conditions like a blizzard. Sometimes, it was so bad that handkerchiefs had to be worn over the nose and mouth, as he had occasionally done at Disaster Gorge. The factory was its usual dusty self when Gideon King walked through the floor. He didn't appear to James to be either inconvenienced or worried by the asbestos fibres in the air. Nobody was.

After a few months in the tide mill, James was moved to the finishing area. He appreciated the new challenge. There was a different group of workers to meet, but the workforce was not dissimilar to that at Disaster Gorge or at the tide mills and in the asbestos gang. There were Italians, Irishmen, Scots and Englishmen. Some Greeks too. The chief difference was that most of the men were married, like James, and had young families. He didn't meet any drunkards like the poor souls back west.

Chapter 16

James kept the finishing machines running smoothly in his new role in the factory. Sheet after sheet of asbestos cement was churned out and stacked in piles, ready to be taken to the loading bay. He didn't need reminding that the asbestos cement sheets were in high demand in the housing sector, but Kruger, the foreman and the leading hands all regularly imparted the message. James played his part in ensuring the company met the demand.

He quickly became familiar with the products in the company catalogues to the extent that he could identify what had been used in the house he and Jenny bought at the end of 1959.

It was not far from their rented cottage.

'There it is, Jenny, 12 Hibiscus Avenue, Bankstown, our new home,' James said as they walked past shortly after buying it. He could see how happy she was even though it was a humble structure, like all the other homes in the suburb.

'I love it, James. It looks so inviting. Just right for us. So much better than where we are now.' James thought it was quite similar, although it was slightly bigger and of course theirs – and that made the world of difference.

The house was set on a gently rising block. Apart from the terracotta-tiled roof, the house was made entirely of Genuine KIL Fibrosheets. The external walls were made of asbestos cement boards cut and patterned to look like the planks of a weatherboard cottage. James knew these were part of a brand-new range of asbestos cement sheets the company had put out. Inside, there were painted flat sheets on the walls of the bedrooms and living areas. The bathroom and kitchen were panelled with new wet-area sheets known as Genuine KIL Tileboard. These sheets were made to look like tiles, using bold modern textures and colours with names like Misty Blue, Seabreeze Green and Kangaroo Paw Red. The builder had used Seabreeze Green in James and Jenny's house, which was James's favourite colour.

Two large gumtrees and a Hills Hoist clothesline dominated the backyard. On the right-hand side of the property sat a garage big enough for the new Holden sedan James had bought a week earlier. At the front of the block stood several wattle trees and bottlebrushes. The path to the front door was edged by uneven blocks of quartzite rocks, emerging from the grass like the dorsal fins of a school of dolphins, gaining speed as they bulleted through the earth from the driveway to the porch.

James and Jenny hugged each other.

'I can't believe it, James. Our own home. I'm so looking forward to moving in.'

'Another four weeks, Jen, that's all.'

'I feel quite odd actually at the moment.'

'What do you mean?' He turned to her anxiously.

'It's like when I was boarding the ship, seeing it pushed away from the dock. That was both scary and thrilling. It's funny having both emotions at the same time. Do you know what I mean?'

'I think so, Jen. For me, it was when I was leaving on the train to London or on the ship to Sydney. The excitement of an adventure mixed with fear about the future. Can you remember your first day at school and you didn't know what to expect?'

'I guess that's it. But I also feel we belong here, James. I know it sounds silly seeing we come from the other side of the world, but it's how I feel right now.'

'I know. It is exciting, Jen. This is ours. Our home. Think of the bedrooms for children, a sunroom, a laundry. Your kitchen. We're going to be so happy here, I know it.'

Chapter 17

'Congratulations on the new baby, James!' Geoff Blaxland said, pumping James's arm vigorously. 'Give my regards to Jenny. I hope mother and baby are doing well.'

The two men sat down at the table in the canteen with their cups of tea and sandwiches.

'Both very well, Geoff. Thanks.' James was still on Cloud 9.

'What's the little blighter's name?'

'Robert Kenneth Henderson.'

'Very distinguished. Did it happen at Crown Street, where Jenny works?'

'Yep. On Saturday.'

'Thirteenth of April 1960; an auspicious date it will unquestionably turn out to be. Now, make sure you pass on Sarah's and my regards to Jenny when you next visit.'

'Thanks, Geoff, I will. Going in to see her and wee Robbie tonight.'

'Good on you, James. I bet you he's a good-looking kid like his mum.'

'You can only hope that'll be the case, Geoff. We don't want any of me ruining his looks, that's for sure.'

Blaxland leaned forward as if he had something serious to say. His expression transformed as if a switch had been flicked.

'Now, the other thing I wanted to mention is that there are going to be a couple of men from the Health Department visiting the factory this week. I'm not sure what's triggered the visit, but it's probably about the amount of dust in the atmosphere. I think there's a general push to make all factories cleaner, and I wouldn't object to that.'

'Should we be worried? They're not going to close us down, are they?' James was thinking of his new family and the future.

'God, no. Nothing like that. We'll be around for decades to come – a good product like ours, they need us. It's not that serious. As I said, a push to make working conditions cleaner. Kruger told me to tell everyone that there'll be a visit, but not to change anything we do. He doesn't know much about it either.'

'That's a relief. Thanks, Geoff, for letting me know. To tell you the truth, I wouldn't mind it if they want us to get the dust down. It gets under your skin sometimes – literally.'

'I know what you mean. Let's see what happens.'

◆

On the Wednesday of that week, Jenny returned home with the baby and the rumoured visit from the Health Department occurred. Although the men were supposed to go about their usual business, James could tell that, like him, they were sneaking looks at the two men wandering around the factory, generally getting in the way.

Bill Kruger initially showed them around then left them to do whatever they needed to. James watched as they pried and poked into all aspects of the factory's operations for three days. Instruments were placed in the vicinity of the tide mill, the finishing area and in the loading dock. James recalled seeing similar devices at Disaster Gorge when Dr Smith paid his visit to the mine and mill with his offsider, Stanley. So, it must be about the dust, James thought.

On the Friday, some of the workers, including James, were asked to go to the nurse's station to be examined. When James entered the room, he was seen by one of the men.

'Hello, young man. I'm Dr White, what's your name?'

'James Henderson, sir.'

'You work in the finishing area?'

'I do.'

'Please sit down here, Mr Henderson, and let me listen to your chest,' Dr White said. 'Take your shirt off for me, there's a good chap.'

James felt the cold bell of a stethoscope against his chest. 'Breathe in deeply,' Dr White instructed. 'And now out. In again. And out.' He moved the bell around James's chest. 'Thank you. All good. Clear as can be. You can get dressed now.'

◆

The next week, there was gossip in the factory about the Health Department visit. How many men were examined, nobody knew. Rumours spread about screening for tuberculosis. Some of the men were sent for chest x-rays. James never found out why the visitors had been there or what they discovered. Although a local GP started coming to the factory some time later to conduct regular clinics, James thought the Health Department men couldn't have found anything important because nothing else changed in the factory. The machines kept cutting and sanding, and the dust spewed forth as before.

Chapter 18

1962

'Are you ready, Jen? I've got Robbie.'

'Almost. I'm trying to squeeze the potato salad into the Tupperware, but it won't fit,' she shouted from the kitchen.

James was standing at the front door holding Robert's hand. He had already reversed the Holden out of the garage and closed its caramel-coloured metal door. It was the Henry King annual picnic at Centennial Park and he didn't want to be late.

'Okay, ready,' Jenny said as she bustled down the hallway carrying a basket. James smiled, amazed as always at her beauty. She was also pregnant, which he knew would be a talking point at the picnic.

'I hope this year's picnic is as good as last year's,' she said as they drove east to the park.

'I'm sure it will be. Look at the weather. It'll be a beauty.'

It was a cloudless spring day and the Henry King families had turned out in force to celebrate another year of prosperity. A rising hubbub greeted James and Jenny as they strolled towards their friends congregating on the grass. Waterfowl honked and squawked, dogs barked, children squealed as they chased one another or tripped over and rolled down the gentle hill, and everywhere men and women were laughing, chatting, cooking, eating, serving drinks and generally having a good time.

'Here he is!' yelled a chunky man as they approached.

'Hello, Norm, how are you?'

'Never better, Hendo. Good to see you've made it. And who do we have here? Young Robbie and your beautiful wife, Jennifer. With child no less. Hello, Jenny, lovely to see you again.'

'Good afternoon, Norman. Yes, we have another on the way. You're looking very fit and healthy. Life must be good.'

'None of that, young Jennifer. You know as well as I do that I'm carrying far too much winter condition.'

'Nonsense. Where's Georgina? Oh, there she is.'

'Hello, Jenny. Glad you could make it. And this big boy must be Robert. Hello to you, young man.' Georgina was a short, plump woman, not unlike her husband. She didn't have far to bend to look directly into Robert's blue eyes. He was plainly uncertain about how to respond to her heartiness. James thought he might even be on the verge of tears. 'Why don't you come and say hello to my daughter, Amy, and her friend, Joanna.' Georgina offered her hand, which Robert took tentatively, and soon he was sitting on a rug with two little girls, eating cake and being told everything it was possible to know about the Airedale sitting aloofly nearby.

'This is very exciting, Jenny. When's the baby due?'

'The doctor says May, just like James.'

'That would be nice, wouldn't it? Are you wanting a boy or a girl?'

'We don't care, Georgina, so long as it's healthy. Are you and Norman planning to have any more children?'

'I think we've got as many as we can handle, Jenny,' interjected Norman. 'Five's enough for any man – any sane man that is,' he replied with a wink at James. 'Why don't you two set up over there near our barbecue and picnic table. We'll keep an eye on your boy for you.'

They spread out their blanket and unpacked the basket next to an impressive folding picnic table. On top, a checked cloth had been spread, covered by what could very well have been every known condiment.

Geoff Blaxland and his wife, Sarah, soon appeared and said hello. James and Jenny easily flowed in and out of conversations with friends and couples new to the Henry King Industries family. James was happy. The company had been good to him. It had given him the start he had yearned for when he'd first thought of travelling from Scotland to Australia. He enjoyed the company of his fellow-workers. They were a good-natured, uncomplaining, rowdy lot. Jenny had met several wives and had forged her own social life with them. The majority had young families. Many were migrants. They were all threatening the horizon together. James and Jenny felt like they belonged. It was a good day.

Late in the afternoon, as James was thinking it was time to leave before Robbie got too cranky, Geoff Blaxland came up to him again. He had on what James knew to be his serious face.

'Look, James, I wanted to talk about this earlier, but I didn't have the chance. It's nothing bad, so don't look worried.' He indicated for James to distance himself from the group by a few yards. 'As you know, I have a brother, Reg, who's a builder. I think you've met him at our house. Perhaps in the loading docks too.'

'That's right.'

'Well, I've been talking to him about you. Steady on, it's okay. Now, as you and I both know, there's a housing boom and Reg is struggling to find hard workers like yourself, James. It's no secret I'm fond of you and would like to see you and Jenny prosper. Well, here's an opportunity. Reg will tell you this himself, but he's happy for me to pass on that he's prepared to give you an 'apprenticeship' on a higher than usual salary, in return for a decent day's work. I know you're getting sick of the dust and working indoors all the time, so this could be the answer. You could one day be your own boss as well. That's got to appeal to you, James.'

'Yes, it does. We've spoken about that before. But I don't know anything about building houses. Wouldn't he be taking a risk giving me a job?'

'Yes, he knows that, but he also knows the risk is negligible. Nothing's beyond you, James – a new skill, an impossible task, overtime – you can do the lot. You've done all the filthy and difficult jobs the other workers baulk at in the factory. And you do them without complaint. Reg would give his eye teeth for a man like you. Look at old Norm over there. He's a capable man, but he only does what he needs to do. Now, if this sounds agreeable, I'll tell Reg and he can set up a meeting with you.'

'Okay, Geoff. I suppose there's nothing to lose. I'll hear what your brother has to say. But please don't tell Jen, not in her condition. She needs to keep calm.'

'Mum's the word, James.'

As he lay in bed with Jenny that night, James wondered whether his life had taken another unexpected term. Was Geoff right? Was James Henderson worth investing in?

Chapter 19

Bill Kruger loomed over James during the lunch break and shook his hand. 'We're sorry to see you go, Henderson; you've been a valuable member of the company. We wish you and your family all the best with your future.' As Kruger attempted unsuccessfully to disappear into the background, everyone started clapping.

'Thank you!' James shouted. The clapping died down. 'I've really enjoyed my time here. The company has looked after me and my family very well. Um, thanks again. I'll miss you all. Goodbye!'

As the clapping and cheering resumed, he again cried out his thanks at the top of his lungs, raised his hand in farewell and walked towards the linishing belts to resume the afternoon shift. A few of the men slapped him on his back as he went. 'Good on you, Hendo.' 'Good luck!'

James felt quite emotional saying goodbye to his colleagues. While he had only been at the factory for three years, he'd met many men like him, trying to get ahead in a new country. Trying to build their own sense of community. He couldn't leave without letting some of them know how much he had appreciated their friendship.

He was shaking hands with Paulo Berendetti, the Italian migrant who'd been his mate in the tide mill area, when Paulo said, 'Hey, Jimmy, who's that man over there with Bill Kruger?'

James looked over his shoulder in the direction Paulo indicated. 'You mean the thin man with the hat on? That's Russell Dymock, the safety officer, who joined us ages ago. Surely you've seen him before, Paulo.'

'No, not him. I know who he is. He's a silly man. Told me to wash my hands before eating lunch the other day. I told him I had, but he told me I must not have done a good job because they were still a disgrace. I told him to get lost. No, not him, the other man, the short fatso one.'

'Oh, him. I couldn't see him behind Kruger. I don't know. Hang on, I'll find out from Geoff.'

Half an hour later, James reported back to Berendetti. 'Geoff Blaxland says he's from the Health Department. He doesn't know his name, but apparently he's here to do some tests on dust levels like those men who came last year or the year before.'

'Everyone knows it's dusty. Why do they need tests to show what we already know?'

'No idea, Paulo. I suppose if they want to try and get it down a wee bit, that can't hurt, can it?'

'But I get paid more for working in the bad dusty areas, Jimmy. I don't want to lose that. Maria's counting on me, you know.'

'I know, I got paid the dust money too when I was in the tide mill. If it's like last time, nothing will happen, and you'll be okay, Paulo. I've got to go. See you later.'

'Ciao Jimmy.'

The rumour mill cranked into gear for the rest of the afternoon just as it had with the previous Health Department visit. The men didn't know what the visitor was up to or what he hoped to achieve. They guessed he wasn't a doctor because no one was physically examined. James watched as the man set up his equipment adjacent to the linishing machine that James had only recently serviced. It was working like a dream.

'Hello, there. Can I help in any way?' James asked the man.

'No thank you, try to pretend I'm not here. Just go about your business and I'll be out of your way in no time at all.'

'Okay. Do you mind if I ask you what you're doing?'

'I'm measuring how much dust is in the atmosphere. If there's too much, I'll be asking the company to try to get the levels down so that it's more comfortable for all of you working nearby.'

'I see. Is there anything to worry about?' James asked, suddenly concerned.

'Hard to say. You don't want to have too much dust floating around when you're working. I'd imagine it's a damn nuisance, getting into your hair, on your skin, up your nose, down your lungs, coughing up lots of phlegm.'

'You're not wrong.'

'Well, if we need to get the levels down, we'll get them down. Shouldn't be a problem. Simply good common sense.'

Russell Dymock, who was hovering nearby, came forward. 'Come on, Henderson, let the man do his job. He's got a lot to do.'

'Sure, sorry to take up your time,' James said. 'I hope the measurements aren't too bad.'

'We'll see how we go. Not too bad so far.'

'Come on, that's enough chatter,' Dymock said.

James was generally quite tolerant of others, but Dymock was definitely not his cup of tea. A weaselly, interfering, nervy man.

After the Health Department officials had visited two years prior, Dymock had been employed to look after safety issues. James wasn't sure he did anything useful. Several months later, the local doctor had started occasionally visiting the factory and examining anyone who was sick. He used the nurse's office as his examining room just as the Health Department doctor had the year before. James had been asked by his foreman to have his annual examination along with a few others in the finishing area. The doctor, a tall, unpleasant man, had introduced himself as Dr Mathers. He listened to James's chest with his cold stethoscope and then dismissed him with the words 'all clear'. James had no idea what he was listening for and no one ever told him. All that mattered was being told his lungs were clear.

James never heard what the latest visitor from the Health Department found or what he recommended to the company. He didn't really care, as all of that was behind him.

What a relief, he thought, as the last farewells receded and he came out of the factory. Into the light! Into the fresh air! He looked up at the sky. The sun was still shining low to the west. To the south, and his home, a warm, bluish glow had settled on the sprawling suburbs.

The next day, he would start his new career with Reg Blaxland & Sons. Things were looking up.

Chapter 20

1964

'Listen, James, now that you have your ticket as a builder, there's something I need to talk to you about.'

'Sure, Reg. What is it?'

They were standing in the mud, drinking coffee from the Thermos flask Reg Blaxland invariably brought to the building site each day. It was a crisp winter's morning and they'd both been at the Fairfield property since 6.30am.

'I've been in the building caper for close to forty years,' Blaxland started, his breath misty in the cold air. 'On days like this, James, I have to tell you it's not as easy as it used to be. My back's giving me gyp. I could hardly reach down to the hammer in my belt this morning when we first got going. It takes an age for the joints to warm up. I'm not sure I've got it in me to keep on getting up at the crack of dawn to hobble around a building site like an old cripple.'

'It can't be that bad, Reg. You're not an old man. Years to go, I'd say.'

Reg bit into the slice of sponge his wife had packed for him. 'That's nice of you to say, James,' he said as the crumbs collected on his chin, 'but I'm no spring chicken and, to tell you the truth, I've had enough. I'm ready to retire.'

'Reg, that's a wee bit sudden, isn't it?'

'I've been thinking about it for some time, James. I'm not getting any younger and Maud and I want to enjoy a nice long retirement down at our house at Gerroa. Wouldn't mind wetting a line every now and then. Take it easy, you know.'

James was starting to become anxious about his own future. For the past two years, he'd worked as hard as he could remember to learn a new trade. Reg, like his younger brother, Geoff, had taken him under his wing. He'd been an excellent teacher. But now James felt that security rapidly evaporating. What was he going to do if Reg closed down?

'I understand, Reg. It's a shock, though, that's all I'm saying.'

'Yeah, that's why I have to start talking about it now and let it sink in over the next few months.' He polished off the last of the cake and took a sip from his cup of coffee. 'We're a good team, I think. The rest of the boys respect you, even though they might've been in the game a bit longer. The problem is that none of them want to take on further responsibility. They want someone to tell them what to do and not have to think. I don't think you're like that, James. You've told me yourself that one day you'd like to be your own boss.'

'Yes, but that's a long way off. It's only a dream I have. It's not really serious.'

'Nah, James, it's not a dream. You'll do it. That's basically what I want to talk to you about. I reckon you've got the energy and drive to make a go of the business when I leave.'

'I'm not clear what you're saying, Reg.'

'Listen, James, I want you to think about it. You know what I'm saying.'

'No, Reg, you're pulling my leg. I don't know enough. I can't run a business. I've only just started in the building trade. It'd be daft for someone like me to even think about it. You can't be serious, Reg.'

'Oh, I am, James, and I know I'm right about you,' he said, then drank the last of his coffee. 'Do you think I knew what I was doing when I went out on my own? Of course not. I was young, stupid, pigheaded. Dad

thought I was a complete no-hoper. He said I was an idiot to start my own business when I'd only just finished my apprenticeship. It wasn't what I'd call a ringing endorsement coming from my own father. But he was as wrong as could be. I enjoyed being my own boss. Took to it like a duck to water. You'll be fine, James. Trust me, I know what I'm talking about. Also, I'm not going to dump it on you without easing you into it. I'll stay on for a few months, making sure the transition's as smooth as possible so that you know all the ins and outs of the business. Maud could even show Jenny how to do the book-keeping if you think she'd like to do that while she's at home with the kids. It worked well for Maud with our girls as they were growing up.'

'That all sounds good, Reg, but what are the others going to think?'

'Don't worry about them. They think you're a top bloke. That counts for something in my book. Chew it over. Talk to Jenny. She'll know I'm talking sense.'

'I don't know about that, Reg. You know she stopped work after Douglas was born, so there's only my wage supporting us.'

'Yeah, and that was two years ago and you've been doing okay as far as I can tell.'

He packed his empty cup and Thermos into the back of his utility and continued. 'I want to hand my business over to a younger man. Someone who can run it for years to come. That's you, James. Now, I've made a bloody good living out of the business and wanted for nothing. I'll make sure the price is something you can manage. I can assure you I'm no rip-off merchant.' He put his hand up as James was about to interrupt. 'No, hear me out. My four daughters have married office types. I've got nobody to inherit the business, so I'm giving it to someone I like, someone I know will run it well. You think about it while we get back into this job. Can't stand here all day gas-bagging.'

James was flattered by Reg's offer but was nervous about Jenny's reaction in light of the need to extend their house with a new baby on

the way. He hadn't yet told Reg that Jenny was pregnant with their third child. Could they afford it?

Later that day, when Reg told him the price he had in mind, it was more than reasonable, but even so, it was a sizeable sum of money. James didn't like going into debt. He couldn't keep on taking these risks in his life. Or could he?

◆

'Hello! I'm home!' James announced that afternoon as he stamped his caked boots on the backdoor mat and tossed his hat onto the laundry shelf.

'Please, James, the boots,' Jenny said as she gave him a quick hug and kiss, brushing the dust that had come from his overalls onto her apron.

He sat down on the back steps and pulled off his dirty boots.

'Daddy! Daddy!' cried his sons, Robert and Douglas, as they belted out of the living room and launched themselves at their father.

'Hey, don't knock your poor dad over,' James laughingly protested.

'Robbie, Dougie! Get off your father. You're getting dirt all over you and I don't want to run another bath. Come on, get off him, now!'

They were too busy giggling to pay attention to their mother.

'Righto, you two, off we get and let me go and have a shower.'

James wriggled free and, still grinning, stripped off his blue overalls and put them in the laundry sink. In his underpants and socks, he tiptoed to the bathroom.

Jenny hurried the boys back into the living room where they'd been playing quietly before James arrived then went into the laundry to wash James's overalls. She considered it important for him to look clean and smart at work. He had a fresh shirt and overalls most days. She lifted the dirty clothes from the tub and carried them at arms' length to the cement landing at the back of the house and shook them vigorously. She didn't know what James did each day to become so dirty and dusty, but his clothes always required a thorough shake before she could put them

in the washing machine. If she didn't, it would clog up with a glutinous muck. And that cost money to fix.

◆

After dinner, James sat at the kitchen table with Jenny. 'How's the new house coming along?' she asked.

'Pretty good, Jen. The timber frame's up and we'll have the outside sheets up by the end of the week. You should see them. They're the new ranch-style Fibrosheets Henry King brought out last month. If we were building now, I think I'd use them instead of the flat sheets.'

'Really? I'm happy with our home, James. It looks good to me.'

'I like it too, Jen. I'm not complaining. I'm just saying these new sheets are pretty smart.'

'Ranch-style? We don't even have ranches in Australia. Are they meant to look like wooden boards, is that what you're saying?'

'That's the idea. Cheaper and longer lasting than real wood. And easy to paint, according to the painter. Apparently, Kings are making a whole range of new sheets with different surface finishes. Who knows, they may even make Fibrosheets that look like bricks.'

'Fake bricks? Ugh. What's wrong with the real thing?'

'Price. That's what. People want their own homes and it's cheaper to use the sheets. Anyway, Jen, talking about new sheets, I've been thinking we should probably extend the sunroom out towards where the jacaranda is now that we're having another baby. We're running out of room.'

'But what about the laundry?'

'Well, Jen,' James said, standing up and moving to the doorway into the sunroom, 'if we knock down the wall from here,' – he demonstrated – 'to over here, there'll be enough room for a corridor and the laundry. I can also push out the back wall a bit to make it as big as it is now. That way, we'll have a new bedroom, the sunroom, which can also be a bedroom, and the laundry.'

'If you say so, James, then I'll go along with it. I really don't want the laundry any smaller. What with Robbie and Dougie's stuff, and your work clothes, I need all the space I can get.'

'You'll be fine, Jen. And there'll be plenty of room for the new baby. If you agree with the plan, I think I can get it done before September when the baby's due.'

'If you think it's a good idea, then let's do it. But I refuse to have any pretend weatherboard or fake bricks or anything like that.'

'It's all right, Jen, I'll only use the standard sheets like we already have.' He returned to the table and sat down. 'Jen, there's something else that's come up today that we need to discuss.' He took a mouthful of water from the glass in front of him. He caught his reflection in the window and looked back at the frown on Jenny's face. 'Nothing's wrong, Jen. We just have to talk about something pretty important. Something pretty good, in fact. Well, something that might be good for us.'

She still looked worried.

'No, really, it's nothing bad. You see, Reg wants to retire. He's had it and—'

'Oh, is that all. Well, of course, I'm sad for Reg and Maud, but—'

'No, Jenny. That's not it. Reg wants me to take over the business. And I really would like to do that, but, you know, I'll need to get a loan from the bank, and we have to make the house bigger, and you're pregnant, and—'

'James, don't be silly. You've got to do it. You want to, don't you?'

'Yes, I think so. It's risky though.'

'Well, I don't care. You should do it.' She moved over to his side of the table, leaned over him from behind and hugged him tightly around the shoulders. 'When have you ever knocked back a challenge? Look at it as a reward for all the hard work you've done in your life. Just look at how much we've achieved in so short a time. This is wonderful news. You deserve the chance. What do you always say? You know, when you're trying to explain the hours you work? "Hard work pays off in the end." Here's proof. We'll manage. We don't need to do the extension yet. Dougie can share with Robbie for a few more years. And the baby can sleep in the sunroom. It'll be a squeeze, but we'll manage.' She hugged him again. 'You make sure you tell Reg that you accept his offer. This is fantastic news! You go and do it right away.'

'Maybe in the morning, Jen. Let me sleep on it. It's a big decision.'

'Don't look so worried, James. It'll work out. You've taken risks before and they've all worked out in the end. Coming here, working up in that awful place in Western Australia, marrying me. Why wouldn't this one work out, too?'

'Marrying you? That wasn't a risk. What are you talking about? Okay, I get it. You're having a go at me.'

'I'm only teasing, James. You don't need to be so serious. Everything we've done has always worked out.'

'I don't know, Jen. Sometimes I feel that things aren't real, that they're going too fast or I'm not in control. One minute I'm in Glasgow feeling miserable and the next I'm here with you in Sydney being offered a builder's business. I don't know why people are so kind to me or what I've done to deserve it.'

Jenny laughed. 'It's because you're a lovely, generous, kind man yourself, that's why.'

'Sometimes, I think I'm doing all these things to prove something. I don't know who to – it could be me. Perhaps it's my dad or my mum. Maybe it's you.'

'Where's this coming from, James? You have nothing to prove, certainly not to me.' She held him more tightly.

'I don't know why I'm talking like this, Jen. I try my best, I know I do. Every now and then I think of what you could have had if you'd married Trevor Hungerford. You would've had so much more than I can give you. You'd probably be living in a mansion in Perth. Sometimes there's this little voice inside me that tells me I'm not good enough or that you could've done better. Maybe I'm trying to prove something to you about that.'

'James, don't torture yourself about Trevor. He's ancient history. I chose you, not him. I wanted to be with you. I don't care whether we have a big house or whether you earn hundreds of pounds or what you do. I just want you and that's all I'll ever want.'

'I'm sorry, Jen. It's a big step and I want it to be a success. I couldn't stand being a failure. It truly would kill me.'

'But you won't be, James. I know this will work because you can do it. Reg wouldn't give it a second's thought if he wasn't certain you could do it. Take his advice, James. I'm with you on this. We all are. Even the baby.'

He smiled wanly. He thought he was an uncomplicated man. Yet here he was, on the threshold of something good, complicating his life with fears about nothing – nothing but the dead past that couldn't possibly hurt him. What was he thinking? He looked into Jenny's eyes. 'I'm sorry, Jen. I guess I'm worried about the future and having a few doubts about whether it'll be as good as I think it might be. You know, it's not only me I have to think of. What I choose affects us all.'

'James, it's all right to feel anxious about big decisions. I'm scared as hell about what's coming, but I also can't wait for it to happen. If you weren't fearful, then it wouldn't mean anything to you and you'd know in your heart not to do it.'

He smiled more convincingly. 'You're right, of course, Jen. We'll be fine. We've always been fine. I think I've always made the right decisions. At least, because they've been mine, I've been able to live with them, even when it's been a struggle to make them work. I'll be better in the morning.'

'Yes, you will. It's time for bed. Just let me tidy up these plates first.'

'I'll give you a hand,' he said and started clearing the table.

◆

When Kate Louise Henderson was born at Crown Street a week overdue in October 1964, James could not have been happier. His firm, James Henderson & Sons, was up and running, building houses in the south-western suburbs of Sydney, specialising in inexpensive KIL Fibrosheet cottages. The business was prospering as it had under Reg Blaxland and James wondered why he'd ever felt panicky at the prospect of accepting Reg's offer.

By the end of the year, James was able to complete the extension to the house at Hibiscus Avenue to give all three children their own bedrooms. He even managed to create a small office in the process so that Jenny had a quiet spot to do the books for the company. It was time-consuming and tedious work, but James knew it gave Jenny a great sense of satisfaction helping him with the business, especially when she asked him to run his eye across the neat columns of figures to see how well he was doing. He didn't, however, need the figures to convince himself how happy he was. He felt it every day he turned over in bed and saw Jenny beside him.

Chapter 21

1970

'Steady that sheet, will you, Nick. I've got to take off four inches along the side.'

'Sure, Jimmy. Got it.'

James went along the length of the Fibrosheet with the fibroshears, the special tool recommended by Henry King Industries. It was a slow process. Given the wide variety of Fibrosheet sizes available, usually little cutting was needed in erecting a James Henderson & Sons fibro cottage. Even so, James was looking forward to receiving his new electric saw that week. His electrician, Colin Frawley, had already connected the site to the power supply. 'Anytime now,' James had been assured by the salesman at the hardware store where he held an account. As that was several weeks ago, the salesman's assurance seemed to mean any time in the next year, James thought. He'd ordered an angle grinder as well. The saw, he'd been told, would cut through a stack of Fibrosheets like a knife through butter, while the angle grinder would allow him to cut the corners off the roofing sheets in no time at all so that he could lay them over the roof in one hit. That task had always been fiddly. James was anticipating being able to almost double his construction rate by the end of the 1970s if the power tools proved successful. He'd seen a demonstration at a trade show where roof fixers were cutting through Henry King asbestos cement corrugated roofing at prodigious rates. One of the tradesmen told James his men were working all day every day cutting roofing sheets or flat sheets. Teams of carpenters did the cutting while others did the installing. Whole suburbs were being built in weeks.

'Nick, this could be one of the last times we'll be using the shears.'

'Can't wait, Jimmy. With the power saw we'll be putting up a house a day. How'd that be?' replied Nick Pastopoulos, one of three carpenters James employed.

'Not too sure about a house every day, Nick, but it'll be interesting to see how they go.'

'Nah, Jimmy, you're too conservative. We'll be building a suburb in a week, like they said at the show.'

'I'm sure it'll be a lot faster than what we do now, but I'm not really interested in building an empire. Sure, I'd like more profits, but I don't want to get too big. I reckon that'll create more problems. Life's good at the moment. The kids are growing up. Jenny's happy. I don't want to spoil that by being too greedy.'

James smiled as he watched Nick cutting the Fibrosheet. He could be very energetic with his opinions, but he was a decent, hard-working young man. Nick's father had worked with James years ago in the Henry King Industries factory in Riverwood. James had taken Nick on as an apprentice as a favour to his dad, Con, who had died the previous year from lung cancer. It was a dreadful shock. Nick told James that he didn't remember his father ever being a heavy smoker. Come to think of it, neither did James. Regardless, it had been enough to turn Nick off the fags for life. He told James he'd stopped smoking the day his dad was diagnosed with cancer. Money had been tight for the family after that. It was imperative for Nick, as the eldest child, to find a job to help out. As he struggled to get a break, James was happy to lend a hand.

'But you could make a killing going out to the southwest or even the north-west. The city's growing, Jimmy, it needs more houses. You've got this great business and it could be huge.'

'Nick, I like your enthusiasm. I don't disagree. Right now, we have to fix this sheet to the frame. Come on, stop yacking and give me a hand!'

◆

The power tools arrived the following week. James was very impressed with them despite the noise and the dust they generated. He hoped Jenny didn't mind the extra dirt he took home on his overalls every day. The angle grinder, in particular, gave off a phenomenal quantity of dust. But he had to agree with Nick; the machines had the potential to revolutionise the industry. His productivity would go through the roof, if he let it.

And that was something he had talked about with Jenny. They were comfortable. The house was almost paid off. They had even bought a block of land down at Kiama on the South Coast, to build a holiday home. Every year, the family trekked down to camp near the town that was little more than a fishing village flanked by sweeping farmland that rolled almost to the sea. The new block sat on a slope of scrub in the elbow of the southern headland above Kendalls Beach. When cleared, it would look north along the sand and out to the east along dark cliffs and the broiling turquoise flow of the ocean.

'I really don't hanker after anything more than we already have, Jen,' James said over dinner at the end of the week in which the power tools had first been put to use. 'Nick and some of the other lads think we should expand. I've heard that some builders are literally buying up acres of land on the outskirts of Sydney, building new suburbs, and selling the houses at huge profits. I don't think I have the energy in me for expansion. I'm not going to become a developer. It's not what I want to do. I don't think it's really me.'

'Then don't, James. I don't need anything more. We already have everything I could ever have wanted.'

'Thanks, Jen. I thought you'd say that. It's not as though I object to any change that makes my job easier. I'd love to do exactly what I do now in less time. As it is, I'm always complaining about not spending enough time with the family – that's the price you pay for having your own business. I can't remember the last time I was able to take the whole weekend off. The owners can be demanding, as you know, Jen. Wanting to meet me on the weekend when I'd rather be watching Kate learn to swim or the boys' football. There's always that extra job that needs to be finished, too.'

'James, we don't mind. You have to be there for the customers. Besides, I know you're proud of the work you do. That attention to detail is what people like. It's how you've built your excellent reputation.'

'I do like being appreciated, that's true, Jenny. I don't want to do it forever, that's all.'

'You don't have to. We've achieved enough. It's already so much more than what we had to begin with.'

'What I want to do, Jen, all I want to do, is keep on doing what I do well. I'll run the business just as it is in the suburbs I know so well. There's nothing wrong with that. I can't see demand for houses dropping any time soon. Before long, we'll be down at Kiama, taking it easy and being free of all these hassles. It's what I dream of as I get up at the crack of dawn each day to go to work. I know it'll all be worth it then. If Nick, or the others like him, want to give something else a go, I'm not going to stop them. There's always going to be work for a good-quality builder wherever they go.'

'Maybe you could pass the business on to Nick at some time down the track if our kids aren't interested.'

'If he's still with me. He likes making money, that boy.'

'He's on a good wicket, James, where he is. He won't leave. He likes you too much anyway.'

James went out to the office and came back with the current account book. Not only did he not want to do what he was doing forever, he also knew he couldn't do it forever. He remembered Reg Blaxland and how he had to give up work because of a bad back. He didn't want his body to fall apart and not enjoy years of retirement with Jenny.

'I've been going through the accounts and checking how we're going this year compared with the returns over the past few years.'

'Much the same,' Jenny said. 'The figures look good to me.'

'Well, Jen, they are good. Actually better than good. We've been growing slowly, steadily, over the years. If it goes along the same lines in the future, I think I can give it away when I'm fifty-five. I know that's a long time off, but it's worth thinking about now. At least, by then, if I feel it's time, I'll be able to stop. Barring an accident or something like that, we'll have no debt, the kids will have left home, and there'll be a lovely big house in Kiama to grow old in, where all the children and grandchildren can visit whenever they want. Who knows, Jen, someday we may even be able to afford to travel back to Scotland and England to show the kids where we came from.'

Chapter 22

In the winter of 1975, James and Jenny took their family back to the United Kingdom for a holiday. They hoped their three children were old enough to appreciate what they would see. They were definitely old enough to appreciate the intolerable tedium of the flight from Sydney to London. It took three good nights sleep in a bed and breakfast near Victoria Station before they recovered sufficiently to travel further. They wondered how their children would have coped with the voyage on the *Neptune*.

As they drove through the English countryside, Jenny recalled fragments of her childhood. It was as if she was recalling a different person, because where she now lived was as good as being on another planet. The soft, diffuse light was like a sprinkling of yellow and silver droplets on a carpet of green. The sky was pale and lacklustre, and merged subtly into the environment instead of opening out like a gigantic, blinding tear in the universe.

They first visited Jenny's family in Sussex. Her two sisters, Patty and Robyn, were still teaching and were both living in the village of Midhurst. Patty's husband was the publican at the Spread Eagle Hotel while Robyn's husband was a plumber. Their homes were ancient in comparison to the fibro house in Bankstown, Jenny thought, and as she found out, the subject of their conversation was similarly antique.

On their first night, over dinner at the Spread Eagle, Patty remarked, 'It's a shame Hugh doesn't talk to you, Jenny. I know that business with

Trevor embarrassed him and soured things a great deal, but it doesn't justify his giving you the cold shoulder.'

'I've written to him a few times, Patty, but I've never received much in reply. It's disappointing, but it's all in the past and we've moved on.'

'It's not good enough, and I've told him so.' James liked Patty, but only in moderation. She was taller and heavier than Jenny with only a sliver of Jenny's good looks. She was a very opinionated woman, which James found uncomfortable. You had to watch out for what might be coming. He supposed it was because she was the eldest. Robyn was much more like Jenny, and decidedly easier to talk to, at the odd moments when Patty wasn't dominating.

'Jenny hasn't told me anything about Hugh for some time. What's he up to? Is he still in Perth?' James asked Robyn, thinking he should engage with his in-laws.

Patty swallowed the mouthful of partridge she was chewing and answered instead. 'Our Hugh is still a specialist in Perth, doing very well for himself. You know, of course, that he married a nurse, and they have five children?'

'Yes, Patty, James knows that,' Jenny said.

James actually did not know and, in fact, had deliberately blotted out all knowledge of Perth from his brain. He wished he had kept his mouth shut.

'Yes, Jen, I remember. He's a podiatrist in Perth.'

'Paediatrician!' Patty guffawed, flecks of fowl shooting out of her mouth. 'You're adorable, James. Absolutely adorable.' They all laughed, James joining in nervously.

'Our dear brother is now a professor. All his children are fabulously talented, or so his wife, Pippa, says. Speaking of which, Hugh's eldest, Lawrence, is marrying Trevor Hungerford's daughter, Prudence. Trevor, of course, is an obstetrician. Hugh claims he's delivered most of the children in Perth.'

Jenny could sense trouble. She needed to stop this talk but couldn't think how. James could feel his thighs moving up and down and reflexively put his hands on them to dampen the jitters.

'How about that? Lucky you broke off the engagement, Jenny, otherwise your Kate might have married your brother's son!' Patty started laughing again. 'What's wrong with you two?' she asked, looking at Jenny and James. The whole table turned towards them. 'My Lord, it's only a joke. If you'd not fallen in love with this adorable little man here, you could even have been living in the same street as Hugh, which is where Trevor and his family live. Quite a well-to-do suburb, Pippa says.' She forked some potato into her mouth.

'I don't know if Jenny and James want to hear that,' Robyn said.

'Why ever not?'

James felt light-headed. He knew his cheeks were bright red. If someone touched his face, they would burn their fingers. He tried sipping the pint of lager before him as if he was ambivalent to the direction the conversation had taken. There was now a vacuum of silence into which all sound had disappeared.

'Patty, you really do have a big mouth,' Jenny eventually said.

Patty was about to bite back, when her husband waved the waiter over for more drinks. 'How about we hear about life in Sydney, Jenny?' he said. 'A top-up, anyone?'

Jenny looked at James's pained face. Mustering her strength, she spoke brightly. 'Good idea, Bob. We now own our house and we've recently started building a holiday house right on the beach in a place called Kiama. It's beautiful there. The hills are as green as they are here on the downs. They roll all the way down to the golden sands our house will look over.'

'Golly, that sounds stunning,' Robyn said.

'It is. We're so lucky to be able to have it.' As she continued prattling on about their lives, she hoped James wasn't conjuring the spectre of Trevor Hungerford once again. She hoped he could hear that she had no regrets. His face was glum and he appeared to have withdrawn into himself.

◆

Over the ensuing days, James's mood improved as he saw the delight of his children enjoying the novelty of cousins, even if they were several years older. The family dinners and picnics they had were large, noisy affairs, so unlike what happened in Sydney. James ruminated over what might have been for Jenny, if she had chosen differently. He could see Hugh and Trevor's families having the same boisterous gatherings where no one ever felt alone. When he looked at Jenny laughing with her own family, he felt guilty for having taken her away from that life.

By the time James, Jenny and the children moved on to Scotland, Patty was back to her opinionated best, her Spread Eagle gaffe long forgotten. They all were sorry to see them go. James wondered whether they would ever see them again. Were they thinking the same thing? He didn't believe so. He had got on well with Jenny's family, but he couldn't displace the feeling of being a nobody outsider. They wouldn't have cared whether they saw him again or not.

He knew nothing of Jenny's private conversations with her sisters, in which she was repeatedly interrogated about her happiness. 'I'm truly very happy,' she assured them. 'No, I'm not making it up, Patty. Can we please talk about something else?' They didn't seem to listen. She was glad to go.

As they ventured north, she noticed James slowly beginning to unwind. The month they planned to be in Britain was his first true break from work since she had known him. Even though they went to Kiama for holidays, he was always available to attend to work issues when required. Jenny realised that he was anxious about more than Trevor Hungerford. Of course, she thought. He was preoccupied with how the business was functioning in his absence. Nick and the other men had guaranteed them both that there wouldn't be any slacking. James, however, was not one to sit back and forget.

As he drove the car north up the spine of England from Cambridge to Lincoln to York and across to the Lakes District, James frequently found himself thinking of Sydney. If the truth be known, he couldn't delegate tasks or not very well. He realised it was the main reason he'd resisted the pressure to allow the business to grow bigger. He had to maintain control of himself, his family, his world. If he didn't, he was afraid he would lose everything. The first few days of the holiday had been torture even without memories of Trevor Hungerford. He was tormented by images of roofs falling in, lawsuits, fingers being smashed by mallets. He was slowly letting them go. Jenny, he was sure, had no idea what was troubling him.

When Jenny looked across at James at the steering wheel, she could see how lost in thought he was. He had carried their burden for so long, she was so happy to see him take a breath. He needed to. Soon though, he was distracted, playing games with the children about what they could spot in the countryside. 'A pig!' Robert yelled. 'A black spotted pig. That's 1000 points.'

'It's not 1000 points,' James said.

'Yes, it is.'

'No, it's not. It's 5000 points!' James said, laughing.

'That's not fair!' Douglas shouted.

'Mum!'

She hoped the laughter would last.

◆

At Windermere, James rang ahead to see whether his sisters, Rosemary and Kate, were up for a visit when he made it to Glasgow. Although she knew James was not a diligent correspondent, Jenny also knew he kept in contact with his sisters, who were still nursing at the Vale of Leven Hospital outside Glasgow.

When the day came, Jenny was pleased she'd finally met them, but she couldn't help noticing how stiff James was in his sisters' presence.

Kate's husband, Bruce, was out of work, and spent the days they saw him drunk. Their children had long since left home. Kate's house was cold. It stank of a busted septic system and cat's piss. Jenny was ashamed of her children's cringing when they were forced to hug Uncle Bruce or had to spend any time in the dank house.

Rosemary was divorced. She lived in a tidy but dark flat in Glasgow from which she commuted by train to the hospital. Jenny could see that she was glad to see her little brother, but no one could escape the sense that something was wrong. Her eyes had no sparkle. It was as if she had lost all hope.

James could see that his children did not enjoy the Glasgow experience. He didn't either. It was truly a depressing place. He had been right to run away from it. He hoped his sisters understood why.

On their final day, after visiting a restaurant on the banks of Loch Lomond, James asked if anyone wanted to see where he was born. 'Of course we do, James. Don't we?' Jenny twisted around to look at the children. James could see in the rearview mirror the feverish shaking of heads. I don't blame them, he said to himself. I have to do it, though. He told himself that he had to connect his present to his past.

He entered the street and drove up to the old terrace in which he had grown up. It was a dilapidated, tiny dwelling. He wondered how his family had squeezed into it.

He parked the car and got out to have a closer look. Nobody else wanted to get out of the car. James walked up to the front gate to look in. The curtains were drawn. The bricks were sickly-brown and dirty. The mortar had crumbled away in some areas. The house had seemed so warm and comfortable when he was a child.

James stood staring at the façade. He could picture himself opening the gate and bursting through the front door. His sisters happy, his mother in an apron, cigarette hanging from her lips, motioning for him to sit down or clean his shoes. His father? Where was his father? He was in that house too. His image entombed in the cottage along with all the other pictures and feelings in James's mind.

His memories of his father were spare. After all, he must have been only six or so when he died. All he had were half-formed images, but the feelings were as pure and potent as they were when he first experienced them. Sitting on the hard sofa, snuggled into his father's left shoulder. He remembered his smell – almost no smell at all. A clean, warm smell. He pushed up into the side of his father and listened to his voice. Soft, kind, yet commanding. The voice of a man he hoped he had become.

His father's words spread over him like a blanket, comforted him, warmed him as far down as his toes. He could almost tuck himself in under their spell. He felt safe, loved.

A child was crying somewhere to his left. A car horn blared. His own children were no doubt restless and complaining in the car.

The faint image was gone. He missed his father terribly. He missed that moment. He had missed it all his life.

James realised how horribly alone he had been in that house once his mother died. He never wanted to feel like that again. He had spent his whole life trying to avoid it. It had been a mistake coming back to this place, he thought. He should never have brought his family here. It was better to leave those ghosts locked inside where they could thunder and storm no more. He turned and walked slowly back to the car. He felt the wet stream of tears on his face. He saw Jenny's concern and the puzzled expressions of his children.

James drove the car away from the grey cleft of land filled by the Clyde and commenced a clockwise circuit of Scotland. He forgot about his old home. In and out of the lochs of the wild west coast, visiting castles, sailing on boats, eating strange food and covering up against the swarming midges, he was happy. He could see everyone else was happy too, despite the absence of a monster in Loch Ness.

In Edinburgh, they strolled down Princes Street, gazing up at the castle on the rock. James put his arm around Jenny's waist as the children walked in front. Jenny leaned into James as she had years before. Robert looked back at his parents. He grinned. He tapped his sister on the shoulder. She turned round and started giggling. Jenny looked at her daughter and smiled. By then the boys as well as Kate were giggling as they walked ahead along the footpath.

By the time they were ready to depart at Heathrow, James's mood had turned full circle. He was so relaxed he couldn't even contemplate work. But he knew he had to. It wasn't yet time to quit. There were many more houses for him to build before he could safely retire. For now, he had to make do with the prospect of years of happiness when he finally downed tools.

Chapter 23

1978

James arrived early at the site in Yagoona to ensure the concrete was poured in the correct place. He never liked to leave that to others. On one occasion, the concreter had poured the concrete outside the well-marked lines as if he was creating a negative of the house's footprint. The man had been up half the night seeing the arrival of his first child, so James was prepared to cut him some slack. He never had the slab poured unsupervised again.

'Good job, Len!' James shouted to the cement-truck driver as the team on the trowels smoothed and levelled the cement. The driver gave him a wave out of the window, the noise from the truck's old engine reaching a deafening crescendo as Len took it through its gears.

Soon afterwards, another truck rumbled up the road. It was a flat-tray Bedford carrying the Fibrosheets for the house. The driver reversed into the yard. The truck had a green body with yellow writing on the doors: 'E.A. Pengilley, Haulage Contractor'.

'G'day, Hendo,' said the driver through the window. 'Anywhere here?'

'Hello, Ernie,' replied James. 'Yes, just over to the left will be fine.' He gestured to a spot downhill from the slab.

Ernie Pengilley climbed out of the truck. It was quite an effort. He was a bulky man with thick pillars for legs. His face was like the crust on a shepherd's pie – courtesy of ten years first-grade rugby league. While

James was convinced the former prop forward could easily manhandle the pallets off his truck, he was relieved to see him use a pallet jack and the hydraulic lowering platform at the back of the tray. Within an hour, Pengilley had unloaded the stacks of Genuine KIL Fibrosheet onto the earth near the embryonic house.

'Thanks, Ernie,' James said as Pengilley asked for his signature on the delivery docket.

'No problems, Hendo. I'll see you next week on that job in Cabbage Road.'

'Might be the week after, Ernie, what with all the rain we've had recently.'

'Yeah, good for the farmers, no doubt, but mucking up the builders for sure. By the way, Jimmy, you should have a close look at the stacks. I couldn't help but notice these new labels on the sheets underneath the plastic. Come over here and I'll show you,' Pengilley said as he walked over to the nearest pallet, motioning for James to follow. He tore a hole in the shrink-wrapped plastic covering and exposed a blue, red and white label about 10 x 15 centimetres. 'Have a gander at that, mate.'

James leaned over the stack and read the words:

CAUTION: Contains asbestos. Breathing asbestos dust might damage health. Work outdoors, use special tools. Power saws require dust suppression. Avoid drilling overhead. Damp down waste and seal it in a bag.

'Well, what do you make of that?'

'I don't know, Ernie. First time I've ever seen such a thing. I'm not sure what to make of it, to be honest. We all know the sheets contain asbestos. They have for decades. I helped put it in the sheets at one time.'

'No kiddin'.'

'Yeah, back in the sixties. No one's ever said anything about Fibrosheets being dangerous or even asbestos for that matter. What's changed? Why are they telling us now?'

'Can't say. Thought you'd be interested. Perhaps it's just this batch. I don't know.'

'No, I don't think it's just this batch. Wouldn't make sense as the sheets have always contained asbestos, as I've said. On the one hand, they say it could be harmful, but on the other, they seem to be saying don't worry about it if you cut the sheets outside and keep the dust levels down. Well, that's ridiculous for a start. Have these guys even been to a building site? It's not exactly a clean place. And anyway, we're always working outside.'

'Yeah, you're not wrong, Hendo. Anyway, I've gotta get going. I'll leave you with it.'

'Yes, see you, Ernie.'

As Pengilley chugged out onto the street, James stood pondering this new development. As far as he could tell, it was business as usual. His work practices, give or take a little, already approximated the recommendations on the sticker. He had some doubt about the use of power saws – they could generate a lot of dust. There was no mention of angle grinders, and they were horrendous. Nonetheless, most of his work was outdoors on houses. The wind took the dust away as effectively as any vacuum-extraction system. Building sites were dirty, dusty places, but most of the mess was from sawdust, cement, plaster and soil. While there was occasional cutting inside, particularly for bathrooms and kitchens, this occupied only a fraction of the overall time spent cutting on a job. It was no use speculating, James thought. The best thing he could do was make a few inquiries. See what it meant.

At morning tea, James travelled home and rang the union for information. Jenny was out shopping. He was put through to Gavin Sheedy, the state representative for the Building Trades Union.

'Yes, pal, what can I do you for?' Sheedy asked.

'Gavin, I'm a builder, and I've just got delivery of some pallets of

Fibrosheet and they've got these warning labels on them about asbestos and I don't know what they mean.'

'Slow down a minute, pal. You're a member, is that right?'

'Certainly am. And so are my men,' James replied.

'Sorry, pal. Gotta check these things, you know.

'Now, you were saying you have an asbestos problem? Tell me where you are, and I'll slap on a ban as quick as you can give a fella the time of day—'

'No, I'm ringing up about these warning labels,' James said, feeling slightly alarmed about the mention of a 'ban' and 'asbestos' in consecutive sentences. 'I've got some Fibrosheets with a warning about asbestos on them. I'm after some more information. Why have we suddenly got warning labels on the fibro?'

'Well, pal, these labels are new.' Sheedy suddenly sounded as though he was reading from a script. 'The labels have been put on to warn users of asbestos cement products that there may be a health hazard if they do not keep dust levels down by working outdoors, using dust extraction equipment, wetting the sheets or scrap, and disposing of waste in sealed bags.'

'Yes, I realise that's what they say, but I want to know what hazards they're referring to.'

'I'm no expert on these things, pal, but I do know you can get cancer if you're exposed to too much,' Sheedy said in a matter-of-fact way.

'What? Cancer!'

'Yeah, sure. But don't worry, pal, you'd have to have very heavy exposure for that to occur. And if you're going to cop that sort of exposure, make sure you get paid danger money. That's what we've been recommending for God knows how many years.'

'I'm a home builder. There's no such thing as danger money.'

'Oh well, some ask for it. Anyway pal, doesn't really apply to you. You don't get much exposure building houses,' Sheedy reassured him.

'Yes, well, thank you, you've been a very big help.'

'No problems, pal. Any other information you want?'

'No, that's been more than enough.'

James regretted making the phone call. It generated even more questions. The mention of cancer was frightening. He needed some more answers to control his rising anxiety. He was reassured in part by Sheedy's confirmation that the health hazards didn't apply to him as a builder, but Sheedy was hardly an oracle. Indeed, James felt he was the opposite. He mulled it over as he sipped his tea. The best option was to telephone one of his old friends from the King Industries factory to see if he knew anything. Straight from the horse's mouth, so to speak. If that failed, he would ask his doctor.

That evening, he telephoned his old mate Geoff Blaxland, Reg's younger brother. Geoff was now a senior foreman at the Riverwood factory and was nearing retirement. James made sure he telephoned while Jenny was with the kids. He didn't want her asking difficult questions and getting alarmed.

'Hi, Geoff. Sorry to trouble you and I appreciate this is a wee bit out of the blue. If now's not a good time…'

'No, everything's fine, James. Good to hear from you. What can I do for you? You sound very serious. Is something up?'

'No, or I don't think so. You see, I received a load of Fibrosheets today and they all had a warning about asbestos. What's going on? I've never seen a warning or any mention of the dangers of asbestos exposure before. I rang the union rep and he said asbestos causes cancer, so, as you can imagine, I'm concerned.'

'Oh, I see. The warnings. Yeah, they caused a stir here in the factory until Dr Mathers, the company doctor, spoke to us. You remember Mathers, James?'

'Vaguely. Tall chap with a plummy voice. He examined me very early on. I think he was checking I didn't have TB.'

'That's the man,' Geoff replied. 'He sat all us foremen down and spoke for quite a while. He said he was "dead against" the warnings and that they were "unscientific". Then he said something like, "If you have heavy enough exposure to asbestos over the years, you can get dusted. That means you get some scarring on the lungs. I've been checking for that for years and I'm pleased to say that none of you men would have had heavy enough exposure to be dusted while I've been at the company. Now, some men who have worked with asbestos have developed lung cancer, but that happens if you have heavy exposure – the sort that gets you dusted. We've made sure none of you get dusted, so you shouldn't get lung cancer. Anyway, all cases of lung cancer have been in smokers. The best thing you can do is quit smoking." I mightn't have got it all because he did go on for a while, but that was the important part. It sounded pretty sensible to me, James. You know, I've become short of wind myself over the years. Nothing much to worry about.'

'What did he say about the warnings? I understand what he said about the factory, but you said the warnings created a stir.'

'They did, for sure, when the men started seeing the labels being applied at the tail end of the process. If customers were being warned, then why not them?'

Fair enough, thought James.

'Mathers assured us it was a bureaucracy thing and unnecessary. He said it was simply a precaution and should be a matter of good workplace hygiene to keep dust levels down. He reckons there's no scientific evidence suggesting carpenters or builders – men like you – are at risk. That's all I know. It made sense to me because we all know that breathing in dust can choke you up and cause coughing and what not. Nobody wants that. We've been putting in equipment to keep the dust down in the factory for years. Why not tell customers to do the same thing? Good common sense, as Mathers was suggesting.'

'Yes, I suppose that's right, Geoff. It was one of the reasons I left the factory to join Reg as a builder – to work in the open air and not have all that dust in my hair or on my skin or in my chest. It can be dusty on a building site, but the wind blows it away. I've never really worried about it.'

'I understand, James. Mathers might be an odd bod, but he's a doctor and I trust him.'

'Thanks, Geoff. That's reassuring. My chest was clear when I left the factory and everything's been outdoors since then. Shouldn't be something I need to worry about.'

'That's how I see it, too. But any time you need anything, give us a bell. We'd love to see you and Jenny and the kids some time.'

'I'll talk to Jen and we'll tee something up soon. See you, Geoff.'

Despite what he'd told Geoff Blaxland, James still felt uneasy.

Two days later, he consulted his general practitioner for a check-up. He was told, as usual, that he was extremely fit and healthy. When he asked the doctor what she knew about the dangers of asbestos exposure, she said that asbestos caused asbestosis, a type of scarring of the lungs. She knew nothing about asbestos causing lung cancer. If Mathers believed there was nothing to worry about and James's own doctor didn't even know that there was a connection between asbestos and lung cancer, then there was nothing more he could do.

In any event, Geoff Blaxland wouldn't lie to him. If Geoff trusted Mathers, then James believed he could too. He worked for Henry King Industries, after all. They'd know if there was a problem. Mathers said there was no risk to carpenters, so there should not be one – as long as James followed the instructions on the labels and kept the dust down as much as possible (which he had been doing since he started) and encouraged the boys at work to do the same.

Even so, James decided he would take no chances. He invested in dust extraction and vacuum bags for his power saws. He made sure his carpenters wore masks when performing the dusty jobs like using an angle grinder to cut through corrugated sheets. They all had confidence in his explanations and the changes he brought in. KIL Fibrosheet still represented the best value building board on the market. There was no reason to cease using it. Because his customers were generally of modest means, he wasn't in a position to recommend other building materials. Besides, once the sheets were installed and painted, there couldn't possibly be an issue, he thought.

The flow of work quickly overtook James's concerns. He had houses to build, deadlines to meet, a home at Kiama to construct and pay for and a family to look after. The labels receded into the background of the many tasks he co-ordinated on his building projects. They became as inconsequential as the name of the manufacturer on a sheet or the brand logo stamped on the underside of a piece of bathroom hardware.

Chapter 24

By 1983, James could not help but notice that the product he had used for so long was changed forever. Genuine KIL Fibrosheets were now asbestos free.

It was not as though he'd been caught off guard by the change. The Henry King Industries sales rep had been talking up the new product for weeks before its release.

'Why the change?' James asked the rep, Vern Larkin.

'Better product. Easier to use.'

'Well, Vern, it would be very difficult, in my opinion, to improve on the old asbestos fibro. Why do you say it's better?'

'Easier to use.'

'So you said. How much easier can you get than the sheets I've been using all my working life?'

'James, they've been tested head to head with the asbestos sheets and those tests show that they cut faster, are easier to handle, take a lick of paint easier, don't break as much and they produce much less dust.'

'Is that it, Vern? The dust.'

'The tests prove that they give off less dust.'

'That's impossible when you're using a power saw.'

'I know it sounds hard to believe, but that's what the tests show. A superior product all round. Same price, better product. No need to start using weatherboards or bricks. This asbestos-free fibre cement is even better than the old sheets. Give it a go, James. You won't be disappointed.'

'What choice do I have when there's no other product now available at the same price?'

'Well, sure, that's the fact, but as I said you'll not notice any difference other than it being a much better sheet to use.'

'What's holding the sheet together? I always thought the asbestos gave it its strength.'

'Cellulose. Paper fibre.'

'Is that right?'

'Yes. It gives it strength and flexibility. I guarantee you'll like it, James.'

When he took delivery of his first order, James observed that the sheets were labelled 'asbestos-free'. He wasn't sure why that feature was highlighted when there were no other asbestos-containing cement boards on the market. He'd never had cause to complain about the quality of the KIL Fibrosheets. The change from asbestos to paper pulp was being emphasised as an advantage. After a week of using the new products, he assured Vern Larkin that they were good. That was all that really mattered, he thought.

That was until Geoff Blaxland telephoned him and said that Reg had died of cancer.

'The family's holding the funeral in Gerringong on the weekend.'

'We'll be there, Geoff. I know Reg was in his seventies, but I wasn't aware he was sick.'

'He wasn't, James. It was very sudden. Some type of lung cancer, which is strange because Reg never smoked. I have to ring a few more friends, but Maud thought you should know, given, you know – well, it's Reg, for God's sake.'

'I understand.'

Jenny noticed James's quietness after the phone call. 'What's wrong, James? Who was that?'

'It was Geoff Blaxland. Reg has passed away.'

'Oh, James, that's so sad. He was a very special man. A very important man in our lives.' She moved in and hugged him.

'He was indeed. We owe him a great deal, Jen. In fact, almost everything.' His voice faltered. Jenny gently wiped the tears from his cheeks before pulling him in tighter.

Reg had been a strong, guiding presence in James's life in Sydney. He often spoke to the older man about the business or as a sounding board when he was confronted by tough decisions. He was reminded of his anguish many years earlier when his mother died, when the last pillar of support in his life crumbled before him, and the profound abandonment which then engulfed him. Reg Blaxland was not family, but he might as well have been.

◆

James had not been to a funeral for decades. He could only remember his mother's funeral as a dour, awful affair. To his surprise, Reg's wake was strangely uplifting as family and friends celebrated and gave colour to his generous life.

'He was a much-loved man, James, as you can see,' Geoff said, glass of beer in hand.

'He was. I owe him so much.'

'We all do. He was my big brother and I idolised him. Can't think why, actually. The sod never gave me a building business—'

'I'm sorry, Geoff—'

'I'm joking, James. It's okay. Really. I was never going to take on a business like that. Too much responsibility. I'm a slacker by nature. I'm happy working for somebody else.' He drained his glass and poured himself another from a nearby bottle. James nodded to be topped up and held out his glass.

'I wanted to talk to you about Reg's cancer.'

'You said it was lung cancer.'

'That's right, an unusual type of lung cancer, Maud said. The doctors told her that it might have been caused by asbestos exposure.'

'I thought lung cancer was caused by smoking,' James said.

'That's what I thought, too, but this one is different and could've been caused by asbestos.'

'But Reg only ever worked as a builder. He used the same sheets I used. I actually inherited his account at Henry King Industries when I bought the business. Are you telling me that the asbestos in the Fibrosheets caused his cancer?'

'That's what I'm saying.'

James stared at Geoff in disbelief. 'Then I could get it too!'

'I'm sure it's rare, or that's what the doctors apparently said.'

James was unconvinced. He recalled what Geoff had told him about the warning labels in the late seventies. He thought it best to keep that memory to himself.

'And another thing, James, the union's been making trouble at the factory recently. Agitating about asbestos and how it can kill workers. The company's out of it now. You'd know that anyway, I suppose.'

'Yes, the Fibrosheets are asbestos-free. The company seems to be making a point about being asbestos-free with its advertising. I was told it was about asbestos-free being superior, but you're telling me something different.'

'It's in part about quality, but there've been so many scare campaigns about the dangers of asbestos that the company decided to get out of it.'

'What? I can't believe you're telling me this, Geoff. Why weren't we told?'

'It's not because there's a definite risk; it's because of all the noise that's being made. The doctors asked Maud about Reg's job and whether he'd worked with asbestos. When she said yes, they told her it could have been the asbestos causing the cancer. They didn't sound too certain.

You've surely heard all the talk about the trade unions demanding action on asbestos.'

'No, I haven't. I rarely read the newspaper or listen to the radio. Not interested in all the doom and gloom out there. So, getting back to the point, when they warned us about the product containing asbestos, that was because there was a real risk of getting some incurable disease like Reg?'

'No. That's not what we were told. It's not what we're being told now either. Dr Mathers says no one knows one way or the other whether the asbestos in the Fibrosheets can cause cancer. He still says the warning labels and going asbestos free are unnecessary. We've been told that it's a response to fear and not science. I understand your concern. God, I'm concerned too. I've worked in the factory most of my life.'

'I was there too.'

'Yeah, I know, but it was only for a short time.'

'Does that matter?'

'Apparently it does.'

'How do you explain Reg's case then?'

'I can't, other than to tell you what I've been told myself. You have to have had very heavy exposure to be at risk. I can't say what Reg got up to in the early days. He was out working before I was out of nappies.' Geoff took another long swallow of beer.

'I appreciate you telling me this, Geoff, but I'm now feeling more than a wee bit anxious.'

'You're fit and healthy, James. Look at you. As if you're going to get sick. Would have happened by now.'

'Reg hadn't been working for years though.'

'I know, but he was never in great condition, as you well know.'

'I suppose not.'

'The asbestos has gone. That's all I know. I don't need to worry about it anymore. I've got a job and I'm grateful for that. It's time to move on. You should do the same. There's nothing else we can do anyway.'

James didn't think Geoff truly believed what he said. On the other hand, if the asbestos cement sheets had been dangerous, nobody would ever have allowed them to be sold. It just wouldn't happen. Those Health Department men he remembered poking about the factory would have stopped Henry Kings in its tracks if there was a problem.

On the trip home from the funeral, James resolved to never discuss the warnings with Jenny or pass on what Geoff had said about Reg and the reasons for going asbestos free. She would become too anxious. He would hold all the fear within him. It was true that he had only briefly worked at Henry King and Disaster Gorge, and Scotland was an eternity ago; the rest of his work had been outside and he had followed the advice in the warning labels to the letter. He looked after his health. Perhaps Reg was simply unlucky or the doctors had got it wrong.

Besides, he had much happier things to think about. Robert was about to complete his Bachelor of Commerce degree at Sydney University and then would start work as an accountant in a large firm, Douglas was studying engineering at the University of New South Wales and Kate had just started nursing. James could not believe that his children were all going to university when he'd had to leave school to work in the shipyards.

Chapter 25

1992

Jenny was looking forward to their week away at Kiama. She had been there often, but this would be the first time she and James were going to stay there and not do any building, painting, landscaping or rubbish removal. The home was ready at long last. All James had to do was decide when to retire.

As James eased the car into the driveway, Jenny looked up at the two-storey brick house. 'It won't be long now, James, and we'll be moving down here for good.'

'Can't wait,' he said. 'Come on, Jen, let's christen the new place.' He winked at her and laughed. He had a mischievous glint in his eye. Jenny was not sure he was joking. He leaned across and kissed her.

'All in good time, James. Let's unpack first and have a swim. I'm hot.'

'If you insist.'

'I do.'

'Right then, let's unpack and get this show on the road.'

As they had already moved most of what they required in earlier trips, James only needed to carry in a couple of light bags and some groceries. Jenny watched as he walked briskly to the front door. He glanced at her playfully just as he disappeared into the shadow of the hall.

Although he was in his late fifties, he was well preserved, Jenny thought. He could have passed for a man fifteen years younger. All that time outdoors had agreed with him. And she hadn't seen him so relaxed for a long time. Building this new home at Kiama had taken its toll – the travelling, the money, the mess. James had done most of it himself. He had earned the happiness he now allowed himself to feel.

Jenny made her way onto the front porch and into the house. She climbed the stairs in the dim afternoon light, discarding her sandals on the way. She could feel the woolly softness of the new carpet on her soles. And then hands reached out and grabbed her, bundling her small body into the bedroom and onto a bed. She and James fell into each other's arms, giggling and groping like newlyweds. 'James,' she said, 'I don't know what's got into you.'

'Well, Jen, I reckon this is the start of the rest of our lives together,' he said. 'This is our new home. I can't believe it. Who would have ever thought we'd end up here when we set out on the *Neptune*? Can you remember that afternoon in the Royal Hotel in Perth?' His body curled around hers on the floral bedspread. It had a satin finish so smooth, they almost slid off it as they moved.

◆

On the beach, Jenny enjoyed, as she always did, the feeling of the sand between her toes and the cool water lapping around her ankles. The sun was setting below the Barren Grounds escarpment, but the air was warm and the golden sand was still bright.

'We'll have to get a dog, James. Can't you see a big friendly black labrador running down the beach?'

'Not really.'

'Oh, don't be difficult, James. Of course you want one.'

'If you do, Jen, then I guess I can learn to live with one too.'

'I do.'

'But not right now. Not while I'm still working and have to concentrate on what I'm doing. And you've still got the books to manage. But we're getting close, Jen. I want to leave the city and be down here just as much as you do. I've had a gutful of deadlines and demanding clients. I know we agreed ages ago that when 1990 arrived and we both turned fifty-five I'd give it away. Okay, I'm now about to turn fifty-seven, but I want to come down here with no debts. There's a wee sum still owing here, and I promised Nick I'd show him the ropes with the business for a couple of years before he takes over completely. It's only fair. We'll have years to enjoy this place when we finally cut the ties.'

'I understand, dear. It's not easy breaking free from our Sydney lives. We're leaving a lot behind. Our friends, our children. I'm ready though, James. It's taken time, but I've come to terms with our kids leaving home and that this is the start of a brand-new adventure.'

They paused to gaze out at the lights of the fishing boats bobbing on the horizon. Jenny thought of her children and felt the pang of loss that often accompanied those thoughts. Robert was married and lived on Sydney's North Shore with his wife and son. Douglas was building bridges and roads with a leading firm of engineers. Kate was engaged to a young dentist, who was hoping to become an orthodontist. And now she was here with the man she loved. She held his hand tightly. She needed him to be with her. He'd said he would be. He had promised he would be with her forever.

Chapter 26

By 1994, James and Jenny owed nothing on the family home, or on the Kiama property. Once the Hibiscus Avenue house was sold, James figured they had more than enough savings to live comfortably for the rest of their days in Kiama. If need be, he could always earn a few dollars as a handyman. He might do it anyway just to keep himself busy. But he was not going to rush into anything. For now, he planned to put his feet up and enjoy the freedom.

Because of all the trips they'd already made to Kiama, the final move was simple, and made even easier by their children volunteering to help.

'We've got this far on our own, I think we can take it from here,' James told Robert.

'No, we're going to pitch in and make sure you're properly settled,' Robert replied.

And so on the day of the move, James led a Henderson convoy down the Princes Highway to Kiama. 'This is ridiculous, Jen. There are three cars behind us blocking all the motorists wanting to get somewhere today rather than tomorrow.'

'You do realise, James, that you're the one in front and they're keeping to the speed you're setting.'

She patted his thigh. He smiled.

'All they want to do is drive down and stay the first night with their parents to satisfy themselves that we're going to be fine.'

'I know, but I don't think they need to. I don't know about you, Jen, but I'm as happy as I've ever been. I don't want to exaggerate, but I reckon we've worked our whole lives to arrive at this point. I've forgotten about Hibiscus Avenue already. Bankstown could be a world away as far as I'm concerned.'

'It's exciting. I can't wait.'

'Neither can I.'

'In that case, would you please make the car go faster?'

◆

Later, after the final boxes had been unloaded and everyone had enjoyed a dip in the ocean, the family assembled on the balcony for a drink.

'So, what are you two going to do with yourselves?' asked Robert as he helped himself to more of the Chinese takeaway he'd bought for the family's dinner.

'A bit of this and a bit of that,' said James.

'That won't take up too much time, Dad,' said Douglas.

'No, but there's plenty of time to work out what else I want to do.'

'The first thing I'll be doing every morning is taking a stroll along the beach,' said Jenny. 'I mean, who else has a beach less than twenty yards from their front door?'

'What about the dog you've been going on about?'

'Dad's agreed I can get one now that we're down here,' Jenny answered, smiling.

'I have?' James said.

'Yes, and don't pretend you haven't,' she replied.

'It will be perfect for a dog,' Kate said. 'You were very lucky buying this place when you did. It must be worth a packet now.'

'A small fortune,' said James.

'Yes, I'd hate to think what we would have to pay for it now,' said Jenny.

'Anyway, here's to Mum and Dad!' Robert led, raising his glass of champagne.

'To Mum and Dad and their new life!' Kate and Douglas chimed in.

James and Jenny smiled at each other, lifting their own glasses to acknowledge their fresh adventure. 'Thank you all for helping out today. You've made it very easy for us. Who could ask for better children than our Robbie, Dougie and Katie!'

'No, who could ask for a better mum and dad,' said Kate.

'Oh stop it, Kate. You're going to bring on the waterworks if you're not careful,' said Douglas. 'Oh my God,' he added, looking at his mother, 'it's too late, she's started already.'

Jenny was crying with joy. James put his arm around her. She laughed and sobbed simultaneously, pulling Kleenex after Kleenex from the box Douglas brought out from the kitchen. They all joined in laughing.

The next day, James was sad to see his children depart, but impatient nonetheless to get on with his new life. He was ready to do nothing.

Doing nothing, however, entailed unpacking boxes and moving items of furniture around to suit Jenny's fluctuating opinion about their correct positions. It took most of the week to accomplish. After that, they began settling into their new routine.

A working lifetime's habit of an early start meant James was up while it was still dark. He had a cup of black coffee while making a cup of tea for Jenny and bringing it to her in bed. There was then nothing more invigorating than the morning walk along the orange sand of the beach. James often dunked himself under the enveloping steel-blue swells, emerging with a loud gasp, the bracing water kick-starting his day. He was no swimmer and was aware he probably looked like a drowned rat. He loved watching Jenny's reaction as he emerged ruddy and cold from the ocean – a beautiful mixture of scorn and pleasure.

After breakfast, James worked in the garden, while Jenny spent a few hours helping out in a local craft shop. On occasion, James did some odd jobs in town. As his reputation as a quality handyman spread, he was forced to teach himself to say no, so that he didn't become overwhelmed by work. For the first time in his life, he started having a short kip in the afternoon. It felt like an indulgence or being lazy, but the feeling passed. After a rest, they went fishing, walking along the headland, travelling to nearby Gerringong or Berry or shopping. Jenny tracked down a labrador breeder and, before long, the unco-ordinated hulk of Tess accompanied them everywhere they went.

It was a dramatic turnaround from the hectic pace of Sydney. James was surprised at how full their lives could be when emptied of grinding stress and noise. He felt he had never known such a profound sense of relaxation. The simplicity of their lifestyle led to escape from the burden of time. He realised he had for too long lived for the future and for the time when some unknown God finally told him he had paid his dues and earned a rest. It was a silly way to have lived, he thought. Running away from the past to get as fast as possible to some future. Blissfully, it no longer mattered.

Sometimes, if the weather was good, they strolled along the beach again in the evening, holding hands the way young lovers do, walking silently in step together, before Tess's barking roused them from their reverie. James enjoyed having her around. He threw sticks into the sea and watched as she careered into the waves to retrieve them. She'd bark for more, and would bound after the pebbles he rolled edgewise across the hardened strip of sand above the lapping water. Eventually she would go quiet and sit, stick in her mouth, as James and Jenny stopped, holding each other, standing in meditative quiet, as the burnished sun slid down the rim of the world and disappeared.

At night in summer, they spent hours sitting on their verandah, talking and looking out along the black water of the bay. They reminisced, laughing at almost forgotten events and characters whose lives had briefly crossed their own. They talked about the children and the grandchildren, the lives that were only just beginning. They would turn off the lights and look out to the moving darkness beyond or across to the twinkling lantern-like houses dotted above the dunes in the trees. Their murmuring voices floating over the soft shshsh-ing wash of the waves. James found these peaceful nights far more entertaining than the television sitting largely unused in the loungeroom.

'I was thinking of buying a wee boat, Jen, so that we can go fishing in the Shoalhaven.'

'But James, you know nothing about boats.'

'Yes, but it can't be too hard and I'm only thinking of a runabout, something easy to handle. It could be fun. Might even do some prawning in the Crooked River. You love flathead and that's where they are. I was talking to George down the street today while I was building the greenhouse for his orchids. He's got a dinghy and would be happy giving me some tips. He said that only last week he caught a five-pounder in the Shoalhaven. That's a big fish, Jen.'

'What if it capsizes?'

'It's not a yacht, Jen.'

'All right, but what if the engine won't start?'

'There'll be oars. We'll have life jackets. No risks.'

'I know you wouldn't do anything foolish, James, but neither of us are strong swimmers.'

'I reckon we'll be okay, Jenny. Don't you worry. Anyway, I'm only thinking about it for now.'

The conversation drifted, as it usually did, to other events in their day, the tribulations they overcame or the moments of happiness or surprise they had experienced. James didn't like to make Jenny feel anxious. He thought momentarily of the things he had done at work over the years. The balancing on roofs, the drill that nearly went through his finger, the wheelbarrow he should never have tried lifting and the asbestos cement dust he'd breathed in. It had all worked out. Boating would be a piece of cake.

PART III

Chapter 27

2001

Bruce Fraser knew people at his law firm, Jacksons, regarded him as an arrogant prick. It didn't bother him unless it was a view held by someone he respected or someone he had romantic aspirations towards. There were mercifully few in the former group for Bruce to worry about. As to the latter, well, that was a different story. He was perennially optimistic, then disappointed. Perhaps he should lower his expectations, he thought. It could be very trying when women regarded you as a tosser.

Bruce was jolted out of his rare moment of honest introspection when he heard footsteps in the corridor outside his office. Not Morahan again, he thought. His supervising partner had already been in to berate him in a minor tactical disagreement about discovery. For a small man, Morahan made a lot of noise. What did he want now?

Morahan, Bruce knew, was one of the leading proponents of the Fraser-is-an-arrogant-shit school of thought. He'd once overheard Morahan at litigation drinks ask another solicitor, 'Don't you find Fraser up himself? He thinks he knows everything. Can't stand him.' The solicitor caught Bruce looking directly at him and offered an awkward nod.

'Yes, Paul, how can I help?' Bruce said without looking up.

'Okay, Fraser, here's another claim against King Industries. Man with meso. Doesn't look anything special. Worked as an apprentice carpenter using Henry King asbestos cement sheets in the seventies. No other exposure. You should be able to handle it. Solicitor is your old girlfriend, Viviana Glosioli, at Shaw & Fletcher. Prognosis probably poor, so you'd better get cracking.'

Bruce picked up the papers Morahan had left and quickly scanned them. Yes, a common or garden variety mesothelioma case. He'd be able to report to the client that afternoon, and knock the whole thing over with a commercial settlement within a few weeks.

Bruce knew he was fast becoming an expert in asbestos litigation. He'd spent countless hours digging as deeply as possible into the history of asbestos use in Australia and reading the scientific literature about asbestos-related diseases. As a Sydney University medallist with honours degrees in science, law and commerce, he knew he had a special capacity to be the leading legal authority on asbestos disease in the country. If that made him a know-it-all, then he'd accept the label as a compliment.

Rather than first producing a letter of advice, Bruce decided to ring Jacksons' client, Charlie Boustead, general counsel for Henry King Industries Limited.

'Hi, Charlie. Paul Morahan just passed the Hawkins case on to me.'

'No brainer, I'd say.'

'Totally. No special features worth litigating. Not a test case. We should get a report from one of our respiratory physicians to confirm causation and then settle as soon as we can. Given his age, I think it will take about $275,000.'

'Sounds fair. You can have that when the time comes. Anything else?'

'No. If there's any change of thinking, I'll let you know.'

'Great. See you, pal.' Click.

Charlie was a cantankerous, rough, sometimes foul-mouthed man, who was fast accelerating towards his use-by date. He had been hit about the head so often by plaintiff lawyers that he was punch drunk, but Bruce found him generally quite accommodating. He was one of the few whose views Bruce respected. He was no fool and knew a great deal about his company's asbestos history.

Bruce put aside what he had been doing and got out his dictaphone to draft a letter of advice to Boustead. He looked at the bundle of documents concerning Mr Hawkins and the covering fax from Boustead to Paul Morahan. God, he hated how correspondence came to the firm through Morahan rather than directly to him. Just because Morahan was a partner and he was only a senior associate. Well, this year at the partners' meeting when new partners were announced, he was confident things would be changing.

Bruce knew he had all the attributes to make partner at Jacksons. He came from a wealthy Eastern Suburbs family. He knew how to connect with people with money and power. He had gone to Sydney Grammar School, like his father and grandfather, where he'd been senior prefect, dux and captain of the fourth eleven cricket team. Bruce still regretted his failure to work himself beyond the fourth eleven. He'd opened the batting as innocuously as the pair in the thirds or, in fact, the second eleven. Oh well, some people just don't know talent when they see it, he mused. He guessed that his background and academic record irked Morahan. Bruce regarded himself as a fine judge of character. It was clear that Morahan was the insecure, jealous type.

Bruce knew he produced work of the highest calibre. Morahan, however, seemed incapable of ever giving him credit. What's more, Morahan's constant taunts about the Shaw & Fletcher solicitor, Viviana Glosioli, were puerile and tiresome. Bruce regretted telling Morahan at litigation drinks that he and Glosioli had been at university together. It was a mistake. Now he had to cope with regular jibes from the entire asbestos litigation team about this non-relationship.

He turned back to the papers before him and started dictating.

◆

The following week, Bruce appeared before Judge Steinblott in the Asbestos Diseases Tribunal. While the judge was amiable enough, Bruce hated going down to the ADT, as it was called. The tribunal was housed in a drab building in the heart of Sydney's retail area, many blocks from both the Jacksons tower, overlooking the Opera House, and the court precinct. Bruce wasn't at Jacksons when the ADT was first established, but was told all about it by Morahan and Charlie Boustead when he'd become involved in asbestos litigation. In the 1980s, there'd been an epidemic of cases of mesothelioma, asbestosis, lung cancer and asbestos-related pleural disease, leading to hundreds of cases being filed in the District and Supreme Courts, which were soon overwhelmed. In order to unclog them, the government had set up a specialist tribunal to hear and determine nothing other than asbestos disease cases. The tribunal was given the same jurisdiction as the Supreme Court without, Bruce thought, any of its intellectual firepower.

As he entered the courtroom before the judge came on the bench, he knew he had to find Viviana Glosioli so he could agree to a timetable in the Hawkins case for the steps to be completed before trial. If he agreed to these interlocutory steps, she would hand up orders to the judge without his having to remain. He quickly located her; Viviana was unmissable. The figure-hugging black suit. The businesslike manner. The severe façade. She acted like someone in charge, or at least someone under tight self-control. You couldn't help but be impressed, Bruce thought. A true believer and drop-dead gorgeous to boot.

He sauntered over to her, his mauve-hued Jacksons notepad clipped to his leather Montblanc clipboard. She was talking to someone about another matter. 'No, we're not agreeing to three weeks extension. Our client is dying from an incurable disease caused by your company's unsafe work practices. You either accept the timetable I circulated or we have an argument about it before the judge. It's a matter for you.' She sounded formidable.

'All right, no need to bite my head off, I'm just the messenger,' the other solicitor said. 'I was told by my boss to ask for an extension. If it's not on, we'll accept the timetable you've suggested. Here, let me sign, so I can get out of here.'

Glosioli turned to Bruce. Was there a hint of a smile? It looked like it.

'Hello, Viviana, nice to see you again. How are you?'

'Good. Are you consenting to the timetable I faxed you yesterday?'

'I am. Have you got a clean copy for me to sign?'

He watched as she flicked through the papers in her folder.

Although Bruce and Viviana had never been friends, he'd spent time with her in tutorials and once had a decent, if drunken, conversation with her at a wine and cheese night. Well, in his mind, it had been a good conversation.

'There you are, Fraser.'

'Thanks, Viviana.' He signed the document and gave it back to her as a loud knock sounded on the door behind the judge's bench. 'All rise!'

Viviana moved to a seat at the bar table. Perhaps he would stay and see proceedings out, Bruce thought. It might be interesting. He should size up the opposition every now and then.

Chapter 28

As he leant back in his chair, sipping his coffee, Bruce ran a few tactics over in his mind. He'd find a way to convince Viviana to settle the Hawkins case for less than $275,000. He'd spent so much time in asbestos litigation that he had come to enjoy the cut and thrust of negotiations; trying to find a point of weakness and then exploiting it. It was comical to think that, years ago, when he'd started at Jacksons, he'd wanted to concentrate on intellectual property. Soon after he entered the litigation department there'd been an explosion in the number of cases against Henry King Industries. The asbestos litigation team needed help. The new graduate solicitor seemed like the right man for the job.

Like all those who joined the team, Bruce first had to read the potted history of the company prepared by an unknown predecessor. He learned that the company was founded by a Dutch immigrant, Henry Konings, in the nineteenth century, and that after the merger with the wealthy Josephson family it grew into a national concern. A tale of rags to riches. It was not unlike the story of his father's pet food business. Dull.

Given the volume of litigation against one of its biggest clients, Jacksons had not held back. It mobilised its vast and expensive resources in aid of Henry King Industries' defence. Strategies were developed. Experts identified and vetted. Company witnesses earmarked for interview. And then there were the documents to be attacked. Squads of junior lawyers were sent to Henry King's corporate headquarters and manufacturing plants to inspect the millions of documents it had stored in filing cabinets and bulging cardboard boxes. The court had ordered Henry King Industries to make discovery. This meant reading every document it held to create a list of all documents that might be relevant to asbestos litigation and then making them available to opposition lawyers. What documents would need to be discovered in the ongoing litigation and what documents could be culled as part of Henry King's newly created and very strict document retention policy? The answer required some lateral thinking.

Although it had been terrifically plodding work, Bruce still recalled with pride how he had read and culled more documents than anyone else. His ability to recommend the destruction of thousands of 'irrelevant' documents was seen as a special gift. He'd soon found himself visiting the homes of former directors and reviewing their private document collections. Many of the old codgers were flattered by Bruce's interest in their work. His knowledge of Henry King Industries grew at the same astronomical rate as his billable hours.

That knowledge led to his having the good fortune, in the late 1990s, to interview the three most influential members of the Henry King board: Gideon and Gordon King and their cousin, Emmanuel Josephson. It was a real feather in his cap when Charlie Boustead handpicked Bruce for the job over Paul Morahan's objections. Nobody had done it before. It was unclear whether the old boys' recollections would help or hinder the company's defence. Bruce was confident he would extract the right answers.

◆

It took him four weeks to interview the octogenarians, generally together, painstakingly cross-referencing their recollections with letters and memos they had created decades earlier, and canvassing general issues in the asbestos litigation. It quickly became clear that the official Henry King discovered documents only told a fraction of the story. That could be an advantage, Bruce thought.

As he drove over the Harbour Bridge each day to visit the three men at the exclusive Turramurra retirement village where they lived, he pondered how he could use the old men's evidence. He couldn't imagine calling them as witnesses. He wouldn't want them cross-examined with a media scrum outside the court. They were way too old. Signed statements, however, could be tendered after they died. That could be useful if Henry King Industries ever had to defend a claim for exemplary, or punitive, damages. Charlie Boustead told him that one day it would happen and they needed to be ready. The accepted wisdom in the ADT was that the company knew about the deadly dangers of asbestos but concealed that fact from its workers and the multitude of builders who used its products. Thus, so the argument went, if a case was brought for exemplary damages, Henry King would be ordered to pay a hefty sum in damages to punish the company for its disregard of people's welfare and also to send a salutary lesson to any other horrible corporation thinking of exploiting the vulnerable. Based on what he'd read, Bruce thought that was bunkum dressed up with a fair splash of hindsight. He was hoping the three elderly men would set the record straight.

'Mr Fraser, we were all very proud about how we built Henry King Industries Limited into the largest manufacturer of asbestos cement building sheets in Australia,' Gideon King had told him on his first visit. 'When I retired, we had factories in each state and territory, except Tasmania, which we regarded as part of regional Victoria. Today, the company has factories in South-East Asia, New Zealand, the United States and even Tasmania. Of course, it doesn't use asbestos anymore. That went out in the 1980s. But it's not a bad achievement when you consider my father's humble beginnings.'

Bruce nodded politely. He was unsure if he could tolerate another 'humble beginnings' monologue. He need not have worried.

'To be honest, Mr Fraser, we couldn't have done it without political assistance. Government was keen to promote our products too, you know.'

This was something Bruce didn't know.

'You look surprised, Mr Fraser. Factories didn't open by themselves, you see. Governments at all levels were involved. They were all keen to help industry. Obstacles that appeared insurmountable at first glance never were, Mr Fraser.' He paused, reflecting, then went on. 'That's actually incorrect, Mr Fraser, forgive me. What I meant to say is that they rarely were a problem. There was one famous exception to the rule, which I guess we will come to: the Tariff Board Inquiry of 1954. That inquiry was an eye-opener for all of us. You've heard of the Tariff Board Inquiry, haven't you?'

'I've read a little about it, but I'd like to know more. In what I've read so far, one name pops up repeatedly, Sir Llewellyn Williams, the former chairman of V&L.'

Gideon grimaced. 'Sir Llew – now there was a character if ever there was one.'

'You knew him?'

'You bet. Larger than life, shall we say. He was responsible for getting the Disaster Gorge blue asbestos mine up and running. Very influential figure. He somehow managed to get both the Commonwealth and West Australian governments to support the mine and pay for important infrastructure like roads and rail, ports, housing. I don't know with certainty how he did it, but I can guess.'

'Crooked deals?'

'In those days, government and business could get away with all sorts of underhand dealings and backdoor agreements. Sir Llew was instrumental in setting up the Northwest Development Committee with the West Australian and Commonwealth governments. You may have heard of it.'

'Vaguely.'

'It was just after the war. The Japanese had bombed Darwin. It was a case of populate or perish. Sir Llew exploited this fear and managed to have the whole of the northwest opened up so V&L could develop its blue asbestos mine. I suspect some ministers in both governments were looked after very well financially. Nothing concrete was ever established. But we at Henry King had our suspicions, particularly after what happened at the Tariff Board Inquiry.'

'Were you there?'

'My word. So were Gordon and Emmanuel. I spoke on behalf of our company. I fear I may not have done a very good job. It was a most troubling situation. They had us over a barrel, that's for sure.'

'What happened?'

'It all started in early 1954 when the company received a letter jointly signed by the Minister for Trade and Customs, John Howell, and the Minister for Industry, Supply and Development, Sir Archibald Hughes, advising us that an inquiry into the tariffs on imported asbestos was scheduled for Brisbane later that year. If you thought Llewellyn Williams was a problem, his crony, Archibald Hughes, was worse. All these airs and graces, but a bigger scoundrel you would not find. I can tell you, Mr Fraser, the idea of an inquiry was a bolt from the blue. It had Hughes's fingerprints all over it.'

'Why?'

'Well, I trust you know by now that the company used the very best asbestos fibre we could get. The quality of our product depended on it. We used to travel regularly overseas to meet with our British, European and American counterparts to find out who produced the best fibre. It all came from Canada and Africa, Mr Fraser. It was good quality material, ideal for the manufacture of asbestos cement boards.'

'Wouldn't it have been cheaper to use local asbestos?'

'It depended, Mr Fraser, on where it was coming from and whether it was of suitable quality. We checked all the suppliers thoroughly. We would not have hesitated to use Australian asbestos if the quality was good and the supply consistent. Our lab staff tested the Disaster Gorge samples and what did they find? I'll tell you, Mr Fraser. It was rubbish.'

'So why did the company end up using it?'

'The Tariff Board Inquiry. It all comes back to that. Everything always comes back to that.'

'I didn't realise it was so important.'

'It changed everything, Mr Fraser. I remember the opening day very clearly and it was over forty years ago. It still irritates me. Cronyism at its worst.'

'Why is that?'

'Let me try to explain. The inquiry was held in Brisbane, I don't know why. Melbourne or Sydney would have been more usual. In any event, it was very hot and the room for the inquiry left a lot to be desired. It was colourless and musty with annoying, rattling ceiling fans. Howell and Hughes sat at a head table with various staffers. In front of them, on one side, sat the V&L team; on the other were Gordon, Emmanuel and me. V&L's head table was occupied by the colossus that was Llewellyn Williams, his chief executive officer, Fergus Hamilton, and a Dr Mitchell Frosby. Journalists sat in the bleachers.

'John Howell was another big man, a sixty-year veteran of federal politics with little claim to fame so far as we could see other than a prodigious appetite for long lunches. A most disagreeable fellow.

'The agenda became clear on the opening day. Howell started by giving a lengthy speech about the purpose of the inquiry. He laboriously outlined the issues, describing the mine at Disaster Gorge in minute detail, huffing and puffing his way through King's manufacturing enterprise, the important role it played in the Australian community, the pressing need for housing, etc, etc. I can tell you, Mr Fraser, that the warm Brisbane air and Howell's droning tones were a soporific cocktail. When he finally finished his opening and looked out at the audience, there were few open eyes to be seen. I could see Sir Llew's watermelon head resting on his shoulder, open-mouthed. He was snoring like a chaff-cutter.'

Bruce stayed silent, torn between hoping Gideon would cut to the chase and admiration at the old man's memory.

'Howell then called for the parties' openings, requesting them to outline their responses to the Tariff Board's proposal to increase the tariff on imported asbestos. The magnitude of the increase was not specified. Howell said that was for another day. The rumour was that a 500 to 1000 percent increase was being sought by V&L, an impost we thought ludicrous. Howell called on Sir Llew first.

'I turned towards the Big Ship, as he was known. He took some time to compose himself and to sponge the drool from his lapel. It was difficult to take him seriously, but you ignored him at your peril.'

'Why was that?'

'You'll see, Mr Fraser.

'Naturally Sir Llew indicated that V&L would vote yes for an increase to the asbestos tariff. He said it was essential for the prosperity of the country and that he couldn't imagine there'd be any valid or convincing argument to the contrary. Then he dropped his bombshell, saying that this being the case, it would be preferable if the inquiry heard from Henry King Industries first.

'"Yes, good idea, Sir Llewellyn," Howell rumbled. "I quite agree. Mr King, would you please go first?"' Gideon had a gift for creating the scene.

'This was not what we had anticipated. Our strategy was to come in over the top after V&L had put what we imagined could only be shoddy arguments of greed and self-interest. This change of agenda felt like an ambush. Sir Llew clearly wanted to speak last. Tactically, I felt this had to be avoided.

'"We would prefer, Mr Chairman, to stick to the agreed agenda and respond to the proposal after our good friends at V&L," I said.

'But Howell insisted we go first. I protested, of course, and Howell said I could fly to the moon for all he cared. He was the chairman and his decision was final. Hughes joined in with the threats. If I didn't get on with it, I wouldn't be allowed to make any submission at all.

'I had expected a fight, but a fair one. I proceeded with our arguments as powerfully as I could. First, I acknowledged the importance of asbestos to the Australian economy and its importance to our society. The country was undergoing massive reconstruction and asbestos played an integral role in that process. It had myriad uses in industry – insulation, housing and construction, friction products, to name but a few. I then pointed out that for more than two decades, the asbestos cement industry had thrived, based in large part on strong relationships with overseas suppliers of asbestos. I informed the inquiry that King Industries mainly used Canadian chrysotile. It was high-grade, pure, cheap and effective. Our machines had been built specifically to handle that type of asbestos. We also imported brown and blue asbestos from Africa for our corrugated roofing sheets and water pipes. Again, the fibre from Africa was high-grade, cheap and totally fit for our manufacturing purposes.

'If the cost of this imported asbestos were to be increased, I said, then our business would become less profitable. The increased costs would have to be passed on to our customers, and the product would be less competitive. And as the biggest asbestos cement manufacturer in Australia, any impact on our business would have a domino effect on the Australian economy, particularly on the housing sector.

'I then pointed out that if there were to be an increase in the price of overseas asbestos, then logically we would have to consider purchasing local fibre – if suitable quantities of good quality fibre were available. And that was the precise problem we had with V&L blue asbestos.

'We had rigorously tested the highest grade V&L fibre in our research and development laboratories. Compared to the overseas supplies it was low grade, almost unusable. If we had to use V&L's fibre, asbestos cement manufacturing would be set back a decade. The technological expenditure required to make the V&L fibre workable would be massive. It was riddled with impurities. It was sharp, long and needle-like. It stayed airborne for hours and would make conditions in the factory unnecessarily dusty and unpleasant. A great deal of the fibre would be wasted, another extra cost. Most importantly, V&L could not supply us with the quantities we required; at best, it would supplement our present supplies, which, if a tariff were imposed, we would have to continue purchasing at a higher cost.

'We understood the Disaster Gorge mine consisted of a number of narrow seams of blue asbestos running into the cliffs. Access was difficult, through small stopes and tunnels. V&L simply couldn't guarantee supply. Its methods were so labour-intensive that V&L blue would be no cheaper than the imported fibre, even if a tariff was imposed. So, I submitted that if the tariff were increased, forcing us to buy Disaster Blue fibre, there would be major problems with the volume able to be supplied and the quality of the fibre supplied. Again, there would be a negative impact on the asbestos cement industry. Given the importance of the industry to the Australian economy, we submitted that asbestos cement manufacturing should be protected, not ruined.

'Finally, I mentioned health issues. There had already been some health concerns in the asbestos textile industry in the United Kingdom. There was no asbestos textile industry in Australia to worry about, but we were concerned that the Disaster Blue fibre might prove dangerous. As I said before, its peculiar shape and characteristics made it prone to remain airborne for long periods. We believed that work conditions using Disaster Blue fibre would be so dusty that they'd approximate those in the asbestos textile industry. We didn't need those additional headaches.

'When I finished speaking, Gordon and Emmanuel leaned over and patted me on the back. "First rate, Gideon. First rate," they said. I admit I felt I had done a very good job.

'But then Sir Llew raised his bulk up in his seat and made his reply. It was insulting, to put it mildly. He said my submissions were laughable, then more or less told the inquiry I was a liar. I think his exact words to the chairman were "You have heard a series of untruths."

'"This is a disgrace!" I think Gordon hissed in my ear.

'But Sir Llew was just hitting his stride. He accused us of putting the self-interest of our company above the larger national interest. Howell sat nodding at his every word. The hypocrisy of it, Mr Fraser! The three of us rose as one to protest.

'Sir Llew then accused us of lacking insight … and that devious toad – excuse my language, Mr Fraser – agreed and ordered us to sit down and shut up.

'What could we do but sit down? Of course, by then we knew the score. It didn't matter how much we shook our heads. We slumped back in our seats, and twiddled our pencils like naughty schoolboys. Totally humiliating.'

Bruce could see it still rankled. There was a lengthy pause before the old man continued.

'Sir Llew went on in his self-serving way. According to him, King Industries had made record profits on the sale of our sheets every year since we began production and therefore should be able to weather what he called the minor storm of a tariff imposition. Hughes was in full agreement. In fact, he agreed enthusiastically with every proposition Sir Llew made, however ridiculous or ill informed. Evidently our so-called record profits should cover the cost of modifying our equipment to handle Disaster Blue.

'And naturally Disaster Blue was a top-notch product – why else would a reputable and prestigious company like V&L go to the enormous expense of developing a mine in a remote part of Western Australia if it didn't think the product was good?

'As for supply, Sir Llew simply assured the chairman that the mine would go on supplying good quality fibre for decades. He went so far as to declare it was good news for this country.

'"Asbestos is a miracle mineral," he boomed. "As safe as a bank."

He called on Dr Frosby, whom he described as an expert in occupational diseases, to back him up.

'Frosby claimed to have made an extensive search of the scientific literature on asbestos. He assured the inquiry that asbestos was safe and that there wasn't a shred of evidence to suggest that Disaster Blue asbestos was in any way dangerous.

'When Frosby sat down, Sir Llew beamed up at Howell and Hughes. Howell nodded and smiled. I felt ill, angry. I looked down at my hands and realised I had snapped my pencil – in three places.

'The inquiry was over before it had started. Regardless of the evidence or submissions, the decision had already been made.

'You see, Mr Fraser, I learned an important lesson back in 1954 and I'll pass it on if you're willing to indulge an old man for a moment more.'

Bruce nodded.

'Please excuse my frankness. The lesson was this: deceit, bullshit and the old boys' club are what matter in our society. Never forget it. I can assure you that I never forgot it after that dreadful time in Brisbane. It might have even changed the way I did business. You would do well to remember it yourself.'

Bruce was somewhat taken aback.

'And that's not all I can tell you about the sorry affair,' Gideon added. 'I'll also always remember my brief meeting with Llew Williams on the final day of the hearing.'

'Yes?'

'I walked into the men's room and observed Sir Llewellyn already at his station. I had no option, Mr Fraser, but to stand next to him.

'It was a very unpleasant situation, being that close to my tormentor. I looked straight at the porcelain, but I could feel his eyes on me.

'"Well, Gideon, looks like we'll be doing business with you," he said. "No hard feelings, old boy."

'"None whatsoever," I managed.

'He chortled and said something about an absolute drubbing.

'I responded with "More like a stitch-up."

'Sir Llew smiled, gave himself a shake and did himself up. "It's always nice receiving a little help from your friends," he said.

'"I bet," I said.

'He then pushed the door open and waddled out, wiping his hands on the sides of his trousers as he went.'

Chapter 29

Several days after signing Viviana's consent orders in court, Bruce found himself again sparring with her. 'I don't know how many times I have to say this, Fraser, but we're not settling for $275,000.'

'Sorry, Viviana. But Mr Hawkins's case isn't worth more than $275,000.'

'I think it is, and so will the judge.'

This is going nowhere, Bruce thought. Perhaps he needed to do the deal face to face. It was far too easy to hide at the end of the telephone line. He was sure he could charm her into his way of thinking.

'Look, Viviana, I'll talk to my client and see what he says. Then we could meet at Cafe Giordino to thrash it out. How does that sound?'

'Appalling.'

'Viviana, I'm trying to do the right thing here for both parties. Give me a break!'

Pleas for logic and justice usually worked for Bruce but this case was unusual. After the respiratory physician's examination, it became obvious Mr Hawkins could pose a PR nightmare for Henry King. Hawkins was only fifteen when he was first exposed to asbestos as an apprentice and now had a young family of four. The media would dine out on a case where Hawkins's children would very soon be without a father, and Hawkins himself had been exposed to asbestos when practically a child himself. Charlie Boustead agreed and had given Bruce instructions to go as high as

$400,000. It was imperative to settle the case and sweep the evidence under the carpet. Even so, Bruce wanted to chisel the plaintiff down a fair way. Most of them settled for less than full value when you put the squeeze on.

'I'll meet you at eight o'clock tomorrow before the directions hearing. If you don't come with sensible instructions, I'll be taking a hearing date for next week.'

'All right, I'll be there tomorrow at Cafe Giordino. It's a date!'

'Shut up, Fraser. It is not a date.'

Bruce couldn't understand why someone as smart as Viviana had fallen for the propaganda about asbestos or why she seemed such a zealot for the rights of injured workers.

He knew from what he had read and his discussions with the old guard that it was not as simple as many plaintiff lawyers thought. Surely, Viviana must know this. Knowledge of the hazards of asbestos exposure was an evolving thing. People didn't wake up one morning and decide it was so dangerous it should be banned. He wasn't going to fight the Hawkins case too hard but where was all this headed? It seemed to Bruce unfair to penalise a company for lawful production of a product that was encouraged by government – if what old Gideon said was correct.

He thought back over what he knew from his own research. It was clear to him that people knew from the early 1900s that heavy asbestos exposure could cause the debilitating fibrosis of the lungs called asbestosis, and that by 1955 it was highly likely that asbestos could cause lung cancer – that was when the famous epidemiologist, Sir Richard Doll, found that an increased incidence of lung cancer was only found in workers with asbestosis. So, thought Bruce, it might be argued that after 1955 it was reasonable for Henry King Industries to think that if it took action to eradicate asbestosis from the workplace, then it would also remove any threat of lung cancer – provided the men didn't smoke; a matter which had nothing to do with Henry King Industries. Nobody had even heard of mesothelioma then, that was clear.

If he could show that Henry King took action on the basis of what was generally believed at the time, Bruce thought, he had a convincing argument. He had read reports from respiratory physicians retained as experts by Henry King who'd understood Doll's findings in this literal way. But was this in fact what was thought at the time or his own defendant sophistry?

It was also critical to know which dust concentrations caused asbestosis. What did experts in the 1950s and 1960s think was a safe level of exposure?

He wondered if he could rely on the 1938 study by Waldemar Dreessen on the asbestos textile industry. That would be an irony, he thought. The Dreessen study was routinely tendered by plaintiffs to prove that asbestos was known to be dangerous as early as the 1930s, but Bruce thought they hadn't properly understood the technical detail of the paper. To him, details mattered. Dreessen and his researchers had measured dust concentrations in factories with a device known as a midget impinger. The results were expressed in millions of particles per cubic foot. They obtained average dust counts, and on the assumption that a worker's exposure was unchanged at the point they worked in the factory, they calculated total cumulative exposure by multiplying the average dust count by the number of years worked. For instance, a worker in the spinning section of the plant may have worked for six years at a particular point in the process where the average dust count was ten million particles per cubic foot. His total cumulative exposure was therefore sixty million particles per cubic foot. That seemed fairly straightforward, but what was significant to Bruce – and should be to the courts, he thought – were Dreessen's conclusions:

Because clean-cut cases of asbestosis were found only in dust concentrations exceeding five million particles per cubic foot, and because they were not found at lower dust concentrations, five million particles per cubic foot may be regarded tentatively as the threshold value for asbestos-dust exposure until better data are available.

The problem for Bruce was that the court had to be convinced Dreessen's conclusions were correct. More importantly, the paper made it clear that a worker's exposure could be below the standard of five million particles per cubic foot even if dust clouds were visible at the worker's station. There was always silica or cement or general dust in a workplace; not all the dust was asbestos. But plaintiff lawyers and the judges in the ADT couldn't seem to get their heads around this fact. Bruce also doubted whether any of the plaintiff lawyers could handle the necessary mathematics.

It was a dry and unappetising subject. Yet judges, plaintiffs and lawyers should be very interested in it, Bruce thought. What Dreessen was saying in 1938 was that as long as the average dust level over a working day never exceeded five million particles per cubic foot, there was virtually no risk of asbestosis, no matter how long the worker was employed at that site. It could not be clearer to Bruce. He just needed proof that that was how it was interpreted at the time.

◆

'Viviana, take a seat. Can I get you a coffee?'

Viviana had entered the courtyard of Cafe Giordino like a sorceress appearing in a bower of greenery. Bruce's composure faltered more than he would have liked to admit. She was in a fitted black dress with her black hair swept back from her face, exposing her bewitching eyes.

'No,' she said as she sat down opposite him.

'Lighten up,' Bruce replied, gazing at her immaculately applied red lipstick. 'What about some water?'

'Could we just get on with this, Fraser? Mr Hawkins wants $600,000.'

Bruce sprayed some of his newly arrived cappuccino across the table.

Viviana looked askance at the chocolate speckles on the glass of water Bruce had poured her.

'Right, I see I'm wasting my time.' She started to rise.

'Hold on, hold on. I have $350,000 to settle his case.'

'$550,000.'

'$400,000.'

'$500,000.'

'That's too much and you know it, Viviana. Don't you need to be putting my offers to your client rather than rejecting them without instructions?'

'Are you a complete moron, Fraser? I obtained instructions before I got here, knowing full well what you'd offer. By the way, don't you have to get your own client's instructions after each offer I make?'

Bruce's composure faltered further. 'I will be now, in light of your outrageous suggestion.'

'Take it or leave it. I'm going. See you in court later this morning when I ask for a hearing date. Mr Hawkins is very unwell. He deserves to have his case finalised before he dies. It will give him some peace after what your client did to him. Goodbye, Fraser.'

After he finished his coffee, Bruce rang Charlie Boustead and, once the swearing abated, obtained more money to settle the case. It was a fair whack, but this matter could not be litigated to Henry King's advantage in light of the inevitable headline: 'Young father of four dies at the hands of Henry King'.

Later, Bruce signed the consent judgment in court while waiting for the judge to come onto the bench.

'Thanks, Bruce,' Viviana said with a dazzling smile when he handed her the document.

Chapter 30

Bruce knew he had to do better than cave in to every demand. The going rate for a meso was slowly climbing. Henry King had to fight at some stage or it would sink under the burden of all these payouts. He was thinking of how best to stop the rot when Morahan bumped into him in the corridor.

'Nice result in Hawkins, I hear,' Morahan said.

'It was a difficult case and could have been a publicity disaster if we hadn't settled it.'

'If that's what you believe.'

'It's the fact.'

'You're sure it wasn't a special deal for your sweetheart, Glosioli?'

'It was not!' Bruce replied, not enjoying the way his voice was increasing in volume. 'What would you have done, Paul? Forced her to accept less?'

'I would have held out. Made her client feel anxious about having to front a trial and being cross-examined. She could have been lowballed once her client told her he wanted out. When you get to partnership level, you know about these things, Bruce.'

He couldn't think of a riposte and walked back to his office fuming. He knew it wasn't his finest hour.

Later that day, he received a phone call from Charlie Boustead about the same matter. It seemed that everyone was on his case about Mr Hawkins.

'Listen, Fraser, my company has invested a lot of money in having you prepare a rock-solid defence to any punitive damages claim that comes along. We expect some dividends, all right? We can't be bending over for every hard case that comes along. We need results, Fraser, not record settlements!'

'I understand, Charlie.'

'I hope you do.'

He had to do something to appease Boustead and to wrest the upper hand from Morahan in their never-ending contest about how Henry King's asbestos litigation should be run. Morahan's approach had always been to let sleeping dogs lie; don't find out what people who were part of the asbestos history actually knew. In this way, he told Bruce when he first joined the Henry King litigation team, the key witnesses would all peacefully pass away and nobody would be any the wiser about what had happened over the years. Bruce had formed a different view. Why not find out what these men remembered? They might just help Henry King's defence. Charlie Boustead largely agreed with Bruce's approach and style. He had endorsed all of Bruce's suggestions to interview witnesses no matter where they lived. He'd even approved Bruce's trip to the west coast of America to interview an aging occupational physician who had authored important studies on asbestos-related diseases. Bruce was worried that the Hawkins matter had put Boustead offside. Perhaps he was thinking twice about Bruce's tactics. But if Charlie Boustead wanted results, he would have to pay for more evidence. There was no choice.

The Hawkins case had also highlighted to Bruce how unprepared Henry King was to defend claims brought by end-users of its products, like carpenters. It was one thing to know that factory workers exposed to asbestos fibre all day every day were at risk of asbestos disease, but how could carpenters working outdoors be in the same boat? Bruce imagined their exposure would be significantly lower. And it wasn't raw fibre they inhaled, but largely cement dust with a bit of fibre locked into it. Most of the time, the fibre in the asbestos cement was white asbestos – chrysotile – rather than the deadly blue crocidolite. When did anyone know that end-users were at risk of mesothelioma or other diseases? Bruce realised it was vital to focus on the company's knowledge of the dangers of asbestos exposure over time. If he could prove it knew as much as, say, governments or researchers in the field and responded to the risks reasonably as they became known, then he would go a long way towards defusing the explosive potential of cases like that of Scott Hawkins. He'd already made some preliminary inquiries of possible witnesses, but he wanted someone credible and compelling.

Gideon King had urged him to do this. 'Don't take my word about our compliance,' he'd said. 'Ask the people who were on the ground at the time, like Dr White and Mr Ferris from the Health Department; that is, if they're still alive and have their wits about them. Or ask the company doctor, Peter Mathers.'

'I've tried talking to a few of these men. Dr Cecil White, he was the chief medical officer of the Health Department, wasn't he?'

'That's right. An odd chap, as I recall, but quite accommodating and reasonable with his suggestions. I don't think my son, Andrew, or our factory manager, Bill Kruger, warmed to him or, indeed, to his offsider – Richards, I believe was his name – but I didn't mind him.'

Gideon's soft, slow, but strong and clear voice was evidence of his still sharp mind, and Bruce had found it hard not to be impressed by the man.

'Henry King's documents include several reports written by Dr White or Mr Richards and documents in which they're mentioned. I've got one of their reports here,' Bruce had said, flicking through the pages on his lap. 'Here it is, A Survey of Exposure and Disease in an Asbestos-Cement Factory by Cecil White and Harvey Richards.'

'Ah, yes. Was it the late 1950s?'

'1960, in fact.'

'That's right. I remember their visit because it was the first time anyone from the Health Department had taken an interest in our little concern.'

'The start of quite a good deal of interest,' Emmanuel Josephson had added.

Gordon King nodded. 'Yes, but nothing we couldn't fix, at least at the start, Emmanuel.'

'If they'd left us to it, Gordon,' replied Emmanuel.

'True, but that was never going to happen, was it?'

It was slow going with the three old company men, but everything they, and particularly Gideon, said was gold.

'How did the visit by Dr White come about?' Bruce asked.

'It was rather a surprise,' Gideon said. 'I received a telephone call from him out of the blue. He said he wanted to measure dust levels in our factory. I asked him whatever for, and he said he had a new device that he wanted to try. He was friendly enough, although his reason for visiting the factory seemed flimsy to me. When I queried him further, he told me he'd fill me in when he and his colleague visited. None of us thought there was any harm in it, so I rang him back and organised the inspection.'

Bruce had done some homework on Cecil White. There wasn't much to find out. He couldn't get any help from the man himself because he was in a dementia ward at a nursing home in Baulkham Hills. He decided against telling the former directors this piece of intelligence.

The meagre facts Bruce's research had uncovered confirmed that Cecil White was the chief medical officer in the Division of Industrial Hygiene of the New South Wales Department of Health in the 1950s and 1960s. Like his counterparts in other states, White was not only the chief, but the sole medical practitioner employed in the department. His sudden interest in asbestos was unusual because the records indicated he was principally concerned with coal mines and power stations.

'I suggested a conference take place in the factory manager's office before White was given access to the factory floor for testing,' Gideon

King explained. 'White thought it a splendid idea, as he could first learn something of the manufacturing process and be given a tour of the factory. He was quite frank about his lack of knowledge of how we worked. Henry King Industries had been making asbestos cement sheets in New South Wales for over twenty years and yet, according to White, no information had ever found its way into the Division of Industrial Hygiene. Extraordinary, when you think about subsequent events.'

'This inspection is pretty important to the asbestos litigation I'm working on. What's your best recollection of what happened?' Bruce was keen to hear more.

Gideon leaned back in his chair, going back in time to relive the moments. 'Well, after the introductions, we moved to the board room. It wasn't much of a board room, you understand, more a large office with a circle of vinyl chairs…

'"What can we do for you, Dr White?" I asked. "We're at your disposal."

'He was a rotund little man, I remember, whose feet barely reached the ground from his chair. He astonished us by suggesting there may be a problem at the factory. Initially, I was worried that there'd been an outbreak of smallpox or similar. He quickly assured us that wasn't the case, then outlined his concerns. He told us that there was increasing evidence that exposure to asbestos could be very harmful.

'"Goodness me, is that all you're worried about?" I think Emmanuel exclaimed. We'd known for some time that the men could become 'dusted' if they had heavy exposure over many years. We rotated them out of the dusty areas before they succumbed. We also tended to employ older men so that they wouldn't have enough exposure to get into any trouble before retiring,' Gideon explained.

'But White said it was a great deal more serious than that. He said the evidence was pretty compelling that asbestos could also cause lung cancer. That certainly took the wind out of our sails, Mr Fraser. Cancer.

It had the potential to shut the place down.

'According to White, the link had been made by some high-class researchers in the UK and we needed to address the problem. Naturally, we were all very alarmed. But White believed there was a way forward. Evidently the research showed that the increased risk of lung cancer only occurred in men with asbestosis. That is, in men who'd had heavy exposure.

'"So, if you prevent asbestosis, you prevent lung cancer?" I asked. "It's that simple?"

'He agreed.

'"But what do you mean by 'heavy'?" Emmanuel asked.

'Would you believe it, Mr Fraser? White said he had no idea. Nor did anyone else.

'I don't mind saying we were pretty nonplussed by this opinion. He was meant to be the expert, not us. Obviously, if you could see dust in the air, you'd imagine it would be pretty heavy, but we hoped Dr White would be able to provide some accurate guidance. And to some extent, he did. He told us that studies had shown that if you kept the dust levels down to five million particles per cubic foot, then asbestosis was unlikely to develop.

'It turned out that the Division of Industrial Hygiene had obtained a dust-measuring device called a midget impinger – what a name eh, Mr Fraser! – and White proposed conducting a survey of the factory to identify any areas of concern. He also wished to examine some of the men who may have had heavier exposure than others to see if they had asbestosis.

'Of course we agreed – what choice did we have? – and offered White and Richards a tour of the factory to acquaint themselves with the manufacturing process. They set off with Bill Kruger, our manager, and Gordon, Emmanuel and I didn't see them again until after they produced a report.

'Bill Kruger told us they spent the following week at the factory,

Richards taking countless dust measurements with his midget impinger, while White examined men from the asbestos gang, the blower room, the tide mill and the finishing area. About two months later, Dr White sent us his report. You have it there in front of you Mr Fraser. Quite an accommodating and reasonable outcome in the end.'

Bruce turned the pages of the report to the conclusion, with which he and the three old men were already very familiar:

The results of this survey confirm the experience of earlier ones in regard to the quantitative relationship between dust exposure and the onset and development of asbestosis. Processes were found where the dust concentrations were high enough inevitably to cause the development of asbestosis provided the employees remained long enough in those particular jobs. Fortunately, these processes employ relatively few workmen, but it is recommended that steps be taken to give these men greater protection against dust. Once the earliest stages of manufacture are past and the wet mix is being prepared in the tide mills, the dust concentrations, with the possible exception of those at scrap reclamation plants, and some cutters and saws, cease to be significant. Therefore, over a major part of the process there is no call for greater medical or hygienic measures than is desirable in industry generally.

'What you won't find in that report, Mr Fraser,' Gideon continued, 'is what he said at the meeting I called for later. I think, Gordon, you were there for that.'

'I was.'

'"Well, Dr White, what can you tell us?" I asked. I hoped there wasn't too much wrong with the factory. Or nothing we couldn't fix with our engineers.

'White advised us that some of the men in the asbestos gang, blower room and tide mills who'd been working in those areas for several years had developed asbestosis. We had to do something to reduce the exposure in these places. The magic number was five million particles of dust per cubic foot, he said. If we got the dust down in those areas, we shouldn't have a problem anywhere else, he thought. White's findings indicated that once the asbestos was locked into the sheets, so to speak, it didn't pose a problem ever again.

'I asked if that went for lung cancer as well.

'White confirmed that lung cancer would only develop in men who had asbestosis. The only men who would get asbestosis were those heavily exposed at the front end of the process. If we tidied that up we should eradicate the risk of cancer in the factory. Do you follow, Mr Fraser?'

Bruce nodded, not wishing to interrupt Gideon's recollections.

'We thanked Dr White for the information and promised to do something about it. Which of course we did. I remember pressing White for confirmation that once the fibre was locked into the sheets, it was safe. I wanted him to understand that the answer to that question was very, very important to us at Henry King Industries.

'His answer couldn't have been clearer. He said that we needed to enclose the dustiest processes, make sure we had the men checked regularly by a doctor and employed someone to measure the dust levels to make sure they stayed below the five million particles per cubic foot limit. If we did that the Health Department wouldn't be bothering us. It would run some checks every now and then, but if we did as White suggested, we would be fine.'

Bruce's mind had whirred as he tried to work out how he could use this amazing evidence.

Chapter 31

The problem for Bruce was witnesses. He couldn't call Gideon King. He couldn't call White and Richards because White was gaga and Richards was dead. Bruce knew he needed someone capable of giving evidence now.

The pressure was on.

From what he'd read in Henry King's discovered documents, the next best witness after White and Richards was surely Edward Ferris, the state's Chief Scientific Officer in the 1960s and 1970s. Charlie Boustead agreed and gave Bruce instructions to interview the man.

When he first met Ferris in the reception area of Jacksons' offices, Bruce wasn't overly impressed. Ferris was a stout, round-shouldered man with a large head, bushy beard and a limp. His eyes, however, were intelligent and his voice rich and fruity. Bruce gradually warmed to him.

Edward Ferris's first job after university was as a scientific officer at Broken Hill. After five years, he told Bruce across Jacksons' conference table, he'd wanted to 'branch out' into other industries. He was sick of the underground work. When he was interviewed by Cecil White for the position of scientific officer with the Health Department's Division of Industrial Hygiene, he told White the same thing. Ferris, to his surprise, was offered the job at the end of the interview.

'Dr White told me that industrial hygiene and occupational medicine were growth areas and that New South Wales took pride in being ahead of the pack. He said there were many industries that required regular inspection to ensure employees were working in safe environments. He was looking for someone with experience and expertise in measuring harmful dusts, mists, smokes and fumes. With my years of sampling conditions in mines, I was the sort of person he needed for the job. I accepted straightaway. It sounded much more interesting than what I was doing at the time.

'On my first day, White gave me an overview of what was expected. I was to measure exposures at the dusty points of workplaces we identified with our devices or which I picked up myself by word of mouth or observation. Then I was to conduct tests as often as required until the problem was eradicated. According to White, the companies we were interested in were all pretty amenable to change. Most knew that if they didn't come up to scratch, we'd shut them down. He warned me not to be complacent in my duties as the health of workers was at stake.

'I was to start by doing some asbestos measurements down at the King Industries factory in Riverwood. Apparently White had been down there the previous year and we needed to check how the company was going with implementing the recommendations he'd made. He and Harvey Richards had been over the place with a fine-tooth comb and written an extensive report. White gave me a copy and I went back to my office to read it. It seemed a simple enough task: keep the dust levels down to below five million particles per cubic foot and all should be fine. I rang up the factory manager, Bill Kruger, and informed him of my plan to make my first inspection of the factory the next day. Kruger had no objections, even though his telephone manner left a lot to be desired.

'The next day, I met Kruger and the factory's safety officer, Russell Dymock, at Riverwood. We shared a cup of tea before moving on to the factory. Tastes in decor have certainly changed since those days, Mr Fraser, but it appeared modern and inviting at the time. In fact, the office block at the factory was surprisingly clean. Much nicer than the factory or the other factories in the area. These were uniformly dirty places. Made from unpainted corrugated asbestos cement sheets covered in splotches of moss and lichen.

'I guess you've heard of Kruger.'

'I have.'

'I'm not sure if he's still with us. He was a stern, imposing man, though he was welcoming enough. He said he thought I'd be pleased with what Henry King had achieved since White and Richards' visit.

'Dymock, on the other hand, was a thin, nervous man. He was too intense for my liking. In any event, I was there to do a job and not be best mates with these fellows, so I got down to business.

'Kruger was very positive. "This company is run by engineers, Mr Ferris," he said. "If there's a problem, they can fix it. You'll be very interested in how we've enclosed a lot of the tide mill processes to reduce the dust levels. We're very proud of the progress we're making."

'I followed Kruger out the door with Dymock and across a loading dock to the factory entrance. Inside the factory, I was soon deafened by the constant humming of conveyor belts, the hissing of steam presses, the jolting, banging and clashing of the machines disgorging raw materials, and the buzzing whirs from the finishing stations.

'"I think you could do with some ear protection here!" I shouted over the din.

'Kruger laughed soundlessly as he showed me around the factory, pointing out phases in the manufacturing process with a mixture of sign language and bellowing. It was easy to follow.

'I was somewhat surprised by Kruger's eager praise for the steps that had been instituted to reduce the dust levels in the factory. Visible clouds of dust rose steadily from the tide mill and the finishing section where the sheets were trimmed and sanded. I couldn't believe the enclosure that had been constructed around the tide mill. All it achieved was the funnelling of asbestos fibres up and into the atmosphere where they could dissipate widely with the breeze blowing through the open doors on each side of the building. Exhaust systems were required. The same plainly applied to the finishing section. I could see I'd be making a few tough calls.

'I completed my inspection that week and sent a report detailing my findings and recommendations to Kruger and Dymock. As it turned out, and much to my chagrin, many of my initial suspicions were unfounded. Although the factory was dusty, not many of the dust count stations exceeded the five million particles per cubic foot threshold even where the dust was visible. I've kept a copy of my report. You've probably seen it before.'

'I believe I have. Would you mind if I see your copy?' Ferris passed Bruce the document. It concluded:

The only station which exceeded the maximum allowable count of five million particles per cubic foot was that located where the bags of asbestos were emptied into bins to be pulverised and disintegrated. High counts were also occasionally found in the tide mill, fibre room and the finishing section where dry sheets were trimmed or sanded. Although there were sporadically high counts, on average the counts at these stations were within acceptable levels. Further efforts are required to enclose those parts of the manufacturing process which generated elevated counts. Overall, however, the results are most pleasing.

After the meeting, Bruce incorporated the conclusion and Ferris's other recollections into a comprehensive statement dealing with everything Ferris knew in the 1960s and 1970s. It was clear that Ferris's knowledge was that of the Health Department. After all, Bruce assumed, Ferris knew as much or as little as everyone else. It was a compelling document, he thought, and he envisaged a fair judge would think the same. The statement proved, in Bruce's mind, that Henry King Industries took all the steps required of it by the government. 'Most pleasing' were the words used by Ed Ferris at the time to describe Henry King's approach to reducing asbestos hazards. That was priceless. Nobody could have predicted the advent of mesothelioma or the specific dangers of blue asbestos. If there was a problem, Henry King could quite reasonably rely on what the government told it – it wasn't up to the company to second-guess what the experts in Macquarie Street were thinking.

♦

Still smarting from his humiliation at the hands of Viviana Glosioli in the Hawkins case, Bruce pondered whether it was time to use Ferris. He had to repair the dint to his reputation. He needed someone who could set the record straight about the past and show that Henry King Industries was not going to roll over every time a plaintiff lawyer demanded an extortionate settlement.

He reviewed the current cases he was responsible for. He had what he thought was a good case to test Viviana's mettle – a former foreman at Henry King's Riverwood factory, Jack Taylor, who was claiming some silly figure in damages for pleural plaques. Everyone, apart from the lawyers at Shaw & Fletcher, knew that pleural plaques couldn't cause any problems. Taylor alleged that he had chronic pain and breathlessness from them. He claimed he got them while working at the factory and that the company never did a thing to prevent his disease or heed government warnings about the dangers of asbestos. This was rubbish, Fraser thought. It was contrary to what White and Richards had said in their report. It was surely time to use Edward Ferris. His statement was bulletproof and he was also still mentally agile enough to be called as a witness.

The more he thought about it, the more Bruce warmed to the idea of serving the Ferris statement and giving Viviana the impression Henry King was going to contest liability. That would put the frighteners on her. Thankfully, Charlie Boustead agreed with this approach. 'Let's see what happens,' he said.

What happened was beyond Bruce's expectations. With the help of Ferris's statement, Bruce managed to settle the Taylor case for $125,000, a miserly sum and, at the time, a record minimum at Jacksons. Charlie Boustead was ecstatic, Morahan sullen. The best part was the hint of grudging respect when Viviana agreed to his offer to settle for $125,000 over the telephone. 'I have instructions to accept your paltry offer. Congratulations, Bruce, for taking advantage of a vulnerable man,' she said in a weary voice.

It was not often that Bruce heard the word 'congratulations' and his first name in the one sentence from Viviana. Definite progress, he thought.

Chapter 32

The success with the Taylor case pointed the way forward for Bruce. He decided to revisit some of the statements he'd taken from the former directors to see if he could use them in some of his cases. Better still, he thought, would be a statement from the Henry King Industries medico, Dr Peter Mathers. He'd have to know something. Bruce felt he might be able to use him to batter some more plaintiff lawyers into submission. Now that he'd had a win, he wanted to keep up the momentum.

'You've got to tread carefully with Dr Mathers,' Charlie Boustead warned. 'None of your predecessors have even got close to getting a decent statement from him. He's an absolute loose cannon.'

Charlie also advised Bruce to watch out for the doctor's trademark temper. Mathers had probably not been asked the right questions, Bruce thought. He pictured Paul Morahan posing technical questions and embarrassing himself completely. No wonder Morahan had told him Mathers would be hostile to the company and to not waste his time.

Even so, Bruce had to admit he felt some trepidation when he travelled to Port Macquarie to interview the former company doctor.

He need not have worried. From the moment Peter Mathers picked him up from the airport in an old silver Mercedes, he didn't stop talking about his years at Henry King – especially after lunch and an accompanying bottle or two of red.

'The French have proven that the secret to a long healthy life is good red wine with lunch,' he explained.

Bruce was far from convinced, but decided it was his duty to drink up. After all, Mathers' wife was absent, staying with one of their children, so Mathers was probably enjoying the company. Bruce stayed a week at Port Macquarie, recording Mathers' opinions, recollections and philosophies on his Dictaphone. Afterwards, he thought he needed a week's holiday to dry out.

Peter Mathers was tall, gaunt and angular. Although in his late sixties when Bruce met him, he could have passed for Gideon and Gordon King's older brother. He had a military bearing that became less pronounced after lunch, when his precise, clipped speech gave way to greater loquacity and then, towards dusk, melancholy.

'I jumped at the opportunity when Bill Kruger asked me whether I wanted a full-time job.'

'Why was that?'

'Well, I had four children under six at the time. I wanted something with decent hours and pay. The job as Henry King's medical officer gave me the chance to do research, gain expertise in the developing field of occupational medicine, travel the world, and pay for my children's education.

'I was provided with a surgery adjacent to the factory with all the equipment I required. Although I often travelled into the city to attend meetings at head office, most of my time was spent at Riverwood. As we already lived in the Shire, I didn't mind. The job gave us the means to buy a nice house overlooking Gymea Bay, and Riverwood was an easy commute.

'I'm a methodical, diligent man by nature and I enjoyed the challenge and discipline in setting up and running the medical surveillance programme at Henry King.'

'What did you do to get it started?'

'Apart from helping with the selection of an industrial hygiene officer to start monitoring dust levels, my first goal was to read all the scientific literature I could find on asbestos-related diseases. Kruger told me I could subscribe to whatever journals I wished and buy whatever books I thought would be useful. I put together a first-class, if highly specialised, scientific library. I procured the relevant legislation on dust hazards and workplace safety. I made contact with the few respiratory physicians in Macquarie Street, and I introduced myself to the medical officers in the state health departments. As you know, Henry King had factories in all the mainland capitals. They had similar problems to those at Riverwood. I had to meet all the bureaucrats in each state. Press the flesh, so to speak. There was a great deal of travel interstate to oversee a national surveillance programme. It was very time-consuming, but I loved it, at least initially.'

'What happened to change your view?'

'We'll get to that, Bruce, don't worry.

'Anyway, by 1965, I was well known in industrial medicine circles and even more so in asbestos disease research. I was well regarded in the health department offices, even if I say so myself. I was proud of how much I'd learned in such a short space of time. I was particularly proud of the national medical surveillance and industrial hygiene programme I'd developed for the King Industries workforce. In fact, Bruce, I regard this as my life's major achievement. With the help of the new industrial hygienist, Bob Frew – a first-class man by the way – I set up an ambitious database in which a worker's full occupational history, smoking history and exposure assessment were recorded. This was well before any of these measures became commonplace or computers were used in business. It was all on paper and entered manually. Frew measured the dust counts at all the employees' work stations so that their cumulative exposures could be tallied. I routinely examined the men for signs and symptoms of lung disease. These findings were also dutifully recorded in my database. What I wanted to do was identify disease early and observe its progression. I ultimately hoped to be able to correlate exposure levels with disease onset, with the aim that, in time, the data would be so thorough that it could be published in one of the international journals I subscribed to. The results would help prevent disease.'

'I didn't realise how good the system was. Did you eventually publish your findings?'

'No, stymied at all posts, as it turned out.'

'I don't understand.'

'Neither did I, Bruce. The data was good, but the company never let me publish it. I don't know why. I'm positive it would have shown what a modern, dedicated medical surveillance programme could achieve.'

'I've spoken at length with Ed Ferris and he told me he was greatly impressed by your achievements when he re-visited the Riverwood factory six months after his first inspection. Presumably that was through your influence.'

'It was. After I read his first report, it was pretty clear the front of the process needed to be fixed up. The changes gradually came. According to Frew, the fugitive dust levels were eventually well below the approved limit.'

'I take it there was no trouble with your recommendations at head office?'

'None. The directors were kept apprised of the changes through the regular reports I sent them. They seemed genuinely pleased to have a robust welfare policy. Healthy workers were happy workers – that's what Bill Kruger would preach to anyone who would listen at the annual factory managers conferences I attended. Few seemed to. To tell you the truth, it was a message he was incapable of delivering with conviction.'

◆

Peter Mathers' desire to tell Bruce everything he could recall did not abate over the course of the week Bruce was in Port Macquarie, nor when he telephoned from time to time to tidy up the statement he was drafting. There were some obvious gaps and plenty of reconstruction, Bruce suspected, aimed at putting the doctor into the most favourable light possible. Of greatest interest to Bruce was Mathers' recollection of the mid-1960s, when he clearly found himself at the epicentre of change.

'I thought, Bruce, I knew everything there was to know about asbestos diseases until I read the 760 pages of the 1965 Annals of the New York Academy of Sciences. The whole volume was devoted to the subject. It was entitled Biological Effects of Asbestos and arrived in my office in March 1966. I remember the date vividly because it was so important. I cancelled the medical examinations that week and had them re-scheduled so I could get stuck into reading almost immediately. It was a massive text, containing all the presentations at a conference of the same name held by the Academy in October 1964. The papers had taken over a year to be published and reach me – that's how slowly things moved back then. I was likely to have been one of the very first in Australia to receive it. I've kept that volume to this very day. Here, wait a minute, while I get it.'

Mathers rose and went into another room. He returned moments later with the tome and dropped it heavily onto the table. He opened and scanned the contents pages. 'There was an enormous amount of material to digest. I remember having a sense of foreboding when I read the preface. Here, look at this.

Bruce read the passage he was shown:

In the four decades during which there has been acceptance of potential hazards associated with exposure to asbestos, solutions to the problems involved have been elusive.

...

Hard-won data have been accumulating which indicate that neoplasia associated with asbestos exposure, especially those of the lung, are perhaps the most important industrial cancers at this time. This importance has been emphasised by the recent stimulating studies of South African and British investigators demonstrating the significant incidence of pleural and peritoneal tumours associated with asbestos exposure and the knowledge that the various neoplasms might follow exposure of limited duration and intensity, inadequate to result in significant asbestosis.

'Neoplasia – that's cancer and mesothelioma, isn't it?' Bruce asked.

'Quite. Very worrying, I thought. I'd heard something of a possible association between mesothelioma and asbestos exposure in my crash course on asbestos when I started with the company, but the scientific proof had yet to surface. If the association were not only true, but related to slight exposure, as was suggested in this preface, then this issue had the potential to devastate the asbestos industry. As I'd only recently started full-time work with the company, I was naturally rather anxious about my career prospects. I therefore read this book from cover to cover. Apart from an obvious issue with blue asbestos, which I'll tell you about in a minute, it was actually quite reassuring. There was a great deal of helpful information. I read about exposure to asbestos and how to measure it. I learned that the midget impinger was no longer the best method of assessing exposure and that something called the membrane filter technique was much better. I learned about the methods of diagnosing asbestosis as early as possible and the reliability of lung function tests with a thing called a spirometer. Of course, we soon bought one as well as a membrane filter device for Bob Frew.'

'So the company remained cutting edge.'

'Absolutely.'

Mathers leafed through the pages. 'There were two articles on the epidemiology of mesothelioma tumours that were particularly compelling,' he said. 'One was authored by Dr Wagner; the other by Drs Muriel Newhouse and Hilda Thompson. I'd heard of Dr Wagner previously. He was one of the South African authors who, in 1960, first suggested an association between blue asbestos exposure and mesothelioma. When I read that early article, I dismissed it as a scientific oddity, only relevant to some distinct patch of dirt in Africa. Dr Wagner then moved to Great Britain to conduct full-time research.'

Mathers showed Bruce part of the paper Wagner had reported to the conference:

At the end of 1961 we had diagnosed a total of eighty-seven pleural and two peritoneal mesotheliomas. In only two cases had it not been possible to establish a history of exposure to asbestos dust and only in one of the cases was there no definite exposure to crocidolite...

Of the eighty-seven cases, twelve had had industrial exposure and the rest came from the region of the Cape asbestos fields. More than half of these people had not been employed by the asbestos industry...

The remainder of the people had had environmental exposure due to living in the vicinity of the mills and dumps in an arid, windswept region. An example of this was a woman who was born in a town on the asbestos fields in 1900. She left there at the age of five and was in good health until she was fifty-five when she developed a pleural effusion. She died from a pleural mesothelioma eighteen months later. Detailed questioning on her childhood revealed that she attended an infants school near an asbestos dump. The children used to enjoy sliding down this on their way home. Two of her playmates at the school have subsequently died of the same condition.

Even among those working in the asbestos mines, the actual exposure seems to have been slight.

Mathers eagerly picked up the story when Bruce finished reading. 'Wagner concluded that there were no cases of mesothelioma associated with exposure to any other type of asbestos, despite intensive investigation.

This was critical, I believed. I realised that I couldn't sit on the fence any longer and dismiss Wagner's earlier study as a one-off. I thought there was little doubt that crocidolite – blue asbestos – was strongly associated with this new, lethal tumour of the lining of the lungs. And it appeared to be caused by only slight exposure years earlier. These people Wagner refers to were only bystanders. They could only have had brief or low-level exposure. I felt the asbestos industry had to change what it was doing or go under.'

Bruce wasn't liking the sound of this. He wasn't sure Henry King had done anything about this new evidence. He hoped the doctor would dispel his anxiety.

'Here, Bruce, let me get you a top-up.'

'I'm fine. Still going with this one.'

'Nonsense.' The doctor went into the kitchen and returned with a fresh bottle of burgundy. 'All this scientific stuff can be rather heavy. This will help.' He splashed the wine into Bruce's glass until it was nearly overflowing.

'Thank you,' Bruce said, wondering how he was going to make it through the afternoon.

'Where was I? Yes, after Wagner, I read the paper by Newhouse and Thompson, "Epidemiology of Mesothelial Tumours in the London Area", and any remaining doubt was dispelled. They reported to the conference on a series of eighty-three patients with mesothelioma, where there was a connection between first exposure and development of mesothelioma of between sixteen and fifty-five years, the mean being thirty-seven years. They found a highly significant association between the tumour and asbestos exposure, particularly blue asbestos.'

'Is this the report that implicated environmental exposure?' Bruce asked.

'You've done your homework. Yes, it found cases in people with no occupational exposure to asbestos but who lived within half a mile of the asbestos factory. It also recognised that exposure to dust brought home by relatives working with asbestos could cause mesothelioma. It was a staggering report. There was also a clear connection with crocidolite. It was lethal. Although I was unaware of any case of mesothelioma in the Henry King workforce, it was probably only a matter of time before I would.'

Bruce desperately wanted to know what Mathers did with this dreadful information and what the company did if and when they found out about it. But Mathers still wanted to talk about the book.

'There was also concern about whether lung cancer could be caused by asbestos exposure in the absence of asbestosis. This could be a potential problem for Henry King too. I'd been led to believe by the study of White and Richards from the Department of Health that lung cancer would only develop if there was asbestosis. If you kept exposure below that which caused asbestosis you would coincidentally remove the risk of lung cancer.

'After I read, and re-read, the important articles, I realised there was still no issue with lung cancer. There was, however, a very big problem with blue asbestos. I convened a meeting with Bill Kruger, Bob Frew and Russell Dymock and impressed upon the three of them that the board had to be told the importance of these findings.'

'And did you tell the board of your opinion?'

'My word.'

Chapter 33

Mathers had given Bruce much to think about. When he returned to his hotel at the end of the day, he spent the evening lying on his bed trying to clear his head of the red wine fug and work out where Mathers was headed. What if the company ignored his warnings? It was difficult to imagine. How could asbestos products still be manufactured when researchers had said in 1964 that you could get mesothelioma from slight exposures? Were all Bruce's efforts destined for the bin?

On the other hand, while he had warmed to Mathers, the doctor's account of how he came to report to the board sounded very convenient to Bruce. He doubted anyone could be so forthright about what was only an emerging science. Mathers had said himself that it was 'new' evidence. Bruce wondered how the next day would unfold.

◆

'You were telling me yesterday, Dr Mathers, that you convened a meeting with Kruger, Dymock and Frew. What happened then?'

'Well, the four of us sat in Bill Kruger's office as I explained the research. Even to a layperson and perennial agnostic like Kruger, the news was grim.

'"Mesothelioma could be caused by even light exposure to blue asbestos decades earlier," I explained. I cited cases of women contracting the disease simply by washing their husbands' work clothes. And cases where the only exposure was literally from the fibre blowing out a factory door to the neighbouring houses.

'Kruger scoffed, but I said, "Bill, if you think I'm making this up, you're welcome to read the 760 pages yourself."

'I could see Dymock and Frew looking at each other. Neither was smiling. They knew I didn't joke about anything to do with my work. I'm sure I had a reputation for being a straight shooter.

'"Bill, this is the end of the road so far as blue's concerned. We must stop using it. It's as simple as that," I said.'

'What did Kruger say then?'

'He put his factory manager hat on and said something like, "That's all very well, Peter, but I can tell you we have tons of blue fibre here to use, and there'll be ships arriving in Sydney, as usual, with further supplies. It's not like it's a tap we can turn off whenever we want."

'I told Bill I understood that, but this was a crisis. The science was clear. Wagner and Newhouse had proved the link with mesothelioma and Cape blue. I then asked about the supplies from Disaster Gorge – that was blue as well, I believed.

'Russell Dymock confirmed that it was.

'I knew that the chief health officer in Western Australia, Neil Smith, had published a case report of mesothelioma in a miner from Disaster Gorge. That was very worrying, and I pointed the implications out to Kruger. I told him Henry King had no choice but to stop using crocidolite.

'Kruger paused, pondering the situation. He was an obstinate man, as I'm sure you've learned. But he asked me to prepare a full, written report to present to the board of directors as soon as he could arrange a meeting. In the meantime, he requested Dymock, Frew and I keep quiet about the findings until the board had an opportunity to look at my report.

'Dymock, who was a terribly nervous chap, had developed a tic under his left eye. It was firing like a machine gun as he asked Kruger the $64,000 question.

'"I want to know if we're going to stop using blue asbestos immediately in light of what Peter's told us," he said.

'Kruger was agitated and answered in belittling terms, questioning Dymock's comprehension and repeating his message about putting the issue before the board. Frew came to Dymock's defence, saying it was a valid question.

'You could tell Bill was stressed. As factory manager he could temporarily stop the use of blue, pending board approval, but such a big step might later be seen as overreaching. He could get himself into very hot water, indeed. It was the first time any of us had seen him being anything worse than curt. It was quite disconcerting. Eventually he inhaled deeply and told Bob, who was also getting aggravated, to "keep his shirt on". He reiterated that we wouldn't stop the blue until the board had considered the position. Henry King was a commercial enterprise employing hundreds of men and decisions as important as this one had to be made at board level. His hands were tied, he said. But he assured the others that he and I would take a firm stance when we saw the directors.

'I looked across at Dymock. His left eyelid twitched again. It was as if he were giving Kruger a playful wink, although I can assure you, Bruce, he wasn't. We were all very worried, although in hindsight, it may not have been for the same reasons.

'Anyway, about a week later, I drove in to head office in Bligh Street to meet the board. I'd spent the remainder of the previous week producing a comprehensive report to Bill Kruger on the current state of knowledge about asbestos-related diseases. He told me he'd provided a copy of the report to each of the eight board members. I assumed the directors would have read it. I'd given the whole thing a great deal of thought and I saw no reason to depart from my main points. I see you have a copy of my report there, Bruce.'

'Yes, it's a very important document.'

'I didn't anticipate any obstacles. Apart from crocidolite, the news was reasonably good. Just get rid of blue and it was business as usual. I hoped the board would see it that way.

'Given Bill Kruger's reaction, however, I wasn't so naive as to think the problem with blue asbestos would be easily solved. Andrew King's secretary asked me to go into the boardroom straightaway. The directors were already seated. I heard the bell of the lift behind me and soon saw Kruger at my side. Andrew King, the new chairman since his father's retirement the year before, stood up, walked towards us and shook our hands energetically. "Very good you could make it, Peter, Bill," he said. He closed the door behind me and motioned for us to take our seats.

'I knew the three Kings, and Joshua and Jacob Josephson, but hadn't met any of the other directors. Andrew King introduced them. I guess all the board was present so that meant Harry Josephson, Jacob's son, was there and Charles Seagrove and Frank Baldwin, the two independent directors. I could see there were a few hard heads, that's for sure.

'"Pleased to meet you all," I said.

'There weren't any what you might call 'grey hairs' on the board given that Gideon, Gordon and Emmanuel had stepped down. Jacob and Joshua Josephson would have been the oldest, although the Kings had also been in the wings for quite some time, watching the family company grow into a large public concern.

'Andrew King smoothly took control of the meeting, reminding us that Henry King was proud to be a smart company, a good company, a profitable company. A company that cared for its workers, and treated them as part of the family. It had experienced setbacks in the past and had overcome them.

'He then turned to my report, which, he said, marked a bit of a crossroads in the company's future. The board members had read it carefully, and agreed they would hate to see the company's excellent reputation tarnished in any way. That would completely dishonour the memory of Henry King and especially Gideon and Gordon King, and Mannie Josephson.

'He then informed me that V&L Ltd had very recently closed down its Disaster Gorge crocidolite mine. There would be no more blue coming to us from over in the west. The company had never liked the crocidolite it got from Disaster Gorge anyway, he added, and only bought it because of some terrible business with the Tariff Board. But to cut to the chase, Bruce, Andrew announced that with the closure of Disaster Gorge and the new health hazards I'd detailed in my report, the board intended to act on my recommendations and stop using crocidolite in the production of asbestos cement.

'The other board members concurred, much to my relief. I think Bill Kruger was even more surprised than I was that things had gone so smoothly.

'Andrew authorised me to inform Frew and Dymock of the decision and said we could purchase as many membrane filters and spirometers as we required – I had also recommended these in my report, so it was pleasing to get their approval on the spot.

'Kruger and I were preparing to leave when Charles Seagrove said he had a question for me. He wanted to know if I had identified any instances of mesothelioma in the Henry King workforce.

'I peered across the table at this Seagrove fellow. He was a well-groomed, rather slick-looking man. I didn't like him, Bruce, I can tell you that much. Far too full of himself. I had naturally prepared for and anticipated such a question. It was the obvious thing to ask. "There have been no confirmed cases," I told the board. The pathological diagnosis of mesothelioma was difficult at that stage, Bruce, as I'm sure you realise.

'Seagrove asked me to reiterate what I'd just said. "I see. No clear cases, then?" he queried.

'I looked at the man asking these pointed questions and nodded. Behind him loomed a portrait of Gideon King, smiling benevolently from the shadows. I felt uncertain. It had been too easy. Andrew King was saying the right things. Did he truly speak for all? I wondered.

'He went on to thank me for my work and asked me to keep up to date with all the latest knowledge about asbestos-related diseases, including disease associations with fibre types other than crocidolite. According to Andrew, the company was most interested in being alerted to any new developments on that front.

'It all seemed too easy, Bruce. I didn't buy it. I could see the issues were still to be debated by the board and with that Seagrove fellow there, I thought there could be trouble.'

'Was there?'

'Well, I've no idea what happened in the boardroom, but as it turned out, I shouldn't have had any doubts. You really had to pay them their dues, because as far as I knew they did stop using crocidolite as I had recommended. I was very happy with the outcome. I felt I had made a real difference.

'But my fears about mesothelioma were soon realised, Bruce,' Mathers added. 'In the three years following my report to the board in 1966, I detected and reported on six cases of mesothelioma in my annual medical survey of the Henry King Industries workforce. All six cases were confirmed by reputable pathologists. All the men had had exposure to crocidolite asbestos, as well as the other fibre types purchased by the company. In light of the long latency period referred to in Biological Effects of Asbestos, I wondered whether the incidence rate would increase. Mesothelioma can develop decades after first exposure, as you know. Disaster Blue was only purchased in the 1950s and Cape Blue in the 1940s, I believe. This meant that men could get the disease in the 1980s or 1990s. I was quite concerned.'

'I can understand why, Peter, but you couldn't have done anything earlier as there was no knowledge of any connection between blue asbestos to mesothelioma.'

'That's true, Bruce. I had a clear conscience. Did what I could as soon as I could.'

Chapter 34

Unfortunately for Bruce's grand plans with Mathers, there was the little problem of Russell Dymock. While Bob Frew confirmed what Mathers said, Dymock refused to talk to him at all. Perhaps Dymock didn't want to dredge up the past. Bruce hoped that was the reason, but he wasn't sure. Did Dymock know something Mathers didn't? He recalled what Mathers had said about Dymock.

He'd been telling Bruce about how he'd always told Bill Kruger what his annual review findings were before they were submitted to the board. In what he thought was 1969, Mathers had told Kruger, who was by then the company's general manager, that there were now six confirmed cases of mesothelioma.

'As we'd started using blue about twenty to thirty years earlier, I told Kruger, as I've told you, that I suspected we'd continue to have cases well into the 1990s because of the long latency period for the disease, but by the new millennium, there should be a gradual decline because we stopped using blue in 1966.

'Kruger agreed, and complimented the job the engineers had done to get the dust counts down. I was feeling quite chuffed at what I'd been able to achieve with my medical surveillance programme and the industrial hygiene measures which also were within my bailiwick. The only hiccup had been the recent resignation of the safety officer, Russell Dymock. He left suddenly without talking to me at all. As I said to Kruger, "He wasn't a bad bloke, although a bit nervy."

'Kruger agreed. "Highly strung," he said, and "probably wanted a less stressful job."

'And that's all I know about Dymock's departure,' Mathers concluded.

'Where did he go after that?' Bruce asked.

'I'm afraid I have no idea. Probably a less stressful job, as Kruger said.'

'Do you think he'll ever give evidence in one of these cases?'

'Who for? The company?'

'Yes, or maybe for a plaintiff?'

'Bruce, why would he give evidence against the company? He saw what I saw. Knew what I knew. He'd say the company did everything I asked it to do and that we stayed ahead of the field.'

'I agree, Peter,' Bruce had replied. 'Just wondering whether his recollection would be any different from yours.'

'Couldn't possibly be.'

'You said he was anxious. Is he the type who'd be willing to be a witness?'

'Doubt it. He was a behind the scenes sort of fellow. I doubt he'd have the gumption to appear in court, Bruce. And what would be the point? He was only the safety officer. It was my programme. My expertise. Not his.'

Bruce wondered whether Mathers was telling the truth. But Bob Frew had the same recollection and he was present when Mathers warned Bill Kruger about blue asbestos.

Yet Ed Ferris, the state scientific officer who had regularly inspected the factory, had mentioned something more troubling about Russell Dymock during one of his interviews with Bruce.

'Dymock often accompanied me on my regular inspections. The factory was in pretty good shape and I gave my usual recommendations to keep up the good work. Can't recall anything more about the visits than that. I do, however, remember a specific occasion in 1969 when, for the first time, I voiced concerns about crocidolite, not that I believed Henry King was using it. It was new information I'd come across and I suppose it was at the front of my mind. I was probably interested in making conversation with Dymock. He could be hard work, you know.'

'"I've been doing some reading lately," I said to him, "and I'm positive blue asbestos causes a new type of cancer called mesothelioma."

'"I know," he said.

'I looked at the safety officer closely. "Why do you say that?" I asked him.

'He said that Dr Mathers had told the company to stop using it in 1966 when he advised the board in no uncertain terms that it could cause mesothelioma.

'I was quite astonished. Bruce, I thought I kept abreast of things, but here I was talking about something three years behind Peter Mathers. He'd got the company out of blue well ahead of the game. In hindsight, I shouldn't have been too surprised as Mathers was a bright man and took his job seriously. It was Dymock's subsequent comments that I found odd.'

'What did he say?'

'He said something like, "But don't believe everything you hear, Ed."

'I asked him what he meant by that,

'He muttered that he'd seen a few things, and heard a bit too.

'I asked him if there was something he wanted to tell me. It really wasn't clear what he was getting at, but it didn't sound good, whatever it was.

'He backtracked and told me not to worry about it. His cheek was twitching. It was quite off-putting. Strange fella, that's for sure.'

Bruce felt he could smell when something was off. The Dymock story had that odour. And yet Mathers' recollection about how easy it was to convince the board to cease using blue asbestos seemed to stack up. He knew there was no contrary evidence in any of Henry King's discovered documents. There was also no evidence that the company knew about the possible connection between blue asbestos and mesothelioma until Dr

Mathers gave the board his memorandum in 1966. None of the directors Bruce had spoken to had any memory of a board discussion about the issue. Andrew King had told him that, as far as he could remember, what Mathers had told Bruce was the fact. That seemed the best way to treat it, Bruce decided. Let Peter Mathers' recollection be the final and only word on the subject. There was no other option.

Chapter 35

While the time with Mathers was extremely useful, Bruce couldn't stop wondering whether the good doctor's account was simply too good to be true? It certainly seemed that way when Mathers was addressing questions about Henry King's duty of care to carpenters and builders such as Scott Hawkins who worked with products outdoors.

'I was extremely pleased, Bruce, to have been invited to join the Occupational Health Committee of the National Health and Medical Research Council in 1977,' Peter Mathers said.

'What was that?' Bruce asked.

'A very important body, Bruce. It was a big deal. I thought that at the time and I still think that to be true. After over a decade in the job, I believed I was finally being recognised as a leader in the field of asbestos disease, and a pioneer in occupational health in Australia.'

'I definitely think you were, Peter. I'm positive, with the statement we finally produce, that that story will shine through in court.'

Mathers smiled. Bruce could see his blatant and repeated flattery was appreciated. 'I enjoyed going to the regular meetings of the OHC, Bruce. I could discuss important issues with intelligent medical men. The committee comprised all the chief medical officers from the states' health departments, men like Neil Smith from Perth and Dr White's successor, Alan Bullcock in Sydney, together with a senior industrial hygienist and the Commonwealth Director of Health, Craig Donaldson, who was the chair of both the NHMRC and its OHC.

'Early on at the OHC, it became commonplace for the members to look to me for all the latest information on asbestos-related diseases or, at least, that was my perception. To tell you the truth, I wasn't quite sure whether the others were spending much time keeping abreast of the literature at all.'

'I'm sure you had some very interesting meetings, but I'm particularly interested in how the asbestos warning labels came about,' prompted Bruce. 'Were you on the committee when that started being tabled?'

'I was. As I've said, I looked forward to each meeting. I remember them well. The meeting in 1977, when we discussed warnings, is no exception.'

'What happened?'

'I'd received personal notice from Alan Bullcock that the meeting would be important. The OHC was going to investigate the safety of asbestos cement and the need for warning labels on asbestos-containing products. This came as quite a shock to me. For years, Ed Ferris had been carrying out inspections of the Riverwood factory, admiring the progress Kings had been making in getting, and keeping, dust counts down. He'd assured the company over and over again that once the fibre was locked into the sheet during the manufacturing process, it no longer posed a health hazard. This had been the Health Department's line since Cecil White first conducted a survey in 1960. When Bullcock replaced White in the mid-1960s, he gave King Industries a similar message. It was a premise on which the entire asbestos cement industry depended.

'Because of the Health Department assurances, I hadn't given the safety of King Industries' customers a moment's additional thought. I didn't consider carpenters, builders, roof-fixers or handymen to be at risk of developing an asbestos disease. There was no need for warning labels. I suppose when one thought about it, and I did briefly, the exposure of carpenters could be like that of the men in the finishing section of the factory, where the power saws cut the sheets to size. But surely that exposure was orders of magnitude higher. Carpenters didn't cut asbestos sheets hour after hour, day after day indoors. In the end, I thought it was a bad analogy. So long as there was no crocidolite in the product, there was no risk of mesothelioma. The exposure of a carpenter couldn't conceivably come close to the level required to develop asbestosis. And if you didn't get asbestosis, then you couldn't get lung cancer. With these thoughts in mind, I was keen to see what the other members of the OHC thought on the issue.

'According to Donaldson, the chair, some of the health ministers around the country were starting to express interest in the subject so we had to deal with it seriously. There were evidently also rumblings in the building unions about asbestos being dangerous. There'd been newspaper reports of men dying of mesothelioma. And Western Australia, he said, was now dealing with a spate of cases from Disaster Gorge, at which point Neil Smith agreed vigorously.

'Someone expressed surprise that we hadn't received any reports of mesothelioma in carpenters, as some of them must have been working with sheets containing crocidolite for years.

'Bullcock pointed out that as they weren't factory workers, they were lost to surveillance and Neil Smith posited that there might already be an epidemic.

'Bullcock cautioned Smith not to get alarmist, saying that we would have heard something about the cases, if there were more than the odd one or two, even taking into account the frequency with which mesothelioma was misdiagnosed as lung cancer. The chest doctors in the hospitals would have told one of us if they'd treated any cases of mesothelioma. He conceded, however, that there must have been a few cases by then. Word of mouth was hardly an accurate method of knowing what cases were out there.

'Donaldson agreed, and suggested that the only way we might pick up end-user cases would be by starting a mesothelioma register like the one in the UK. But that was a matter for another day. Right then we had to focus on the risks to consumers.

'I suggested we try to estimate what a tradesman's exposure would be on a typical day on the tools, and work out what his time-weighted exposure would be – would it be above the current threshold limit value?

'I believed we'd be able to work out what the exposure was likely to be when a tradesman was cutting sheets and then extrapolate what the exposure would be over the whole day. We'd have to make an assumption as to how often a worker would spend cutting sheets and generating dust. It wouldn't be too difficult. For my part, I thought that none of them would spend more than twenty to thirty percent of their time on the tools on any given day.

'Most of the others, even those with testing experience in the field, agreed with my estimate and thought it fair: a carpenter wouldn't be cutting sheets all day. He'd be cutting wood, making wooden frames, screwing, hammering, carrying gear, loading, driving and so on. But Donaldson said we were simply guessing what proportion of the day would be spent cutting. Some operators might have dedicated teams doing little else, as if they were on the production line in a factory. What if they did the cutting indoors, as must occur quite frequently? There were so many variables, he said, that it would be absurd for us to say the asbestos products were safe for carpenters. He worked up quite a lather, I can tell you, Bruce. A slight alteration to the assumptions or a change in the location where the cutting was done could see the threshold limit value exceeded, he insisted. At the very least, we should be warning users to keep dust down.

'"Warning labels?" I asked him, probably sounding rather dubious, Bruce.

'Neil Smith jumped in. He thought it wasn't a bad idea. After all, we were all concerned to keep dust exposure to a minimum. In the factory situation, it was relatively easy, because the workers were a captive audience, so to speak. But on worksites, nobody really knew about asbestos or threshold limit values. Builders could do what they wanted. He thought they should be warned.

'I was unconvinced, at first. Everyone knew warning labels weren't worth the paper they were printed on. I pointed out that the warnings on cigarette packets hadn't stopped people smoking.

'Donaldson quickly shut me down. Smokers choose to smoke, he said – it was a personal choice. But carpenters weren't being given any choice at all whether to protect themselves or not.

'Bruce, he was, of course, right, but I didn't concede that at the time.' Mathers chuckled.

'Despite my recalcitrance, the "Code for the Handling of Asbestos for Small Users" was the end-result of our discussions. We produced that document and then a warning label and finally a "Statement of Health Hazards Associated with the Use of Asbestos in the Construction Industry". You've probably got all of them there with you, Bruce.'

'I do.'

'Would you mind if I see the code for a minute? Yes, here it is. Sensible, general advice, but not of any medical significance, in my view. We stated:

Asbestos cement (fibro) is a hard-surfaced material, in which the asbestos fibres are reasonably bonded by cement. Work with this material can be carried out safely with hand saws and other hand tools and also with power drills. Occasional power sawing does not present a problem if limited to an operation of say, fifteen minutes in a shift, and if carried out in the open air. For longer periods, dust-extraction equipment should be used or the dust should be suppressed by the use of water or an approved respirator should be used.

'And then in 1978, Henry King Industries rolled out its first consignment of sheets with warning labels stuck to the back. The labels were printed in bright blue and red and stated:

CAUTION: contains asbestos. Breathing asbestos dust might damage health. Work outdoors, use special tools, power saws require dust suppression, avoid drilling overhead, damp down waste and seal it in a bag.

'It was commonsense advice about keeping dust levels down. I mean, who wants to work in a dusty atmosphere? But of no medical relevance. I think I did my job very well in keeping it fairly bland.'

'Did you have to make recommendations to the board about the warning labels?'

'No, the board made the decision without my involvement. Kruger told me it was a fait accompli once the Health Department endorsed the NHMRC recommendations. It was evidently good business to keep the Health Department happy.'

'Do you think the warnings were adequate?'

'Yes, I do. You have to understand, Bruce, that nobody, and I mean nobody, was thinking of any connection between mesothelioma, lung cancer or asbestosis and the use of our sheets by tradesmen. There was no blue asbestos in the product and the proportion of asbestos in the whole mix was something like ten to fifteen percent. There was no fatal disease to warn about. As I've already said, advice to keep dust down was mainly a matter of good housekeeping.'

'The warning does include a statement about the possibility of harm.'

'It does, but it was an awfully nebulous statement and when I later spoke to the trade union representatives about it, they were happy with our explanation that it was simply a precautionary measure. Nobody had established a definite risk, and if workers kept dust levels down they wouldn't run into any trouble, whether real or imaginary.'

♦

When he eventually got Mathers to sign on the dotted line, Bruce believed that with his statement he had a powerful weapon against plaintiffs in asbestos litigation. While he considered that Mathers' narrative was largely self-serving, Bruce also knew that there was probably no living witness to contradict him. He only wished he'd spoken to Mathers before settling the Scott Hawkins case for so much. Next time would be different.

PART IV

Chapter 36

Every Wednesday morning, the asbestos team at Shaw & Fletcher's Sydney office held a planning meeting during which the lawyers discussed the tactics for, and progress of, all current matters. Mesothelioma cases were given priority. Viviana Glosioli always had the biggest case load to present to her colleagues.

She knew some of the male solicitors resented her for what they perceived as favouritism. It didn't take Einstein to work out why. They predictably considered her rise to the top to be more about her relationship with the senior partner, Gary Shaw, than her ability.

She gazed around the table of fifteen lawyers. Some were writing in their pads, others shuffling papers and reports. Some of the young men looked challengingly in her direction. No one held her gaze. How pathetic. She could make them squirm, if she chose to, provoke angry impulsive outbursts or streams of garbled foolishness. The fact of the matter, however, was that Viviana really didn't want to do that. It was game-playing and she was dead tired of it.

And then Gary Shaw entered.

Viviana found her own heartbeat rising, her breath becoming shallow. She didn't want to feel like this, but she couldn't control it – at least not yet.

Gary smiled at her as he sat down at the head of the table to her right. Viviana stiffened and then recoiled as his thigh brushed against her own.

Although in her mind their relationship was over, and had been for many months, Shaw seemed to see things differently. He certainly didn't know how to keep physical boundaries or cease using unpalatable familiarities and innuendo. How she wished it had never started. Why had it even started in the first place? What had she been thinking?

'Morning everyone,' Shaw said. 'Pass me that plate of croissants will you, Nikos? Thanks.' He took a big bite, flakes and crumbs falling on his lap. 'Okay, that's better. Let's get started. First on my list here is Berendetti. Viviana?' He turned to look at her, pastry adhering to his upper incisor creating the appearance of a gap in his teeth.

'Thanks, Gary. Mr Paulo Berendetti was employed at the Henry King Industries factory in the 1950s and 1960s. He has a right-sided mesothelioma confirmed on histopathology by Professor Philbrick. It's inoperable and according to his treating oncologist, he has about three months to live.'

'Are there any special issues with his case?' asked Shaw.

'There's one thing that might interest everyone. Mr Berendetti claims to have seen bags of blue asbestos being used as late as 1969.'

'That can't be right,' said another solicitor, Carlo Saccheri. 'They stopped using it, according to their discovered documents, in 1966.'

'What if that's wrong? What if it's a cover up?' Viviana countered.

'Doubt it.'

'I don't think we should dismiss this out of hand,' said Shaw. 'If we can convince the tribunal that Henry King was using blue after they said they'd stopped it, then we may well be able to finally prove they should pay punitive damages. His evidence might match that of other witnesses.'

'But Disaster Gorge closed the mine in 1966,' another of the lawyers, Nikos Papadogolous, chimed in.

'That doesn't mean there weren't bags of it still in a warehouse at Henry King's, does it, Nikos?' retorted Viviana. 'And besides, they could have got blue from South Africa.'

'Can Mr Berendetti identify where the blue asbestos came from?' Shaw asked.

'No, unfortunately. He does recall that Henry King got its blue from both Disaster Gorge and Africa. He worked in the pulverising plant for some time and remembers seeing the bags. In 1969, he moved to a different part of the factory, but he could still see blue asbestos in the mix. It was unmistakable. I've been looking through the affidavits of other plaintiffs over the years trying to find someone who corroborates Mr Berendetti's evidence. So far, no luck. I'm thinking of talking to some of the former company witnesses about it, but I won't be able to get to them by the time Mr Berendetti's case comes on for hearing.'

'Well, Viviana, I think you should definitely include these recollections in Mr Berendetti's affidavit. Might extract a premium when it comes time to settle,' said Nikos. There was a collective nod from most of the lawyers at the table.

'If I were in Bruce Fraser's shoes over at Jacksons, I wouldn't pay more. There's no reason to believe a sick old man's memory when the contemporaneous documents say something different.'

'Perhaps you should apply for a job at Jacksons, Carlo. Do you think you're on the right side, here?' Viviana did not like Carlo.

'What's this about sides? I'm just talking about the evidence.'

'Are you? What would you do if it was your case?'

'I'd—'

'What? Not use this evidence? Not believe what a dying man told you was the honest truth?'

'I didn't say that. I wouldn't say that. I'd probably use it too,' Carlo said, shifting his gaze to the files in front of him.

'Okay, okay, let's move on,' Shaw interrupted. 'Nothing like a good debate about the issues, right? Now the next case is Strudwick. Viviana, over to you again.'

Chapter 37

After the team meeting, Viviana fixed herself a coffee in the staff kitchen and returned to her office. She was keen to discover if any of the hundreds of former Shaw & Fletcher clients had sworn affidavits about the use of blue asbestos at Henry King Industries after 1966. She sat down at the computer and started scrolling through the firm's database. If she didn't find anything, she could try Russell Dymock, the company's safety officer in the 1960s. She had approached him recently and he'd said he would think about making a statement, but he didn't sound overly keen.

She was still searching the database when she sensed a change in the energy in her room. There could be only one reason. She looked up. There he was, a tall hulk of a man, grinning slyly at her in the way she hated so much. She could feel her blood pressure rise. Stop it! she silently commanded herself.

'Viv, thought I'd congratulate you on that find with the Berendetti case. Good work. Could be very important.'

Of course it could be, she said to herself. Stop pretending. You know exactly why you're here and it makes me sick.

'Thanks, although I'm only reporting what Mr Berendetti tells me.'

'Yes, but not all of the team would have paid attention. You heard them this morning. Rather than record it, they'd ignore it.'

'Possibly.'

'No doubt about it. Viv, you're one of a kind.'

Viviana hoped Shaw would not take a seat. He did. She stared at him blankly as he prattled on about a restaurant, his car, his boat, himself.

At some stage, her focus sharpened. Gary Shaw really was an unattractive man, with his round pock-marked face and fleshy frame. He had the air of a man who believed it was to his advantage to sound and appear simple. It didn't work with Viviana – not anymore. The air about him was now what she always should have felt but somehow misinterpreted – noxious and enervating.

'That's very interesting, Gary, but I'd like to get back to searching for some corroborative evidence.'

'I hear you, I'll get out of your hair. Perhaps we could chat further over lunch.'

'I don't think so.'

She tried to appear as calm as possible despite her racing heart. He looked at her with his cunning, piggy eyes. His curly mop of black hair was trimmed like buxus. She felt like cowering, but by conscious effort she kept her face hard and cold. He shrugged, got up and left.

This can't go on, she thought. I have to get out of here.

Viviana had done well at university. She had worked absurd hours to achieve her first-class honours degree, sacrificing any meaningful social life for good marks. Once she entered the workforce, there never seemed any time to go out and meet people. Yet somehow the affair with Gary Shaw happened. She wasn't sure how or why. When she was near him now, she felt sick with embarrassment. It was a source of endless self-loathing. She desperately didn't want it to ruin her career or her life. She owed it to herself and to her parents not to waste the opportunities they had given her.

Viviana's Italian immigrant parents had worked hard, dirty jobs to put her and her two sisters through university. They were immensely proud of her, even though her father constantly urged her to fatten herself up whenever she visited them at their Punchbowl home. They would be devastated if they discovered the sordid truth behind her stellar legal career or found out how unhappy she truly was.

She had to keep the wall up for as long as she could. It was her only protection.

The phone rang. Bruce Fraser. Not now, she thought. 'Okay, put him through.'

'Hello,' she answered as flatly as possible.

'Viviana, good to talk to you. How are you?'

'Well.'

'That's good.'

'What do you want, Fraser?' She was amazed that someone so intelligent could be so witless at the same time. It had largely been like that at university too, as she recalled.

'I want to know whether you want to settle Paulo Berendetti's case.'

'Why the hurry? We've only just started.'

'Sure, but there seems no reason to prolong things. He's got a terminal condition.'

'I know. Your client's pressuring you, is that it?'

'That might be so, but that doesn't mean we can't settle sooner rather than later – that is, Viviana, unless you want to rack up your costs first.'

'That's offensive.'

'Okay, I apologise, but I can't think of any other reason to delay settlement.'

'I can – to make sure his case is investigated fully so that he can get the maximum damages he's entitled to. Just follow the timetable, Fraser; you know, the one you consented to, and then we'll consider whether settlement's possible down the track.'

'Well, if that's your attitude—'

'It is my attitude.'

'Okay, I'll wait for you and Gary Shaw to rack up your costs and then we'll talk. I only hope Mr Berendetti's well enough to give instructions at that time.' He hung up.

Viviana suppressed her anger. Bruce Fraser was going to get a nasty surprise when he was served with Paulo Berendetti's affidavit. She could already picture his bespectacled Cheshire cat face turning white.

But while she might extract some satisfaction from seeing Bruce Fraser pay an extortionate sum to settle the case, in the end these antics were tiresome. She couldn't help feeling that she was being forced to be someone she was not. Was it law? Was the profession so bad that it made all involved aggressive two-faced monsters or incapable of making good decisions in their own interests? Did she even belong in it?

Her results at law school had given her access to jobs at the major law firms. She'd even worked at Jacksons alongside Bruce Fraser as a summer clerk. She considered it ironic that she now came up against that firm with her asbestos work. Her time at the firm had been rewarding so far as training and experience in litigation was concerned, but she'd known that she didn't belong among the lawyers who worked there. The majority had gone to private schools or had family members already 'in the law'. They seemed much more interested in money, buying a house in Mosman or skiing in Aspen than interacting with real human clients. They'd spent their summer clerkships engaged in astute, selective smarming. Law to them was a device to be used to get your own way rather than a set of principles to achieve justice. Perhaps she was naive, but these principles mattered to her.

When the time came to apply for jobs as a graduate lawyer, Viviana had ignored the big end of town firms and got a job with the Bankstown Legal Centre. She'd met and acted for criminals, injured workers, the dispossessed and the needy. She loved the responsibility and the steep learning curve. Her friends were puzzled at her choice, but she never regretted it. They told her they were doing a 'massive discovery' exercise or a 'difficult security for costs' application or similar. She, on the other hand, was in court before magistrates, arguing cases, testing her mettle.

The centre wanted her to stay with them, but after two years she'd decided to apply for work at a plaintiff law firm. To her surprise, she received countless offers. In her interview with Gary Shaw and Herb Fletcher, she was told that it was unusual for a first-class honours graduate to work at a plaintiff firm. They offered her top dollar to join them. She did, but it wasn't for the money. Viviana knew Shaw & Fletcher was the leader in the field of asbestos litigation. She wanted to sue the companies responsible for her uncle's asbestosis. Like Viviana's father, her uncle had worked many menial jobs to support his family and ensure his children received a good education. He was a cleaner in factories, office buildings, sports arenas – wherever he could find work. After all this effort, Uncle Tommaso now spent most of his time strapped to an oxygen machine. Providing for a family should not be a death sentence, Viviana believed.

She continued scrolling through the list of former Shaw & Fletcher clients. Many had worked in the Henry King factory in the 1960s, but the affidavits were silent about the use of crocidolite. This could not be by accident, Viviana thought. Whoever drafted the affidavits seemed to concentrate only on asbestos in general, rather than the specific fibre types used in the process. She read the names of the solicitors on the record for these clients – Carlo Saccheri, Nikos Papadogolous, Cindy Triffitt ... Gary Shaw! Viviana sat back, astonished. She looked at the name again. She couldn't believe that her boss, one of the nation's leaders in the asbestos field, had omitted to inquire about exposure to blue asbestos or the types of fibre being used by Henry King Industries over the years. How could he have been so complacent?

Chapter 38

At home in her apartment with her cat, Echo, an affectionate Burmese, Viviana reflected on what she had discovered. It was hardly earth-shattering, although it had the effect of cementing in her mind what she had long suspected. Shaw didn't care about his clients anymore.

Her sister, Francesca, rang, interrupting her ruminations.

'Hi, Vivvie, how are you? How's Echo?'

'Fine, everything's good. He's as loud as ever – here, listen to him purr.' She put the receiver near the cat. She could hear her sister talking to him: 'How's my beautiful boy?' Echo's yellow eyes closed momentarily in reverie.

'What's up, Fran?'

'Nothing much. I was over at Mum and Dad's, and they want to know if you can join us for lunch on Sunday.'

'Why couldn't they ring me themselves?'

'They don't like to disturb you, knowing how busy you are.'

'But you're a doctor, you're busy too.'

'Apparently not as busy as they think you are.'

'Okay, I'll come over if I can.'

'No, that's not good enough. They want a definite yes or no. Apparently, Dad's invited the Ferrantes over and their son, Andrea, will also be coming.'

'Oh no, not one of these lunches again where Dad tries to marry me off to a 'good Italian boy'.'

'Yes, I'm afraid so. Anyway, Andrea is cute, you said so yourself.'

'That was when I was fifteen. He's probably turned ugly now.'

'He hasn't, I've seen him. He's handsome and rich and quiet.'

'I don't care if he's rich. What does he do, anyway?'

'Property developer.'

'God, no. Spare me.'

'Come on, you have to come. Dad will be upset. He's worried about you.'

'What for? I'm not ready to marry yet.'

'But you don't even have a boyfriend.'

'I do – I mean I did. I'm getting over it.'

'Really? You never told me you were going out with someone. Who was the lucky guy? A good-looking barrister?'

'No. Just someone from work. You wouldn't know him. You wouldn't want to know him.'

'What was wrong with him?'

'Everything.'

'Then why did you go out with him?'

'I don't know. It was a mistake.'

'Tell me, what happened?'

'I can't. Just leave it, Fran, please.'

'Okay, but if you need to talk about it, I'm always here.'

'I know. I'll get over it in time.'

'All right. I'll tell Mum and Dad you'll be there.'

As Echo sat in her lap purring, Viviana leaned back and closed her eyes. The law had taught her how to rationalise most decisions and outcomes in her life. Even her relationship with Shaw she could probably justify if she would only be kind to herself. She wasn't sure she deserved that.

When Gary Shaw walked into her office on her first day of work, she hadn't seen a corpulent, vile, menacing man. She saw a confident, charming colossus. A leader. Someone who fought for a fair go for ordinary people like her family. She was now embarrassed at the memory. She was so naive, so trusting. She wanted to punch herself in the head at the shame.

'Welcome, Viviana! We're so glad you decided to join our firm,' he had said. 'Someone with your special abilities will go far here. Most of the big end firms think they have a mortgage on the brightest stars from university. Well, not anymore! You're going to have the opportunity to fight the good fight, to make new law, change the way society thinks about corporate conduct and greed. I'm sure you'll be up for the challenge.'

'I believe I am.'

She recalled Shaw staring at her, grinning, nodding, for an uncomfortable minute. 'Yes, Viv, you're going to do very well, I'm going to make sure of it. I'll make it my special project.' She remembered blushing as his eyes wandered over her. He laughed in what she'd thought was a kind, understanding way. 'I'll let you settle in and then we'll go down to the ADT together.'

She'd felt an amazing lightness. Now, she felt bleak.

Chapter 39

Shaw had certainly taken Viviana under his wing. He'd had her join him for the weekly directions hearings in the Asbestos Diseases Tribunal, eventually letting her run the lists. Viviana had appeared in court many times while working for the Bankstown Legal Centre so she quickly adapted to the new role. As for Gary Shaw, he could not have been more attentive. He was patient and gentlemanly, introducing her to opposing solicitors and barristers, and taking her into the judges' chambers for morning tea so that they could get to know Shaw & Fletcher's prized recruit.

Shaw had described the judges as 'very plaintiff friendly'. Viviana hadn't seen any obvious evidence of this, but she had witnessed considerable compassion towards her clients. Because many of the plaintiffs were extremely ill or dying, the tribunal had devised several ways to expedite the hearing of proceedings. They would often conduct hearings at hospitals and homes, sometimes travelling interstate or overseas to accommodate the very ill. In fact, on at least two occasions, Shaw had instructed her to serve a writ on a defendant on a Friday and obtained orders from the tribunal to take the dying plaintiff's evidence on the following Monday. The aim was to permit a victim to know the outcome of his case before he died. He could then die in peace, knowing his family would be financially secure with an award of damages.

Viviana had observed Shaw in court. In the ADT, Gary Shaw was king. And he knew it. He proceeded through cases with enviable efficiency. Viviana could sense his power and self-control, towering over the lectern, brandishing his arms like weapons. She was mesmerised by it. She thought she wanted to have it too. But for that she would need to toughen up.

About three months into the job, Shaw persuaded Viviana to lunch with him – at first once a week and eventually every day of the week. He talked tactics with her and guided her decision-making with the increasing number of urgent cases she took sole control of.

'Stick with me, Viv, and I'll make it happen for you. You can have everything I've achieved if you put your heart and soul into it.'

'It's very kind of you, Gary, to show me the ropes. I really appreciate it.'

'Viv, I'm now the senior partner of what will become the largest plaintiff law firm in Australia,' he said. 'We're expanding into every state. There'll be enormous opportunities for someone like you as we grow.' He gesticulated handsomely, his hands moving apart as if holding an expanding balloon.

'I've become very wealthy taking on some of Australia's biggest companies. I'm the one who ran all the test cases in the 1990s. Everybody knows it was all my doing. Now companies like V&L and Henry King are eating out of my hand. There's a constant stream of asbestos victims knocking on my door. What I've done will keep teams of lawyers busy throughout Australia. I want you to be part of it, Viv. You've got something in you that I recognise in myself.'

Viviana now winced at these recollections, but at the time she stared at him with adoration.

'You've got the same will to win, the same ambition to prove all the doubters wrong, to fight for justice, as corny as that sounds.'

'Is that what you see?'

'That's what I see. I always see what a person has inside. I can read you, Viviana. You're a dangerous, dark, beautiful force.' He reached across the table and squeezed her hand. She didn't know what to do, so she left her hand there until he moved his own. That was the start. There was more to come.

Every year, Shaw & Fletcher put on an 'asbestos spectacular'. They hired a bar, restaurant or space in a hotel, and invited their lawyers, the barristers they briefed, secretaries, and all the regular experts. Viviana experienced her first spectacular the night she settled her first solo mesothelioma case. She was weary but elated.

Now, she found these evenings tiresome. There was something vulgar in celebrating a business based on dying men and women. While husbands, fathers and grandfathers lay slowly choking to death, fat, oily men and ambitious sycophants were chatting up secretaries, groping in the dark and sliding their tongues down each other's throats.

Of course, they weren't all like that. In fact, only a few could justifiably be criticised. Viviana appreciated she had become far too judgmental. If the truth be known, asbestos litigation was a depressing, emotionally draining business. An annual splurge was not unreasonable. The first time she went, she welcomed the opportunity to release some of the energy she had been bottling for the previous months.

'Hello there,' a nondescript middle-aged man with a skew-whiff tie and a sodden suit said to her soon after her arrival.

Viviana was holding a glass of champagne, standing at the periphery of a group of solicitors from Shaw & Fletcher. 'Hello,' she replied, casting a critical but kindly eye over the obviously inebriated man.

'I'm Gregory Lucas, barrister-at-law.'

Viviana wondered what she now would have said to Lucas if the same thing happened. At the time, however, she was in a loose, friendly state. 'Hello, Mr Barrister-at-Law, Gregory Lucas. I'm Viviana.'

'I know.'

'You do, do you? How do you know who I am?'

Lucas pointed at Gary Shaw. 'I asked someone who knows.'

'And why did you want to know?'

'Because I wanted to meet you. You could possibly be the best thing that's ever happened to asbestos litigation in this country.'

'Is that right?'

'It is indeed. How about a dance?'

'I suppose now that you've given me so many compliments, it would be rude not to.'

Lucas took Viviana's hand and led her into the writhing mass of revellers. He wasn't terribly co-ordinated, but he made up for this deficiency with boundless energy, gyrating wildly, his beer splashing over his shirt and trousers, his mouth gaping as if a doctor had asked him to say 'Aahh'. Viviana laughed as she moved to the music.

She danced with Lucas for about twenty minutes before Gary Shaw loomed behind the barrister and tapped him on the shoulder. 'My turn, Greg,' he shouted in the din. Lucas skulked off as Shaw's sweaty belly started heaving haphazardly to the beat.

Viviana felt electrified. She couldn't remember ever feeling so free. Shaw stared at her intently, seeming to Viviana to share her joy. When the set finished, they danced to the next one until they were both exhausted. Shaw took her hand and led her outside for some air.

'I'm so happy, Gary. What a night!' She laughed, tossing her hair back out of her face.

'I knew you'd enjoy it, Viv, after all the hard work you've done. You've got to be able to let off some steam, you know, otherwise you'll go crazy. You have to let go sometimes.'

He moved closer to her, his big hand relocating to the small of her back, pressing her steadily towards him. Soon, he lowered his wet face right before her, and then they were kissing. Kissing with a frenetic energy that was both scary and exhilarating. She could not stop. She knew she could be seen, but did not at that moment care. She now wished she had.

She peered around Shaw's shoulder as the bloated ogre slid his big spade of a hand down the inside of her skirt. At the other end of the lane behind the restaurant, Carlo Saccheri stood with a small group of solicitors watching her. She still recoiled at the memory.

Chapter 40

After two weeks of staring at her computer, Viviana gave up on the search for another past plaintiff who could confirm Paulo Berendetti's evidence. It didn't stop her, however, extracting a very large sum from Bruce Fraser to settle the case. This was the second time within the year that she had delivered a great result for a client. While Fraser maintained his annoying bravado and feigned disinterest when she raised the point with him, she could tell he was anxious to settle and that proved his client was too. Viviana felt there was definitely some truth to Mr Berendetti's recollection. Henry King Industries may well have used crocidolite after 1966. She hoped this could be exploited in other cases.

The next case she had to resolve, however, involved a man with pleural plaques, Herb Caxton. He complained of chest pain and shortness of breath, but Viviana struggled to believe him. She knew when men and women were crippled by asbestos disease. He was not one of them. He had a history of heavy cigarette smoking, obesity and emphysema. If pleural plaques were responsible for anything in his case, it was only several white flecks on a chest x-ray.

To make matters worse, Bruce Fraser had again served a statement from the Health Department's industrial hygiene officer from the mid-1960s, Edward Ferris, in which he claimed that all the Henry King safety measures were 'ahead of their time' and 'pleasing'. Fraser had already played the Ferris card in the case of Jack Taylor, a former foreman at Henry King, forcing her to recommend a modest settlement to the client. Caxton could end up being the first plaintiff to lose an asbestos case. That was not going to happen. She had to settle.

'Do whatever you think appropriate, Shaw had said at the recent team meeting. I'm sure you'll do the right thing by Mr Caxton, just like you did for Mr Taylor.'

'What's that supposed to mean?'

'Nothing.'

Viviana knew what she had to do. She had to settle for whatever she could reasonably extract from Fraser's client. Fortunately, Caxton did not want to go to court and was willing to take advice.

It proved difficult to remain composed as she subsequently handed up the terms of settlement in the ADT. Judge Steinblott feigned incredulity when he read the document and looked at her with surprise. It was a galling moment, especially as Bruce Fraser asked the judge, 'Pardon me, your Honour, what was the amount of the settlement again, so I may make a note of it?'

'$100,000 as you well know, Mr Fraser.'

'I'm indebted to your Honour. $100,000 it is.' Bruce gazed about the tribunal so that all the other solicitors with cases in the list, essentially all those who practised in the area, could hear of his brilliant result.

'Your Honour, I wonder whether Mr Fraser might stop his showboating so that I could get to the next case in the list,' Viviana interjected.

'Yes, Ms Glosioli, proceed. Mr Fraser, you may leave.'

'May it please the court,' Bruce said and bowed.

When she returned to the office, Viviana ruminated over Bruce Fraser's use of experts who were in the field at the key moments in history. While she'd had two recent successes with record settlements, they had been interspersed with two poor results. The goal posts were shifting. She needed her own 'real' expert to fight back. The experts the firm relied on were generally self-proclaimed with tenuous links to industry or occupational medicine at the relevant times. She'd already spoken to several kind old men who knew the history of the evolving awareness of the dangers of asbestos. It was time to dust off their draft statements and convert at least one of them into a threatening witness. Dr Neil Smith was the one she chose. She had already spent a lot of time with him, getting his statement into reasonable shape. He was a good man. He would make a very good witness.

Chapter 41

The time Viviana first spoke to Dr Smith was also something of a turning point in her personal life. Gary Shaw wanted to come with her when she told him she had persuaded the former chief medical officer of Western Australia to be interviewed about the developing awareness of the dangers of asbestos. Viviana had other ideas.

As the affair went on, she'd started to feel differently about the man who seemed habitually to have his sweaty palms close to her person. His interest in her life, emotions or aspirations gradually dwindled. Conversely, he never stopped telling her everything about his life. Conversations were repetitive soliloquies, and were usually followed by sex. Shaw's personality became steadily less engaging and his physical appearance more off-putting.

'Neil Smith is an important witness,' Shaw had said. 'This is the first time to my knowledge he's agreed to talk to anyone in person.'

'I know. He potentially could be very good for us.'

'That's why I need to come.'

'It's only going to be for a few days. I can do it myself.'

'I have the time. You don't know as much as I do about the asbestos 'story'. I'll be able to ask him the questions you won't think of.'

'Gary, I've read enough. That's all I've been doing now since I joined the firm. Nobody else has thought of speaking to him, including you.'

Viviana watched as Shaw's face coloured at the slight. 'Besides,' she lied, 'he was very reluctant to talk at all. I assured him that it would only be me.'

'I could come and simply be with you over there. I don't need to see him. It would be good for us.'

'I want to be able to concentrate on the job, Gary. It is, as you've said, very important.'

Viviana stared him down until he acquiesced. He patted her hand affectionately, but received nothing in return. Her resolve against him was hardening and the shame she felt began to encrust itself over her. She was slowly changing, becoming hostile to the outside world. She despised the feeling, but seemed powerless to stop it.

◆

Dr Smith hadn't much of a telephone manner. When Viviana entered the lobby of her Perth hotel to meet him, she was concerned he was going to be monosyllabic. The opposite was true. Neil Smith in person was a humble, spritely and knowledgeable gentleman. He had much to tell her.

'When I started in the Health Department, Ms Glosioli,' he began, 'I must confess to thinking that Chief Medical Officer was a strange job description when there was only one medical practitioner employed by the Western Australian government – me. Like my counterparts in the other states, my job required me to handle a range of health problems: from vaccination to venereal disease, epidemics to occupational health; safety at mines to tropical medicine. Even so, I recognised early that safety at Disaster Gorge was not only within my jurisdiction, but something I needed to give a great deal of attention to.'

'Why was that? I haven't found anything bad about the mine until your article in 1962.'

'That's true in terms of published papers. Stories about the dusty environment up at the Disaster mine and mill had nonetheless filtered down to me in Perth over the decade the mine had been operating. As the mainly immigrant mine workers left the town, some would invariably end up in Perth, many in Perth hospitals. They provided, by any standard, lurid descriptions about life in Disaster Gorge. The tales, as I recall, had four common ingredients: the heat, the dust, the booze and the boredom. I'm not sure if you've ever been up there, but the Hamersley Range and the Pilbara are rugged, beautiful places. You can still find blue asbestos on the ground, you know.'

'I haven't, although one day I'd like to. I'm wondering, was there a watershed moment for you about Disaster Gorge, Dr Smith?'

'Yes, there was. It was relatively early in my job. 1957. I heard a horrifying second-hand account of conditions at Disaster Gorge from my hygiene officer, Stanley Carter. Carter had recently returned from the Kalgoorlie gold mines where he'd been measuring dust levels. There were some Irishmen in town who told him of the awful dust in the mill at Disaster Gorge. They said they knew men whose lungs were so choked with asbestos that they could barely breathe. I resolved straightaway to look into Disaster Gorge to see if these stories had any truth to them.

'Up till then, I knew little about asbestos. It didn't feature in my medical studies. I wasn't even sure if it was associated with any medical conditions. I was, however, determined to find out.

'I pulled out a couple of texts on occupational lung disorders and respiratory diseases from the library. I flicked to the index and was surprised to see that asbestos was mentioned. I turned to the relevant pages and learned about a condition called asbestosis. It was in a section on the pneumoconioses, fibrotic lung diseases caused by inhaling various materials, including asbestos fibres. Asbestosis caused scarring of the lungs. It restricted breathing, resulting in reduced lung volume. Asbestosis could become severe enough to cause respiratory failure and death. This was appalling. I was worried that it was happening at Disaster Gorge on my watch! I read as much as I could find.

'I found a reference to a recent journal article linking lung cancer and asbestos written by Dr Richard Doll. He was the scientist who found a connection between cigarette smoking and lung cancer in 1950. He was a very famous man. I filled in a requisition form and sent it off to the departmental librarian – there was no internet then, Ms Glosioli!

'While waiting for the article to arrive, I wrote to Fergus Hamilton, the CEO at V&L Ltd, requesting an inspection of the mine. Hamilton was slow to respond. When he finally did, he said his company would be only too pleased to host me on an inspection of the mine. He told me that the V&L Ltd medical officer, Dr Mitchell Frosby, would accompany me. He said he hoped to dispel some of the myths circulating about the mine.'

'When did you go? Were the myths dispelled?'

'We went up later in 1957. And no, the myths were not dispelled in my mind. It was an extraordinary trip. The V&L people put on quite a performance. It was pantomime at its best.'

Chapter 42

'Am I going too fast?' Dr Smith asked Viviana.

'No, not at all.'

'Stop me if I am,' said Smith. 'My wife says I talk too quickly when I'm excited about a subject. I suppose I am at the moment. Now, let me tell you more about that time in 1957. It was a long time ago, but you don't forget things like Disaster Gorge in a hurry.'

The old doctor settled back in the armchair in the hotel's conference room.

'The flight to Disaster Gorge was a milk run to every populated dot on the West Australian map. Fortunately, there weren't many dots despite the Commonwealth government's populate or perish policy after the war. While Stanley Carter and I had been on a little twin-prop plane to visit some of the gold mines in the state, the V&L men, Dr Frosby and their industrial hygienist, Gary Crick, looked decidedly ill at ease. We were packed in like sardines in this bobbing, noisy aircraft. Frosby was as pale as a ghost, undoubtedly battling the horrors of claustrophobia, aerophobia and acrophobia throughout the journey.

'Then, as the plane entered the Disaster Gorge region, we hit a dust storm. It was exhilarating. I recall the pilot shouting, "This may feel a bit strange!" as he commenced the descent. As the aircraft dropped into the storm, we all yelled out. Frosby and Crick sat dead still, white-knuckling the armrests and screwing their eyes shut. They missed the dust parting to reveal the glorious panorama of red earth, dark, eerie rivers and the orange and blue chiselled cliffs. The plane landed like a tennis ball bouncing on an ant-bed court.

'We were led to a highly polished car parked adjacent to the corrugated-iron terminal. I looked up and down the runway. It was a bumpy bed of crushed red dirt tinged with the blue tailings of the mine. The blue-red colour stretched along the road from the airport and beyond like an elastic band pulled tight.

'The mine manager, Fred Stephenson, drove us into town to the company headquarters, another corrugated-iron building. Inside, the place was clean and cool. It was a relief, as outside it felt like the temperature was above boiling point. I was naturally impatient to get down to business and to check out the mine, but the large spread the company had put on was very tempting. As we ate, Stephenson went through the history of the mine, the discovery of asbestos and the importance of asbestos to Australia's development. It was actually pretty interesting. Two hours later, however, after all the plates had been cleared, I had the distinct impression that the V&L employees were stonewalling. When Stephenson started on the benefits of the north-western railway, I knew it was time to inspect the mine.

'After a long delay while Stephenson gathered our security passes and safety gear, we started crawling along the dirt road to the mine. I wondered whether we would ever arrive. Stephenson kept up a monologue as we drove. His rambling, however, couldn't detract from the grandeur of the scenery. This was an ancient place. The cliffs easing down into a funnel of red and blue rubble. I was amazed, I can tell you, Viviana. What a place! And then the mine came into view. That was less impressive. A hotch-potch of squat, dirty buildings dug into the scrub and dirt.

'When we arrived, there was a further hold-up while one of the men at the mill was sent to get some masks for us to wear. A pleasant young Scottish chap, as I recall. It was a dirty place even outdoors, so I was grateful for some protection. Stephenson droned on about safety and then we were ushered past the transport bay into the mill. I asked Stanley to take photographs of all the sites we visited. Inside, the machines were dormant. Even so, a thin cloud of grey-blue dust hung in the air. I looked around at the workers. They weren't doing anything, just looking at us. They all wore masks.

'I had no doubt that V&L was trying to sanitise the work conditions. I was prepared to play along with the charade for a while, but I hadn't travelled that far to be fobbed off.

'As I said, there was a blue, silvery dust everywhere. Chunks of crocidolite were scattered on the floor. I picked up a piece. I don't know if you've ever seen blue asbestos, Viviana, but it has a unique appearance and feel.'

'I've only seen photos.'

'When I first touched it, I felt an urge to play with it. It's hard to explain. I pulled the fibres apart. The more I pulled them apart, the finer the fibres became. I held the teased-out sheet of crocidolite up to the light and saw how it was made up of myriad tiny blue darts, which I could imagine with a breath of wind spearing through the air, being inhaled, and if they went deep enough, piercing the lungs.

'I asked Carter to take a few measurements. Frosby had Crick do the same. It was as if he didn't trust us or wanted their own counts in case there was a debate in the future about how dusty it was. After Carter finished his dust sampling, I asked Stephenson why the mill was silent.

'I can't remember exactly what he said. Whatever it was, it sounded like complete rubbish, but he wouldn't budge when I pressed him to start it up. We then traipsed up to the mine while waiting for the mill to commence operations.

'The mine entrance was a steep sweaty climb from the mill. In the tunnels, I saw filthy, blackened faces staring at me, the whites of their eyes and the flashing brightness of their grinning teeth stark in the dark, cramped surrounds. It was impossible to hide how bad the conditions were. I asked Stanley to take some further measurements, which of course meant Crick set up his own device right next to Stanley. I could see he was becoming quite peeved at the V&L antics. He wasn't the only one. I was glad when we emerged back into the glare of the light an hour or so later. The images of the airless, cramped mine have haunted me to this day. Carter took a few photographs to ensure that there was a proper record of the conditions. We returned to the mill in silence. It should have been operating.

'"What's going on here, Stephenson?" I asked. "This is unacceptable. You must have known for some time that we were coming to do an inspection and yet all operations in the mill are suspended."

'He assured me that they would try to have things fixed by the following day so that measurements could be taken.

'I asked him what the men were doing there if the mill wasn't working. He claimed they were waiting to start work again as the problem might be fixed any moment. He couldn't say what the problem was – he just fobbed us off with a mumble about a technical matter.

'I felt thwarted, but unless the mill was operating the next day, which my instincts told me was unlikely, there was little I could do. Carter would have to extrapolate his results upwards to give an estimate of the dust levels with the mill fully functional. It was unsatisfactory because I didn't wish to have any debate in the future about the conditions at the mill.

'Back in town, V&L had organised rooms for us at the Empire Hotel. It was basic, but comfortable. It was also V&L management's watering hole.

'Stephenson had booked a private room for dinner. He clearly thought that a further serving of V&L hospitality would smooth over any of the rough edges at the mine and mill.

'I thanked Stephenson for his hospitality and said I'd like to ask a few questions about health matters, which we'd had little chance to discuss, given his incessant monologues.

'So, as the meal was served and consumed, I endeavoured to find out what V&L knew about the hazards of asbestos exposure at Disaster Gorge. This proved difficult as Stephenson repeatedly hijacked the conversation, particularly as the number of beers he drained increased. Towards the end of dessert, I'd had enough.

'I pointed out that when I'd asked head office to allow me to inspect the mine, I was concerned there may be problems at Disaster Gorge. I told Stephenson that from what I'd seen, conditions in the mine were appalling and I assumed the mill would be very dusty when it was operational. I explained that asbestos could cause asbestosis and, it seemed, lung cancer. I wanted to know what V&L had to say about that.

'Frosby put down his drink and asked Stephenson to let him answer. He declared that V&L took safety in the mine and mill seriously. The conditions were challenging, but V&L was doing everything possible to keep the men healthy. He ignored Stanley's spluttering. Men were instructed to wear masks when working, he claimed, as the company recognised the need to reduce the men's exposure to asbestos. Even so, many of the workers were only at Disaster Gorge for a short time and so weren't at risk of disease. It was only those men who were exposed heavily for many years who were at risk, he said. As for lung cancer, there had never been a case in the workforce. He assured me that the V&L employees were happy and healthy.

'I thanked him for his helpful comments, but advised that nevertheless I'd be recommending regular examinations of the workers as well as periodic dust sampling to make sure every effort was made to keep the employees as healthy as he claimed them to be.

'Stephenson nearly spat out his beer in surprise. He suggested that it would be quite expensive to implement such a regime.

'I agreed, but said that if V&L wished to continue mining at Disaster Gorge, then that was what they'd have to do. I took my leave with Stanley. You should have seen their faces. Staring at each other dumbfounded.

'As I lay awake in bed that night, I could hear yelling and swearing in the streets. The noise from the brawls came roaring across the still, hot darkness until, exhausted, I finally fell asleep.

'Predictably, the mill wasn't operational the following day. We crammed into the little plane again and flew home without any further samples taken. What a debacle!'

'Did you write a report about the visit and your recommendations?'

'Of course. I submitted a copy to both the Minister for Health and the Minister for Mines. You should be able to get a copy from the government archives.'

'I've never seen a report. It doesn't exist.'

'It does or, at least, did. But to tell you the truth, Ms Glosioli, I'm not surprised.'

'Why?'

'A few weeks after the trip to Disaster Gorge, I was paid a visit by the Secretary for the Department of Health. He told me that the minister and his counterpart in the Department of Mines had been contacted by V&L executives about my proposals. He said that V&L had assured the ministers that they were taking steps to ensure the safety of the workers and that government interference wasn't justified. I tried to explain that the conditions were dreadful and that so-called 'interference' was imperative. He then shut that argument down by saying that we'd give the company the opportunity to do the right thing itself. I was flabbergasted. He went on to talk about the importance of the mine to the state and the nation. I'd heard it all before. It was to be business as usual at Disaster Gorge.'

Chapter 43

Weeks after settling Mr Caxton's case and deciding to return to Neil Smith's statement, Viviana was able to present what she regarded as the final product to Gary Shaw. His response was tepid.

'What's wrong with it?' Viviana asked.

'Nothing, it's a good start.'

'Are you kidding? I've spent countless hours finessing it with Neil. I even travelled to Perth again to go over it with him, as you know.'

'Simmer down, Viv, I'm sure you'll get there in the end.'

He reached out to touch her arm, but she withdrew it.

'What's going on, Viv? What's happened to you? I thought we were doing well together.'

'Gary, it's over. I don't want to be in any kind of relationship with my employer. You're also married. It looks bad, people are talking about it, and I regret it. I'm sorry. I can't do it anymore.'

'Who cares what others say? I'm the boss. They wouldn't dare say anything.'

'But they do.'

'Who?'

'I can't say. I don't want to say. The fact that we're even having this conversation proves how wrong it is.'

'It's only an office romance. They happen all the time. What's there to feel bad about?'

'Gary, I don't want it anymore. It's not good for me.'

'Not good for you? I don't understand. It was perfectly good for you when I was showing you the ropes and helping you get ahead. It was perfectly good for you when you were enjoying the three-course meal at Arpeggio. It was perfectly good for you when we had the long weekend at Killcare.' His voice was taking on that unpleasant tone Viviana disliked so much. It made her feel small and vulnerable. 'We can work through this, Viv, I'm sure we can.'

'I don't want to work through it, Gary. I want to end it. I'm sorry. I know it's not what you want, but it's what I want and need. I'm grateful for all you've done but I have to move on.'

He glowered at her. A tense silence was developing. She struggled to keep her nerve.

'Very well,' he said. 'I'll give you some space. But the Smith statement still needs work.' He rose and left her office.

Viviana's heart rate slowed. She looked down at the Neil Smith statement. It was faultless, she believed. It could cause significant damage to both V&L and Henry King Industries. Was she missing something or was Gary trying to undermine her?

She read through the opening paragraphs. Shaw was playing games, manipulating her. Anyone with any knowledge of asbestos litigation could see how explosive the statement was.

'After the visit to Disaster Gorge,' Smith had said during her second visit to Perth, 'my knowledge about asbestos diseases effectively stalled. Nothing of interest was published. There were no new developments. Nonetheless, I thought if I kept my eyes open and ears to the ground about the V&L mine, something might pop up, which is basically what happened in 1961.'

'What happened then?' Viviana had asked him.

'I received the latest volume of the British Journal of Industrial

Medicine. Of course, by 'latest', I mean the edition published in 1960 in Britain.'

'The Wagner article?'

'Precisely. "Diffuse Pleural Mesothelioma and Asbestos Exposure in the North Western Cape Province".' He'd smiled appreciatively. 'I suppose everyone knows about it now.'

'It's tendered in cases all the time. But I'd like to know more from those who were practising at the time rather than the reconstructed version of history touted by defendant lawyers.

'For instance, some have said the Wagner article wasn't that important and only suggested a possible association between asbestos and mesothelioma and then just in South Africa with its peculiar form of fibre and appalling health standards. Most experts and lawyers say it was much later, in the mid-1960s, that the connection with mesothelioma was established. And then they say the mine was closed promptly and blue asbestos removed from asbestos cement products.'

'Utter hogwash!' Smith had expostulated. 'I was there on the ground reading this evidence for the very first time. I know what it meant to me.'

'What was that?'

'I'll explain. Have you got a copy there?'

'Yes.'

'Thank you.' Dr Smith had scanned the pages of the photocopy. 'As you can see, Viviana, the article was received for publication in April 1960, so we're talking about thirty-three cases that had been accumulating for years before then. The findings were so bizarre they had to be true. You see, Wagner and his colleagues were reporting an unusual concentration of this rare cancer among a population exposed exclusively to blue asbestos. The authors described eight case histories. I was interested in two of the cases which concerned white females with what could hardly have been considered heavy exposure to asbestos.'

'Why do you say that?'

'Only the black or coloured workers were in the mines. Only they had heavy exposure.'

'I see.'

'The evidence was fairly convincing in my mind. An addendum to the article recorded a total of forty-seven cases of mesothelioma by the end of June 1960 with forty-five of these having an association with crocidolite exposure. The disease was essentially non-existent in the general population. It could only have been explained by exposure to blue asbestos. I can assure you, Viviana, that I immediately thought I needed to check whether I was missing a similar connection in my own backyard up at Disaster Gorge.

'I told Stanley Carter that we had to find out if Disaster Blue also caused mesothelioma. "I'm not going to be fobbed off this time," I said. I was determined to get V&L to start screening its workforce up there: the men should be examined annually, chest x-rays should be performed, and we'd see if we came up with any cases. We also had to get hold of V&L's employment records and trace the men who'd left the mine and might be living here in Perth.'

'Stanley stated the obvious – V&L weren't going to like it and would do their best to shut us down as they had the previous time. Frankly I didn't give a damn what V&L thought about it or me. I now had a clear obligation to carry out medical surveillance or, at least, get V&L to do it and let us know the results. The department couldn't ignore the threat of mesothelioma, no matter what V&L told them.'

'What happened?'

'After some to-ing and fro-ing and a little pressure from the minister, I secured a meeting with Dr Frosby in Sydney. In those days, it was a long flight, but I was happy to do it. I can't recall exactly when I flew to Sydney, but it was probably about the middle of 1961. I was only there overnight, but I felt I made some headway, at least about surveillance.

'Frosby was rather blunt with his opinions. It was as if I was talking to a different man from the one who'd tried to obfuscate at Disaster Gorge back in the late 1950s.

'He told me point blank that he knew he was going to be pestered by me as soon as I became aware of the Wagner paper. And he realised V&L could hardly refuse me access to the mine population if I wished to examine them. But he pointed out that it was a long way for me to travel. It would be far better in V&L's view if it screened its own men and reported to the government on a regular basis.

'I'd certainly have preferred that the department did the screening, but knew that Frosby had a point. The department simply didn't have the resources to fly Stanley and me to Disaster Gorge regularly. So I agreed – but I impressed upon him the gravity of the matter.

'If we identified cases of mesothelioma in the Disaster Gorge workforce, there would be serious repercussions for V&L.

'Frosby, of course, had his doubts about any connection between mesothelioma and the crocidolite at Disaster Gorge – he'd never seen any cases and the mine and mill had been operating for almost fifteen years. But he knew as well I did that most of the workers only stayed at Disaster Gorge for a short while. So he had no idea what became of them. I was insistent that, in future, V&L not only carry out medical surveillance but also retain contact details for all former employees so we could determine whether any might go on to develop mesothelioma.

'Frosby got a bit huffy and reiterated that we wouldn't find a single case of mesothelioma among the Disaster Gorge workers: the company supplied the men with masks, and had recently been installing exhaust equipment. But he agreed to send me the records V&L already held.

'I continued to push my own barrow, Viviana. I argued that the fact there'd been no cases of mesothelioma at Disaster Gorge might well come down to inadequate follow-up – he didn't like that much – or that there might be a long latency period between exposure and onset of the disease, as Wagner suggested, of something like twenty to forty years and it was just too early to diagnose any.

'He continued to assert that it was much more likely that Disaster Blue didn't cause mesothelioma. If it were truly responsible, he'd have seen a case by then. In any event, he said, most of the men were only in the mine for a very short time. They were foreigners, indentured men, itinerants. Many were from the UK, migrating here on the Bring out a Briton scheme after the war. They weren't at Disaster Gorge long enough to have the exposure necessary to develop mesothelioma, even if Disaster Blue was capable of causing it.'

'I couldn't see how he could be so confident that short exposure at Disaster Gorge couldn't cause mesothelioma.

'Frosby had clearly read Wagner's article thoroughly. He pointed out that the people in Wagner's study basically lived on top of the mine or worked in it for years. There wasn't anyone like that at Disaster Gorge, where the workers lived well away from the mine and mill.

'But for the full working day they were in the middle of it, I countered. The V&L mine workers had to put up with terrible conditions. The company even used mine tailings in the town on the roads.

'Frosby wasn't backing down. The dust measurements taken by Stanley had failed to establish dust levels above the Dreessen standard, he reminded me. Though he omitted to mention that the mills weren't operational at the time. And the mine tunnels might be cramped and dark, but that in itself wasn't a health hazard or anything to do with mesothelioma.

'I hoped his predictions might prove accurate, but I very much doubted it. I honestly thought V&L should close the mine before we witnessed an unfolding disaster over the coming decades – although I had no grounds for enforcing that, of course.

'I stared out of the office window at the slate-grey expanse of Sydney Harbour. It was a dull, cloudy day. The water and view disappointed. "Your company will eventually come to regret its involvement in this mine," I told him.

'Frosby drew my attention to a painting on the wall. It was a portrait of an austere, corpulent, grey-skinned old man.

'It was the late Sir Llewellyn Williams, the former chair of the company, Frosby said. He was the one who'd driven the decision to get into asbestos. A decision that helped develop this country after the war. "No one at V&L would ever regret opening the Disaster Gorge mine," Frosby assured me. "Everyone who'd ever worked there would always be thankful for the opportunities it gave them, especially those men who'd come to Australia without a job, with nothing. V&L made them."

'Viviana, I decided not to debate the issue any further. This man seemed to believe his own rhetoric. He was gambling with the lives of his workers, in my view, but I couldn't do anything other than check the data and hunt for cases among those men who'd left the mine. I felt the outcome was inevitable. As we now know, I was right.'

Chapter 44

'I didn't have to wait long for my proof, Viviana. My first case of mesothelioma,' Dr Smith had said.

'How long?'

'A year.'

'That soon?'

'Yes, and I was sure it wasn't the only one out there.

'I found out about him in early 1962 from a physician at Kalgoorlie District Hospital. The man was an Italian who'd worked at Disaster Gorge for only thirteen months in 1949 to 1950. He was diagnosed at the end of 1959 and died in early 1962. He wasn't even fifty years of age. An autopsy revealed asbestosis and mesothelioma, so he'd clearly had asbestos exposure. I couldn't determine whether he'd had exposure to asbestos elsewhere. Despite Frosby's protestations, I believed V&L now had to face the facts. I published my findings in the Medical Journal of Australia in 1962 and wrote to Dr Frosby at the same time. I also wrote to the Minister for Health. I said something like "Disaster Blue asbestos is a very harmful and lethal fibre. The interval between exposure and the development of the tumour is much shorter than has been previously reported, which confirms its dangerous qualities. The relatively short period of exposure in this man also confirms the impression from the Wagner study of 1960 that these tumours may arise after transitory exposure to crocidolite in susceptible persons." Let me tell you what happened after I sent Dr Frosby a copy of the article. You need to know the type of man I was dealing with. He rang me up, furious.'

'What did he say?'

'It was a real harangue.

'"Now listen here, you damn fool, you can't be going around publishing unsubstantiated case histories like this, claiming a connection between Disaster Blue asbestos and mesothelioma. Who do you think you are, peddling a cockamamie, scaremongering theory that would risk a vital national industry? You have no proof. None at all." That was the gist of it, Viviana.

'I countered by reminding him that he'd claimed we'd never turn up a case of mesothelioma. That there would never be enough exposure. That Disaster Blue was different. There would be no proof. V&L's workers were untraceable. And that's what I'd told the minister, who wouldn't be pleased with this latest development.

'It was only one case, and we couldn't close Disaster Gorge over one case, he responded.

'But wasn't one case enough, I asked him. What if this was the start of something awful like the South Africans were experiencing? They'd been mining blue asbestos for longer. Surely that was why we hadn't been deluged with cases – yet.

'He paused for a moment then told me patronisingly to stop being so excitable and to evaluate things rationally. There hadn't been any other cases and this one was probably an aberration.

'I couldn't believe what I was hearing, Viviana. An aberration? Unless Frosby was clairvoyant, he couldn't possibly know what would happen down the track. I told him again: the case I'd reported would be the death knell of the mine.

'He insisted that one isolated case didn't prove anything. Perhaps the worker had experienced exposure back in Italy or elsewhere.

'I felt he was just making things up to hide the facts. In my view, something drastic had to happen. I was determined not to let things slide into a catastrophe. I suggested he start acquainting his board with reality.

'He'd certainly be doing that, he said. And making sure it understood perfectly my tendency to exaggerate!

'Viviana, I was seething when he said that. I had never before been accused of exaggerating. My article was restrained. He knew it.'

'He sounds abysmal.'

'He was.'

'Is he dead?'

'Yes, many years ago. I suppose he was just doing his job.'

'That's not a job anyone should be doing.'

'Anyway, I held my breath for about ten seconds and then told him he was offensive and wrong. His company, and Frosby in particular, needed to open their eyes. He laughed when I said that. Laughed!

'In his weaselly way he told me that scientific developments needed to be put into their proper context. There was never only a single way of looking at something and others would see his point of view.

'And that was the last time I heard from him. You wouldn't think it possible, but again V&L executives lobbied the government, particularly the Mines Department, and I got nowhere. My own department supported my stance, but they seemed powerless against other interests – vested interests, I suspect. The government and V&L wanted more evidence, they said.'

'Incredible.'

'I felt humiliated given my earlier threat in Sydney to close them down.'

'I'm sure you did.'

'Even later, when we traced other cases from the mine, often using immigration records, I couldn't force its closure. I couldn't get ministerial support. But that's not the main point. What I'm telling you, Viviana, and this is the important point – there was sufficient evidence for the company to close that mine as a health hazard by 1962. I knew it and I guarantee Frosby knew it. Anyone who didn't was pretending. The fact that the government stepped in to support V&L didn't in my opinion ever justify the company continuing to operate the mine. It didn't need government approval to close it down. It could do it itself if it wanted to. You draw your own inferences from that. What's more, given that Henry King Industries used Disaster Gorge blue in their products as well as Cape Blue from South Africa, they should have known too. I knew what fibre they were using from visiting their plant in Perth. They could have quite easily ceased using blue asbestos by 1962. They certainly couldn't argue that, if V&L kept mining crocidolite, it must be safe. Nor in my view could they maintain that they had to wait for V&L to tell them it was unsafe. Henry King was a big asbestos user. They were sophisticated enough to know when something wasn't right.'

'Yes, but the defendants all argue that it wasn't until the 1965 publication of the Biological Effects of Asbestos that there was proof of an association between blue and mesothelioma and that action was only required within a reasonable time after that.'

'Of course they'd say that, Viviana. Government would say that too. They were the ones that let these companies continue to operate with blue asbestos. They all have to pretend they acted reasonably. I'm telling you they didn't.'

'According to what I've read in its board minutes, V&L closed the mine in 1966 for financial reasons.'

'I'm no accountant, Viviana, but I don't buy a word of it. By mid-1966, Frosby must surely have given the board a damning report on the hazards of blue asbestos based on what he'd undoubtedly read in Biological Effects of Asbestos. Crocidolite caused mesothelioma. He must have advised the board to get out of it to save money down the track. There's no other explanation.'

'I'd like to put all this in your statement, if that's okay.'

'It is. I want to be on record saying it. It's all absolutely true.

'But don't be fooled by any statement from V&L about looking after its workers when they closed the mine. Once the remaining bags were shipped, and the mine closed, the workers dispersed, often still illiterate, unqualified, with a burden of fibre in their lungs that could claim them at any time no matter where they went. And another thing, V&L might have ceased its supply of Disaster Blue to Henry King Industries' asbestos cement factories throughout Australia in 1966, but what happened to the tons of blue fibre transported to its factories in the months leading up to the mine closure? I have no idea.'

Chapter 45

Viviana was convinced that the health department doctors around the nation would have had the same reaction as Dr Smith to the emerging knowledge about mesothelioma and blue asbestos in the 1960s. If they'd waited until after the publication of Biological Effects of Asbestos to demand action by V&L, Henry King Industries or any other asbestos user, then they'd waited too long. Sadly, there were no documents proving any health department doctor thought the same as Dr Smith – and his report had seemingly been buried. Maybe all the incriminating evidence had been destroyed. Perhaps it'd never existed, the opinions never committed to writing.

This meant Dr Smith's word would need to be accepted without corroboration if plaintiffs were ever going to be awarded punitive damages from these killer companies. His evidence could be supplemented by the evidence of some of the former mid-level employees, maybe Russell Dymock if he ever spoke to her, and a bundle of the medical and scientific literature that had been published over the years. It wasn't perfect, but Viviana believed strongly in Neil Smith's objectivity and persuasiveness. She was sure a judge would too.

'And another thing, Viviana, you should also know what I know about Peter Mathers, the Henry King in-house medico,' Dr Smith had told her.

'What do you mean?'

'I sat on the Occupational Health Committee of the NHMRC with Mathers for over a decade while Henry King was using asbestos. All the state health officers were on the committee. We met regularly to discuss asbestos health matters. He told me a few things about when he first joined the company, initially part-time and then full-time.'

'What did he say?'

'He told me that Henry King must have known about the Wagner article in 1961 and my journal article in 1962 because he knew about them himself. If a part-time employee like Peter Mathers knew these things, I'm sure the powers that be at Henry King must have known.'

'I haven't seen any document establishing that.'

'Doesn't surprise me.'

'What was Mathers like?'

'Well, he was exactly the sort of doctor Henry King was after; someone we'd now call a 'fall guy'. Someone who'd read the minutiae on every asbestos health issue so that he could argue with conviction against his peers at seminars, conferences or what have you. It worked like a charm. Peter Mathers was a pleasant enough man, but he certainly had a very high opinion of his abilities and knowledge. When he fired up, he was like an attack dog. He was forever giving us lectures about asbestos and telling us not to be so worried. Mind you, and to his credit, he was fervently against blue asbestos after he read Biological Effects of Asbestos in 1966. With respect to everything else, he was a denier. He obstructed all the OHC's attempts at regulation, changing recommended threshold dust levels and warnings. Don't you let anyone tell you that warnings came in at a reasonable time. They came in only after Mathers was sidelined, after people got sick of listening to him talk about trusting the science.'

'Can I say this in the statement?'

'I think we have to be careful with how we phrase it and I don't want my personal speculations ventilated, but I don't mind signing up to something to the effect that both companies ignored what was obviously the start of an asbestos epidemic. I believe that to be true. I wish I could have done more.'

'Like what?'

'I'm not sure. It's a lingering sense of guilt I have. I was asked to do a job by the Health Department and when I tried to do it – to protect the health of West Australian workers – I was blocked at all turns. It seems to be a common human failing to wait until the problem is blindingly obvious before acting. Everyone's always arguing about when evidence is sufficient to justify action. Asbestos was no different.'

As she perused the final signed version of Dr Smith's statement, Viviana believed she'd created a weapon in the fight against the asbestos companies. The extra time she'd taken to complete it had been worthwhile. She hadn't changed a thing despite Shaw's initial comments. He didn't seem to know.

'I've circulated Dr Smith's statement to the team,' Shaw told her. 'It'll be good to get their feedback and see whether anyone can use it.'

'I was hoping to be the first to call Dr Smith as a witness. I'm looking at my cases now to see if any are suitable.'

'He's not your witness, Viviana, he's my firm's witness.'

'I understand that, Gary, but I don't understand there to be any pressing need to use him on any old case. We need to identify the best possible case.'

'That's what I'm proposing. The best case may not be yours. It could be one of Carlo's, for instance.'

'No.'

'Now listen, and listen carefully,' Shaw said, towering over her. 'I will determine when and how to use Smith. Not you. I determine what happens in this firm.'

'The firm might be yours, Gary, but you had no interest or any intention of ever calling Dr Smith, let alone talking to him. I did that, not you. I should have some say in the matter.'

'You don't. Get over yourself.' He strode out of Viviana's office, the friction between his plump inner thighs creating a loud rasping as he departed.

At home, later that day, with Echo purring on her lap and a glass of wine in her hand, Viviana sat oblivious to the programme on the television. As she chewed over her relationship with Shaw, trying to soften its distasteful aspects, she realised she couldn't swallow the embarrassment whole. It would not go down.

'What a joke I've become,' she said aloud. Echo looked up and pincushioned her thigh with his claws. 'I suppose you think so, too.' He closed his eyes and purred.

◆

Everywhere Viviana looked at the firm, she saw enemies. She imagined the secretaries were gossiping about her. She was sure the other solicitors were talking about her, making snide remarks, belittling her. She began to feel trapped. Her legal work was becoming unpleasant. The opposition took the fact that they operated in an adversarial system to heart. Everything was hostile, a fight. She felt alone in the office and in court. She was a litigator, and it could be rough, but it shouldn't feel as though she was the one on trial.

Her only sanctuary was her unit. Her only support, Echo. She could never tell her family what had happened or what it was like. They would never understand. Francesca had tried to get her to talk, but she didn't feel she was ready. She built higher and higher walls around herself.

As the weeks passed, Shaw's huge shadow swirled into view time and again like a circling shark. Mostly he left her alone, but when he appeared suddenly in the staff kitchen or walked past her office, she stiffened. She yearned for the day she could leave the firm and set up her own practice or possibly even go to the bar. But she didn't have enough savings to go anywhere, and she felt strongly about her clients. She needed to build a reputation, but not in the way it appeared to be heading.

She must toughen up, she told herself. Emotions were for the weak. What she needed was a case in which she could immerse herself, something to which she could bring all her skills and intuition. Something that would give her an opportunity to find herself.

PART V

Chapter 46

2002

'Slow down, Jen, let me get my breath back,' James panted as he tried to catch up to his wife who was striding along the sand with their dog Tess. It was a warm, still November morning. Even so, after his plunge in the cold sea, James felt he couldn't get going. The soft sand gave way even to his featherweight. He could gain no purchase with his clawing toes.

'Okay, slow coach, I'll wait for you,' she called, coming to a halt. Tess barked as if annoyed at having no one to throw her a stick or stone. 'You're really blowing today, just look at you. Old age suddenly caught up with you?'

'Well, I'm sixty-seven and some days the water literally takes your breath away.' He reached out, took a towel from Jenny and draped it over his shoulders. 'The warm currents haven't arrived yet. It's still a wee bit nippy.'

They continued their walk but it seemed to take an age for James to regain his usual equilibrium. Jenny wondered if he was coming down with something. She couldn't remember the last time he'd been sick. Indeed, the GP had given James a clean bill of health at his most recent check-up. But he again fell behind as they ascended the path at the end of the beach close to their home. He held grimly to the handrail, pausing twice to catch his breath. James always hosed off and dried Tess, but that morning Jenny had to do it. They'd been living in Kiama for eight years, walking daily along the beach, even when the rain blew in sideways over a violent ocean. James had never appeared so distressed.

'Are you feeling okay, James?'

'I'm not sure,' he replied breathily. 'I feel a bit tight in the chest.'

Upstairs, James showered and went back to bed, pulling the bedclothes over himself. 'I'm aching all over, Jen. Let me go back to sleep and I'll be right.'

Jenny looked at her husband snuggled up in the blankets despite the mild day. The flu was never pleasant, no matter how strong you were. She placed the back of her hand on his forehead. He felt slightly warm. 'Okay, I'll leave you in peace. Let me know if you need anything. I'll check on you later.' He was asleep before she finished speaking.

James spent most of the day in bed. Around four o'clock in the afternoon, Jenny heard a groan and looked up from her cross-stitching. Her husband shuffled feebly into the loungeroom. His hair was wild, his striped pyjamas were awry with some buttons undone and the fly agape.

'Hello, dear. How are you feeling?' She wanted to ask him to rearrange his pyjamas, but she didn't have the heart when she saw his pitiful hangdog expression.

He slumped into a chair. 'God, I feel like a bomb's gone off in my head.'

'Would you like something to eat? You haven't eaten all day, you poor thing.'

'Maybe later, Jen. Let me sit here for a while.'

Jenny returned to her craftwork, peering up occasionally over her reading glasses to look at him. Half an hour later, he pushed himself up out of the chair and walked gingerly to the bedroom.

Jenny followed him and watched him get back into bed. He refused a glass of water and was soon fast asleep. The best thing for him, thought Jenny. If he wasn't better in the morning, she'd suggest he see the doctor.

Thankfully, James said he was much improved in the morning and, over the next few days, he seemed to be back to his normal self. Jenny was relieved, not least because Robbie was expected down for the weekend. She was pleased to see that James had no difficulty walking, although he stopped taking his early morning dips – 'Don't want to risk catching cold until the water temperature improves,' he'd said. And over the next few days he'd not only mown the lawn but pruned the hedges and dug out some weeds.

The garden was looking beautiful and Jenny was proud of what they'd achieved after retiring to Kiama. It had taken a few years, but now it was one of the highlights in the street – the long screening wall of murraya, the patchwork splashes of colour from the azaleas, rhododendrons, oleanders and hydrangeas, the perfume from the four frangipani trees and the border of gardenias that ran from the letterbox to the front door. Even James's roses blossomed in the sunshine of the north-facing side garden. He'd spent many hours tending them, ever hopeful that they would take off against the odds.

Robert arrived on the Friday night, and the next morning he, Jenny and James set off on a fishing trip down the Shoalhaven River in the little tinnie James kept for such occasions. It was a relaxing although wholly unrewarding excursion.

'The river's so beautiful this time of year,' Robert said as he again replaced some bait on his hook.

'It's beautiful every day of the year, Robbie. You should try this more often. You and Prue need to take a break every once in a while.'

'Come on, Jen, let's not pester the boy on his weekend off.'

'Dad, it's all right. I agree with Mum. I can't keep up the hectic pace of life in Sydney forever. But the cost of living's going up and the schools aren't cheap. Then there's all the extras like guitar and flute lessons and subscriptions to the theatre and the like.'

'My word, the theatre. Never been in one in my life. Guess I never will.'

'James, things are different these days. There's more on offer. I wouldn't mind trying something new.'

'That's not what you were saying when I suggested we get a boat.'

'That was different. Fishing isn't theatre.'

'It can be.'

'Like when you fell in the water holding up the biggest flathead ever seen?' Jenny said, laughing.

'It was!'

'We'll never know seeing how you lost the fish when you fell in.'

'You saw it too, Jen.'

'I didn't have long enough before you were overboard. Could have been a tiddler, for all I know.'

James looked at his son and his wife, grinning. 'See what I mean, Robbie, there's plenty of theatre down here all the time.'

'I can see. Anyway, Prue likes to go to the plays and I don't mind them either. It helps get your mind off things. The job's very stressful now that I'm a partner, but I can handle it for now. These big accountancy firms demand their pound of flesh from you so I've got no choice. One day we hope to buy a place on the coast too and enjoy a slower life with more freedom. But it's a long way off.'

'Robbie, I've heard it all before,' Jenny said, smiling at James.

◆

For lunch on the Sunday before Robert left, James cooked some steak and sausages on the small barbecue on the verandah. Jenny stood with Robert, looking out at the glistening ocean and the colourful activity on the beach. 'I think I could take this view every day of my life,' Robert said to his mother.

'It's not too bad, is it? Look over there, Robbie.' Jenny pointed. 'Dolphins!'

Robert spotted the grey shapes running with the swells. 'Wow! Look at them go! Fantastic! You certainly don't get that in Pymble,' he said.

'You're not doing it too hard, I know, despite your complaints about school fees and petrol prices or whatever you go on about.'

'You could come and stay with us in Sydney every now and then.'

'I know, but your father isn't a terribly adventurous cook. I'm not even sure he could boil water for some peas or beans if I left him for a few days.'

Robert looked over at the barbecue. 'I see what you mean.'

He turned slightly away from James and lowered his voice confidentially. 'Actually, Mum, there's one thing I've been meaning to say. Have you noticed how much weight Dad's lost? Is he on a diet?'

'No, he isn't. And no, I haven't,' she said. They both turned to look at James through the smoke billowing up from the hotplate. He smiled at them as he turned the sausages.

'His clothes are hanging off him.'

'I really haven't noticed, Robbie.' She looked again at James. Perhaps he was thinner. 'I suppose he may have lost a couple of pounds. He was very sick for a day or so earlier this week. A bad dose of the flu. I guess he hasn't been eating as much since then. It must have taken a bit out of him. You know, the older you are, the longer it takes to shake these things off.'

'What are you two talking about?' James came over to them. 'Whispering about me, no doubt.' He grinned.

'Yes, sprung!' Robert replied. 'I was just telling Mum that I thought you'd lost some weight.'

'It's all this healthy living and exercise. Can't help but be nice and trim,' James joked.

'I told Robbie you might have lost a bit after being sick.'

'Yes, that didn't help. If I've lost any weight, that would be why, because otherwise I feel great. Couldn't be better. Now, you'd better start eating if you want to get back to Sydney before dark,' James said.

'You're right.' Robert strode over to the table and eyed the plate of meat James had lifted from the barbecue. 'I see your cooking skills haven't improved despite all this free time,' he said with a smile, picking up a burned steak with some tongs.

Chapter 47

'James, the tea's ready!' Jenny shouted out the kitchen window. She put the two mugs on a tray and walked downstairs to the pergola in the backyard. James was already seated there, rubbing the right side of his chest.

'What's wrong?' she asked.

'I'm not sure. I think I might have pulled a muscle using the shears.'

He twisted in his seat and took a mug of tea from the tray. After his first sip, he started coughing. His hand went reflexively to his side. 'Ahh! That hurts.' Jenny watched him wince with each cough. It was as if he were endeavouring to hold his chest together. 'Bloody hell!' he exclaimed after the fit of coughing ended. 'That hurt. It's like I've got broken glass scattered in my chest, cutting into me when I cough.'

Jenny was concerned. The weight loss, the pain, the episode of shortness of breath and the so-called bout of flu: something was wrong. All the instincts she'd developed over years of nursing in hospitals were on alert. She got up and put her hands against James's chest. 'Is this where it hurts?'

'Yes.'

She pushed gently inwards. 'Does that hurt?'

'No.'

She pushed more firmly around the area. There was no tenderness. Jenny thought that strange. 'It can't be a muscle, James. Surely it would be sore to touch if you'd torn one.'

'Might be a deep one.'

'Is your breathing okay?' James didn't look like he was having difficulty breathing, but he took a deep breath to test. He quickly stopped, again wincing in pain.

'God, that hurt as well,' he said.

Jenny looked at her husband. He was trying to appear calm, but she could tell he was anxious. 'James, I think it's time to see the doctor. I'm only a nurse, but it doesn't add up.'

She saw he was about to protest, but when she added, 'No excuses,' his shoulders slumped slightly. 'Okay, Jen. Tomorrow,' he said.

There was little sleep that night. After a lot of adjustments to his position, James said he could only feel comfortable propped up on four pillows. He moaned pitifully whenever he breathed in too deeply or coughed. Jenny thought of calling an ambulance when she heard his distress in the darkness. But she didn't want him feeling more uncomfortable at the local hospital, so she kept quiet, her anxiety rising.

She drove him into town to see their local doctor, Jerry Petzheldt, at the first available appointment the next morning. Dr Petzheldt listened to James's history and passed a stethoscope over his chest. 'I can hear a few crackles low down on the right. That's the painful side, isn't it?'

'Yes. It's only on that side.'

'What could it be?' Jenny asked.

Dr Petzheldt was non-committal; his poker face gave away nothing. 'I think we need to see a chest x-ray before we talk about possible diagnoses. I'd like you to have this done as soon as possible,' he said, scribbling some words on a referral pad. He handed Jenny the document. 'I'll telephone the radiology firm and say it's urgent. Once you're there, you should be seen straightaway. Come back with the films once they've been reported on. Do you need anything for the pain?'

'Yes,' Jenny said.

'No,' James said firmly. 'I've had some Panadol this morning.'

Jenny knew that it hadn't touched the sides, but could see James wasn't going to be swayed.

She drove James around the corner to the radiologist. Shortly before lunch, he went in for the x-ray. They allowed him to sleep on an examination couch while they waited for the radiologist's report.

Finally, James and Jenny returned to the GP with the films and the report late in the afternoon.

'Mmm, looks like you've got something going on at the bottom of the right lung,' Dr Petzheldt said, holding up the x-ray to the light from the window. He put the film down and read the report. 'Yep, you've got some fluid around the right lung and something else – could be an infection or a type of growth. Can't tell on a plain x-ray.'

'What does that mean exactly?' Jenny asked.

'Well, Jenny, James. It could be something like TB, pneumonia or a tumour. I need to send you off to a lung specialist in Wollongong so that a biopsy can be taken to see what it is. Hold on a minute, while I give him a call.'

Jenny looked at James nervously as Dr Petzheldt telephoned the specialist. She held James's fingertips tightly as he leaned forward on his seat, seemingly dumbfounded.

'Okay, that's sorted. He wants you up there tonight,' Dr Petzheldt said, putting the phone down.

'So soon? How serious is this?' Jenny asked.

'I can't hear much air making its way down to the bottom of the right lung with my stethoscope. So, I think it's for the best that they sort it out now. And you can't have another night like the last. You need to go home, get a few things and make your way to Wollongong Hospital. Go to the emergency department; they'll be expecting you. Please take the x-rays with you.'

'Could it be from asbestos?' James whispered.

'What do you mean, asbestos?' Jenny asked.

'I don't know about that, James,' Dr Petzheldt said. 'The lung specialist will give you more answers. Have you been exposed?'

'Yes.'

'I suppose it's possible, but you really need to have a biopsy. It could be a bad case of pneumonia. That's what I think it is, but Dr Freeman, the specialist, will tell you exactly what's what. Let's wait for him to work it out. You'll be in very good hands, James, I can assure you of that.' Dr Petzheldt stood up and handed the x-ray package to James. 'They'll get on top of it in no time,' he added, in an attempt at encouragement.

Outside in the waiting room, Jenny and James stood motionless, trapped by the sharp, inquisitorial stares of patients and the thick sticky air of illness. Dr Petzheldt's receptionist saw their dismay and gently beckoned them to the counter. It was a relief to pay the bill; to be able to do something. To resume function. 'Take care, Jenny, James,' the receptionist murmured. 'Please ring if you need help.'

Chapter 48

The drive north to Wollongong was largely in silence. Twice, Jenny told James that she was sure everything would be fine. Twice, he muttered a reply that was inaudible. She realised her words were hollow and decided it was probably better for her just to be with him, to comfort him if required. She desperately wanted to know why he'd asked about asbestos, but he didn't want to talk. She kept her questions to herself.

As Dr Petzheldt had explained, James was expected in the emergency department. He was processed quickly. Blood was taken, a drip set up and a CT scan of his chest performed. Within a couple of hours he was lying in bed in a room with three other men. Thanks to a prescription for pethidine written by one of the ward doctors, he was relatively pain free. The doctor told him that he would see the specialist the next morning.

James didn't touch his dinner of mashed pumpkin, soggy cabbage and corned beef. Jenny tried a few mouthfuls and thought James had made the correct decision. Before long, he was fast asleep. Jenny tearfully kissed his cheek as she said goodnight and was shown the accommodation for relatives. She sat down on the small, sagging bed with an olive terylene cover and cried.

She showered and, before retiring, telephoned their children, informing them of the day's events and reassuring them it was no doubt pneumonia, and all would be well. They bombarded her with questions she couldn't answer. 'We'll know more in the morning,' she kept repeating. 'I'll ring as soon as I hear anything.'

Her words sounded false. She knew she wasn't fooling anyone. Then she chastised herself for being such a pessimist. The last thing James needed was the burden of worrying about an anxious wife.

She was back in the ward by 8.00am, when Dr Paul Freeman, a respiratory physician, saw James on his ward round. He was a tall, jovial man in his fifties with shiny jet-black hair. Jenny found it difficult, despite her anxiety, not to be sidetracked wondering whether his hair was dyed. Dr Freeman was accompanied by two younger doctors and the charge nurse, Sister Robinson.

'Good morning, Mr Henderson. I'm Dr Freeman and I'll be looking after you,' the doctor began. 'If you wouldn't mind sitting up a bit, I'd like to listen to your chest.'

James pushed himself up as the head of the bed was raised. He lifted his pyjama top and hunched forward as Dr Freeman produced an impressive stethoscope to listen to James's lungs. Its bell seemed as wide to Jenny as a toilet plunger. The doctor closed his eyes as he concentrated on James's breath. The room was silent.

'Thank you, that's fine. You can relax now,' Dr Freeman said as he coiled his stethoscope and returned it to his pocket. Sister Robinson helped James ease back against the pillows and lowered the head of the bed.

'Well,' Dr Freeman continued, 'we're still unsure what's going on down there. I've looked at last night's CAT scan. There's definitely some type of inflammation around the lower lobe of your right lung. We need to put a long needle into the area today and take some tissue to send to the pathologists. We'll also drain some of the fluid that's built up around the lung, which will make your breathing easier. It's going to be painful for a minute or two, but once the fluid's gone you're going to feel very much better.'

'Will he be okay, Dr Freeman? What's wrong with him?' Jenny asked.

'Well, Mrs Henderson, it's too early to know. It could be a number of things, some of which are quite benign. I don't think there's anything to be gained by speculating at this stage. It'll take a couple of days to analyse the fluid and biopsy from today, and then we'll know more. Dr Fellowes, here, my registrar,' Dr Freeman said, pointing to one of the doctors, 'will perform the pleural aspiration and biopsy later this morning.'

'So I'll be in for a few days yet, doctor?'

'I'm afraid so, Mr Henderson. I'll be back to see you once we have the results. Sister Robinson will ensure you have everything you need to be as comfortable as possible. Goodbye for now.'

Within an hour, Dr Fellowes returned with Sister Robinson to perform the pleural tap. Dr Freeman had certainly spoken the truth about the pain. There was an intense spiking sensation that almost caused James to sob with horror as a bloody pink fluid drained from his chest. Once the procedure was over, however, he found he could breathe normally again. The pain he experienced when he inhaled deeply remained, although it was less severe. He continued to imagine there was something sharp scratching the outside of his lung. He shut his eyes, trying to keep his thoughts hidden from Jenny. It pained him to see her so distraught.

Two days later, James saw Dr Freeman again, accompanied by the same two doctors and Sister Robinson.

'Hello, Mr Henderson, Mrs Henderson,' Dr Freeman said. 'Good to see you again.' James and Jenny looked at him hopefully. 'Well, then, we've got the results back from the pathologist.' Dr Freeman nodded to one of the doctors and sat down on the edge of James's bed. The young doctor walked behind Jenny and pulled at the yellow partitioning curtains to enclose the space about them, as if the three other patients in the room couldn't hear through cotton. Jenny's heart sank. She knew something terrible was about to happen. She could feel the tears filling in her eyes.

Once the curtain was drawn, Dr Freeman continued. 'I'm afraid the news isn't good.' He put his hand on James's arm. Jenny trembled. Tears fell on the bedclothes as she leaned towards James, grasping his hand tightly. 'I'm sorry, but the results show you have a rare type of lung cancer called mesothelioma. It's a very aggressive cancer and there's not much we can do about it. Your best chance is to have surgery to remove as much as we can and then to undergo chemotherapy. I'm afraid I can't really tell you any more. I've arranged for you to be transferred today to the Royal Prince Alfred in Sydney under a thoracic surgeon where you'll have the surgery tomorrow. I'm so sorry.' He rubbed James's arm. 'Sister Robinson will make the arrangements as soon as she can. I'll probably see you again after the operation when you're transferred back here for rehab.'

James lay back, staring at the yellow curtain, numb. 'It was asbestos, wasn't it?'

'I'm afraid so. There's no other cause that we know of. I assume you've had exposure in your work.'

'I have. I was a builder.'

Jenny looked up, confused by the talk of asbestos. 'I don't understand.'

'Mrs Henderson, asbestos exposure can cause this cancer. We know that now. I'm so sorry about this,' Dr Freeman repeated. 'We'll leave you alone. If there are any questions, please let us know.' He patted James's arm again and stood up. 'Goodbye.'

In the next bed, an elderly man coughed as he emptied his bladder into a bottle with a long, tinkling, hesitant flow.

Chapter 49

James and Jenny travelled in an ambulance from Wollongong to Sydney. Their three children, Robert, Douglas and Kate, were there to meet them and accompany James to the ward. This time, James had a room to himself. There were fresh examinations, more blood tests and meetings with a blur of medical and nursing staff. The specialist thoracic surgeon, Dr Tony Haug, introduced himself within an hour of James's admission.

'Now, Mr Henderson, I'm going to explain what I'll be doing tomorrow morning. I understand this will be quite a lot of information to digest in one go, but I trust you'll get the gist of it,' Dr Haug said. 'I'll be performing what's known as a thoracotomy, pleurectomy and pleurodesis. In simple terms, I'll be making a 15 to 20-centimetre incision between your ribs, just here,' he explained, touching James's back low down on the right side. 'I'll then stretch the ribs apart to give me some room to work in and then I'll strip the tissue around the outside of your right lung, which is called the pleura, along with as much of the tumour as I can safely excise. It's like peeling the rind from an orange. The mesothelioma is a cancer of the pleura, the lining of the lung, and not of the lung itself. I've looked at the scans and although the tumour has pushed a little way into the lung, I'm confident I'll be able to remove most, if not all, of it. Once I've cut all the pleura and tumour out, I'll stick the lung to the inside of the chest wall using some powdered talc. This is called a pleurodesis. It will stop fluid building up around the lung in your chest, which I know was making it hard for you to breathe. Now, Mr Henderson, you're going to be in pain for a week or so. It can't be helped. I'll make sure the staff give you plenty of painkillers to make you as comfortable as possible while the wound heals. After that, we'll transfer you back to Wollongong Hospital for further recuperation and treatment. You'll be there, I think, for another week – that will be up to Dr Freeman and the oncologists – and then home.'

Dr Haug's confident air was exactly what James required.

After the surgeon left the room, James's children closed in around him. It was a tearful, awkward reunion. Only a few months ago James had been fit, happy, healthy. Now he lay in a hospital bed, seemingly a condemned man. His children found it difficult to know what to say, or what to ask him after he assured them he wasn't in pain. In the end, they sat in chairs around the bed, chatting about their own lives, as James listened silently, his attention wavering as a host of fearful thoughts took turns at stealing what remained of his equanimity. As they talked, he reflected on what Dr Haug had described. He forced himself to believe it was all going to be very straightforward. Now that he was on the rollercoaster, he knew he had to become impervious to the travails ahead.

When the dinner tray arrived, the three children kissed their father and departed.

'I'll see you tomorrow,' James said as brightly as possible, even though he knew his face was giving them a different message.

'Yes, Dad, we'll be here before the operation. We'll be here when they wheel you out,' said Kate, bending over her father. 'Make sure you get a good night's sleep. You'll need it for tomorrow.'

'Don't worry, I'll be turning the light out early. Not much else to do. Might even ask for a tablet to make it easier.' He looked at Jenny. 'Might even ask them to give your mother one too.' They all smiled bravely.

When Jenny left to get some sleep, James found himself staring at the wall opposite. He wondered whether he should ask the nurses for a sleeping tablet. He couldn't get the negative thoughts out of his head. He kept on seeing that morning in Fairfield decades ago when his boss, Reg Blaxland, suggested he take over the business. After some hesitation, James had agreed to take over the business. And, like Reg, for the next few decades he'd built houses in the south-western suburbs of Sydney, specialising in inexpensive Fibrosheet cottages. He'd never wanted to look back. Now he couldn't help it.

He saw himself at Reg's funeral not so many years ago.

'The doctors said that Reg had an unusual type of lung cancer. A cancer that might've been caused by asbestos exposure,' Reg's brother, Geoff, had told him.

'But Reg only ever worked as a builder. He used the same asbestos cement sheets I used. Are you telling me that the asbestos in the Fibrosheets caused his cancer?

'That's what I'm saying.'

James recalled staring at Geoff in disbelief. 'Then I could get it too!'

At the time, James resolved never to mention the conversation to Jenny. He'd put it out of his mind. He now thought of Reg Blaxland and knew the same thing was happening to him.

Chapter 50

James was unsure how many days after the surgery he woke. His conscious world was tubes, pain, and strange or familiar faces running together in a filmy-grey montage. Reality flooded forth and receded just as quickly.

'James, James,' he heard whispered in his ears. He saw Jenny's distressed face. He squeezed the fingers he felt clutching his own. The corners of his mouth lifted tentatively into a smile before the wave of unconsciousness swept over him again.

His next waking sensations were an awareness of the shallowness of his breathing and the sharp stab of pain in his chest when he moved, coughed or tried to breathe more deeply. He thought Dr Haug had said he'd fix that problem. He tried not to make a noise when the pain hit. He tried to remember not to do anything that brought it on. It was hard going. He allowed himself a soft moan at night as he stared into the yellowy darkness created by the incandescent bulbs in the corridor. He tried never to let Jenny see how much pain he was in. He was only just holding on. It would break the fine twine from which his world hung heavy and hopeless to know that Jenny was aware of his suffering. He had to be strong for both of them.

The pain gradually eased over the first week. The nurses removed the drip in James's arm. He was able to sit on a chair, and later to walk slowly along the hall to the nurses station and back, supported by a physiotherapist on one side and Jenny on the other. The physiotherapist was teaching him how to breathe again.

Two weeks after the operation, he saw Dr Haug. 'It's taken a little longer than I would have liked, but I can see that we've finally got there in the end.' He sat on the chair on James's left. James couldn't recall seeing him since the day before the operation. 'As I've already told your wife, Mr Henderson, I cut out most of the cancer and gummed the pleura together as promised. That all went well. The pathologists have confirmed the diagnosis of mesothelioma. Unfortunately, there was a small amount I couldn't remove. That's to be expected with this type of malignancy. You'll need to undergo a course of chemotherapy down at Wollongong Hospital to target that. I know you've had a rocky time of it, but the pleurodesis is now working and I don't expect your chest to fill up with fluid in the future.'

'Thank you, doctor,' James said, holding Jenny's hand. 'What are my chances now?' He heard Jenny gulp in a breath of air.

'Well, Mr Henderson, I know you've wanted it straight all along, so I'll tell you. This cancer you have, mesothelioma, is incurable.'

He paused as Jenny gasped. She moved so that she now held James's hand with both of hers.

'The chemo and surgery will buy you time, but I have to tell you that you're unlikely to make it to Christmas this year. It's a very aggressive cancer and all we can do now is slow it down a bit and blunt the pain when it comes. Some are able to survive for many years. But they are the lucky few. I'm sorry to be so blunt, but that's how it is. Do you understand?'

'Yes, thank you,' James said softly. 'I appreciate you telling me the truth.'

'I know it's is a great deal to cope with. But you need to know the facts. Now, I also should tell you that the only known cause of mesothelioma is asbestos exposure—'

'I've heard that before. It doesn't matter anymore, does it? I mean, now that I have it,' James said.

'Well, Mr Henderson, we've known about this connection with asbestos for quite a few years. Most of my patients have had a long history of working with asbestos-containing insulation or fibrocement or some other exposure like that.

'I'm no expert, and this discussion is for another day with another person, but to me it's wrong. Plain wrong. It shouldn't have come to this.'

'To be honest, doctor, I've had quite a lot of exposure over the years. I was a fitter and turner in Glasgow, I've worked in an asbestos mill and factory and I've been a builder for decades.'

Dr Haug smiled grimly. 'That sadly sounds all too familiar. You see, this disease can start up three or four decades after you get the asbestos fibres in your lungs. They sit there and can't be eliminated by the body. And then one day the trigger is pulled, so to speak, and the cancer goes off, growing out of control. We don't really know what starts it off when the fibres have seemingly been sitting there for so long doing nothing.'

James thought for a minute about what Dr Haug had said earlier. 'What did you mean by 'quite a few years'?'

'Oh, we've been aware of the connection since the 1960s,' Dr Haug said matter of factly. 'Naturally, I wasn't practising then, but most of us thoracic specialists know that to be the case. You seem surprised, Mr Henderson, if you don't mind me saying.'

'I am. I feel … I don't know, stunned. Shocked. I don't know how to describe what I'm feeling.'

'I'm afraid most of my patients feel the same way when I tell them about asbestos.'

'I was never told.'

'Few were.'

'In fact, I was told the opposite. That it was safe.'

'What are you saying, James?' Jenny asked. 'What have you known?'

'Not this, Jen. Not this at all.' He stared straight ahead at the back of the chart hanging over the end of the bed.

Dr Haug reached into his coat pocket and pulled a business card from his wallet. He gave it to James. 'These are lawyers I know. They do a lot of work for victims of asbestos exposure. When you're feeling up to it, you might want to give them a call. They help a lot of people like you. Think about it. Some of these asbestos companies knew about the dangers years before they did anything about the problem. You need to see if they should be paying you compensation. Anyway, you'll be down in Wollongong this afternoon, and again in the good hands of the respiratory unit. I wish you both all the best.' Dr Haug shook James's hand. As he reached out to shake Jenny's, he was surprised to be met by her embrace. 'Thank you, Dr Haug. Thank you for all you've done for James. I know you've done your best.'

James looked on as the surgeon appeared to be at a loss to know what to do with his hands. In the end, he patted Jenny on the back like a child until she withdrew.

Chapter 51

James and Jenny returned to Wollongong Hospital in an ambulance. James still felt weak and dozed for much of the journey. As she held James's hand, Jenny wondered about the future. What an awful Christmas they would have. How would she cope without James? Would he be one of the lucky ones – he'd always looked after himself and had never smoked or drunk to excess, so why wouldn't he survive for years? What could she do to help him?

She felt useless. He shouldn't have to go on this fearful journey alone. Yet she couldn't share any of his experiences. The disease was driving a wedge between them and she felt like a fly buzzing pointlessly against a window pane – destined to batter herself to death trying to reach the other side.

While Jenny sat in a turmoil of fear, James again thought of the past. The doctor's words had conjured images he thought were no longer stored in his brain. He could see the sepia haze in the hulls of ships on the Clyde where he'd worked as an apprentice fitter and turner in Glasgow before he sailed for Australia. The dust as thick in the air as the fog rolling off the grey water. He saw the grinning, drunk, sweaty faces of the Italians and the Irish after a hard day's work at Disaster Gorge, the rash from the blue-grey fibres turning into welts across their backs where they scratched their skin during the long, suffocating hours in bed. He pictured himself in Sydney shovelling barrow loads of clumped fibre into the chutes of the Henry King factory. The men around him doing the same. Paper masks dangling around their necks, cigarettes tucked into the corners of their mouths like small pipes connected to some invisible source of clean air. Then there were the years of cutting Fibrosheet. Dust everywhere as he and his crew shaped the boards with power saws and grinders. Where had all the men he worked with gone? Were they still laughing, drinking, telling yarns of past deeds and future conquests? What had become of men like Jack Taylor, his foreman at Henry King's, or Paulo Berendetti, the friendly Italian labourer in the tide mill of the factory? He'd spent hours with these men. Were they alive? He opened his eyes to stop the reel. But all he could see was a warning label: 'CAUTION Asbestos'. What did these companies know? Why didn't they tell the truth? While he thought he was working hard for his family's future, he was actually killing himself. They never told him anything remotely about what he was now going through. And Dr Haug said they knew from the 1960s! He hated himself for letting this happen. He'd worked precisely long enough to end up dead at the time he should have been enjoying the benefits of his hard work. The horrible irony! James felt cheated. He couldn't look at Jenny. He turned away from her towards the side of the ambulance. As he fell back on the bed, he wished he would never wake up.

◆

James startled awake as he was transferred on a trolley by the ambulance officers to his hospital bed. He wasn't overjoyed to be back in the respiratory ward. The hospital smells and noises were noxious. To the extent that his physical reserves permitted, James settled into a restless funk. Depression, anger and panic created a tempest in his mind, with no end in sight. Jenny's attempts at calming him only aggravated the situation. He could sense her own agitation in everything she did.

'Please, Jen, you have to go home. I have to be on my own for a while.'

'I don't want to leave you on your own, James.'

'It's okay,' James said hoarsely. 'I really need to be alone. Just let me think about this for a bit. Let me work out what to do.'

'Don't push me away, James, I need to be with you. To help get you through this.'

'I know you do, Jen, but I'm barely keeping it together and I need to find some space where I can deal with it in some way. I don't know how, but I can't cope with your pain on top of mine right now. Please let me be for a wee bit. Only a day or so.'

Jenny could see he was almost in tears. He looked exhausted, if not defeated. So much had happened in such a short space of time. Although it hurt her deeply to admit it, she could see her distress wasn't helping him.

As if on cue, a nurse came into the cubicle. She'd been on duty when they were last in the hospital. She looked at James and then at Jenny.

'Hello, Mr and Mrs Henderson. It's good to see you again. Now, Mrs Henderson, I have to do a few things with your husband – examine him, take some observations. Make sure he's settled in. You look as though you haven't slept for days.'

'I haven't.'

'Well, you really do need to get some sleep. Your husband needs you to be strong for him. You can't do that if you're not sleeping well. Why don't you go home and get some rest?'

'But we live in Kiama. It's miles away. I'll sleep here.'

'It's not that far. I suggest you take the time to go home. Stay there for a couple of days. The break will do you the power of good. I'm sure your husband will agree that it will be for the best.'

Jenny knew the advice was sound, but she hesitated to agree. 'Well ... I can see your point ... but James, dear, what do you think?'

'Jenny, please go. Come back on the weekend when you've had a good rest. You never know, I might even feel happier myself.' He managed a wan smile.

Jenny started to cry. She wished she could get a better handle on her emotions. This shouldn't be happening to them. No one had the right to hurt James like this. What did he ever do to deserve this? Oh, stop crying, you fool! she thought. How is this helping James? She kissed him and pressed gently downwards around his shoulders in a tentative hug. 'Okay, James, I'll go. Make sure you tell the nurses to ring me if you need anything.' She could barely look at him. 'Please take care of him, sister.'

'We will, Mrs Henderson. Try not to worry and, please, get some sleep.'

Jenny withdrew slowly from the room. She turned to see James one last time before she left, but his face was obscured by the nurse's body.

After Jenny's departure, James lay with his eyes closed. Despite his fatigue, he couldn't settle. A sudden thought came to him and he reached into his bedside drawer. Pulling out the card Dr Haug had given him, he looked at the inscription. In navy ink, were the words:

Shaw & Fletcher
Solicitors
We get you more

Chapter 52

Jenny wandered outside the house she and James had built, towards the path to the beach. The sun had long since fled the day. The house stood gloomy, silent, dead. It was two days since James had dismissed her from the hospital in Wollongong with the instruction to get some rest but her brain was still full of noise.

Nearby, she could hear the waves crashing and sucking a clattering stream of pebbles end over end into the wash. Everything was turbulent. Jenny made out the pale, sandy cleft of the path between the dark bushes and followed it to the beach, Tess moving silently behind her. After she'd retrieved her from the neighbours, Tess was reluctant to leave her side. The dampness of the sand soaked into Jenny's stockings. She didn't care. Her legs carried her forward down the camber of the beach and into the water. The cold bite of the sea at her thighs jolted her out of her trance. She felt the deathly tug of the undertow. Her legs were pulled from underneath her and she fell backwards with a slapping splash into the rapidly moving shallows. She crawled up to the soft, dry sand, panting with the effort and lay motionless until her breathing slowed and her awareness returned. Tess nudged at her with her muzzle. Jenny slowly got to her feet, shivering and sobbing. She found the path to the house and shuffled numbly up through the shrubs.

Inside, Jenny stripped out of her wet, sandy clothes. She went to the bathroom and had a long, hot shower, standing under the water until some feeling returned. She dried herself and fed Tess, then got into bed, curling into a ball beneath the covers. She was soon asleep.

When she woke, it was early in the afternoon. She hadn't slept in for decades. She gazed up at the ceiling, waiting for the urge to rise from the bed. It wouldn't come. Jenny couldn't care less. She rolled over and drifted off again to sleep.

Later, at night, Jenny climbed out of bed to wash her clothes and make herself a toasted sandwich. Tess returned through the dog door as if to check on her. Feeling guilty, Jenny gave her a bowl of food. Despite spending almost twenty-four hours in bed, she still felt tired. She looked at the photograph on the sideboard on their wedding day. It was black and white, but she could recall all the colour of the occasion. Two young people from the other side of the world starting a new adventure together. And now this.

After watching television for an hour or so, she went back to bed. She had no inclination to read. She closed her eyes and let her thoughts take her where they wished.

She remembered how they first met travelling on the *Neptune* from Britain for a better life in Australia. He was a wiry, handsome fitter and turner from Glasgow and the kindest, strongest person she had ever known. They fell in love on that voyage and had rarely been apart since. She couldn't bear to see his hair plastered to his head with sweat and his glittering blue eyes dulled by sickness. But she couldn't think of anything else.

The next day, Jenny returned to the hospital, leaving Tess again with the neighbours. James was much brighter. He too looked as though he had slept deeply and recovered some vitality. Although it hurt Jenny to see James still in discomfort and so thin and weak, his mood was clearly better.

'Dr Freeman came in yesterday, Jen, and said I would probably be able to go home soon. I don't need as many painkillers. My breathing has also definitely improved. I can now walk up to the end of the corridor and back three times a day with the physiotherapist's help.'

'That certainly sounds like progress, dear. What about the chemotherapy? Has anyone talked to you about that?'

'The oncologist came in at the same time as Dr Freeman and went through what was involved and what it would be like. I've got to tell you, Jen, I'm not keen to do it right at the moment. It's been hard as it is. I need to get my strength back before I think about chemo. It doesn't sound good at all.'

'Don't do it, James. That is, don't do it if it's not necessary right away.'

'Well, the oncologist – her name's Dr Cindy Pryde, a very nice woman, I thought – she said I could be treated as an outpatient after I've fully recovered from the operation. So long as I didn't mind the weekly drive to Wollongong. I told her I was happy to put up with the inconvenience but it's up to you, Jen, because you'll have to do the driving.'

'I'll drive. Of course, I'll do it.'

'Thank you. I want to be home in my own bed, with you, Jen.'

An occupational therapist then came into the room to talk to Jenny about a home visit, to ensure they had all the appropriate aids and equipment when James was discharged. She explained that, over the following months, they might need a shower chair, commode, adjustable bed, dressings, an oxygen tank, mask, and many other things.

After she left, James told Jenny that it would be easier for her if she only spent every second day at the hospital.

'No, James, I'm coming up every day.'

'I don't think that's a good idea, Jen. I've thought this through. By not driving up from Kiama every day, you can busy yourself preparing for my return and co-ordinating the delivery of whatever equipment's required.'

'I suppose.'

'In any event, I get visitors every day. The children take it in turns to see me, as you know. And some of my old workmates have popped in to visit.'

James didn't say that, despite his friends' best efforts, most of their visits proved sombre and demoralising, and that, after his children left, he didn't think he could go on.

'I also want you to do something for me.'

'Anything, James.'

'I've been thinking about something Dr Haug mentioned after the operation.'

'How long you've got? James, he also said that some survive and—'

'No, Jenny, not that. I've been thinking about the cause of my cancer. You know, asbestos.'

'I thought you somehow already knew about that.'

'Well, I knew a few things. Nothing like this. We were told right the way through that there was nothing to worry about so long as we did certain things. You know, keep dust levels down, which I always did. Anyway, no one ever said a thing about this cancer, this mesothelioma, if that's how you say it. Jen, I'd like to look up those solicitors Dr Haug told us about. I've kept the card. It's in the top drawer. Would you mind getting it out for me, dear?'

'James, do you really want to be talking to lawyers? Don't we have enough on our plate without doing this? I don't want you spending what time might be left...' She started crying. '...in a court case with lawyers hanging around and stressing you and taking advantage of you.'

'Look, Jen, I know what you mean. And I have my doubts, just like you. Bottom line for me is that I can't stop thinking about all that asbestos I was exposed to over the years. I can't believe nobody knew about its dangers. It doesn't make sense. Dr Haug said they knew about it in the 1960s. That's decades ago.

'He also said that these solicitors have helped other people with the same sort of disease, so they must know something. I want to know, Jen, if this shouldn't have happened. I want to know the truth. I want to know whether I've been lied to. It's not much to ask for now … now that I'm here … dying.'

'No, don't say that, James. Please don't say that.'

Jenny could see that James had been thinking about the matter for some time. If that was what he wanted, then she could hardly fight him. But she didn't want him to become mixed up with people who were only interested in making money and couldn't give a damn whether they made a dying man's last months a misery. She wanted to protect him against anyone who might cause him further pain. But she also had to try to help him find the truth.

'All right, James. I understand. What do you want me to do?'

'Jen, I want you to ring these solicitors and tell them about my case. I want to know if they can help. Whether they can give me some answers.'

'I'll do it, but on one condition. If they say you have a weak case, or put unreasonable demands on you, then you'll drop it.'

'Okay, I agree. We'll suck it and see for now.'

Chapter 53

Jenny delayed telephoning Shaw & Fletcher. She didn't like going into unknown territory. But when she saw how exasperated James was when she continued to reply 'not yet' to his regular inquiries, she knew it was time to muster the courage.

She put on her glasses and dialled the number on the card. After explaining the situation to a receptionist, she was put through to a female solicitor, who was described as 'one of our senior dust lawyers'.

'Good morning, Viviana Glosioli speaking. How may I help you?' The words were friendly, but the voice had a hard, businesslike edge to it, something Jenny had never dealt with before. She immediately felt apologetic as if she shouldn't be wasting the woman's time.

'Yes, ah, thank you for taking my call,' she started.

'What can I do to help you?'

'Well, you see, it's my husband, James. Sorry, my name is Jenny Henderson...'

'Yes, hello, Mrs Henderson.'

'Oh, hello... '

'Viviana Glosioli.'

'I'm sorry, I'm not used to doing this.'

'Please, Mrs Henderson, take a breath. That's better. Now take your time and tell me how I can help you and your husband.'

Jenny relaxed a little. She appreciated that the hardness she had sensed might be imaginary or merely reflected her own anxiety. The woman at the end of the phone was simply doing her job and trying to get to the point and find out what needed to be done. She took another deep breath. 'My husband, James, has been diagnosed with mesothelioma. He's in Wollongong Hospital ... and he was given your firm's card by his surgeon, Dr Haug.'

'A top surgeon. Very caring man.'

'Yes, he was, is … My husband asked me to ring you to see if he has a claim.'

'Has he been exposed to asbestos?'

'Well, yes, he has...'

'How sick is he, Mrs Henderson?'

'He's just had a big operation and he's to start chemo soon...'

'I assume he's under Dr Freeman's care?'

'Yes, that's right.'

'Is the oncologist Dr Pryde?'

'I believe that's her name.' Jenny's initial frustration at being interrupted eased as she realised this woman knew what she was talking about and was trying to elicit the salient facts as quickly as possible.

'All very competent doctors. Has Dr Freeman given you an opinion on prognosis?'

Jenny hesitated. She didn't like talking or thinking about James's prognosis. 'Yes, he has. It's a bit better than Dr Haug's opinion. Dr Haug said he wouldn't make it to Christmas. Dr Freeman said he might make it to Australia Day next year...' The tears pooled in her eyes and spilled onto her chest.

'I understand. We have no time to lose. We'll need to come and see your husband in hospital. Would Thursday be convenient, Mrs Henderson?'

Jenny felt that this Glosioli woman was oblivious to her anguish. She was being rushed. She didn't want this.

'Um, yes, fine ... I mean if it's okay by the hospital,' she replied.

'It will be, Mrs Henderson. This has happened before.'

'It has?'

'Yes. Is 10.30am okay?'

'I guess so. But what do I need to do? I don't know anything about—'

'Mrs Henderson, I understand that this is all new and in many ways frightening for you and your husband. One minute he's well, the next minute he's in hospital and lawyers are bossing you about. It's going to feel very strange for a while, but we do need to act quickly so that he can spend as brief a time as possible with lawyers and experts. I need to find out as much as possible about your husband's work as soon as I can.

'To do that, I have to get cracking. You don't have to do a thing except tell your husband when we're coming. I'll contact the hospital. They'll be ready.'

'That would be a big help.'

'It's part of my job, Mrs Henderson. I want to help your husband. I want to make it as easy as I can for him. For you.'

Jenny felt increasingly relieved. Now the woman sounded warm, compassionate.

'Mr Shaw and I will come down on Thursday. Would you please ensure that Mr Henderson is expecting us?'

'Yes, of course. Who's Mr Shaw?'

'He's the firm's partner. He sees all new cases.'

'Will I like him?'

'He's very good at his job, Mrs Henderson.'

'I see. He's the 'Shaw' on the card.'

'That's right. Now, if there are any problems, please contact me immediately. Otherwise, we'll see you and your husband on Thursday at 10.30am.'

'Thank you.' Jenny felt she should say more, ask more questions, but she didn't know where to begin. She put down the phone wondering what she might have unleashed. There wouldn't be any time to settle into this new phase. Fear rose up through her like damp. She felt squeamish, her heart racing out of control ... again.

Chapter 54

James and Jenny looked up in unison as Viviana and Gary Shaw entered James's room at Wollongong Hospital.

'Hello, Mr and Mrs Henderson. I'm Viviana Glosioli, senior associate at Shaw & Fletcher. This is Mr Shaw, the senior partner. I spoke with you, Mrs Henderson, on the telephone. Nice to meet you in person.'

Viviana watched the couple's fragile, earnest response. She felt truly embarrassed to be associated with Gary Shaw. She retreated as he walked forward with his hand extended, full of his phoney bonhomie, filling the room like an elephant.

'Hello, hello, Mr and Mrs Henderson,' he said, shaking their hands in turn. 'Pleased to meet you.'

'Glad to meet you,' James said quietly. 'I hope you'll be able to help me.'

'Thank you. I hope so too. Do you mind?' He indicated the chairs beside the bed.

'No, please sit down,' James replied.

'And do call us Gary and Viviana. We're going to get to know each other very well in the next few months.'

'Months?' Jenny asked.

'Afraid so, Jenny. Sorry, you don't mind if we call you Jenny and James?'

'Not at all, but—'

'Thank you, Jenny.'

Shaw lowered his bulky frame onto a chair. James twisted in his bed so that he could face the lawyers, Jenny sitting on the other side, holding his arm, looking at Shaw warily. Out of the blue, as she watched, Viviana recalled hiding behind her mother's legs at the gorilla exhibit at a zoo.

'It will only be a few months, Jenny,' Shaw began. 'Not even that. We'll be largely out of your hair. Viviana here will be looking after your case, James.' Viviana smiled as warmly as possible as James turned to acknowledge her. She needed to instil confidence in the poor man and his wife and keep her dislike for Shaw concealed. 'She's a very experienced litigator,' Shaw continued, 'and has already got some pretty big judgments under her belt. You'll be in very capable hands. I, of course, will be overseeing everything and will always have my finger on the pulse of your case, so to speak. There's always that safeguard for you. Does that sound acceptable to you both?' James and Jenny nodded, dazed. 'Good. Now, what we need to do is take a very detailed statement from you, James. This will form the basis of an affidavit we'll need to prepare down the track. The affidavit may be used at trial, if it comes to that.'

'What's an affidavit? And what do you mean "if it comes to that"?' Jenny asked.

Shaw took the question in his practised stride. 'Viviana will talk to you about the technical details in due course. As to your other question, Jenny, I can say a few words about that. Most of the asbestos disease cases we handle settle before trial, some as late as at the door of the court. You see, we've already run the big test cases against the asbestos companies and, frankly, after the walloping they received, they're a little gun-shy about going to court. So, once Viviana's taken a statement, we should be in a good position to advise you about your prospects and what will happen when we commence proceedings. Ninety-nine out of a hundred cases settle. We have a very good track record. The best in fact. There's a very small risk that the case might come to a trial, but you shouldn't worry about that in the slightest. If you have strong evidence of exposure to asbestos from one of the usual suspects like Henry King Industries, then the chances of going to court are infinitesimal.'

'I worked at Disaster Gorge, in King Industries' Riverwood factory, and I was a builder for years.'

'Well, there you are. The likelihood of a trial, Jenny and James, is slight. Your story sounds fairly typical, I'm afraid, James. I don't foresee too many problems. I'd hope to have everything wrapped up before Christmas. Obviously, we'll know more after a detailed statement, but at first blush I'd say this is going to be seamless. The only hassle will be that you may have to be examined by a few doctors retained by both you and the potential defendants. That's standard practice. The rest of the preparation, you leave to us. We know which doctors to engage, those who are plaintiff-friendly, as we say. Viviana will go through it all with you. She's incredibly thorough. It may take a couple of days so she'll probably stay locally to ensure it's done.' Viviana smiled dutifully at the right moment.

'Now, I should also mention what your case will be about. It will be in negligence. What that means is that you'll need to prove that the particular defendants breached their duty of care to you and that that breach caused you to develop mesothelioma. Sounds quite simple, doesn't it? It should be. We'll argue on your behalf that they knew about the dangers of asbestos but did nothing to protect employees and customers from exposure. They should have insisted on masks, exhaust equipment, warning labels, or stopped using asbestos altogether. You follow? Good. Anyway, as I said, Viviana will run through it in more detail after she takes your statement.'

'Are you saying these companies knew about the dangers of asbestos or of mesothelioma all along?' James asked.

'Yes, I am. It's a national disgrace.'

'Why didn't they warn us?'

'Greed, I'd say. Money over safety. Look, we'll get into more of that down the track. You'll be fully informed as we move along with the investigation. Viv here will take a detailed history from you.' Viviana winced at the familiarity and saw that Jenny had noticed it too.

'I'm very concerned that all the questioning will tire James,' Jenny said.

'It's okay, Jen, I want it over and done with as soon as possible. I can start whenever you're ready,' James said. 'Will you need Jenny to be here as well?'

'No, she doesn't need to stick around for this. It will be terribly boring,' Shaw replied.

'No, I'll stay,' insisted Jenny, staring straight at Viviana with determination.

'Very well. Now, if there are no more questions, I'll be off. I have some other business to attend to.'

Shaw rose, shook James and Jenny's hands again and lumbered out the door. His gut wobbled beneath his thin silk shirt. If only he'd wear a singlet, Viviana thought.

When she turned back to James and Jenny, she again noted Jenny's questioning gaze. She smiled at her awkwardly. To Viviana's surprise, Jenny nodded with the faintest hint of comprehension.

Chapter 55

'I know I said to get into it straightaway, Jen, but this is getting me down,' James admitted to Jenny after the first session with Viviana. 'Does she have to write down everything? It's so slow.'

'Do you want me to tell her to stop; tell her that you've changed your mind?'

'No. I'm sure she's doing her best. She says she needs to know everything from when I was an apprentice in Glasgow to the time I hammered in my last nail as a builder. We have to trust that she knows what she's doing. I know it's necessary and I know I was the one who wanted this. I want to go home, that's all.'

'I know you do. I want to see you back there, too, James. Let's allow her to do her job. It'll be over before you know it.' Jenny realised how unconvincing she sounded. The process was progressing at a snail's pace. James needed to rest every hour or so and sometimes became hazy with his recollection after he took painkillers. Viviana was methodical, but patient. She seemed genuinely caring, and had reassured James and Jenny more than once that she was on their side.

Such a contrast to how she dressed, thought Jenny. Every day she came in to see James, Viviana was dressed in the same black figure-hugging suit. Presumably she hadn't brought a change of clothes. Her long legs were encased in black stockings. Her feet in their glossy high-heeled shoes stayed side-by-side throughout the interview, as if they were stuck in a pot of black tar. The only colour she permitted the world to see was her blood-red lipstick and her matching hair comb, which pulled her black shoulder-length hair tightly off her forehead. Her eyes were dark, Mediterranean; her eyebrows thick and elegantly arched. She was a beautiful young woman, Jenny thought, and yet she dressed as if in mourning.

But it was none of her business. All she wanted was for Viviana to do a good job and to look after her husband and his case properly. She seemed to be doing that very well. So why this fascination with her?

Jenny pushed these irrelevancies to the background. She was becoming much more concerned at the history of asbestos exposure James was recounting. As the days passed, she sat through it all, aghast at how much of the substance James had come into contact with over the years.

What's more, the exposure had started when he was just sixteen. As James spoke, Jenny began to understand the horrors of the putrid ship-building works on the Clyde, the blue fug of crocidolite in the mine and mill at Disaster Gorge, the fibrous blizzards at the Henry King Riverwood factory and the daily coating he received of asbestos cement dust over the many years of running his own business. She remembered James's disgusting overalls he left in the laundry tub. And all that and more had gone into his lungs! It was a nightmare.

'If my hunch is right, James, you must have been at Disaster Gorge when the Western Australian Health Department inspected the mine and mill?' Viviana asked at one stage. 'I've interviewed a doctor who was part of that group.'

'There was a visit by some men, including a doctor, who must have been important because they arrived by plane. I remember because that rarely happened.'

'Dr Smith?'

'That's him.'

'What do you remember about the visit?'

'I recall that when I arrived for work that morning, the machines in the mill were turned off and we were told to do other chores, like filling bags with fibre and cleaning the floor. Later, five or so men, including the doctor, arrived in a car and were taken on a tour of the mill. After they left for the mine, I never saw them again. The plane flew out the next day.'

'Thank you, James, that could be very important.'

Jenny sat listening, becoming angry. Why didn't that doctor do something? He could have stopped what had happened to her husband.

And as Viviana continued to extract further details about his work, Jenny wondered why James hadn't told her about the asbestos warning labels that were eventually stuck onto the Fibrosheets, or the suspicions about Reg Blaxland's death. She would have done something. At the very least, she would have told him to stop being a builder.

Later, she felt silly thinking these things. She knew the answer. Why James had never told her. He wouldn't have wanted her to worry. What did he really know, anyway? Nothing. James said he'd been reassured that everything was okay.

No matter which way Jenny looked at the situation, it simply wasn't right. She felt betrayed on James's behalf. She felt guilty that he'd worked as he had for her and the children.

◆

Once what Jenny thought of as the 'inquisition' ended, Viviana assured James and Jenny that they could leave everything to her.

'I'll contact you regularly for updates, and inform you well in advance about medical appointments so that everything's as stress free as possible. Apart from these inconveniences, the case will forge on without you, James.'

'I'm happy to let you run the show, Viviana. I'll do whatever you want. I only want them to pay in some way and to admit they did the wrong thing.'

'I believe they will, James. I think you have a strong case against V&L for your time at Disaster Gorge and an even stronger claim against Henry King Industries for your exposure to asbestos at its factory and from asbestos-containing products while you worked as a builder.'

'Thank you, Viviana, that gives me some peace of mind,' James said softly.

Next, Viviana explained Shaw & Fletcher's costs agreement, a lengthy document she placed on James's lap. He nodded along as she spoke, but Jenny knew he'd not understood or listened to a word. She barely understood it either. It seemed to say that Shaw & Fletcher stood to be paid a sizeable sum of money out of James's damages when the case settled. She had no idea how the amount was calculated.

'In terms of quantum, which is how much the defendants might pay you to settle the case, I expect you'd be paid over $400,000,' Viviana advised.

'That doesn't seem enough, Viviana,' Jenny blurted out, feeling aggrieved that James wouldn't be receiving a multi-million-dollar sum.

'It's not about the money, Jen,' James said. 'It's about making them admit they did something wrong.'

'I understand, James, but the more they pay, the more they learn. We have to teach them a lesson, don't we? Viviana, isn't that right?'

'I'm afraid, Jenny, we're not living in America. Over there, juries award millions of dollars in what's known as punitive damages. It's not like that here – or not yet.'

'What are punitive damages?' Jenny asked.

'They're a special type of damages, sometimes called exemplary damages, that may be awarded in particular cases when a defendant's conduct is reprehensible – you know, very, very bad.'

'Isn't that what happened to James? They covered up the truth?'

'I absolutely agree, Jenny. I promise I'll be looking into it very carefully. We might be able to claim punitive damages in James's case, but it hasn't been done before, so there are risks. We have to be cautious and prepare the case meticulously. James's case will progress quickly. I don't want to rush in with the wrong evidence on this issue. I also don't want to drag things out unnecessarily or give you any false hope. That won't help anyone. If we do this the right way, we'll make these companies pay.'

Chapter 56

Finally, after weeks in hospital, the day came when James could return home. His strength and stamina were rapidly returning. He was able to walk the length of the ward without assistance. Even though he knew that chemotherapy was on the horizon, he allowed himself to experience a small white light of hope. It was fragile; he didn't want to frighten it. He kept it tucked away in his mind, trying to keep it alive, but scared to let it grow.

As he left the respiratory ward, he felt like his imprisonment was over. Dr Freeman, the junior doctors and the nursing staff all wished him and Jenny well, joked about not wanting to see them again, and said their goodbyes. James carefully thanked them each in turn.

'We've got the ambulance ready for you outside the emergency department. We'll take you down there in a wheelchair,' Sister Robinson said.

'No, thank you, sister,' James said. 'I'm fit enough to walk out the door myself and to go home in my own car.'

'My apologies, Mr Henderson.'

Jenny hugged her. They walked slowly to the lifts and out the door.

Despite his resolve, James found travelling home difficult. It was a sunny day. The glare made his eyes water and blink; he hadn't been outside for so long. Jenny drove carefully, but the winding road soon induced motion sickness. James wasn't good at being a passenger. He sighed softly at some of Jenny's decisions. And when he put his foot out as if pressing down on a brake pedal, Jenny nearly veered off the road as she turned to him and said, 'Stop that, James. You're really giving me the pip. I'm driving the car. Let me do it my way.'

'Sorry, Jen.'

'Apology accepted,' she said with diminishing sternness.

The car eventually pulled into the Kiama driveway. A wave of joy washed over James. He pushed open the door and inhaled the smell of the ocean, tasted the salt and seaweed in the air, felt the blaze of sunshine on his chest. He was still alive. He was home.

Jenny helped him up the stairs and into the lounge. He sat down in his favourite chair as she made a cup of tea. Later, they sat together as if the past weeks had never happened, gazing out at the light dancing on the undulating sea. The sky was pale blue, almost white. Seagulls arced over the headland. An oil tanker crawled along the horizon. James felt the warmth of the tea through his mug. He sat back, smiling, feeling the heat climb up his fingers to his hand and into his wasted arms and shoulders. The heat and light of the day entered his joints and muscles, swelling, expanding, running through him in a great surge of wellness.

Chapter 57

James was glad for the break before he started the chemotherapy because it gave him a frightful battering. While the oncologist, Dr Cindy Pryde, was one of the kindest doctors James had met, that had not made it any easier.

'I'm sorry, Mr Henderson, but the cocktail of agents I'm going to use on you is, frankly, experimental,' she warned. 'Surgery has always been the frontline treatment for mesothelioma. There have been various clinical trials with chemotherapeutic drugs, but they've proven to be rather hit and miss.'

'I don't mind. Let's give it a wee go,' he assured her, despite his earlier reservations.

'Okay. I have to tell you, however, that you'll experience nausea, vomiting and fatigue.'

No warning could have described the reality of the treatment.

James couldn't keep anything down. He vomited so hard that Dr Pryde was worried he might tear a hole in his stomach or rip his oesophagus from its attachments. The torrent of nausea roared through his system within hours of the drugs passing into his veins. Anti-vomiting medication did nothing to arrest the feeling. His insides heaved and twisted. And as he hung his head over a bucket, all that came up was a trickle of frothy yellow acidic liquid. He leaned back in his armchair in the brief periods of respite, moaning like a dog, trying to rest before it started all over again. He felt out of control and out of his body. When he managed to gain focus, all he saw was Jenny struggling to cope. He became so weak that Dr Pryde was eventually forced to admit him to hospital for the final two cycles.

Jenny helped James as much as she could, feeling as though the man she loved was shrivelling before her eyes. She felt powerless, rubbing his back, mopping his brow, wiping away the bile from the corner of his parched, cracked mouth, offering sips of water he could barely keep down. Her utterances of love started to sound to her like platitudes. She began attending to James in silence. She refused to talk to the children or allow them to come down and see their father in his haggard state.

And then it was over.

'I think I've turned the corner, Jen,' James muttered from his armchair three weeks after the final cycle.

'You do?'

'I feel I've got a fraction of my strength back. It's not much, but I wouldn't mind trying to walk outside.'

'Are you sure?' Jenny hoped he was telling the truth and not pushing himself.

'I am. Come on, Jen, give me a hand.'

She helped him push upright from the chair. He wobbled unsteadily for a few seconds and then shuffled forward. 'Be careful, dear. Slowly now.'

He beamed at her as he walked carefully out onto the balcony and rested with his hands on the railing.

He closed his eyes and experienced the glow of the sun on his grey face.

Within days, James had managed to totter down the path to the beach a few times, Jenny vigilant at his side, an ecstatic Tess in danger of bowling him over. He was overjoyed to feel the soft sand massaging his feet.

'I hope my ghastly appearance isn't going to upset any of the others on the beach, Jen.'

'Don't talk such utter nonsense, James,' Jenny scolded. 'Get those thoughts out of your head this instant. If anyone, I mean anyone, even remotely looks askance at you, I'll give them a real what for.'

As it turned out, all the passers-by greeted him warmly and were pleased to see him out and about. His neighbours' kind thoughts buoyed James. The feeble hope of being able to beat the cancer welled up. All he needed was to get his strength back, then he'd be right.

His appetite improved. His face gained some colour. The more time he spent in the sunshine, the greater grew his optimism. 'This is so beautiful. It makes me feel so good. Better than any drug they gave me in hospital,' he said to Jenny one morning as they sat on the beach, his toes digging into the yellow sand. He picked up handfuls of it and let it pour from his fist. He looked at the small mound he had made. He trickled another clenched fist's worth onto the peak, seeing the specks tumble down the sides, never able to hold their position, the pinnacle never gaining in height no matter how many fistfuls he decanted from his palm.

Jenny put her arm around James's shoulders. Regardless of the number of times she did it, she couldn't get used to how thin he was.

'You're sounding much better, dear. It's a shame we couldn't have had all the chemotherapy here, but I suppose it was really too difficult at the end. It was knocking you about so much.'

'Maybe, but I'm telling you, Jenny, I don't want to leave home again. I couldn't take it. The way I'm feeling, I hope it won't come to it, but if I suffer a relapse or get sicker, promise me, Jen, that you won't let them take me back to hospital. If I'm going to die, I want to die in my own home.'

He stared out at the sea. A fishing boat swayed in the swells past the headland. Netted arms stuck out from its hull, appearing to move as the boat yawed, like the wings on a giant seabird, struggling to take flight.

Jenny was on the verge of tears. She rubbed his back, squeezed his knobby shoulder. There was so little of him now. He didn't seem capable of putting on weight and it was disturbing to feel the bony wings of his shoulder blades or the hard corrugations of his ribs under her hand.

'Of course, I promise,' she assured him. 'If anything happens, I'll look after you here. We'll manage. We've got all this equipment that the occupational therapist organised sitting in the house. We'll get by. James, I couldn't stand to see you one more time in that sterile, smelly hospital. You're going to be here for good.'

She looked at his wasted profile, the blue blaze of his eyes. She rested her head against his. The sun dried her tears as the shadows shortened. A sea breeze picked up over the bay, exhaling quietly, warmly, across their skin.

◆

Jenny endeavoured to be positive, yet every day was a painful, waiting game. She waited for James to declare himself better or a doctor to say he was cured. She waited for James to gain a couple of kilograms, to come out of the shower able to breathe, to put his feet in the surf. She waited for him to be dressed so that he could sit in his armchair and wait some more. Waiting. Just waiting for something to happen. And while she waited, she lied to herself, pretending life was normal, pretending that she cared about the weather or the garden or the television programme or about anything in the world other than her husband's life. Was he going to die? What did that sneeze mean? Running up the steps from the laundry when she heard a cough, bursting into the loungeroom ready for action. Relaxing when she saw her husband sip from his pottery mug and offer an amused smile. She would turn on her heels and traipse back down to the tub, embarrassed. She was angry at herself for being paranoid. The waiting had her wound up like a top, ready to unravel in a frenzied whir of useless activity at the sound of an alarm.

She lay awake at night listening to James's laboured breathing. Sometimes, there were pauses in the in and out of the cycle. She would find herself about to shake his broken body when, with a gasp, he would start breathing again.

Every night she listened and waited for the breathing to stop for good.

She listened until, in a trance, she started counting his breaths like sheep, counting and counting until she could no longer distinguish reality from dreams. When she finally awakened from an exhausted sleep, the first thing she thought was whether her husband was still there. She would roll over and watch nervously to see his chest rise and fall and hear the low gurgling of his breath. Then she would get up to prepare for the day ahead.

James felt Jenny's distress. Their lives were in limbo. If he could fast-forward a few weeks, he knew there would be obvious changes. He knew he was slowly, very slowly, gaining weight, but Jenny couldn't or wouldn't see the improvement he was positive was taking place. By early November 2002, however, he knew even she could not deny the improvement. The entire Henderson clan was travelling to Kiama to celebrate James's 'recovery'.

James had secretly planned the day with Robert. He told his son that he'd missed having everyone around and that, as he felt better, why not have a get-together? He knew that if he mentioned the celebration to Jenny, she would flatly refuse on the grounds that he was too weak to cope with the excitement. He didn't want to disclose his optimism to her, if only to avoid cursing himself with bad luck. He kept his thoughts to himself and hoped it would be a surprise.

♦

James and Jenny were sitting on the verandah nursing their morning tea when they heard the 'honk! honk!' of a car horn.

'Who's that?' Jenny asked, displeased at the thought of visitors. 'For God's sake stop that blaring horn,' she started complaining until she realised that the person honking was her son, Douglas. And after Robert and Kate arrived in convoy, she was elated. She rushed down the stairs to greet them, James leaning back in his squatter's chair, grinning.

'What are you people doing here?' Jenny asked as if annoyed.

'We've been invited to a family barbecue; didn't you get the invitation,

Mum?' Douglas said as he embraced her. Soon she was engulfed by Robert and Kate, their partners and her grandchildren. She hugged them all, smiling, talking, laughing, her voice rising in her excitement. The gaiety went on for so long, James wondered whether they'd ever make it past the front door.

The greeting he received was disappointingly subdued in comparison. He could see that they were wary. They squeezed him tentatively as if afraid that he would snap like a twig in their arms. No matter how well he said he felt, everyone knew he had something bad inside him. It kept them at bay, forced them to change how they spoke to him, and how they behaved around him. James thought he could handle anything his cancer could throw up at him. But he couldn't manage the distance it drove him from his loved ones. He was a marked man, and he believed they knew it. He wanted to show them otherwise.

Over the course of the day, James felt the gap between them close. He managed to play with his grandchildren on the beach – dug holes, built sandcastles, watched them paddle in the shallows. He had the strength to again throw sticks along the beach for Tess to chase. He helped cook the meat on the barbecue, burning the sausages with aplomb. He spoke to everyone, and the subject never turned to himself. He immersed himself in his children's lives, their work, the holidays, the talents already discernible in his grandchildren, their houses, their views on politics, sport, travel.

He noticed Jenny watching him, smiling or frowning depending on how much energy he put into a task. He wanted to ask her whether she could see that he wasn't a man worried about his life. She tried to coax him into an afternoon rest, but he was having none of it. He was enjoying himself. He wasn't going to let himself recede into the background of his family life like an invalid. Perhaps, he thought, she might be thinking he was getting better. She might even be daring to think for a second that he'd be one of the lucky ones. He hoped so. It was what he felt.

'Quiet, everyone!' James said. His voice wasn't strong. He had to repeat himself: 'Quiet!' The family was out on the deck in the bright afternoon sunshine. James had propped himself up against the door from the loungeroom. 'Thank you.' Jenny looked at him, as if he was going to topple. 'As you know, I've been through a bit of a rough spot. Thank you all for making the trip down so that I can see you all in better circumstances and enjoy my family once again. It's been a fantastic day and hopefully a huge surprise to at least one person.' Jenny laughed as she nodded in agreement. 'Jenny, you're as beautiful as the day I first met you as we travelled to Australia on the *Neptune* over forty years ago. I couldn't have made it here without you.' A chorus of 'oohs' and 'aahs!' lifted off the deck and floated into the sky like balloons released at a fete.

'What's Grandpa doing?' asked Robert's son, Duigald.

'He's saying how much he loves Grandma,' Robert explained. Duigald looked again at his grandfather then resumed sipping from his cup of lemonade.

'I know, Jen, it's been hard for you looking after me recently—'

'Don't be silly,' she interrupted.

'Well, this is to say thank you, dear, for everything. For making me so happy, for giving me this beautiful family, for making me the luckiest man in the world. I love you!'

Jenny was a blubbering mess. She walked over to James, kissed him and clasped him with all the love and hope she could muster. She hugged him as if she had no fear of crushing him. The family cheered and clapped. Tess barked enthusiastically and frightened the grandchildren.

◆

Jenny could see James was exhausted the following day and he put up no opposition when she suggested an afternoon nap was in order. 'I hope you didn't overdo it yesterday,' she said as she watched him slowly walk towards the bedroom.

By the end of the week, however, James's energy levels had improved.

Jenny contemplated ringing up the hospital to return the electric bed and other accessories. The tranquillity of Kiama descended on them as before. Jenny could see the future calm and purposeful before her. It would be all right. He was going to get through it.

Chapter 58

In her dream, Jenny could hear James whispering her name: 'Jenny, Jenny, Jenny.' She was floating in the cool, buoyant body of the ocean. Though her eyes were closed, she gazed into a yellow-red darkness that seemed to stretch for miles. She drifted with the motion of the sea, floating over newly formed waves, listening to the lap, lap, lap of water in her ears.

Suddenly, she was twisted over and engulfed by the roiling ocean. Her arms flailed and spun like a propeller. Disturbed sand rose from the floor as smoke, blotting out the sun, coursing around her as she gulped in salty water, felt it rushing up her nostrils and into her throat. Then she was airborne, wet with spray, slammed carelessly into the shells and grit at the water's edge. She lay gasping, a gleaming bream expiring on the sand. Through the tumult, she heard James again whisper her name: 'Jenny, Jenny, Jenny.' She dozed, prostrate on the sand, only to be brought back by the whispering call: 'Jenny, Jenny.'

She jolted awake, staring up at the ceiling with eyes like dinner plates. 'Jenny, Jenny, Jenny.' She heard James's hoarse, soft voice. She turned towards him. He was sitting up, supported by three pillows. His face was white, terrified. His lips were blue. He could barely breathe.

'James, what's wrong? Oh my God, what's wrong?'

'It hurts, Jen. It really hurts to breathe,' he wheezed.

Jenny lurched out of bed, stumbled and fell to the floor. She got back up and raced for the phone. She called the GP, no answer. She called Wollongong Hospital, but Dr Pryde wasn't available. In desperation, she called an ambulance to take James to hospital. 'I'm sorry, darling, I'm sorry, I had to,' she told James as he was carried out of the house by the ambulance officers with an oxygen mask over his nose and mouth. 'I didn't know what else to do.'

◆

James spent two days in Wollongong Hospital.

Each day, Jenny was bombarded with explanations about procedures and diagnoses. It was difficult to take it all in after such a promising lull. It was almost impossible after Dr Freeman pulled Jenny aside into the patients' lounge and said quietly, 'Expect the worst, Jenny.'

X-rays had revealed a significant bleed into James's chest from the mesothelioma. Dr Freeman's registrar managed to drain some of the fluid, but James's breathing remained laboured. He required oxygen to help him breathe and morphine for the pain. He was sent home with both. Community nurses came to visit every day to check on his progress and to provide instructions to Jenny about how to keep James comfortable.

'So, this is our life from now on,' she thought.

PART VI

Chapter 59

After polishing James's statement for a few weeks, Viviana had a version with which she was comfortable. She drove down to Kiama to have James sign it. She was surprised at how thin he was. She needed to get things moving. The next day, still tired from the long drive, Viviana presented his case at Shaw & Fletcher's weekly asbestos team meeting.

'Thanks, Gary,' she said after he invited her to summarise the new case for the team. He continued to sit uncomfortably close. His volatile cologne was suffocating. 'The new file involves a 67-year-old retired builder called James Henderson, who's recently been diagnosed with mesothelioma. He had exposure in Scotland as a fitter and turner, then in Disaster Gorge, then in Henry King's Riverwood asbestos cement factory and finally from King's asbestos cement products for decades as a builder.'

'You've got to be kidding!' said Carlo Saccheri. 'Hard to think of a better case. In fact, I can't think of one in all the years I've been here.'

'Thanks, Carlo, but how long has it been? Two years, not even that, since you started?' asked Viviana.

'I don't think that's relevant, Viviana. I know a good case when I see one. Wish I had more.'

'If you keep playing these games, Carlo, anything's possible.'

'What games?'

'I think you know.'

'That's enough,' Shaw interjected. 'Carlo's right, though, Viviana, that exposure history is extraordinary. He could sue anyone.'

'Exactly my point, Gary.' Carlo looked around the table, gloating, until he saw Viviana glaring at him. He looked down again.

'As I was saying,' she continued, 'Mr Henderson's exposure spans multiple periods of employment and involves the usual suspects in Australia. I'm worried, however, about how a court will treat the very heavy exposure in Scotland. I don't know whether it will affect causation. We can't trace the company that employed him there. Probably long gone. So, we have to press on without a defendant we can sue for that period.'

'Just ignore it, Viviana,' volunteered another associate, John Beall. 'You only have to prove that the Australian exposure contributed to his mesothelioma to win. You don't have to prove that the Australian exposure was the sole cause of his disease.'

'That sounds correct, John, but I'm still worried. What if the defendants argue that it was only the early, heavy exposure in Scotland that caused the mesothelioma? What if the court can't decide which exposure was responsible? He could lose. I think it'd be a good idea to get two or three decent expert reports on causation to be safe.'

'Good idea, Viv,' said Shaw. 'Although I wouldn't worry too much about it. You know as well as I do that the case will settle like they all do. V&L and Henry King will pretend to put up a fight and then fold once their expensive lawyers have billed enough fees to pay for the artwork in their boardrooms. They're not going to recommend defending the case. They haven't in the past. They won't now. Besides, it's not up to Henderson to volunteer information about asbestos exposure in Scotland. They're able to find that out themselves! Let them do their worst.'

'You're probably right, Gary,' Viviana replied. 'But I decided not to omit the Scottish exposure from Mr Henderson's statement, as you suggested I do. It smells.' She noticed Shaw colouring. She hoped the comment stung.

'Nonsense. As I said, the defendants can find that out themselves. We only have to prove that the Australian exposure contributed to his mesothelioma. Let's just pay attention to what happened in this country.'

'I suppose so. I'll organise some expert reports on breach, causation and damages. I hope we'll be able to file the statement of claim shortly and settle the case before Christmas. Mr Henderson seemed to be wasting away when I visited him yesterday. Even worse than when we first met him in hospital.'

'Poor bloke. Better get cracking, Viv,' Shaw said. 'Now, what about Mr Baldwin's matter? Nikos, you've been handling that. Why hasn't it settled?'

Chapter 60

Back in her office, Viviana looked over James's statement once more. It was extraordinary, that much was true. And yet she continued to feel uneasy. She couldn't explain why. She knew the odds were that James Henderson's case would be another easy settlement. Knock it over and then on to the next one. Stay aloof, keep your distance, she instructed herself. Law was only about reason, about facts.

She pondered the choice of experts to use, sometimes a problematic part of case preparation. So many self-professed experts had queued up to prove that the dangers of asbestos were known years before the Disaster Gorge mine had opened, it was becoming embarrassing. Everyone claimed expertise about how asbestos caused mesothelioma or lung cancer. There were retired doctors, engineers, industrial hygienists, occupational physicians, even librarians. Viviana was unsure whether they were motivated by a desire to cleanse themselves of their own guilt about being asleep at the wheel while the asbestos industry boomed, whether they wanted to get in at ground level in what could be a lucrative expert witness gig, or whether they were genuine. Perhaps a mixture of all three. She was wary of using the same hacks over and over, but the defendants usually didn't put up a fight, so any expert would usually do. Their reports were mostly the same – a few changes here and there before spitting out a document from a word processor.

Her instinct, in James's case, was to retain the most eminent experts in the Shaw & Fletcher stable to deal with the question of causation. She accepted the team's advice that it was unnecessary to worry about breach of duty. She would initially obtain the 'standard' report from Dr George Phillips, about what was known about asbestos over time and what steps should have been taken in consequence.

Dr Phillips was a retired lecturer in geology from Melbourne University. He purportedly lectured students about dust control and disease prevention from the late 1950s and provided advice to industry on the same topic over this period. As far as Viviana could see from reading transcripts of his evidence in past cases, nobody had ever tested his credentials. If they had, they would have discovered that Dr Phillips had acquired most of his knowledge on dust suppression equipment, masks and warning labels from texts and articles read specifically to become an asbestos litigation expert. She accepted that his reports were well written. They chronicled a sorry tale of neglect in circumstances where effective safety equipment had abounded but been ignored. He provided numerous references, many in obscure journals. Viviana could see that Phillips's aim was to revise history, and to catalogue the developing awareness of asbestos diseases through the prism of hindsight. He didn't seem to care, but neither did the judges who routinely admitted his reports into evidence without objection. Some of Phillips's best work was to extract from Wagner's seminal study of 1960 the conclusion that all asbestos companies from that moment onward should have been aware that slight exposure to any type of asbestos could cause mesothelioma. It was a fiction on which all asbestos litigation was based. It had never been questioned. Viviana hoped it never would be.

Viviana next considered barristers for the case. This raised another thorny problem. She wanted to brief barristers she knew were diligent. She even, at a pinch, would accept those who were competent. Shaw, however, insisted that only barristers from the firm's panel were to be briefed. That panel comprised ten barristers, all of whom Viviana would describe as 'roll your arm over' merchants. They all greased up to Gary Shaw and seemed incapable of making independent decisions.

Viviana dutifully prepared briefs to go out to Geoffrey Sutton SC and Gregory Lucas. She then organised a conference with them in Sutton's chambers later that week.

◆

Sutton's chambers were in the Selborne-Wentworth Chambers complex adjacent to the Supreme Court. The majority of Sydney's barristers practised out of this rabbit warren and had done so since the 1950s.

Viviana walked east over the hill from Darling Harbour, where Shaw & Fletcher was located, and up Martin Place, a more than decent hike in office clothes. She resented the effort she had to make to see barristers she preferred not to brief. The building housing the chambers didn't improve her mood. It was a ghastly monument to poor taste – an architectural style usually reserved for a university engineering faculty.

Sutton had a large room that commanded a view through white plantation shutters to the rugby league club across the street. Inside, by contrast, a polished wooden floor had been put down, over which a vast, Middle Eastern rug was sprawled. Sutton's desk was the size of a ten-seater dining table complete with velvet-cushioned mahogany chairs. One wall was covered from floor to ceiling with books. The other wall had open shelves containing an impressive assortment of glass and ceramic bowls, bottles, vases and urns. The worst offence imaginable (to their owner) was to call them 'pots' (a mistake Viviana didn't wish to repeat). The remaining wall space was taken up with the oils and etchings of celebrated artists. Sutton's desk was covered with an eclectic panoply of objets d'art – a troupe of miniature rodents in brass playing various musical instruments, an ornamental dagger from Thailand, a piece of Huon pine turned into a chrysalis.

When she'd first conferred with Sutton in another case, he'd caught Viviana looking at the objects on his desk. 'Viviana, you're not the first person to be amazed at my collection.'

'It's very ... interesting,' she'd said.

'I work very hard, Viviana, and have for many years. I confess that I've been handsomely remunerated for my endeavours. Art, you see, is my passion. These urns over here are Etruscan. This, over my shoulder, is a Smart. It gives me immense satisfaction when I catch solicitors and clients gawping. Please don't feel embarrassed.'

'I'll try not to,' Viviana had answered. He no doubt thought that, outside, people were commenting on his unique chambers and what a character he must be. In truth, Viviana knew that most, including herself, regarded him as a pretentious wanker.

As she entered the room, Sutton gushed, 'Viviana, good to see you again,' his eyes focused on her chest. 'Please take a seat. You know Gregory, of course.'

'Yes, thank you,' Viviana replied, considering Lucas's starched appearance while recalling his sweaty dance moves at the firm's shame-making party.

'Right, okay then,' Sutton continued in a slightly more professional tone, 'let's get down to business.'

'Gladly,' Viviana said. 'This is my concern. How do we deal with Mr Henderson's Scottish exposure? Will it affect causation?'

'Well, Viviana, I can't see why it would be a problem. It's not the first time we've had a case where there's been an element of asbestos exposure for which no defendant will be accountable. The defendants' lawyers won't do anything about it – particularly if they never find out he had it. We're not obliged to volunteer the information. It's not part of Mr Henderson's case. His case is that he was exposed to asbestos in Australia. That exposure materially contributed to the development of his mesothelioma. The law doesn't require anything more. The Australian exposure doesn't have to be the sole cause, just a cause. What do you think, Greg?'

'That's right, Geoffrey. That's what the law says.'

In Viviana's opinion, Greg was an archetypal yes man. It was like hearing Sutton's echo.

'I do have concerns about this, though,' she persisted. 'You're assuming all asbestos exposure contributed to the development of Mr Henderson's mesothelioma. I thought exposure only put a man at risk of later developing it. Nobody knows how or why the disease starts. How do we know which exposure caused the disease? What about taking fibre type or concentration into account?'

'Look here, Viviana, I've been practising at the Bar for over thirty-five years. I note your concern, but if I say it isn't a problem, it isn't a problem.' Sutton waved a hand airily. 'Everyone knows all asbestos is dangerous, all asbestos causes mesothelioma. So long as the defendants' negligence caused one of these exposures, that's enough. There's not a single judge in the Asbestos Diseases Tribunal who'll find otherwise. Right, Greg?'

'Right, Geoffrey,' said Lucas, nodding his head like one of those bobbing animals people put at the rear of their cars.

'See. Nothing to worry about. And besides, as if those bastards at Jacksons or that other lot at Berry Hall are going to run this case. Relax, Viviana, it'll all be fine. We'll tell you what to do.'

'I disagree. I've read a great deal about this causation question, both the case law and the medical literature. I'm genuinely concerned about the issue in Mr Henderson's case,' Viviana replied. 'I want us to look at it closely.'

'Viviana,' Sutton said after a long pause, 'we've given you our considered opinion. You may be confident that we know what we're talking about.'

He smiled at her, pleased no doubt that he had put her in her place. 'This is what I propose,' he said. 'You should obtain a report on breach from somebody like George Phillips. He's usually all we need. I would then obtain two reports on causation from Mr Henderson's treaters, Dr Haug and Dr Freeman. I then suggest you ask for an additional opinion on causation from Professor Schaffer, the oncologist. Greg will help you draft the letters. I want you to specifically ask them to outline the histories they elicited about Mr Henderson's Australian exposure. I want them to say that, on the balance of probabilities, all the Australian exposures caused Mr Henderson's mesothelioma. I don't think we should say a peep about the overseas exposure.'

'You don't think that will look a little obvious?' Viviana asked. 'Shouldn't we accept it as a fact and mould our case around it? I mean, it's going to come out at some stage.'

Sutton's face suddenly turned the colour of rhubarb. 'How dare you—' he started, spittle at his lips, his voice rising in what Viviana imagined would be a hysterical tirade. There was a knock and the door opened. Barbara, Sutton's long-serving and probably long-suffering secretary, walked in with coffee. 'Oh yes, thank you, Barb,' Sutton said, his voice composed and moderate, his handkerchief dabbing at his mouth. 'Just here, thank you.'

An awkward silence fell as Barbara fussed over the coffee. Sutton sipped as daintily as his pudgy fingers permitted from a porcelain cup. All the time, he glowered at Viviana. After Barbara left, he carefully placed his cup on the desk and cranked up the decibels. 'How dare you question me! This is the way we're going to do it and that's that!' He jabbed repeatedly at Viviana with a woodpecker finger.

'Yes, I think I understand, Geoffrey. You've explained yourself very well. Pardon me, while I take a note of your opinion, so that I may inform Mr Henderson of it if the need arises,' she said demurely.

She opened her notepad and slowly, deliberately, recorded the conversation. She could sense Sutton glaring and fuming. The only sounds were her pen scratching on the paper and Lucas's annoyingly noisy swallowing. When she finally looked up, she was greeted by Sutton's hostile red face. She smiled. 'All done.'

'Good. I'm glad we've sorted that out,' Sutton said with finality. 'Now, back to business. Once you provide us with the expert reports, Greg will draw the pleadings and we can start the claim off and get on with settling the case in the usual way. If there are no further questions, Viviana...? Good. Then that's the end of the conference. Greg, you stay. I want a word with you.'

Sutton and Lucas stood as Viviana closed her folder, pulled her handbag over her shoulder and departed. She closed the door behind her, aware that the two men were probably staring at her buttocks moving under her tight skirt.

Chapter 61

Despite her doubts, Viviana followed Geoffrey Sutton's advice, especially once Shaw reinforced it later that day, explaining that he'd received an 'informative' telephone call from Sutton during which the conference was discussed 'at length'.

James's treating specialists, Drs Haug and Freeman, sent in reports soon after they received the requests. They'd provided many reports in the past and knew what to say.

To obtain a report from Professor David Schaffer, however, Viviana had to organise a return flight from Hobart to Sydney, overnight accommodation in a five-star hotel overlooking the harbour and a hire car to and from Kiama so that the professor could examine James. She figured it was worth it because past experience had taught her that he was likely to be the best expert she was going to get on causation.

Schaffer had been an oncologist in Sydney for decades. Although he'd ceased clinical practice and moved to Tasmania, his medico-legal services were still in high demand on the mainland. Plaintiff lawyers like Shaw loved him. Viviana understood why. She'd seen first-hand how judges were transfixed by him. Tall, authoritarian, handsome, with just the right amount of grey in his hair, Schaffer had a gift for condensing abstruse concepts into simple phrases. His voice was mellifluous, his delivery impeccable. He was quick-witted enough to enjoy the occasional joust with a cross-examiner. Indeed, he was far too clever for most barristers who 'did dust', including, Viviana mused, Sutton and Lucas. The accepted wisdom at Shaw & Fletcher was that he was untouchable in cross-examination. Even though his expertise, as a practising oncologist, had been in malignancies of the blood rather than those of the lung, it didn't seem to matter. Professor Schaffer had read widely on asbestos-related diseases since his retirement and was the published co-author of a textbook on chest malignancies, including mesothelioma, something which guaranteed his credibility. His reports were well written, well researched and precisely referenced. Viviana doubted that anyone ever read the medical articles referred to in his footnotes. She was unaware of any instance where a barrister had seriously challenged his expertise or the validity of his references.

Viviana travelled down to Kiama to be with James when he saw Professor Schaffer. He travelled separately with a driver. She wanted to provide support, but also to have James swear an affidavit so that it could be filed at the same time as the writ. For the first time in a long while, she didn't wear black. It had been a spur of the moment decision. She wasn't sure why, and as she neared Kiama she began to feel uncomfortable.

Jenny wanted to sit with James, but the professor politely waved her away. 'It is critical, Mrs Henderson, that I see the client alone. It will be very straightforward, I assure you.'

'It's all right, Jenny, perhaps we can have a cup of tea in the garden while we wait,' Viviana suggested.

'Don't worry, Jen,' James chipped in.

'Very well, I'll be outside if you need me, dear.'

Viviana and Jenny moved downstairs to the pergola with Tess. 'How many times will James have to be examined?' Jenny asked.

'Once more, possibly twice,' Viviana replied. 'I'll object to anything more than that. But it's important, Jenny, that the defendants examine James so they can't later complain that they weren't given the opportunity to defend the case. I'll insist that any examinations occur here, and the sooner that happens, the sooner the case can settle. That's the plan anyway.'

'Do you think that will happen?'

'Everyone says it will.'

'But what do you think, Viviana?'

'I agree that's the most likely outcome, but I have to be honest, Jenny, I sometimes get worried about how a judge will be able to work out which period of exposure caused James's mesothelioma. It could be one period or a combination of a couple of them or all of them. It's very complicated. I don't want to worry you unnecessarily.'

'I don't think it's possible to worry more than I am already, Viviana, but I appreciate your honesty. We both need to know the truth. Since this happened, I don't believe what I'm told as easily as I once did. I don't like being like that, but there it is. It's why I need to tell you that I don't like your boss – that Gary Shaw fellow.'

Viviana felt uncomfortable. She didn't want to undermine the firm that permitted her to act for people she cared about, like James and Jenny. 'He's very experienced and he's done many good things for asbestos victims,' she managed. That much was true.

'I'm sure he has, but I don't trust him. I can sense you don't like him either.'

Viviana bent over and patted Tess. 'I guess we don't always see eye to eye,' she eventually said.

Jenny smiled at her. Viviana couldn't understand how this woman was able to both unsettle her and calm her down. 'It's healthy to have debate within a legal team to ensure a client gets the best possible advice,' she explained.

'I see. Tell me about Geoffrey Sutton. Is he going to do a good job for James.'

'He's an experienced silk – that is, a senior counsel – in the field. He'll do his very best.'

'But do you like him, Viviana? Do you trust him?'

'Jenny, I can't say any more than I have. He's a leader in the field. He's represented many clients and achieved excellent results.'

At that moment, Professor Schaffer peered down from the verandah above them. 'All finished here. Please come up, ladies.'

◆

After the expert departed, Jenny asked James how it had gone.

'It wasn't at all difficult. He's a very kind, caring man.'

'I hope he was gentle with you.'

'He was.'

'What did he ask you?'

'Am I able to say, Viviana?'

'Yes. It won't be an issue.'

'Well, he first asked me about my illness and when I got sick. Then he asked me about our family life. I felt he was interested in what I said. Before long, I was describing my work history again. That was the only tiring part. I know it's important, but I wonder how many times I'll have to do it before this is finished. He seemed to listen carefully and jotted down a few notes, but I thought his main concern was the Australian exposure. I could be imagining it, but he wasn't much interested in my exposure in the Clyde shipyards. I'm starting to think it has little relevance to my claim. What do you think, Viviana?'

'The barristers don't think it's particularly relevant, James, but you must always answer truthfully when other doctors query you about your asbestos exposure. Don't hide it, no matter what anyone tells you.'

James and Jenny looked puzzled.

'I wouldn't,' James said.

'I know, James.' Viviana smiled at him.

'Then what did the professor do?' Jenny asked.

'He listened to my chest, felt my tummy and took my pulse and blood pressure. As I said, it wasn't tough at all.'

'That's good, James. I now need to go over your statement with you,' Viviana said. 'I've converted it into an affidavit that I want you to swear now in case you become very ill or suffer some type of complication. I don't want to alarm you. It's simply a precaution so we don't have to bother you for a while. I'll serve it when we file proceedings in the court. The only other thing I have to bother you with for the time being is a visit by an occupational therapist to check how much help Jenny and other family members have been providing—'

'Heaps. I wouldn't be here if it weren't for Jenny,' James volunteered, squeezing Jenny's hand.

'I'm sure that's so, James. The OT will ask Jenny all about that. She'll also provide us with an opinion about the future care you'll need. It's all about damages. Trying to get as much money as we can for you. It won't be too difficult. Okay?'

'Fine.'

'Good. Back to the affidavit. Based on the advice of Mr Sutton, your senior barrister, and Mr Shaw, I've cut back on some of the description of your Scottish exposure. Mr Sutton thinks it has nothing to do with your claim against V&L and Henry King Industries. Now, as I said before, we're not trying to hide it. If anyone asks you about it, then you have to tell them. You can read the whole thing quietly to yourself. It's exactly what's in your statement, but I want to draw your attention to the portion about your Scottish work. Here, this is the pared-back version we want to use:

From about 1951 to 1957, I was employed in the shipyards on the Clyde River in Glasgow, Scotland. I worked first as an apprentice fitter and turner and then as a licensed fitter and turner. My employer was a firm called McGlinty & Dunrobin. I worked in ships and in workshops alongside plumbers, boilermakers and laggers.'

Is that okay, James?'

'Yes, I think so. It's the truth even if it's a wee bit shorter than in the original.'

'Excellent. Now, please read through the rest of the affidavit. If you're happy with it, I'll witness you swearing on the Bible that it's true and correct.'

◆

A week after her trip to Kiama, Viviana received Professor Schaffer's report. She forwarded it to Sutton and Lucas. They told her that they were very happy with the conclusion:

Although Mr Henderson may have had some asbestos exposure in the early to mid 1950s when he was employed as a fitter and turner, by far his greatest exposure was in Australia from 1957 to 1994 when he worked in the infamous Disaster Gorge mine and mill, the Henry King Industries Riverwood asbestos products factory, and then for many years as a builder where he used genuine King Industries Limited Fibrosheets on a daily basis. In my opinion, and on the balance of probabilities, this long, intense exposure to asbestos in Australia was the cause of Mr Henderson's mesothelioma.

The occupational therapy report had also come in. Viviana had all she needed to launch the litigation. It wasn't the expert evidence from a gun epidemiologist or some other expert on causation she wanted, but it would have to do.

On 21 November 2002, she commenced proceedings on James Henderson's behalf in the Asbestos Diseases Tribunal of New South Wales. There was no turning back. It was familiar to her, but for James and Jenny it was a leap into the unknown. Viviana thought about what everybody kept telling her – it's a no-brainer; over before Christmas; don't worry. But she did worry. She needed to get a grip and make sure all happened as predicted.

Chapter 62

Returning from court with a piccolo, Bruce Fraser found a pimply-faced mail clerk hovering by his desk.

'How can I help you?' he said.

The clerk startled. 'Fax, from Henry King Industries, with a note from Mr Morahan,' he stammered.

'Okay, leave it on the desk, thanks,' Bruce said, walking into his office, a glass cube seemingly perched in thin air, overlooking Sydney Harbour and the Opera House.

He put the piccolo on his desk, hung his suit coat in the wardrobe and sat down. The note from Morahan instructed him, as usual, to 'Get an advice to the client by 6pm.'

The coversheet to the fax underneath read:

Dear Morahan,
Another one.
Regards,
Charlie Boustead.

Why couldn't Boustead send the fax to him directly? It was very irritating. Not for too much longer, Bruce thought, as he sipped his coffee and looked at the court seal on the attached statement of claim. Filed in the ADT on 21 November 2002. Just this morning, he realised. Plaintiff: James Henderson. Defendants: V&L Ltd and Henry King Industries Limited. Solicitors: Shaw & Fletcher, as usual. Solicitor's reference: VG – Viviana, yet again. This could be fun, he thought.

Fraser binned the coffee cup and read on. The statement of claim was accompanied by expert reports and an affidavit. Viviana will want to finish this one by Christmas, he thought. Why not try to thwart her plans and make her work during the vacation? He wasn't doing anything, so maybe he could make it difficult for Shaw & Fletcher. He chuckled, picturing their anger and how much they'd hate him for it. How much she would have to think of him.

He turned back to the pleadings. God, how many times had he seen V&L and Henry King Industries listed as defendants? They'd been sued so many times before that Bruce imagined receipt of a fresh writ barely raised an eyebrow at their head offices.

They were, of course, large, important companies. Their boards, naturally, considered it appropriate to instruct large, prestigious law firms. While they unquestionably believed their respective law firms were the best in the land, Bruce well knew that the firms were indistinguishable. Both occupied multiple floors in steel and glass towers on Phillip Street. Both had almost 250 partners throughout Australia. Both plundered the university law schools for the brightest students. And both sucked every single molecule of creativity, sympathy and humour from their employees. It was only then that they would be ready for partnership. Bruce knew the game. He believed he could play it.

Jacksons had always enjoyed a very strong association with Henry King Industries. The connection remained solid as the current King Industries chairman, Terry Abrahams, was a firm friend of Paul Morahan, the senior litigation partner. They golfed weekly at the Royal Sydney Golf Club, enjoyed watching the cricket from the members stand of the Sydney Cricket Ground, and liked to organise their holidays around tour dates for the Wallabies. Bruce hoped one day to have the same pull with the company and with other big corporations in Australia. He saw himself as a future managing partner with directorships in several Top 100 companies. One big win for Henry King against the odds was all it required for him to be on his way.

He read on.

Henderson's history of asbestos exposure was incredible. Disaster Gorge, Riverwood – Hang on, Bruce thought, Henderson must have been at the Henry King factory at the time White and Richards did their inspection and also when Peter Mathers started working there. This might be very interesting, especially if Shaw & Fletcher decided to pursue punitive damages, as Bruce was sure they'd been itching to do for some time.

The defence of a punitive damages claim was not, however, the only thing Bruce had been plotting. He'd been waiting for the right mesothelioma case to test his theories on legal causation.

Henry King was paying out millions of dollars every year to plaintiffs and their lawyers and Bruce could see no end in sight. Most cases involved asbestos exposure decades in the past, often with different periods of exposure with a variety of employers. Frequently, Henry King was only responsible for a proportion of a plaintiff's overall exposure and yet it was usually the only defendant sued or one of the few sued. Cases were settled for almost full value without any discount for the fact that asbestos exposure from other sources was also responsible. It was simply assumed that the Henry King exposure contributed to the development of a plaintiff's mesothelioma and was therefore sufficient to sheet home full liability. The company was basically carrying the can for all the 'empty-chair' defendants. To Bruce's black-letter-law mindset, this was wrong. It didn't matter how delinquent King Industries may have been in managing the asbestos problem, it shouldn't have to pay for everyone else's mistakes. He now knew from his witness interviews and discovered documents that V&L Ltd and the Commonwealth and state governments were in it up to their necks.

Sure, mesothelioma was a frightful disease, but plaintiffs still had to prove their cases. They weren't all deserving. Far from it. Their stupid, lazy lawyers should be made to do some work instead of holding their money-grubbing hands out for exorbitant fees. Bruce wanted the circus to stop. He was the man to do it.

He wasn't convinced that any of the usual experts knew how a mesothelioma arose or which asbestos exposure out of many could be incriminated in an individual case. All the scientists knew was that each exposure increased the risk that a person might develop mesothelioma in the future. That risk varied, depending on the type of fibre to which a person was exposed and how long ago the exposure occurred. Blue asbestos was the worst, brown debatable and white – well, there was no good evidence that it could be implicated. The earliest exposures were the most likely to cause the cancer.

Each time Bruce read a new statement of claim, he hoped it would be the long-awaited test case on causation. Was James Henderson the case he was looking for?

As Bruce read the pleadings once more, he felt his heart rate increasing. There was exposure to blue asbestos at Disaster Gorge, the Henry King asbestos cement factory and during decades of work as a builder. This was promising. He turned to the expert reports. Henderson was originally from Scotland. The experts referred to asbestos exposure in Glasgow as a fitter and turner before Henderson arrived in Australia, but dismissed it as irrelevant. Henderson's affidavit was similarly brief. Bruce quickly read between the lines. This sort of subterfuge might appear clever to the clods at Shaw & Fletcher, but it wasn't fooling him for one second. He was disappointed in Viviana for being so stupid. Mr Henderson's Scottish exposure was being deliberately underplayed. The details of that exposure would have to be teased out by the respiratory physician he would engage to examine Henderson. Given the likelihood of this early, heavy exposure together with early contact with blue asbestos at Disaster Gorge and the man's disparate work history in Australia, Bruce began to believe that the James Henderson case could be the perfect vehicle to test his views on causation.

But if he were going to run a test case, he would have to get V&L's solicitors to see it the same way. In the past, that had proved difficult. V&L's solicitors, Berry Hall, saw the history of asbestos exploitation in Australia somewhat differently from Bruce. It was a reconstruction of history that held V&L blameless, and Henry King culpable. Bruce found it hard to fathom. Thanks to his research and witness interviews, he knew all about V&L's dirty past. In his mind, it had a lot to answer for. How could he get its solicitors to see it his way?

Chapter 63

Bruce decided the best course to follow if he was to run a test case on causation in the Asbestos Diseases Tribunal was to meet Lurlene Maguire, the partner in charge of V&L's asbestos litigation at Berry Hall. He phoned Charlie Boustead and received instructions to tee up a meeting. At the last minute, Paul Morahan pulled out, citing an urgent injunction in the Federal Court. Bruce was always happy to take the lead, in fact preferred it, although he anticipated being treated as an underling by his Berry Hall opponent.

Entering the meeting, Boustead told Bruce he had every confidence in him and that he was keen to get stuck into V&L, yet Bruce found himself in the unusual position of having doubts.

He'd frequently wondered what would happen if Henry King sued V&L or even the governments for contribution to all the damages it had been paying out for years. He would have to prove that they were as blameworthy as Henry King for all the mesotheliomas and lung cancers men and women had suffered. His hubris told him that it would be easy, as V&L had supplied the deadly blue fibre that went into the Henry King products, and it was clear that the governments had been in on the whole thing. The counter-argument, however, seemed unassailable. It would be very rich indeed for the largest asbestos products manufacturer in the nation, Henry King, to say that V&L hadn't told it how harmful blue asbestos was or that the governments kept mum as well. He feared being laughed out of court. Everyone knew that Henry King Industries knew everything about asbestos. It didn't rely on the expertise of V&L or the knowledge of the state or federal governments. It made its own decisions. Peter Mathers had said as much. As he sat in the conference room, Bruce suppressed his nagging doubts. Boustead had given him the green light to at least try.

'I think V&L should have minimal financial exposure in this case. Henderson only worked at Disaster Gorge for a year or two. By far his heaviest exposure was at Henry King's factory and from using its products as a builder,' Maguire said.

'That's true, Lurlene,' the V&L in-house counsel, Stewart Renouf, agreed. 'We won't be chipping in more than a nominal sum.'

'Cut it out, Renouf,' Boustead said. 'That's rubbish. First in time, first in line to pay.'

'The science is very clear that the earliest exposures, particularly to blue asbestos, are the most causally relevant,' Bruce argued. 'And you both know as well as I do that V&L supplied Disaster Blue to Henry King's until 1966 and that blue asbestos is the most potent cause of mesothelioma on the planet. Don't forget also that King's was forced to buy your fibre because of the Tariff Board Inquiry in the 1950s.'

'I appreciate that, Bruce, but that's the government's problem, not ours.'

'No, you're missing the point, Stewart – your company exposed Mr Henderson to almost a decade of blue asbestos. First in your mine and second in our products.'

'But no plaintiff has even come close to alleging that V&L is responsible for the blue in your products and I can't see your client cross-claiming against us for supplying blue. Can you imagine the stink, let alone the hypocrisy of Henry King arguing that it relied on V&L to tell it about the dangers of asbestos?'

'Yes, yes, we know all about those arguments,' Bruce replied. 'What you fail to understand is that, if we cross-claim, all we have to prove is that if the plaintiff had sued you in negligence for supplying blue to us, he would be successful. We don't have to establish that we relied on your advice at all. Independent of our duty, your client had a duty to an end-user like Mr Henderson to warn him about the risk of mesothelioma. Do you seriously think Mr Henderson wouldn't be able to prove that the supply of crocidolite to Henry King Industries was negligent?'

'It's about time V&L started operating in the real world,' Boustead added. 'You were experimenting on your own workforce in that regard.'

'Steady on, Charlie,' said Renouf. 'If anyone was experimenting, it was your client.'

'Yeah, with your fibre.'

'This is going nowhere,' Bruce interrupted. 'We know what your arguments are. You know what ours might be. The reason for this meeting is to discuss whether in Mr Henderson's case we can put that disagreement to one side and instead present a united front on the question of causation.'

'What's so special about his case?' Maguire asked.

'You may not yet have noted, Lurlene, that Mr Henderson worked as a fitter and turner in the Clyde shipyards in Glasgow for about five years. That exposure was probably heavy and in confined spaces. My understanding of the epidemiology is that a person's earliest exposure is exponentially more likely to cause mesothelioma than later exposures. In other words, before he came to Australia he was doomed. In addition, the law is that a plaintiff fails if all he can show is that his mesothelioma was caused by one of a number of exposures, any one or more of which were negligent. Mr Henderson will not succeed in proving one or more or all of his exposures were causative.'

'Look, Fraser, that's all well and good, but no ADT judge is going to accept either of those arguments.'

'I appreciate that, Lurlene, but the Court of Appeal might, and that's where we should be going.'

'Appeals are very expensive.'

'So is settling every case without analysis. While you may believe your plan of keeping a low profile and letting Henry King take the running on everything, including settlement negotiations, doesn't need modification, we're here today to tell you it does. If you keep refusing to pay very little, then one day soon we'll cross-claim against you and let a court uncover the whole sordid tale of V&L and asbestos.'

'We're not going to bow to threats.'

'It's not a threat, Lurlene, but a reality. We know that Henry King Industries invariably takes the lead in defending a claim, and what we do usually has the benefit of also assisting V&L, even though V&L never pays a cent for the help. No more.'

'Why not, Bruce? It works well,' Maguire said. 'You love showing us how clever you are – organising the medical examinations, engaging in pointless bickering with Shaw & Fletcher over discovery or interrogatories or whatever, paying over the odds.'

Bruce knew this was true. He also knew that Charlie Boustead was at the end of his tether with this strategy. It was the antithesis of the V&L approach and was costing his client hundreds of thousands of dollars every year. Maguire was a good operator, but Bruce had to push through.

'Lurlene, I realise that might have been the case, but those days are at an end.'

'Is that right?'

Bruce suddenly remembered how annoying he found Maguire. Berry Hall was a breeding ground for intellectual snobs. He had to strike.

'I have here a draft cross-claim against V&L that Charlie's given me instructions to file if we can't reach an understanding.' He reached across the table and slid a copy to both Maguire and Renouf. 'You'll see that the various allegations mirror what I've outlined this morning.' Bruce watched as they flicked through the document.

'This is a bluff,' Renouf said.

'Afraid not, Stewart,' Boustead replied.

'We'd be surprised to learn, Lurlene, that you weren't sufficiently across V&L's discovered documents or hadn't interviewed the major protagonists in its history to know the risks to V&L bubbling under the surface. You've created this defence, this 'nothing to see here' fiction, but I'm guessing you and Stewart know full well that it only takes one case to shatter that illusion, to foment media frenzy about V&L's dark past or to see its share price fall. It's not a threat, as I've said, but a reality.'

Bruce watched their faces as he spoke. They were good, he'd concede that.

'Obviously, V&L is rarely a defendant unless a plaintiff had exposure at Disaster Gorge,' he pushed on. 'Plaintiff lawyers are lazy, you know that. They go for the low-hanging fruit and sue Henry King rather than worrying about having to prove V&L was at fault for supplying blue asbestos to us. We want to make it easier for them to do so. Mr Henderson's case could be the start.'

'What's your proposal?' Maguire asked.

Bruce felt he was making an impact. 'We recognise that this could be difficult for V&L to accept without taking time to digest the draft cross-claim. What we propose in the interim is that you allow us to take the lead as we usually do in organising expert evidence, developing the legal arguments and taking the case all the way to the High Court if necessary. And also that you contribute fifty percent to the cost of all of this.'

'Out of the question,' spluttered Renouf.

'Naturally, if we can settle the case with Mr Henderson for a reasonable sum, one reflecting the risk of failure he faces, then we'll do that – but again on condition that V&L pays half of the settlement.'

'Absolutely not.'

'Matter for you, Stewart,' Boustead said. 'You have until the first day of the hearing, whenever that is, before we file that cross-claim.'

Chapter 64

As he waited for the V&L response to the propositions he'd put to Lurlene Maguire and Stewart Renouf, Bruce Fraser became convinced he'd unearthed the perfect case in which to test his arguments on causation. He would have liked to fight breach of duty as well, but it seemed preferable to limit the trial to one central issue rather than fighting across multiple fronts. The court wouldn't tolerate a hearing that dragged on for weeks when the plaintiff was critically ill.

Even so, Bruce thought it was a shame not to contest breach of duty. Although asbestos was known to cause asbestosis from the turn of the century, mesothelioma had only been shown to be associated with asbestos from the 1960s, and then only from blue asbestos. But judges in the ADT had lumped all asbestos types together and concluded that all were equally dangerous. That was simply wrong.

What peeved Bruce even more was that the courts had found in favour of men with mesothelioma whose only asbestos exposure had been in the 1940s or even earlier, times when mesothelioma wasn't known to exist as a separate pathological entity. How could a defendant protect a worker from a disease that was unknown? The courts' answer was that a defendant was liable if it should have foreseen that its negligence could result in any form of respiratory disease. If asbestosis were foreseeable, then so was mesothelioma. Bruce thought the logic so strained that it smacked of political expediency rather than legal principle. It was a waste of time, however, to challenge this dogma. Bruce was convinced that the lawyers involved in the original test cases on breach of duty had got it wrong. They'd had only one chance and they'd blown it. That's what you got for instructing nincompoops, he thought.

The question of causation, however, was uncharted territory. It had never been subjected to rigorous analysis. Here was his opportunity. If he were correct, and his arguments were successful, then he would be made a partner in record time. He could almost feel the congratulatory pats on the back as he attended his first lunch in the partners' dining room. He wouldn't have to put up with Morahan's infantile jokes anymore. He knew he deserved success. He was very good.

As he emerged from his daydream, Bruce got on to organising the examination of James Henderson by one of the city's leading respiratory physicians, Professor Herbert Parkinson, who also had specialist qualifications in occupational medicine. Parkinson was rarely asked to examine plaintiffs and provide opinions because he was too busy seeing his own patients. He was also very expensive. Bruce liked to use him in special cases where there was a prospect the matter might go to trial. Parkinson's objectivity and independence could not be questioned, although the ADT often tried.

◆

It proved tricky persuading the professor to go to Kiama to see Mr Henderson. It was almost impossible to calm Charlie Boustead down when he saw the bill. But it was worth the aggravation.

Professor Parkinson's report read like a treatise on the causes of mesothelioma. He'd taken a careful history from the plaintiff and examined him thoroughly. The problem, so far as Parkinson saw it, was working out which period of exposure was the culprit or whether all Henderson's exposure contributed to the outcome. The final page of his report read:

Mr Henderson has had four separate periods of exposure in his working lifetime. It is impossible to say whether one, some, or all have been causally responsible for his mesothelioma. Medical science does not yet fully understand the pathogenesis of this rare tumour. Epidemiological or population studies have shown that the risk of mesothelioma is associated with the type of fibre to which persons are exposed, the intensity of the exposure and the time since exposure…

You have asked me whether Mr Henderson's exposure at the Riverwood factory and to Henry King Industries' asbestos cement sheets caused or contributed to his mesothelioma. I cannot say. I do not think medical science can provide an answer. All that can be said is that such exposure increased the risk or chance that he would subsequently develop mesothelioma. It does not mean that it did.

Professor Parkinson referred to numerous epidemiological studies. While he was knowledgeable, he wasn't a qualified epidemiologist. Bruce considered it prudent to obtain an opinion on causation from a proper epidemiologist to bolster Parkinson's opinion. He was aware of several important cohort and case-control studies that were likely to be relevant. He telephoned Charlie Boustead to get approval to identify a suitable epidemiologist to provide a report. If Boustead consented, then Bruce was confident that James Henderson would become his long-sought-after test case on causation. If those fools at V&L would only agree to share the expenses, then his job would be so much easier.

'Charlie, I think we should try and find a real expert this time, you know, some sort of professor at a leading university. Maybe from the States.'

'That's going to cost a bomb, son. You sure it's worth it? What does Morahan say?'

'To be honest, I haven't mentioned it to him yet. I'm sure it'll be fine. Yes, it'll be expensive, but, as you know, I've discussed the need to test these issues with proper experts. This case is ideal. I'm optimistic V&L

will start chipping in at some point.'

'Yeah, I hope so, too. But when the bill comes in from some Harvard professor for a junket to Australia, I have to explain it to the board. I agree we've got to try a few things. We're leaking like a sieve over asbestos. Anything capable of stemming the flow's worth a shot. Keep those greedy, ambulance-chasing plaintiff lawyers honest, I say. Go ahead, Bruce. See if you can find someone. I'll ask a few questions myself.'

Fraser loved working for Boustead. He knew Charlie was desperate to land a blow before he retired. Bruce was going to make that happen.

He wasted no time looking into suitable overseas candidates. His search soon turned up an epidemiologist who'd been lead author on many important articles, including several on the aetiology of mesothelioma. John McGuinness was a professor of epidemiology and biostatistics at Yale University. He'd given evidence for both plaintiffs and defendants across a range of product liability suits. He'd played a key role in successful cases against tobacco manufacturers in the United States. He was the man.

Bruce set his alarm for 3.00 in the morning so that he could contact McGuinness at work, as agreed in an exchange of faxes. With some apprehension, he dialled the number. His heart double-pumped as he heard the trill of the numbers running together as the call went through.

'Hello, John McGuinness.' McGuinness's tone was friendly, warm, assured.

To Bruce's intense relief, McGuinness professed himself happy to take a look at the case, and after a preliminary chat quickly diagnosed the core issue as one of aetiologic contribution – multiple exposures to asbestos and the need to know which was responsible for James Henderson's cancer.

'You see, Bruce,' McGuinness explained, 'that's a common problem over here with asbestos litigation. It's nigh on impossible to work out who's to blame. Epidemiology can only take it so far. You may have read some of my articles on the subject. I get approached regularly to provide opinions on the issue, and I'd be happy to branch out and look at an Australian case. Might get a trip downunder, Bruce.'

'Well, you may need to come out if the case goes to trial.'

'That'd be swell, Bruce. But before we do anything, you'll need to agree to my terms of engagement as an expert. I'm not cheap.'

Fortunately, Charlie Boustead was on the other end of a telephone line when he saw John McGuinness's fee agreement. He gave Bruce a serve, accusing McGuinness of being a bloody Seppo rip-off merchant. Even so, he gave Bruce the go-ahead to retain the American expert. He hoped it was a relatively small price to pay for success.

By early December, after numerous early morning telephone conversations and multiple faxes, Bruce had the report he wanted. He'd also learned more about McGuinness over the course of their exchanges. The professor was a smooth operator. He knew precisely how lawyers and court cases worked. Bruce reckoned McGuinness would need all his smoothness to win over a judge of the ADT. His report was a fine start. He could picture Viviana's face when she first read it. She would have kittens.

McGuinness had written:

Epidemiology has established that the risk of mesothelioma increases with the passage of time since asbestos exposure. This relationship between mesothelioma rate and time since first exposure has been investigated in several studies involving different populations throughout the world. The studies establish that the mesothelioma rate increases according to time since first exposure, t, raised to a power of between three and four (a constant k which by convention is 3.5). The rate is also dependent on cumulative exposure, c, being the product of exposure concentration and duration of exposure. The risk of mesothelioma has been reduced to the following formula:

Rate = c x t^k.

The type of asbestos is also important. Crocidolite has the highest risk for mesothelioma, chrysotile the lowest. The risk from amosite exposure is intermediate.

This formula can be used to calculate the contributions of several periods of exposure to asbestos to the risk of an individual's developing mesothelioma. By adding the sums calculated in this way for each year in which an individual is exposed, the total contribution to risk from all exposures can be obtained. The contribution from a particular period of employment can be calculated by dividing the contribution from that period by the total.

In Mr Henderson's case, there have been unequal relative risks in his various periods of employment because of differences in the intensity of his exposure to asbestos and differences in the type of asbestos to which he was exposed. The relative risk for Mr Henderson's exposure in Scotland, probably to amosite and crocidolite, is two times that from his exposure to asbestos cement building products. His exposure at Disaster Gorge to pure crocidolite has a relative risk five times that when he was a builder and exposed essentially to chrysotile. The relative risk for his exposure to blue, brown and white asbestos at Henry King Industries Riverwood factory is two times that when he worked as a builder.

Because time since first exposure is the major determinant of the magnitude of the risk of developing mesothelioma, the contribution to the risk of developing mesothelioma from his Scottish exposure is vastly in excess of that from his work in Australia, particularly as a builder. Indeed, as my calculations demonstrate, Mr Henderson's exposure in Scotland carries a 73% risk of his developing mesothelioma.

If one were to view the risk of mesothelioma as the equivalent of actual contribution to the individual case, then I consider that, on the balance of probabilities, Mr Henderson's mesothelioma was caused by his exposure to asbestos in Scotland (73% probability).

'Good luck with that, Mr Henderson!' Bruce exclaimed, as he signed off on the letter serving the report. His secretary looked up from her workstation in surprise.

Now that he had acquired all the necessary ammunition to defend the case, Bruce thought it was time to brief a barrister to represent Henry King Industries should the case proceed, as he hoped, to a contested hearing. He wasn't hamstrung in his choice; he could brief whoever he believed was the best and, coming from Jacksons, he could dictate the terms. Most members of the Bar desired a brief from Jacksons. Their smart silver ring-binders were impressive additions to any chambers – a sign that a barrister had made it.

Bruce wasn't a big fan of senior counsel. He considered silks to be generally pompous over-chargers. He preferred to brief a 'senior junior', someone on the threshold of becoming a silk, but who still had the commitment and work ethic to descend into the fine print. Fortunately, there were several to choose from. He needed a person who was unflappable. If the case went to trial, it was likely to get ugly. This type of litigation was highly emotional. It was often intensely adversarial. Jeremy Lawson was just the man for the occasion.

Lawson was forty-two, and a black-letter lawyer like Bruce. He had little oratory flair (unlike himself, Bruce believed) but knew the law back to front. Two years earlier, Bruce had briefed him in a very difficult contractual dispute. He'd been impressed by Lawson's appetite for working long hours, sometimes ringing Bruce as early as 5.00am with a new argument. He could be relied upon to master the facts. The court had found in favour of Bruce's client largely because of Lawson's performance. He proved a formidable advocate simply because he was invariably right. And because he was always courteous, it was never possible to bully or berate him into submission.

What Bruce especially liked was that Lawson didn't come from a long line of lawyers. He couldn't rely on an old-boy network for success. His reputation had been won legitimately. He was renowned for taking on hard cases and arguing them as fearlessly and forcefully as he was able.

Bruce had briefed him several times in the ADT when there was a prospect of a matter going to trial. He remembered a case about bowel cancer, said to be caused by asbestos exposure. It had been hopelessly prepared by the plaintiff's solicitors, but the judge in the ADT had nonetheless got the plaintiff up. Lawson had no qualms about appealing the decision to the Court of Appeal and, when he lost there, appealing to the High Court. The case settled before the High Court hearing for a nominal sum. It was as good as a win. Bruce had been impressed by Lawson's perseverance and the accuracy of his legal analysis.

Most judges in the Asbestos Diseases Tribunal now knew that when Lawson announced his appearance, the matter might be appealed if they didn't get it right. They then spent most of the hearing second-guessing themselves so much that they often got it wrong, with their judgments being 'carted' to the Court of Appeal. For this reason, Lawson wasn't popular in the tribunal. Bruce liked to annoy the judges by briefing Lawson when he could.

Like Geoffrey Sutton, Jeremy Lawson had chambers in the Selborne-Wentworth bunker in Phillip Street. Whereas Sutton was extravagant in his efforts to divine a suitable feng shui, Lawson made no effort at all. His chambers had sufficient shelf space to house his law reports and briefs. His desk had no props. In front of him lay the brief he was working on; perhaps a cup of tea. Nothing else. His only splurge was on a comfortable chair for himself.

Conferences with Lawson were in the nature of brain-storming – all participants free to express their views to reach the best possible tactical solution. That was another reason Bruce enjoyed briefing Lawson. He felt part of the team.

'I think, Bruce, your ideas on causation are worth running,' Lawson said in their first conference. 'My research suggests that a plaintiff can't win on causation if all he can prove is that the defendant's breach of duty increased the risk of his suffering injury. If that's all he can prove, then he's only proving a possibility. As you know, the law requires proof of probabilities, not possibilities.'

'So, you agree Parkinson and McGuinness's reports are sufficient for the argument?' Bruce asked.

'Yes. They're excellent. I also think we should admit breach of duty. I know the client will be reluctant to admit anything, but it should in this case. It won't look good to be running the issue when every judge in the ADT thinks it's a dead duck. This is a case only about causation.'

'I agree. I might have a hard time convincing Charlie Boustead. Perhaps you'll need to speak to him as well. I'm sure Paul Morahan will support it as he knows the futility of running a breach of duty defence better than anyone. I don't know what V&L will do. Probably nothing. Ask you to go first with the cross-examinations and then say 'Nothing further'. I don't know who they've briefed yet. I suppose it'll be one of the usual crew like Gerald Woods, Joel Dangerfield or Pat Sandaver.'

'Probably. My guess is that they'll tell the court that breach of duty isn't admitted, but that they won't contest it either. The plaintiff will tender George Phillips's report and that will be enough evidence to prove breach. Henry King could also do that if Boustead can't stomach admitting that his company breached its duty of care to Mr Henderson.

'After announcing to the court that it won't be contesting breach of duty, V&L will call no witnesses on any issue, let Henry King have all the running on causation and then support our submissions at the end with one exception—'

'Yeah, and that exception will be to argue Henry King is liable for the lion's share of the damages if the plaintiff wins!'

'You've got it.'

'Because Henderson had only two years' exposure in its nice clean mine at Disaster Gorge.'

'That's it,' Lawson said. 'Pathetic, I know, particularly when we all know V&L supplied Henry King with blue asbestos to make its asbestos cement sheets. Unless Henry King wants to have a massive stoush with V&L, I say it should cop it. Leave that fight for another day. Let's focus on causation in Mr Henderson's case.'

'I agree, although I haven't given up hope of V&L joining the party. I'm actually waiting for Berry Hall's response to a recent proposal I put to them.'

'I hope they agree. It's always better to have a united front.'

'Jeremy, what if the plaintiff amends his case to claim punitive damages? They always make the threat. Will an admission of breach of duty make it easier for him to succeed?'

'No, different legal test, although some of the facts will be common. I think we'll be all right if they do it.'

'I really don't want to be stuck in a distracting fight about punitive damages. I'm sure we'll lose at first instance and then I'll get a blasting from the client.'

'They couldn't possibly amend without having a star witness to support the punitive damages claim,' Lawson reflected. 'Any ideas who it could be?'

'I'm unsure, but from what I've gathered from speaking with the old company doctor, Peter Mathers, it's likely to be Russell Dymock.'

'The safety officer?'

'Yes. He left Henry King very disgruntled. I don't know if he has the guts to testify, but he's had years to stew on the way he thinks he was treated.'

'How was he treated?'

'Wasn't taken seriously, as I understand. An officious twerp.'

'I see.'

'And if they do allege punitive damages, I may have some surprises for them.'

'Really? What have you got in mind, Bruce?'

'I've been working on a few things. You know about Ferris. I've used his statement before, but we could possibly use Peter Mathers. He recommended the company cease using blue in 1966 and is convinced it did just that.'

'That would have been a pretty prompt response, given that Biological Effects of Asbestos was only published in 1965.'

'I agree, but what if they kept on using blue asbestos despite saying they'd stopped?'

'It wouldn't be good. Do you know something I don't?'

'I know there are no documents in our discovery contrary to Mathers' version of events.'

'What's the problem, then?'

'Shaw & Fletcher had a recent mesothelioma case where the plaintiff said just that. That Henry King was still using blue after 1966. A Mr Berendetti. It settled.'

'They're not going to call a sick man to give evidence.'

'I suppose not.'

'I wouldn't worry.'

'What do you think Shaw & Fletcher will do when they read Parkinson and McGuinness's reports?' Bruce asked, changing the topic.

'Ignore them. They might try to get their own high-powered epidemiologist, or they might just rely on Schaffer and Mr Henderson's treating doctors. I mean, they've got plaintiffs over the line before. That's what we're banking on. They might get anxious for a while, but then go about it the same way they always do.'

'I suppose that's right. We're running a point that goes against the accepted wisdom down at the tribunal, so they'll have whoever the judge is onside right from the start. No judge down there's going to upset the apple cart – that's for the Court of Appeal.'

'You say Geoffrey Sutton and Greg Lucas have been briefed, Bruce?

Well, they're not what you'd call intellectual powerhouses, so I can't see them thinking up some clever counter-plan to McGuinness and Parkinson. My guess is that the one we'll need to watch out for is the human blancmange, Gary Shaw. He's a wily bastard. You never know what trick he might pull.'

'We'll see what happens at the next directions hearing in the tribunal. We'll also find out then who the trial judge will be.'

◆

Within forty-eight hours, Bruce Fraser had obtained instructions from Charlie Boustead to inform the tribunal that Henry King Industries would not be contesting breach of duty. Boustead had fumed at the suggestion to admit breach. 'There's no way, son, that this company will ever admit that it was negligent!'

Chapter 65

'Predictably, they've unearthed Mr Henderson's asbestos exposure in Scotland and basically made it the issue in the case,' Viviana said at the asbestos team meeting after she'd been served with the expert reports of Professors Parkinson and McGuinness. She wished she'd trusted her instincts and not agreed to minimise the Scottish exposure. It would have been out in the open sooner, and might even have been overlooked because there would have been no suggestion of a cover-up or the need to dig deeper. Regardless, it was just a bad look and she hated being associated with it.

'Couldn't you have told the bloke to shut up about it or say that he couldn't remember?' Carlo Saccheri said.

'No, I could not!' Viviana said. 'What sort of question is that?'

'I'm sure Viviana explained the nature of his case to Mr Henderson, and let him know all its, let's say, special or trickier features,' Gary Shaw cut in, the sickly odour of a new cologne wafting over those around him. 'He'll have known what to say.'

'The truth.'

'Of course. That's what I meant.'

'Didn't sound like it.'

'Come on, don't be so testy, Viviana. We know you're concerned about this issue.'

'As I've said before, the Scottish exposure shouldn't be a problem so long as his Australian exposure made a material contribution,' John Beall said. 'As I understand it, you already have expert evidence saying that.'

'Yes, I do. But McGuinness is a new witness. A real expert in this area. The Scottish exposure is a big confounding factor.'

'It can be as much a confounder as they want,' Beall argued. 'It won't matter if the Australian exposure contributed to Henderson's mesothelioma, even if it was only a minor contribution. That's the law.'

Beall was an irritatingly smug lawyer, but Viviana accepted he was one of the smarter ones at Shaw & Fletcher. 'Did the Australian exposure actually contribute to the mesothelioma or did it just put Mr Henderson at risk of contracting it?'

'That's a distinction without a difference,' Beall replied, 'but I appreciate it might be an issue for some.'

'Like whom?' Viviana asked.

'I still think Jacksons will settle. They're only serving this evidence to scare us,' Shaw said. 'Oldest trick in the book. Trying to create some panic, hoping to drive the settlement dollar down. Well, two can play at that game.'

Viviana turned to her flabby employer. What was he thinking? She really wanted to find a heavyweight professor of epidemiology herself. She had contacts at the American Trial Lawyers Association in Chicago who could help her find someone to match Professor McGuinness's expertise.

'What I'm contemplating is that, if needed, we amend the statement of claim to include punitive damages. That'll put the wind up the bullies at Jacksons.'

'But that will prolong the hearing and make it some bigger-than-Ben-Hur production. We don't have the time to do that,' Viviana said. 'I assured James and Jenny that it would all be over by Christmas. As I recall, so did you, Gary, when you met them in the hospital.'

'I know. I haven't forgotten. No, I think we'll still be on track. What I propose is that if they don't pay the right price when we take Henderson's evidence, which must be soon, we apply to amend to claim punitive damages as late as possible – you know, before the rest of the trial proceeds. Henry King's lawyers will jump up and down about it, but the judge will allow it. Their barrister will ask for an adjournment, which will be refused because of Mr Henderson's parlous physical state, and they'll be railroaded into settling for a huge sum.'

'I like it,' Carlo enthused and one or two others at the table nodded.

'I wouldn't want to be Charlie Boustead having to explain to the Henry King board how thousands of dollars were wasted paying for a useless report from some US academic,' Shaw continued.

'I'd still like to obtain a report from an epidemiologist, just in case,' Viviana said.

'I appreciate your concern, Viviana, but I don't think it'll be necessary. Get Schaffer to respond to their reports. He'll say the right thing.' He put his fat hand on her thigh. The muscles throughout her body tensed. Only the colour suffusing her throat and face betrayed the horror she felt. 'I know a few people to look up who may be able to assist when the time comes to establish punitive damages,' Shaw said, smiling. Viviana was certain he could feel her tension through his pulpy fingers. 'If it comes to that. No need to pull the exemplary damages trigger just yet though.' His hand remained on her thigh like a tarantula, as if challenging her to brush it off. Viviana took a deep breath. She didn't want to make a scene and give him some horrid victory. Eventually the tarantula scuttled away when Shaw realised she was going to outlast him.

After the meeting, Viviana needed some air. She went down the elevator and walked the long distance to the Botanic Gardens. She sat down on a bench in the middle of a field-like lawn. Across the grass there was a grove of ancient trees, and beyond that, a glittering curve of Sydney Harbour. A pod of joggers sped by, the murmur of their breathless conversation hanging momentarily near Viviana before the breeze sent it on. She had always wanted to be one of those joggers, but work came first. It was now who she was.

Back at the office, Viviana shut her door and telephoned Geoffrey Sutton to ascertain his take on Henry King's expert evidence. Unsurprisingly, he agreed with Shaw's approach of asking Schaffer to reply. He suggested, however, asking a local epidemiologist, Tom Forgan, to provide an opinion.

While Forgan had worked with Schaffer on various research projects and had impeccable credentials, he was a poor witness. Viviana had seen him give evidence several times. He mumbled and blithered his way through his testimony. The transcript of his evidence always read badly, although if you looked carefully between the 'ums' and the 'ahs', the occasional pearl could be found. He would be no match for McGuinness, but it was something.

'I'm not sure this is the right case to allege punitive damages, but it might work,' Sutton said. 'Gary knows what he's doing, so let's run with it. If we threaten to drag the hearing out long enough, the defendants are bound to settle because otherwise their plans for the Christmas holidays will be disrupted. Heaven forbid if they have to cancel their flights to Whistler. I strongly doubt we'd even need to call anyone to prove exemplary damages. They'll settle before it comes to that.'

Viviana wasn't keen on the punitive damages strategy. It was a flimsy and obvious stunt. How could she get it ready in time when it wasn't even clear that they'd need to do it? Dr Smith would have to be contacted and prepared for evidence. It was an ill-conceived rush job. Exactly what she'd told James and Jenny Henderson wouldn't happen.

Viviana requested a report in reply from Professor Schaffer and Dr Forgan. Schaffer confirmed his view that James's Australian exposure was the overwhelming cause of his mesothelioma. Tom Forgan concurred. The battle lines had been drawn. It was time to go to court.

Chapter 66

The day before the pre-trial directions hearing, Viviana received a telephone call from a tearful Jenny, explaining that James had suddenly deteriorated after seeming to have been on the mend. Jenny told her of his urgent admission to Wollongong Hospital and Dr Freeman's grim prognosis. Viviana immediately rang Sutton, who agreed it would be necessary to ask the tribunal to take James's evidence that week and to expedite the hearing as soon as possible. He advised Viviana to obtain evidence from a doctor familiar with James's condition so that the defendants couldn't complain about being ambushed by an expedited hearing. Viviana followed his advice and obtained a short report from the oncology registrar at Wollongong Hospital to the effect that James could die any day and that it was vital his trial be heard without delay. Viviana felt everything was in readiness for an expedited hearing, apart from the punitive damages claim, which she wished to avoid if possible.

She rang to update Jenny.

'We've drawn Judge Byrnes as the trial judge,' Viviana said. 'She's a good draw. Very pro-plaintiff.' She didn't tell Jenny that her judgments were overturned in the Court of Appeal more often than any other judge of the Asbestos Diseases Tribunal.

'We'll ask her tomorrow for the hearing to start this week. James will need to give his evidence within a day or so.'

'So soon? I don't know if he'll be ready.'

'It'll be all right, Jenny. We have to do this now.'

'I'll tell him. I'm worried, Viviana, he's so weak.' Jenny was sobbing. Viviana dreaded these conversations with family members; she hated upsetting them further.

'It's only one day, Jenny. Judge Byrnes will make sure James is comfortable. She's a kind and compassionate person.' Viviana hoped that were true.

She had only met Belinda Byrnes two or three times. The first time was at a function hosted by the Women in Dust Lawyers Association, and Viviana had found her to be a sour-faced, wide-bottomed, complaining woman. She didn't like her.

She hadn't run a case before her, though and relied on Gary Shaw's assurance that she had a heart of gold. He knew her well. They'd been at university together. She was a fine lawyer, he told Viviana, but let her emotions cloud her judgment and rule her decisions. Viviana now understood the dilemma. Lately, she was struggling to suppress her own emotions.

'Belinda Byrnes was the first female judge appointed to the ADT,' Gary had explained. 'That's quite an achievement, being appointed to the bench in such a demanding area of the law, particularly for someone who came from nothing.'

'She didn't strike me as being all that happy,' Viviana had countered.

'Well, she was hoping for something else when she was appointed.'

'What do you mean?'

'As a barrister, Belinda did 'compo' work. Made pots of dough. When there was talk of the government curtailing that work with statutory reforms, Belinda had her brother, a Labor mover and shaker, lobby hard for a judicial appointment. She was expecting the Court of Appeal. She got the ADT.'

'I see.'

'It was a slight in her mind, I guess. You'll warm to her, Viviana, I guarantee.'

'Really?'

'Yes, although I accept she can be prickly and, as you've seen, she has a few distinctive features which can be off-putting.'

'Like her teeth?'

'Yes. She copped a lot of teasing at uni about her appearance. Childish stuff like 'Bucky Beaver' and much worse. You can't blame her for having a chip on her shoulder. But once you get over that, you'll find she's a real softy. If you get on her good side, you'll find she'll always get your punter up.'

PART VII

Chapter 67

The lawyers in the courtroom bowed as Judge Byrnes, resplendent in kaftan-like purple and black robes, walked in, squared her shoulders and sat down, scowling at the audience. 'Call the first matter,' she ordered.

Her tipstaff called, 'James Henderson and Henry King Industries Limited and another.'

Greg Lucas stood up. 'May it please the court, I appear for the plaintiff.'

'May the court please, I appear for the first defendant, Henry King Industries Limited,' said Jeremy Lawson.

'And I appear for the second defendant, V&L, your Honour,' Pat Sandaver announced.

'Yes, very well. What's this all about, Mr Lucas?' Judge Byrnes asked.

'Your Honour, Mr Henderson has mesothelioma. He is very ill and may not survive a month. We would ask the tribunal to take his evidence as soon as possible, hopefully this week, and to then expedite the hearing of this matter.'

'Mr Lawson?'

'Your Honour, this is the first we've heard about this. We're not ready to take a hearing date, yet.'

'Mr Sandaver?'

'Our position is the same. This comes as a surprise.'

Lucas leaned over Viviana as she whispered instructions in his ear. He straightened. 'Your Honour, my instructing solicitor served the plaintiff's notice of motion on my learned friends' solicitors yesterday. They were also served with an affidavit by my instructing solicitor annexing a report from a Dr Yeong, which indicates that Mr Henderson is in a bad way—'

'Bad way? Is that a medical term, Mr Lucas?'

'Ah, no, your Honour—'

'Then what is the situation? Have you copies of the affidavit and report for me?'

'Yes, your Honour.'

'Then hand them up.' Lucas gave the documents to the tipstaff, who gave them to the judge's associate who in turn passed them to the judge. She quickly read the documents. She leaned over to talk to her associate before informing the barristers, 'This is clear-cut. Mr Henderson is in extremis. I am told by my associate that we can take Mr Henderson's evidence on Wednesday or Thursday morning. What day suits?'

'Wednesday, your Honour,' Lucas said.

'Mr Lawson?'

'I object, your Honour. We haven't seen either of the documents. We're not ready.'

'Mr Lawson, I'm told by Mr Lucas that your solicitor has already been served with the documents. If counsel tells me from the bar table that that has occurred, then I accept him at his word. Are you suggesting Mr Lucas is a liar?'

'No, your Honour, but—'

'You know as well as I how precarious the situation can be with mesothelioma patients. I won't be delaying the hearing of this matter. I propose taking Mr Henderson's evidence on Wednesday and to continue with the rest of the witnesses next Monday. You'll just have to fit in.'

'Your Honour, taking the plaintiff's evidence this week is one thing, but we cannot possibly be ready by Monday for the balance of the trial. We have an international expert to call.'

'What? An international expert? Why have you got an international expert? Who is it? What are the issues in the case?'

'The expert is Professor John McGuinness. He is an epidemiologist from the United States. His evidence goes to the question of causation—'

'Causation? How can causation possibly be in issue? I've read the pleadings. I've read the affidavit. Mr Henderson was exposed to your client's products, wasn't he?'

'That is what he says, your Honour.'

'Look here, Mr Lawson, I've read Mr Henderson's affidavit. Pretty convincing. I don't know how you propose refuting his claim. It's a matter for your client, of course, but I will not have this court's time wasted by needless arguments about matters not genuinely in dispute. Do you understand what I'm saying?' The judge fixed her black eyes on Lawson in his dapper navy suit.

'Yes, I do, your Honour. I understand perfectly what you're saying. At this stage, I can inform the court that my client admits Mr Henderson was its employee at Riverwood as alleged. Henry King does not dispute breach of duty of care or exposure to asbestos although it does not formally admit breach. It puts in issue causation, the extent of his exposure to asbestos and quantum but does not dispute the diagnosis of mesothelioma.'

'Thank you, Mr Lawson. I hope commonsense prevails after today and that my preliminary views are heeded. What about your client, Mr Sandaver?'

'Same position as Mr Lawson, your Honour.'

'I can't say I'm surprised. Now, Mr Lucas, I assume we'll need to travel to see Mr Henderson. Will we be taking his evidence at his home or in hospital?'

'At his home.'

'Very well, if your solicitor could liaise with my associate with the details, I'll order that Mr Henderson's evidence be taken at 10.00am on Wednesday 9 December 2002. Nothing further? Very well, I'll see you all on Wednesday.'

After the hearing, Bruce Fraser assured Jeremy Lawson that he hadn't received James Henderson's affidavit.

'It doesn't matter, Bruce. Byrnes would have made the same orders even if Lucas said it had never been served. You know how it goes – railroad us through, trying to force a settlement by catching us unawares.'

'Yeah, I know.' Even though Bruce had seen it before, each time he experienced the tribunal's aggressive, unfair approach, he found it unsettling. It was as if the judge considered everyone associated with Henry King to be evil.

'The main thing, Bruce, is to ensure you have McGuinness and Parkinson teed up for next week or the week after to give evidence. I don't care if you have to fly McGuinness and his wife out and keep them sustained on lobster mornay and Roederer for a fortnight. We must be ready to run by Monday if we're to make a go of the causation defence.'

Chapter 68

After his discharge from hospital, Jenny set James up in the loungeroom in the adjustable electric bed the occupational therapist had organised, so that she could keep a close eye on him during the day. James required oxygen via nasal prongs. He couldn't lie flat. If he did, his breathing became tortured, broken by horrifying wet, gurgling sounds. Meals and toileting were an ordeal. James was far too weak to manage them alone. He suffered drenching night sweats. Every morning, the sheets needed to be changed and James's pyjamas washed. After a shower, James was even more distressed. He panted like a dog for almost thirty minutes before his breath came under control. The oncologist had prescribed liquid morphine for his pain. Every three to four hours, Jenny asked him whether he needed any pain relief. He usually did.

Jenny didn't know how she would have coped without their daughter Kate's assistance. They took it in turns to feed James and to help him into his special lounge chair while they stripped the bedclothes and put on fresh sheets, though James would only let Jenny wash him and take him to the toilet. When he felt well enough, Kate would read to her father, and both women tried to keep his spirits up with chat and reminiscences.

Jenny had little time to indulge her emotions. But at night, when all the tasks were complete and James lay aslant his levee of pillows, she sometimes allowed herself to wallow in her overwhelming sorrow. She feared those quiet times when she had time to herself to think.

♦

On the Tuesday before the hearing, Sutton, Lucas and Viviana called in to see James and to outline what could be expected the following day.

'Hello, Mrs Henderson, I'm Geoffrey Sutton, your husband's senior counsel,' Sutton said at the door. Jenny looked at him blankly. He was a porky fellow with a put-on voice. 'This is my junior, Gregory Lucas.' He motioned to his rear where a middle-aged man wearing steel-framed spectacles stood smiling at her. He seems remarkably old for a junior barrister, Jenny thought.

'Pleased to meet you, Mrs Henderson,' he said with too much cheeriness.

'May we come in?' Sutton asked.

'I'm terribly sorry, where are my manners?' Jenny said. 'Come in, please.' She let them pass her into the house. 'Hello, Viviana,' she said with more enthusiasm.

'Hello, Jenny. I'm sorry this has been a rush, but we need to take James's evidence as soon as we can.'

'It's okay, Viviana, we understand.' She turned to James, propped up in the bed in the loungeroom. 'James, Viviana and the barristers are here.'

His blue eyes opened and peered over the rim of the oxygen mask. He gave a slight nod in greeting.

'Hello, Mr Henderson. Geoffrey Sutton, barrister.' The silk laid his hand on James's shoulder.

'Hello,' James said in a whisper.

'Now, Mr Henderson, I'm sorry to bombard you with so much when I've only met you, but I need to ensure that you have an idea about what will be happening tomorrow.'

'Do what you have to do,' James said, pulling the mask down to speak.

'The judge, her staff and all the lawyers will sit around your bed here.

I'll sit as close as I can to you. The judge's tipstaff will take your oath to tell the truth and then I'll tender your affidavit as your evidence-in-chief. I'll then supplement the affidavit by asking several further questions, some of which may be difficult. I apologise in advance for these questions, but they're necessary so that the judge can get a feel for what you've been through.'

'What questions are you going to ask?' Jenny interrupted.

'I'd rather not say as I only want your husband to have to answer them once.'

'You're not going to upset him, are you?' Jenny said.

'Only to the extent necessary, Mrs Henderson. I assure you, I have to do it.'

'If you say so.'

'I do, I'm afraid. Now, after I finish, the judge will hand over to the barristers for the two defendants, who will cross-examine you.'

'That's what I'm really worried about,' said Jenny. 'I don't want them bullying James and upsetting him.'

'You needn't worry about that, Mrs Henderson. I won't allow it and neither will the judge. Judge Byrnes may seem hard on the outside, but deep down she's like a marshmallow. She will be extremely sympathetic to James's plight.'

'I hope so. I want this over as soon as possible.'

'It will be. I doubt whether James's evidence will take more than two hours. Once he's finished, he doesn't need to be bothered again. Viviana will keep you posted about events, but the reality is that tomorrow will be James's one and only involvement in the trial.'

Sutton went on to outline the sort of issues that were likely to be explored by the barristers for the defendants. Towards the end, he said, 'I anticipate that they'll ask you a lot of questions about your exposure to asbestos in Scotland.'

'How am I meant to answer those questions?' James asked quietly.

'You must answer the questions truthfully, although I don't see how your Scottish exposure can be relevant. I'll probably object to the questions and, you never know, the judge may disallow them. But if she allows the barristers to ask you those questions, then you must respond truthfully. Remember, however, the most important exposure was in Australia. Do you follow? Exposure in Australia. Remember that and all will go smoothly.'

'Okay.'

'We'll be here tomorrow morning about an hour and a half before everyone else arrives. I'll go over a few of the topics again so that you're prepared. Try and get a good night's sleep.'

'That's unlikely, but we'll do our best,' Jenny said.

◆

Jenny and Kate had James fed, washed and back into a clean bed by 8.00am the next day.

'You're looking quite spry this morning, dear. Are you ready for your morning dose of morphine?'

'I don't want it, Jen. I need to have my wits about me for the cross-examination. I'm ready to go right now.'

'They'll be here soon enough. I'll get you a tea.'

As promised, Sutton and the rest of James's legal team arrived at 8.30am. Viviana helped Kate and Jenny arrange the furniture so that all participants, especially the barristers who had to ask questions, would be in a close arc around James's bed. Viviana manoeuvred James's comfortable armchair to the centre of the arc for the judge. Jenny pressed the buttons on the control for the bed and propped James up at about 60 degrees. By the time these arrangements were in place, Judge Byrnes arrived. Sutton hadn't had time to ask a single question in rehearsal, although he leaned over James when Viviana announced the judge's arrival. 'It's about your Australian exposure, Mr Henderson. Remember, that was the worst of it,' he said, nodding as he spoke, encouraging James to nod in unison. 'Good man.'

At the door, Viviana watched as the judge emerged from a government Holden Statesman with her associate and tipstaff. The court reporter pulled up moments later in a beaten-up Toyota Corolla. Belinda Byrnes appeared less than pleased at seeing Sutton's sleek 7-series BMW hogging the Henderson's driveway.

The judge wore what could never be considered a smart or fashionable suit. It was a drab affair with pin stripes like bars on a prison window. The matching blouse did nothing for her complexion. In any event, when Viviana greeted her at the door and ushered her into the Hendersons' home, none of the participants were overly interested in her attire. They were interested in her mood. It would affect how smoothly the morning progressed. Sutton's car had clearly not been helpful to her Honour's temper, but when she entered Jenny and James's loungeroom, her ill humour quickly disappeared.

Viviana watched as she bustled over to James and introduced herself to him, clasping his outstretched hand with both of hers. 'Good morning, Mr Henderson, my name is Belinda Byrnes. I'm the judge who'll hear your case. How are you feeling? Are you comfortable? Are you up for it? Please tell me if you can't do this today.'

'Pleased to meet you, your Honour,' James said, holding the mask away from his face. 'Yes, I think I'll be able to manage.' He smiled. The grey spittled skin around his mouth threatened to tear like wet paper.

'You make sure you let me know if you need a break at any time. There's no hurry. You don't need to tire yourself out.'

James nodded. The judge turned to Jenny. 'You must be Mrs Henderson. Hello, I'm Belinda Byrnes.' She moved towards Jenny, again gripping her hand with both of hers, pulling herself in towards Jenny.

'Pleased to meet you, your Honour.' Jenny found the judge's proximity unnerving, the judge's teeth almost making contact with her nose. 'Can I get you a cup of tea, water, or something?' she asked.

'I wouldn't mind a cup of tea, if it's not too much trouble.'

'No, not at all. Would anyone else like tea or coffee?' Jenny asked the other lawyers in the room. Before she knew it, she was preparing seven cups of tea and coffee. She didn't mind. She needed the distraction.

Forty-five minutes later, Viviana looked out the window and saw two more cars parking in the street outside the Hendersons': Jeremy Lawson's silver C-class Mercedes and Pat Sandaver's Alfa Romeo Spider. She watched as they checked out Sutton's BMW, muttering, 'Wanker,' simultaneously to each other, then they went to the door for her to let them in.

'Viviana, would you mind letting the judge know we need a few minutes before we come in? In any event, we have to wait for Lurlene Maguire,' Bruce Fraser called as he shut the door of Lawson's car.

'Here she is now,' Viviana observed. 'I'll only ask the judge for five.' She went inside.

Bruce turned to see Lurlene Maguire stepping clumsily along the grassy footpath and down the driveway in her high heels. 'They could have built a decent footpath,' she complained. 'Has anyone announced our arrival to the judge?'

'Viviana Glosioli is doing that now,' Bruce replied.

'Well, let's get on with it, I don't want to be stuck down here all day,' Maguire said.

'If it's all right with you, Lurlene, we'd like to discuss the case before going in,' Bruce said.

'What is there to talk about? Your client's responsible for Mr Henderson's mesothelioma and, if it's not prepared to settle with him, then we should simply get on with it.'

'That's very amusing. Do you think that Mr Henderson's exposure at your mine and mill made no difference to his outcome?'

'Yes, I do, as a matter of fact. The exposure he received at Disaster Gorge was a drop in the ocean compared to the exposure he had in Scotland or at your client's hands.'

'We're still waiting for your client's response to our offer and cross-claim.'

'You'll be waiting a very long time, Fraser.'

'The trial starts on Monday. Our offer in relation to the cross-claim expires then.'

'We're aware of that fact.'

'Very well, but before we go down that path, don't you think we should try and resolve this before cross-examining Mr Henderson?' Bruce said.

'It's up to you.'

'Now, settle down you two,' Jeremy Lawson interjected. 'It's in both our clients' interests to resolve this matter on a commercial basis before committing to the time and expense of a trial and, no doubt, an appeal. We think that there's a good defence in this case based on causation, as I'm sure Bruce has told you. The plaintiff should be willing to resolve the case for a heavily discounted sum to reflect the risk that he could lose – that's if he's been properly advised – and, yes, I realise that's a big assumption to make.'

'What do you have in mind, Jeremy?' asked Sandaver.

'Well, I think the claim's worth about $450,000 at full value. A fifty percent discount's appropriate to reflect the chance that Mr Henderson could lose. So I think we should offer up to $225,000 plus costs to resolve the matter. Bruce has told me that he has instructions to contribute fifty percent to any offer up to that amount. What's your position?'

'Well, I'd need to discuss it with Lurlene, but—' Sandaver commenced.

'V&L is never going to contribute fifty percent to any settlement in this case. It may be persuaded to offer a token sum such as $50,000 all up, but that's about it,' Maguire asserted.

'That's ridiculous, Lurlene,' Bruce expostulated.

'That's my client's position.'

'And what does your client's barrister think? Pat?'

'He does what he's told,' Maguire insisted.

Bruce thought that although V&L might still agree to contribute fifty percent if the case ran on Monday, rather than risk a cross-claim by Henry King, that prospect seemed increasingly hopeless given Maguire's comments. Anticipating such a stance, Charlie Boustead had given him instructions to try to settle the case up to $225,000 with whatever contribution he could get from V&L.

'Right, if your client is only prepared to contribute $50,000 towards any settlement, we'll take that. I propose that we make a once-and-only offer to settle for $225,000. Henry King will contribute the remainder of the amount. Agreed?'

'That's fine. But understand this, Bruce: V&L isn't contributing to costs. Its $50,000 is what it will contribute to both damages and costs.'

'I understood that the first time, Lurlene.'

'Well, now that that's agreed, I think I should relay the offer to Geoffrey Sutton and find out if we're going to proceed with taking Mr Henderson's evidence,' Lawson said.

Viviana had been watching the antics from the door. Jeremy Lawson walked up the steps towards her.

'Hello, Viviana. Nice to see you again. Could I please speak to Geoff Sutton?'

'Come in, but you should probably ask the judge for the time.'

'Thank you, I will.' Lawson walked into the loungeroom. 'Good morning, your Honour. Good morning, everyone. Your Honour, would you mind if I have a moment with Mr Sutton? It may shorten the matter.'

'Very well, Mr Lawson, but not too long.'

'Why don't you step outside to my office, Jeremy?' Sutton said with a guffaw, beckoning Lawson to accompany him onto the verandah. Lucas went with him. Before they knew it, Viviana was outside as well. 'This is between barristers, Viviana, if you don't mind.' Sutton's tone was dismissive.

'I do mind and it's my case. I want to hear what Jeremy has to say.'

'This is most unusual,' Sutton huffed.

'It's okay, Geoff, but I'll have to get Bruce Fraser in as well.'

'If you must.'

Once Bruce was on the verandah, Sutton shut the sliding glass door behind him. 'Yes, Jeremy, what can I do for you?'

'I thought, Geoff, that before we embark on this hearing, we should at least try and settle the case.'

'Very well, what have you got for us?'

'The defendants are prepared to offer no more than $225,000 plus costs in full and final settlement of Mr Henderson's case.'

Sutton rolled his eyes. 'You're kidding! The case is worth more than double that, and you know it.'

Viviana looked furious.

'Maybe, Geoff, but we think Mr Henderson is going to lose on the question of causation. We think he should be prepared to settle his case on a heavily compromised basis as a consequence.'

Bruce watched Sutton's reactions carefully. It was evident that the silk wasn't sure whether Lawson was joking. He shouldn't have been in any doubt. Jeremy Lawson wasn't the type of man who played games.

'I'll pass the offer on, Jeremy, but I don't hold out much hope.'

Sutton, Lucas and Viviana went back inside. Bruce saw them speak briefly with the judge before walking down the hallway to another room in the house. Bruce and the others waited on the deck, watching the waves rolling onto the beach. Twenty minutes later, Sutton and Lucas returned. Sutton's fat face was inflamed. He was clearly angry about something. When Sutton informed them of his side's response, Bruce understood why.

'That offer is rejected, Jeremy. I am instructed to put in reply an offer of $500,000 plus costs to settle the matter.' The counter-offer was plainly not Sutton's decision.

Everyone knew that Sutton was a settler. His nickname at the Bar was 'Arthur Phillip', after the first settler of the colony in New South Wales.

Sutton was retained by solicitors on a 'no win, no fee' basis, which meant that if a plaintiff lost, he wouldn't be paid. Like all other barristers briefed on the same basis, Sutton did not like running cases because he could end up devoting a great deal of his time towards a matter for which he might never be paid. Bruce also guessed that Sutton was avaricious. The expensive toy sitting in the Hendersons' driveway was a give-away.

Sutton had probably been told what to do by Gary Shaw, Bruce thought, pulling the strings from a distance. He suspected that James Henderson would accept whatever advice he was given by his solicitors, even if it meant rejecting an offer that he was happy to accept.

'Well, Geoff, that is disappointing,' replied Lawson. 'As I said before, the defendants aren't prepared to make any further offer.'

'What? You're not going to negotiate any further?' Sutton asked.

'That's right, Geoff. Even if I wanted to negotiate further, I can't. My instructions are clear.'

'I'll pass that on to the client and my instructing solicitor,' Sutton said and went back into the house with Lucas.

When Bruce looked into the loungeroom, he couldn't see Judge Byrnes. She must have been asked to leave James and his team alone for a period. He could see Viviana and Sutton talking intensely to one another. Lucas stood to the side, hands in his pockets. Mrs Henderson and her daughter appeared fretful. Sutton and Glosioli turned to Mr Henderson, each speaking in turn to him. They saw him shake his head slowly. Bruce knew before Sutton reappeared that the answer was no. The case was going to run. Bruce had what he wanted. He couldn't now or in the future be criticised for not genuinely trying to settle first.

Fifteen minutes later, the lawyers were stationed around James's bed. The court reporter had set up microphones on the floor in front of the barristers. He had attached another microphone to the railing on James's bed. Jenny and Kate stood in the kitchen, observing, in case James needed attention. The judge sat in the centre in James's lounge chair, her court book open before her to enable her to make notes. The judge's associate sat upright on the edge of the kitchen table, leaning over a narrow console.

Judge Byrnes looked at the court reporter, who nodded to her. She then stated that the case was ready to proceed. 'I think you may begin, Mr Sutton.'

Geoffrey Sutton was seated on a sofa. He found it difficult to lean forward to ask questions and he couldn't rock himself out of its deep hollow. As a consequence, he was compelled to semi-recline in the seat, propping his notebook on his protuberant belly. 'I tender the affidavit of James Henderson, your Honour,' he said.

'Very well, that will be exhibit PX1.'

'I object, your Honour.' Lawson said loudly.

Judge Byrnes turned to her left and gave Lawson an admonitory sneer. 'Mr Lawson, I'm not having Mr Henderson's time wasted by needless objections. I take it you do not object to the affidavit going into evidence, but rather you object to parts of the affidavit. Is that correct?'

'Yes, your Honour.'

'Well, I'll deal with those objections in court next week. I will allow it in on that basis. Satisfied?'

'Yes, your Honour.'

'Mr Sandaver?'

'No objections, your Honour.'

'Yes, Mr Sutton, proceed.'

'Thank you, your Honour. I have a few additional questions I would like to ask Mr Henderson. Mr Henderson, can you hear me?'

'Yes.' James said. His mask was around his neck for the examination. The judge motioned to the court reporter to adjust the microphone. He got up and moved the microphone closer to James's head.

'Mr Henderson, we all know that you have developed a mesothelioma. Would you mind telling her Honour what that diagnosis has meant to you?' Sutton said.

Lawson and Bruce looked at each other. *What sort of question is that?* Bruce thought.

James was equally concerned. 'It's been devastating,' he began. 'It's been the worst thing that's happened to me. It's horrible. I can't breathe. It's like I'm drowning, slowly going under. The pain is unbearable.' Chinks were appearing in his composure. He looked to Viviana to be crumbling.

'Thank you. And could you also tell her Honour what it's like knowing you are going to die from the mesothelioma?'

'I object!' Jeremy Lawson almost yelled. 'This is outrageous, your Honour.'

'What's your objection, Mr Lawson?'

'Your Honour, what type of question is that to ask a person in Mr Henderson's condition? There's no dispute from my client that mesothelioma is a dreadful disease. There's no dispute that Mr Henderson's life expectancy is severely curtailed. There can be no dispute that to be given the diagnosis and to be told its consequences must be a terrible experience for a person,' he said passionately.

'Yes?' asked Judge Byrnes.

'It's bad enough to be given the diagnosis, but do we all have to sit here and see a grown man lose his dignity by being made to cry by Mr Sutton?'

'That is absolutely unwarranted, your Honour!' Sutton burst out. 'These are legitimate questions to ask Mr Henderson.'

'You see, Mr Lawson, while your sentiments are admirable, unless your client is prepared to admit that Mr Henderson should receive the maximum damages for pain and suffering, I'm afraid I have to let Mr Sutton continue. How else am I to determine how badly he's been affected by his diagnosis than to hear him tell us how he feels? I allow the question.'

'Mr Henderson, could you please answer my question,' Sutton said.

James's response was barely audible. There were long pauses between sentences as he wept and told his mournful story. Jenny and Kate dabbed at their streaming eyes, balled tissues clutched in their hands. It was an insensitive thing to do to a dying man, Jenny thought, but she couldn't intervene.

After James had struggled through a series of almost identical questions from Sutton, the judge called a short break. James's thin face was awash with tears, snot trailing from his nose, his hands reaching for something to put over him to cover his shame. Jenny was weeping uncontrollably. Judge Byrnes needed the time not only to go to the bathroom, but to regain her own equanimity. Viviana sat in her chair staring vacantly ahead.

Thirty minutes later, everyone was seated again in the loungeroom. 'Mr Lawson, you may commence,' the judge said.

'Thank you, your Honour.' Jeremy turned to James. He looked into his red rheumy eyes. 'Mr Henderson, my name is Jeremy Lawson. I am the barrister representing Henry King Industries Limited. I'll try to be as brief as I possibly can.' He spoke in a measured, kindly tone. He didn't know it, but James had already formed a favourable opinion of him after he objected to Sutton's questions. Bruce knew from experience that Lawson approached difficult cross-examinations with courtesy rather than charging in aggressively. It was the best method for extracting concessions. 'I would like to first ask you about your exposure to asbestos in Scotland. You haven't referred to exposure in Scotland in your affidavit, but it is the case, isn't it, that you were heavily exposed to asbestos while working on the shipyards in Glasgow.'

'Yes, that's correct,' James admitted.

'Objection!' Sutton shouted, far too loudly for the small room.

'Mr Sutton, I fear you may have been a little late with your objection,' Judge Byrnes said dryly.

'Sorry, your Honour, but I do object to this line of questioning.'

'On what basis?'

'Relevance, your Honour.'

'Yes, Mr Lawson, how is this possibly relevant? You admitted earlier that your client doesn't dispute the fact that Mr Henderson was exposed to asbestos while working at your client's factory and to its products while he worked as a builder. If that remains the case, and I am hardly going to allow you to withdraw such an admission, how is this evidence about Scotland relevant?'

'Your Honour, it goes to the question of causation.'

'Causation? In what possible way? Based on my initial perusal of Mr Henderson's affidavit, causation seems a dead issue. I stress that this is only a preliminary view, but you're well aware that judges of the tribunal have accepted for years that proof of exposure to asbestos at a defendant's hands is enough to sheet home liability against that defendant. Convince me that this approach should not be taken in Mr Henderson's unfortunate case.'

'We will argue, your Honour, that the Scottish exposure was the most probable cause of Mr Henderson's mesothelioma. At the very least, we'll argue that the tribunal is unable to determine which of his multiple exposures was responsible for his mesothelioma.'

'That sounds a tad far-fetched to me, Mr Lawson. Surely, all asbestos exposures are causally responsible for a man's mesothelioma, and the law, as you know, permits a plaintiff to recover damages in full if he proves that a defendant's exposure materially contributed to his mesothelioma. It doesn't have to be the sole cause.'

'We say, your Honour, that you will not be able to be satisfied that the defendants' exposure made a material contribution to the development of Mr Henderson's mesothelioma. My questions about his Scottish exposure go directly to the point. It's a point that's supported by expert evidence, as your Honour will hear next week, if the matter proceeds.'

'Of course it's proceeding next week. I haven't heard any application by you to adjourn the further hearing of the matter. Now, I'll let you continue with these questions, but you're on a short leash, Mr Lawson. I'm not convinced that the questions are relevant. I'll consider next week whether I shall strike out the evidence you obtain from Mr Henderson on his Scottish exposure. Proceed.'

'Thank you, your Honour. Now, Mr Henderson, let us return to your exposure in Scotland...'

Two hours later, James's evidence was complete. Despite Sutton's protestations, Bruce was impressed by Jeremy Lawson's having elicited a detailed history of very heavy exposure to asbestos during the time James worked in Scotland. Lawson was able to lead James along a path on which he admitted that his Scottish exposure was far heavier than anything that he'd experienced in Australia. Despite Pat Sandaver's objections, Lawson also managed to have James agree that his exposure to blue asbestos at Disaster Gorge was 'like a snowstorm' and 'at least ten times heavier' than his exposure as a builder.

Sandaver, in trying to reclaim some lost ground, cross-examined James about his exposure at the Riverwood factory. He agreed that it was extremely dusty during the time he worked in the blower room and tide mill. Sandaver then committed the cardinal cross-examiner's sin of asking one question too many. 'So, Mr Henderson,' he said, 'that exposure at the Riverwood factory must have been at least as heavy, if not heavier, than your exposure while working at Disaster Gorge. Is that right?'

'It was dusty, I agree,' James answered haltingly. 'But having put up with the Disaster Gorge mill, I never expected to see blue asbestos again. And when I worked at Riverwood, I had to empty bags and bags of Disaster Blue. The bags had V&L's name stencilled on them. I couldn't believe my eyes when I saw that stuff again. It was as if I was never going to get away from it. And that's the fibre I had to shovel into barrows and down chutes while at Henry King's. The same dirty dust I had to work with in Western Australia. Of all my exposure in Australia, breathing in V&L's blue asbestos was the worst.'

'I object to the second part of Mr Henderson's answer to my question, your Honour. It was non-responsive and should be struck out,' Sandaver requested.

'No, Mr Sandaver. I think Mr Henderson's answer was perfectly responsive to your question. I allow it.'

'You idiot,' Bruce heard Lurlene Maguire say sotto voce beside him.

'I beg your pardon. What was that?' Judge Byrnes inquired, angrily looking around the room. There was no response. She turned to James and spoke kindly. 'Thank you, Mr Henderson, for all your patience this morning. I'm sure I speak for all lawyers here today in wishing you all the best. The matter is adjourned for further hearing on Monday.'

Jenny rushed to James to try to make him comfortable. She pulled the oxygen mask up over his nose and mouth. 'It's all right, Jenny. I'm okay,' he managed.

Once the defendant lawyers, the judge and the judge's staff left the house, Sutton gave a de-briefing to Jenny and James. 'That went very well, Mr Henderson, very well, indeed,' he proclaimed.

Jenny and James didn't appear as convinced. 'Is there any chance of settling, now?' Jenny asked.

'There's always a prospect of settling, Mrs Henderson. But the money has to be right.'

'They're not offering you enough, James,' said Viviana. 'We've spoken to Gary Shaw about the offer made by the defendants. He's adamant that it's not enough. You'd be selling yourself short if you accepted that sort of money. I agree with him. The judge is very sympathetic. After hearing your evidence, she's likely to give you close to $500,000 in damages.'

'I hope you're right, Viviana,' James said through his mask.

'As I said at the start today, you'll not have to do anything again during this hearing, Mr Henderson. It's plain sailing from here on,' Sutton said. 'What do you think, Greg?'

Greg Lucas had said little the whole day. Viviana thought that was preferable. For some reason, Sutton always came with Lucas. It was like a comedy act.

'I agree wholeheartedly with Geoffrey. You have a strong case, Mr Henderson.'

'You rest up, Mr Henderson. Viviana will keep you informed of developments next week,' Sutton said.

'Thank you, we trust you to do the best for us,' Jenny said. Kate looked at her mother from the kitchen, shaking her head. Jenny felt ill, a sense of foreboding gnawing away in the pit of her stomach.

Chapter 69

Viviana Glosioli found herself staring at a squirrel-like creature playing a violin. She sat in front of Sutton's desk looking at the silly figurine while James's legal team discussed tactics the day after James gave his evidence. Gary Shaw insisted on attending, 'to ensure that appropriate strategies were deployed', as he told Viviana during their walk to Phillip Street.

'I've read the transcript of Mr Henderson's evidence and I think it went as well as could be expected in the circumstances,' Shaw said. 'I mean, we couldn't do much about concealing his Scottish exposure, particularly after he blurted out in great detail how bad it was. Sounds as though he found a new friend in Jeremy Lawson when you look at the number of concessions he made. Anyhow, it's too late now. We always knew it could come out if the defendants dug a bit. Shouldn't, however, change a thing about causation and our general strategy.'

'I agree, Gary,' said Sutton. 'I'm not sure he could have been prepped any more thoroughly about the importance of the Australian exposure. He was aware what was at stake. I made that plain. We'll need to send the transcript of his evidence to Schaffer and Forgan to make sure they're on board.

'Viviana, would you please attend to that?'

The hypnotic pull of the violin-playing rodent was broken. 'Of course. I'll do it right after we're finished here.' She felt as though the conduct of her case was being taken away from her. Shaw and Sutton were far too confident about the outcome. While Judge Byrnes was likely to get James up, it could be different in the Court of Appeal. That was where Lawson would take it if he lost. And settlement seemed improbable.

'I think the next thing we should do is serve a proposed amended statement of claim on the defendants' solicitors late on Friday afternoon,' Shaw said. 'So late that they have no chance of bringing the matter before the court to complain until the hearing recommences on Monday. What do you think?'

Sutton mulled over the suggestion while sipping from a bone china teacup. 'You mean the exemplary damages amendment?'

Shaw nodded.

'I don't think it really matters when we serve a proposed amended statement of claim,' Sutton continued. 'It's so close to the continuation of the hearing that the defendants will scream blue murder whether we give it to them today or tomorrow afternoon. But let's serve it on them as late as possible. That way, they'll squirm about it all weekend. Lawson can forget about the events on his social calendar, that's for sure. Henry Kings will be pooping themselves about exemplary damages. They'll settle for full value on Monday, mark my word. They don't have the stomach for bad publicity.'

As she watched the three men laugh, Viviana decided she wasn't yet prepared to see her case derailed. It was one thing to talk tough about punitive damages. It was another thing altogether to have evidence to establish the legitimacy of the claim. You needed to have clear, convincing evidence. She knew what evidence she would want to call – Dr Smith's, for a start. If he were to be used as a witness, she needed to connect his visit to Disaster Gorge with James's work there at the same time. It could be dynamite against both Henry King and V&L. But it needed careful planning. Not this. For one thing, James hadn't even been asked about Smith's visit during his evidence because nobody had seriously believed the punitive damages claim was coming, except, of course, Gary Shaw.

'I have one question,' she said. 'How do you propose proving exemplary damages against Henry King?'

'I was waiting for that.' Shaw smiled. 'You see, what I know and nobody else knows is that I've tracked down the former safety officer at Henry King's Riverwood factory, Russell Dymock. He's prepared to give evidence against them. And what he'll say will be like a bomb going off. He says that, in 1966, he was present when Henry King's doctor, Peter Mathers, told the factory manager, Bill Kruger, that crocidolite asbestos was lethal, and that Henry King should stop using it immediately. He also knows that crocidolite was used for at least three more years despite Mathers' advice.' He looked around the room as if for applause.

'My God, Gary, that's sensational. Henry King can't possibly fight the case after they hear that sort of evidence. Mr Henderson had exposure to its products when blue asbestos was still in it.'

'I know, Geoff. And they'll be even more anxious to settle when they see a few news reporters sitting in the audience taking notes.'

Then it dawned on Viviana – that's why Dymock hadn't wanted to talk to her. Shaw had told him not to. He wanted it to be a surprise. She watched him smiling widely at his cleverness. He couldn't help himself. 'I'm going to organise for Dymock to come in and speak with you tomorrow so that you can call him as your first witness on Monday. What do you reckon?'

'Sounds an excellent idea to me,' said Sutton.

I bet it does, Viviana thought. He was clearly feeling more comfortable about the prospects of settlement and charging cancellation fees for the one to two weeks he'd set aside for the hearing. There was nothing quite like the feeling of being paid in full for work not actually performed, Viviana surmised.

'And after we call this Dymock fellow, we can call George Phillips to give evidence about the developing awareness of the hazards of asbestos exposure and how it was known by 1960, or at the latest 1965, that blue asbestos was particularly dangerous at low levels of exposure.'

This was nonsense, Viviana thought. She knew Gary Shaw loved trials by ambush, but it was at serious risk of backfiring in this case. 'Surely, we need more and better evidence than Dymock's hearsay or Dr Phillips's invention. As you know, Gary, I've spent days working on Dr Smith's statement, getting him ready to give evidence in an exemplary damages claim. He needs to be contacted and brought over here if we're serious about this. What's more, his evidence could justify a claim for exemplary damages against V&L as well.'

'No, we don't need him. Dymock and Phillips will be fine. Henry King is the soft target. They'll pay if we put the blowtorch on them.'

'Who's Dr Smith?' Sutton asked.

'He was the chief medical officer for Western Australia from the 1950s. Knows all about Disaster Gorge, Dr Mathers, the dangers of crocidolite. He'll make a great witness.'

'We're not using him, Viviana, so drop it,' Shaw cut in. 'Dymock will be a shock to them. They'll fold like a deck of cards.'

Viviana wasn't ready to concede. 'This undermines all the work I've done. We may only have one shot at punitive damages. Shouldn't we do it properly, if only for Mr Henderson's sake?'

'No. That's my decision. Move on. We've got work to do.'

'Look, Viviana, I think Gary's right about this,' Sutton said. 'The strategy is to generate a bigger settlement. I don't think we need to worry about the actual claim being litigated in full – that's for another day. They won't know it's coming and so they'll be very keen to settle.'

Viviana sat back glumly in her chair. Perhaps she was too cautious, simply not suited to or agile enough for high stakes litigation. She nodded acceptance.

'Very well,' Shaw said, turning to Lucas. 'Greg, would you draw the amended pleadings alleging punitive damages? If you can do that by this afternoon, Viviana will be able to serve it by fax tomorrow at, say, 4.00pm. We should be looking at settling the case for close to $600,000 plus costs. What a result that would be! A new record.'

Chapter 70

Bruce Fraser sat at his desk reading the proposed amended statement of claim Viviana Glosioli had faxed to him. The pages were still warm. 'Shit! Shit! Shit!' he said as he read the underlined amendments. 'The bastards.' He looked at his watch and saw that it was 4.15pm. Too late to ask to have the matter listed before Judge Byrnes. 'Shit!'

Bruce knew that if the Asbestos Diseases Tribunal allowed the proposed amendment, he was looking down the barrel of being the solicitor acting for Henry King when an award of punitive damages was first found against the company. That would be quite the achievement, he thought. A distinction he would prefer not to have on his curriculum vitae. But that wasn't the main problem.

He faxed the proposed amended statement of claim to Charlie Boustead and Jeremy Lawson. He then rang Lawson. 'This could be a disaster, Jeremy. I don't think we have any choice but to settle. Henry King won't want us to run a case in which there's a risk of going down for exemplary damages. I think we can fight the claim, but the client won't want to. And that's what I'm angry about.'

'Why?'

'What this ploy means is that we'll never be able to run a good causation argument. Every time we try, like in this case, they'll lob up a claim for exemplary damages and the client will settle. Shit!'

'I know this is blackmail, Bruce. And the client shouldn't give in. I still think the causation argument is sound. I realise it will be risky, but the question of punitive damages won't arise if Henry King wins on causation. It may have to suffer the adverse publicity from a finding of exemplary damages at first instance, but once the Court of Appeal overturns Judge Byrnes's decision on causation, nobody will remember.'

'That sounds logical, Jeremy, but I doubt whether Charlie Boustead will have the stomach to gamble the company's reputation.'

'What reputation? What on earth does it have to lose?'

'A great deal of money, I suspect. Besides, there might have been a few questions you could have asked Henderson in cross-examination that might have helped.'

'Such as?'

'Well, I think he was at the Henry King factory when White and Richards did their report on safety there; you know, when they said that all was good if the company got dust down in a couple of places, which happened.'

'Yes, I know about their report.'

'Henderson might also have been there when Dr Mathers started medical surveillance of the workforce.'

'So, if Henderson was, in fact, there at the same time, we could prove that Henry King was acting reasonably and that an award of punitive damages would be inappropriate.'

'Exactly.'

'That's a shame, but it doesn't detract from the main game – causation.'

'There's also the issue about Henry King continuing to use blue asbestos throughout the 1960s. That's another one of their allegations in this amended statement of claim. As you know, we say it was reasonable to stop using it in 1966 and not before. We also say Henry King did not use it after 1966.'

'Bruce, let's think this through for a minute. There's not a single discovered document supporting the claim that blue asbestos was used after 1966. Didn't you tell me that you personally worked on culling documents pursuant to the document retention policy? There's no smoking gun. Nothing exists anymore.'

'Okay, okay. Then who's their key witness? It could only be Russell Dymock. If that's correct, then why don't we use Mathers to counter him? I can contact him to see how he's travelling and whether he's capable of giving evidence. We could serve his statement. Then there's the Ferris statement I've prepared and one or two of the directors signed very helpful statements before they died – you know, Gideon and Gordon King.' Bruce realised the tightrope he was walking, and how it made him uncharacteristically nervous.

'I think we can decide what evidence we might call after we see what happens next week. I really want the issue in the case to be quite narrow if at all possible – causation only.'

'I agree with you; it's why this ruse is so irritating. I think we can win this case on causation. I don't want the exemplary damages claim to put that at risk.'

'Why don't you ring Charlie Boustead and see if you can get him to come to my chambers for a meeting at 5.00pm.'

'Okay, I'll see what I can organise. He may have already gone home; it's Friday after all.'

◆

Charlie Boustead was still at his desk when Bruce telephoned. He was reading the amended statement of claim, and sounded irate. 'This is no good for my health, son. Every day, the prospect of a stroke gets nearer. Tell me you've got good news. I need it.'

Later, when Bruce sat next to Charlie as Jeremy Lawson outlined his plan, Charlie's face looked redder than usual. The cauliflower ears from his rugby days jutted out from his head like two bits of chewed gristle. It was as if he had been mauled. That's certainly how he sounded to Bruce.

'You're telling me that Henry King should bat on regardless of the threat of punitive damages. Is that what you're saying?'

'Yes, Charlie. That's exactly what I'm saying. Surely, it's time to draw a line in the sand and stop being blackmailed by these plaintiff lawyers.'

'That's all well and good, Jeremy, but what if these allegations are actually true and that the company knew, in fact, that crocidolite could cause mesothelioma, even with minimal exposure, in the early 1960s, or that even after Biological Effects of Asbestos it still went on using the blasted stuff for another three, four, five or so years? Let's cut the crap – if that's the truth, then it's almost criminal.'

'I agree, it would be disastrous, Charlie. But the plaintiff has to prove that Henry King actually turned a blind eye to the danger. There has to be proof that senior management or the board at Henry King specifically knew that crocidolite was dangerous in the early 1960s before the Biological Effects of Asbestos or that after Mathers' warning in 1966, it continued to use it. How are they going to prove this? Well, I can answer that question. They will call George Phillips, the retired geologist, to give evidence on the first point. He's the only witness dealing with the developing awareness of the dangers of asbestos exposure. I think I can deal with his evidence. After all, he's no doctor and he was never there at the time making decisions about asbestos. They would need someone credible, not Phillips. As to the second point, I'm not sure who they could call as a witness. There's no document saying that Henry King continued to use crocidolite after 1966, so they'd have to call an eye witness. To have any sway that witness would need to know more than Dr Mathers or be in senior management. I can't imagine they have either. It remains open for us to maintain that Henry King always acted promptly and responsibly.'

'Well, Jeremy, that sounds plausible, but do you think a halfwit judge in the ADT or those Einsteins in the Court of Appeal are going to buy it?' asked Boustead. 'I have my doubts. Besides, I wouldn't like a precedent set where every plaintiff from here to eternity can claim exemplary damages. The company's liability for exposing people to asbestos is big enough as it is without adding to it.'

'What if the burden of any award for exemplary damages could be lessened or shared with another company?' questioned Lawson.

'What do you mean?'

'Well, Henderson gave pretty clear and damaging evidence that he was exposed to V&L's Disaster Blue fibre while working at the Riverwood factory. We know we can prove from shipping records that V&L supplied all its crocidolite to Henry King for use in asbestos cement products. If the plaintiff succeeds in proving everyone ought to have known about the dangers of minimal exposure to crocidolite from the early 1960s, then surely V&L is in the firing line just as much as Henry King.'

'But it will never agree to contribute anything towards punitive damages, if that's what you're driving at. It's hard enough getting them to contribute a dime in an ordinary case. And we've already met with them threatening a cross-claim, which they appear to be ignoring.'

'Yes, but what if an agreement could be reached at a higher level? What if, for example, the chairman or one of the board members politely explained the situation to his counterpart at V&L and suggested that Henry King was adamant it will be cross-claiming against V&L for the supply of Disaster Blue?'

'I like that idea – bypassing the lawyers,' Bruce chipped in. 'If the chair finds out about Henderson's evidence and about the offer to contribute fifty percent or face a cross-claim, he may well tell Renouf and Maguire to change their tune.'

'Yeah, I can see that it might work,' conceded Boustead. 'They have until Monday anyway to accept or reject our offer. There's not much time to make this work.'

'If V&L agrees behind the scenes, so to speak, to pay half of any award of punitive damages, then it may soften the blow to Henry King if the judge awards them to Henderson. If you obtain such an indemnity in this case, we can press on with the causation defence. At worst, we can review the situation during the trial. It may be necessary to pay a premium to settle the case, but that's better than bailing out now. What do you think, Charlie?'

'I'm all for batting on, don't get me wrong. I guess after some type of media furore, the dust will settle so to speak – no pun intended – and it'll be business as usual. I'm happy to talk to the board about this, but it's not going to be easy.'

'Good. Very good. You have to give it a try as soon as possible, Charlie.'

'Yeah, I get it.'

'And who do you think, Charlie, they might call as their eye witness to prove punitive damages?'

'I bet it's Russell Dymock, the former safety officer,' Boustead said. 'Bob Frew tells me that Gary Shaw made contact with Dymock last year in the hope of calling him as a witness at some time. Shaw, of course, believes we're all in the dark about this. But there are only a few former Henry King health and safety employees around. They tend to know each other's business.'

'Dymock? That's what we suspected.'

'He's a fool, according to Frew, although Bob thinks he could say anything. The best we have on Dymock is whatever he signed off on with his regular memos to Bill Kruger about factory conditions. His views were pretty non-committal or ambiguous, as I recall. You should probably have a look at them, Lawson.'

'I'm aware of that bundle of documents, Charlie, and I'll look at all the other discovered documents we have where Dymock's mentioned. There'll be a few. If they're truly going to call him, we may be able to do something to defend the punitive damages claim right at the outset. I'll see what I find. He's hardly what I would call a lynchpin in the case, but if they think he is, then let's see how he fares. Of course, I'll still object to the amendments to plead punitive damages, but they'll be allowed. Byrnes isn't going to stop now and permit an adjournment. Once she builds up momentum, she's like a runaway train, particularly if she warms to a plaintiff. And there's absolutely no doubt that she liked James Henderson. I mean, so did I. He's a lovely man and it's an absolute tragedy what's happened to him. But we all have a job to do here. And the law is the law. So far as the legal principles relating to causation are concerned, I think they're on our side.'

'Sometimes, you even have me convinced, Lawson,' said Charlie Boustead. 'I'll let you know how I go with the board. Another thing – shouldn't we be mobilising our own evidence on punitive damages? Bruce has done a mountain of work on the issue, talking to all the old directors and even Peter Mathers when he was compos.'

'We think we should wait until next week to see who they call and how it goes. The best outcome is that it goes nowhere and we don't need to do anything so that the case remains only about causation.'

'I guess that's fair enough. Listen, you two keep on working on this case as if it's going to run to judgment. I'll let you know if there's any hiccup with the board. I'd love to see Gary Shaw's face or Sutton's ugly dial when they realise on Monday that we're not giving up. Henry King's liable for a lot of things, but it ain't liable for Henderson's mesothelioma.'

'I hope we get the chance to prove that, Charlie.'

Chapter 71

Although she'd been in the Asbestos Diseases Tribunal many times, Viviana loathed the place. It comprised two floors of six courtrooms in a sandstone building in Castlereagh Street. The whole place exuded a negative energy. She wondered what it would be like to have months to live and to spend your precious time in this building. Fortunately, on the Monday at the resumption of the hearing, James Henderson was spared the trauma. Viviana looked at her surroundings. The courtroom was overburdened by dark wooden panelling and an absence of natural light. Judge Byrnes was perched behind a fortress-like structure, her head and shoulders barely visible. With her jaw clenching and unclenching, she resembled a beaver poking up from the wooden parapet of its dam.

At the long bar table below the gnashing judge sat Geoffrey Sutton SC, Gregory Lucas, Jeremy Lawson and Pat Sandaver. The barristers were dressed in their traditional black robes and wore wigs of varying shades of grey. Five metres behind the bar table was another long table at which Viviana and the other instructing solicitors sat. The two tables were fenced in by banks of trolleys stacked with numbered A4 ring binders containing discovered documents, clinical records, expert reports, journal articles and extracts from textbooks. At the back of the court were two rows for interested spectators. Gary Shaw sat in one of the chairs alongside three female journalists, identically kitted out in tailored shirts and skirts, with faces painted by the same heavy brush.

'Now, Mr Sutton, you have an application of some sort, I'm told by my associate,' said Judge Byrnes. Apart from her teeth, her features were hard to define in the gloom of the courtroom. There was, however, no mistaking her mood. Forbidding.

'Yes, I do, your Honour. If I may hand up a document.' Sutton passed some papers to the tipstaff. 'Your Honour will see that the document is a proposed amended statement of claim. The only relevant changes are those marked up at the end of the claim. Your Honour will see that the plaintiff wishes to amend his statement of claim to allege punitive damages against Henry King Industries Limited, the first defendant.'

'Has this document been served on the two defendants?'

'Yes, your Honour. It was sent to the solicitors for both defendants on Friday afternoon.'

'And what is your client's position, Mr Lawson?'

'We object to the amendment or, if the amendment is granted, then we apply for an adjournment so that we may properly investigate the allegations and, if necessary, obtain evidence to meet them.' Lawson was forthright in his objection but displayed little or no emotion. Viviana was impressed by his self-control, which so far had ensured that the trial hadn't descended into a running battle with the judge. That was the mode by which most cases in the tribunal were usually heard.

'I assume, Mr Sandaver, you have no objection to the proposed amendments?'

'Indeed, I do object to the amendments, your Honour,' Sandaver declared. Viviana thought he had lost some of the coolness he'd had the previous Wednesday. His face was flushed. Lurlene Maguire sat behind him, also looking less relaxed than the previous week.

'Why do you object, Mr Sandaver? How can this amendment possibly affect your client?' the judge asked aggressively. 'If you're wasting the court's time, Mr Sandaver, there will be serious consequences.'

'In light of Mr Henderson's evidence last week about the use of Disaster Blue at the first defendant's Riverwood factory, the amendments may have serious repercussions for my client.'

'That is ridiculous, Mr Sandaver. I can see your point if the allegations were directed against your client, but they are not. They are solely against Henry King. I need not hear further from you.'

Sandaver stood speechless at the bar table as the judge turned her attention to Jeremy Lawson. Viviana had no notion of what was troubling Sandaver and Maguire.

Bruce Fraser did. Sandaver and Maguire believed that Henry King would be filing a cross-claim against V&L Ltd if it did not agree to pay a fifty percent contribution to damages and costs within the hour.

'Now, Mr Lawson, why can't your client meet these allegations now?'

'Your Honour, it's a very serious step for the plaintiff to take in claiming exemplary damages from my client. If he were proposing to claim such damages, then he should have done so right from the outset. We have not received any new evidence or any new expert report supporting the allegations. This is trial by ambush and should not be permitted, with respect, your Honour.'

'I don't see much difference, Mr Lawson, between the fresh allegations and the plaintiff's present claim. The plaintiff already alleges that Henry King ought to have known that blue asbestos was hazardous and shouldn't have been used at all from the early 1960s. The amendments simply reiterate the allegation but now allege that it actually knew of those dangers but chose to ignore them. There is a difference, but the difference is not great. If your client was in a position to meet the existing allegations, I fail to see how it cannot be in a position to meet these new allegations when they're based on basically the same facts.'

'The difficulty is, your Honour, that we haven't been served with any evidence supporting the allegations. There's been no expert evidence on the subject. But more importantly, because of the seriousness of the allegations, my client needs time to investigate the issue and to obtain evidence to meet the allegations. That may be expert evidence, it may be lay evidence. I do not know at this stage.'

'Mr Lawson, if you don't know how you're going to meet the allegations, that's hardly the plaintiff's problem, is it? If the plaintiff calls evidence which he was already going to call and it proves additionally that your client is liable for exemplary damages, then I fail to see how your client is prejudiced. Your client is a large multinational company. I'm sure it has the resources to meet any of these allegations. It's not as though they are new. Mr Henderson is not the first plaintiff to threaten exemplary damages. And you are briefed by one of the largest law firms in Australia with armies of solicitors and paralegals at its disposal. Yes, thank you, Mr Lawson, I reject your arguments and allow the amendments.

'Now, Mr Sutton, where are we going with this matter?'

'Your Honour, the matter is proceeding. The plaintiff's next witness is Mr Russell Dymock.'

Sutton announced Dymock's name as if he was reading out the winning lotto numbers. Bruce thought Sutton might have expected a cheer. Instead, he got silence. Lawson sat imperturbably at the bar table. Sutton appeared slightly cheated and bent down close to Lawson's ear. Although he whispered, Bruce could hear what he said from the table behind. 'Wait till you hear what he says. I'd get your client's chequebook out if I were you.'

'Thanks, Geoff, I'll let Bruce know.' Jeremy Lawson spoke without expression.

Bruce watched as Russell Dymock padded noiselessly to the witness box. He wore a white shirt, a celery-green tie, a grey suit and a pair of sensible grey shoes – more like sneakers than leather dress shoes. His face was thin, worn-out. From beneath bushy, white eyebrows, nervous eyes flickered. His tentative voice was nearly inaudible as he was sworn in to tell the truth and nothing but the truth.

'Mr Dymock, if you wouldn't mind speaking up, please. Relax, take your time and listen carefully to counsel's questions,' Judge Byrnes advised him. She smiled warmly as if to encourage him. As Sutton led him through his full name, date of birth, his address and marital status, Dymock slowly seemed more at ease.

'You are now retired, Mr Dymock, but you formerly worked in occupational health and safety, is that correct?'

'Yes.'

'And did you ever work in that capacity for Henry King Industries Limited?'

'Yes, I did. From 1961 to 1969, I was the safety officer at its Riverwood factory.'

Sutton stood like a preening peacock, gazing across at Dymock. Bruce found his antics risible. One side of Sutton's body was to the judge, the other to the audience. His left elbow rested on the lectern on the bar table. His right arm pulled his silk robe backwards to allow the four fingers of his right hand to sit in the small bottom pocket of his black bar jacket. As he asked Dymock questions he turned to the reporters in the gallery, occasionally emphasising a word by removing his hand from his pocket and twirling his wrist with a flourish. 'I just asked you about the conditions at the factory. You said intolerable, I believe. Did I hear you correctly, Mr Dymock?'

'Yes.'

'I see, intolerable conditions, you say. Now, Mr Dymock, what tasks were you obliged to perform in the capacity of safety officer?'

'I was responsible for ordering safety equipment, ensuring the men followed safety instructions. I helped with measuring dust levels in the factory. I reported safety incidents and concerns to the factory manager and ... that was about it.'

'Who was the factory manager?'

'Bill Kruger.'

'And was there a doctor at the factory in the period you were there?'

'Yes, Dr Peter Mathers.'

'Who did the dust counts?'

'The industrial hygienist, Mr Bob Frew.'

'Did you ever attend meetings or have discussions about safety issues with Mr Kruger, Dr Mathers or Mr Frew?'

'Yes, regularly throughout the time I was employed at the factory.'

'Did any of those discussions ever concern asbestos?'

'I object, that's leading,' said Jeremy Lawson.

'Oh really, Mr Lawson, sit down. That's not leading,' the judge said. 'Continue, Mr Dymock.' She appeared to be moving closer to him, riveted by his evidence. Soon, she would climb over her parapet and fall into his lap.

'Yes, they did,' Dymock said directly to her.

'Did any of the discussions ever concern blue asbestos?'

'I object,' interjected Lawson.

'Please! Mr Lawson. I allow the question.'

'Yes, they did.'

'How many discussions did you have about blue asbestos?'

'I can remember only one. I'll never forget it. It's as clear as a bell to me even now.' Dymock seemed angry as if he was reliving how he felt on a day more than three decades past. From sitting in on Dymock's interviews with Sutton, Viviana knew about his indignation, his embarrassment. She could see it take hold of Dymock and grip him tightly. This may be his undoing, she thought. 'It was in 1966. I remember the year because it was the year my son was born. It would have been about a month before that. As I said, I can picture it as it happened,' Dymock continued. 'Peter Mathers was there, Kruger, Frew and—'

'If you wouldn't mind pausing there, for a moment, Mr Dymock,' Sutton interrupted. 'What was the topic of discussion?' He puffed out his chest and stole a glance at the most attractive of the female reporters in the gallery.

'It was about the company not using blue asbestos.'

'Yes. And what was said?'

'Peter Mathers told Bill Kruger that blue asbestos was lethal, it caused mesothelioma, and we should stop using it immediately.' Viviana surveyed the room. Dymock looking at the audience defiantly. Sutton's gloating face staring up at the judge, Gary Shaw's triumphant smile, the three reporters writing feverishly and Lawson's unflinching face tilted down at his notes.

'Lethal, is that what you said?' Sutton queried, rotating back to the audience.

'Yes.'

'Blue asbestos was lethal. Yes, go on,' Sutton coaxed after a suitable pause.

'I told Kruger I agreed with Mathers. Frew also said he agreed. Kruger said it was an over-reaction and that the whole thing had to go to the board.'

'Did it go to the board?'

'Peter, that is, Dr Mathers, said it did. He told me he wrote a report for them and—'

'Objection!'

'Sit down, Mr Lawson, I allow it.'

'Your Honour, this is hopeless hearsay.'

'Be quiet! I've ruled. Are you cavilling with my ruling?'

'No, your Honour.'

'Then let this man continue.'

'Thank you, your Honour,' said Sutton. 'Did you ever see the report, Mr Dymock?'

'No.'

'I call for the report of Dr Mathers to the Henry King board dated 1966 concerning blue asbestos.'

'Not produced,' announced Jeremy Lawson.

'Why is that, Mr Lawson?' asked Judge Byrnes.

'The plaintiff already has a copy, your Honour. It's one of my client's discovered documents.'

'I see. Is that correct, Mr Sutton?'

'Let me take instructions, your Honour.' He looked at Viviana, who nodded. 'That's correct, your Honour.'

'What was the point of the call, then, Mr Sutton?'

'My apologies, your Honour.'

'Get on with it, Mr Sutton, this isn't a jury.'

'I suppose, Mr Dymock, you moved around all of the areas in the factory as part of your job?' Sutton asked.

'Yes, I did.'

'You inspected or observed the front end of the manufacturing process where raw fibre was unloaded?'

'Yes, I did. I saw the bags being opened and emptied into the chutes.'

'Were you familiar with the types of asbestos fibre used at the factory?'

'Yes, I was. It was part of my job.'

'And did you observe blue asbestos being used at about the time of this meeting in 1966 with Mathers, Kruger and Frew?'

'Yes.'

'Did you see it being used after 1966?'

'Yes, I did. Right up to when I resigned in 1969.'

'So, to your direct observation, despite Dr Mathers' advice in 1966 to stop using blue, the company continued to use it for another three years, knowing it was lethal according to the doctor they employed to tell them such things. Is that right?'

'I object!'

'Yes, Mr Sutton, I think that conclusion is self-evident.'

'I withdraw it. Nothing further, your Honour.'

'Mr Lawson.'

'Thank you, your Honour.' Jeremy Lawson waited until the murmuring behind him subsided. He waited as the reporters left. He waited until the courtroom door ceased swinging. In the silence, Dymock started fidgeting. Viviana watched as his nervousness returned. 'Why did you resign, Mr Dymock?'

'I told Kruger I couldn't stand working for the company when it still used blue asbestos.'

'Is that so?'

'Yes.'

'Not personal health reasons?'

'No.'

'Positive?'

'Yes.'

'You didn't tell anyone you resigned for health reasons?'

'No.'

'You certainly didn't tell Kruger you were resigning for health reasons?'

'No.'

'You told him it was because Henry King still used blue, is that what you say?'

'Yes.'

'It was an important point of principle for you, wasn't it?'

'Yes.'

'There was no way you were going to hide that important point of principle by pretending you were resigning for health reasons?'

'Not on your life.'

'Very well, Mr Dymock.' Lawson looked down at his papers and riffled through them. He settled on a single page. 'Please take a look at this document.' He handed the page to the tipstaff, who passed it to Dymock. 'Take your time.' The colour drained from Dymock's face. 'That's a copy of your letter of resignation dated 26 September 1969, is it not?'

'Yes,' Dymock admitted quietly.

'Would you read out the first sentence? Nice loud voice, if you don't mind.'

Dymock slowly read, 'I regret to inform you that because of ill health I will be resigning from the company, effective immediately.'

'Thank you, Mr Dymock. Would you mind handing back the document? Thank you. You agree now that that was precisely what you gave as the reason for resigning?'

'Yes.'

'Nothing about principles?'

'No.'

'No mention of blue asbestos?'

'Not in that letter.'

'Now, let us move on to your knowledge about blue being dangerous. You say you agreed with Mathers when he said blue was lethal, is that right?'

'Yes.'

'And what was the source of your knowledge?'

'Ah, that was Wagner's article, I think.'

'I see. Is that Dr Wagner's 1960 article?'

'Yes.'

'And when did you read it?'

'1960, I guess.'

'You guess?'

'Okay, I'm sure I read it then. The year it was published, I know that.'

'And, do you say, after you read it that you knew blue asbestos was lethal and Henry King should immediately stop using it?'

'Yes.'

'And this was in 1960?'

'Yes.'

'When you were not even employed by Henry King Industries?' Someone laughed.

'Quiet in the court!' Judge Byrnes roared.

'No, I was not employed then,' Dymock said.

'Were you working in the asbestos industry in 1960?'

'No.'

'Where were you working?'

'What is now known as Australia Post.'

'Doing what?'

'Looking after the employees loading and unloading deliveries.'

'Bad backs?'

'Yes.'

'Wry necks?'

'Yes.'

'Nothing about asbestos?'

'No.'

'Why on earth would you have read Wagner's article, let alone had access to it?'

Dymock shifted in his seat. He took out a handkerchief and mopped his brow. 'I might have been wrong. I probably read it later.'

'After you were employed by Henry King Industries?'

'Yes, that's probably right.'

'Before this meeting in 1966?'

'Yes, I'm sure it was. Maybe 1961, soon after I joined the company.'

'This was very important information. Did you tell Kruger?'

'Probably.'

'Probably?'

'Definitely.'

'You certainly wouldn't have been telling him that blue asbestos was safe, would you?'

'Definitely not.' Dymock was squirming. His face was hot, flushed. Viviana did not like where Lawson was going with these questions.

'Every quarter, you were required to provide a report to Kruger about safety matters, isn't that right?'

'Yes.' What had he written? Viviana couldn't remember the content of all the discovered documents. It couldn't be good.

'If you thought blue asbestos was lethal, that was a safety matter, wasn't it?'

'Yes.'

'It was so important, you wouldn't have concealed your concerns from Kruger?'

'No, I wouldn't have, but...'

'But what?'

'But those safety reports weren't about asbestos,' Dymock stammered.

'A moment ago you said the subject of blue asbestos was something that would go in these reports. Now you're saying it's not. Which is true?'

'The second – it wasn't something for those safety reports.'

'I see. So, your first statement was false, is that what you're saying?'

Dymock looked up as if beseeching the judge to intervene. Viviana could almost see his pulse hammering at his temples.

Judge Byrnes obliged. 'Mr Lawson, I think we'll have a break. Mr Dymock is clearly confused with your questions. I can't blame him. I call the morning tea adjournment.'

'If it pleases the court.'

◆

During the twenty-minute interval, Bruce Fraser called Charlie Boustead. V&L had agreed to contribute half to any damages, including a secret contribution to any punitive damages award, together with whatever the costs might be. The Henry King board was prepared to see the case out to judgment. Bruce was elated. Lawson, who was already in the groove, was also pleased. There was a long way to go, and a trial always had its ups and downs, but things were progressing well. Very well.

In the corridor outside the courtroom, Bruce was approached by Viviana. 'Could I have a word?' she asked.

'Sure.'

They moved to a corner near a water fountain. Viviana's face was emotionless. Her skin was smooth apart from a tiny blemish in the middle of her forehead. Viviana could see Bruce's eyes wandering to the zit. She wanted to ask him whether he had any problems with her complexion, but instead said, 'I'm instructed to offer the defendants $600,000 plus costs to settle the matter.'

Bruce was amazed that she could deliver such an offer with a straight face. 'That's $100,000 more than last week,' he said.

'Mmm.'

'Well, all I can say is thanks, but no thanks. The offer is not accepted.'

'Okay.'

Bruce watched as Viviana, all in black, slithered away like a viper. Even when he felt bullish, she could unnerve him. He stooped and took a sip of water from the fountain. One of the legal teams was clearly wrong. He doubted his team was the one in error.

◆

After the adjournment, Lawson bored into Dymock about his safety officer reports. After being shown several of his reports, Dymock conceded that the health hazards of asbestos were, indeed, an important topic in the reports.

Bruce turned around to check on Gary Shaw's reaction from time to time. He was looking less cocky in his seat at the back of the courtroom. Fortunately for Shaw, Bruce thought, the three journalists had left before Dymock's cross-examination so they could file reports for the next day's paper or that evening's news. In fact, as he subsequently ascertained, at the very time Dymock was bumbling his way through his responses, one of the reporters was being filmed giving an overview of the morning's evidence, describing how 'Henry King Industries knew of the killer dust, but did nothing about it.'

As Lawson's cross-examination continued, Geoffrey Sutton sat sullenly in his chair, no doubt thinking about the work he would be obliged to undertake if the case did not settle, as now seemed almost certain, or the potential financial loss he would incur should James Henderson lose.

Watching him, Viviana knew his and Shaw's strategy had been half baked all along. Dymock's evidence was unravelling. She feared she might never again be able to argue punitive damages.

'Mr Dymock, given how strongly you felt about blue asbestos from 1966 after the meeting with Dr Mathers, you surely would have reported your concerns in your quarterly safety officer reports?'

'I can't remember.'

'Are you saying that you're not sure whether you advised Mr Kruger of your concerns about blue asbestos in those reports?'

'Well, I may not have. I can't be sure.'

'But surely, Mr Dymock, given how concerned you were about blue asbestos and the issue being a point of principle to you, you at least would not have told Mr Kruger the opposite – that is, that there were no safety issues with blue asbestos?'

'Definitely not. I would have told him it was bad!' Dymock asserted. 'Are you suggesting I'm dishonest? That I would have hidden the danger from Kruger?' Viviana could see that Dymock, having had his credibility shaken, was angry again.

'Now, now, Mr Dymock. I don't think counsel is suggesting that at all. Or are you, Mr Lawson?' Judge Byrnes asked.

'No, your Honour,' Lawson replied before returning to the witness. 'Now, Mr Dymock, I want to get this clear. You're telling her Honour that, while you can't specifically recall reporting to Mr Kruger about the danger of blue asbestos, one thing is certain, and that is that you wouldn't have told him that blue asbestos was safe. Have I got that correct?'

'That's what I'm saying.'

'Good. There is no way you would have told Mr Kruger that blue asbestos was safe?'

'I think we've been over this, Mr Lawson,' said Judge Byrnes irritably.

'Thank you, your Honour. If that's clear. Now, Mr Dymock, if I could show you this document, a copy of your safety officer's report of October

1968.' It was passed up to him. 'Mr Dymock, if you would please turn to page three and the first paragraph of your conclusion. Please read out to her Honour what you have written there.'

Dymock blanched. Viviana could see that he wanted the ordeal to end. He quickly read the following words to the court:

'The dust counts at all stations complied with the Health Department recommendations and the asbestos exposure standards recommended by the NHMRC. Mr Ferris, the field safety officer from the Public Health Department, has advised that, so long as the company maintains the dust counts at these levels, then there should be no safety concerns with its workforce. I concur.'

'Now, Mr Dymock, in that report, you have advised Mr Kruger that you did not consider there to be any health hazards from asbestos so long as the dust counts were kept at the recommended levels, that is so, isn't it?'

'Yes.'

'Assuming blue asbestos was still being used at the factory, your opinion applied to all types of asbestos, didn't it?' Dymock hesitated. 'Didn't it?' Lawson repeated quietly.

'Yes.'

'You didn't single out white asbestos or brown asbestos or blue asbestos as being different in any way from one another, did you?'

'No.'

'You didn't, for example, say something like, 'With the exception of blue asbestos, there should be no health hazards, etc,' did you?'

'No.'

'In fact, it was reasonable for Mr Kruger to interpret your conclusions as being that blue asbestos – if it was being used – just like brown asbestos and just like white asbestos, posed no particular health hazard or safety issue to the workforce at Henry King Industries if the dust counts were kept at the recommended levels, do you agree?'

'Yes, I suppose so.'

'Here, Mr Dymock, please take a look at this safety officer's report, your final report before you resigned.' Russell Dymock reluctantly read the three pages of the report handed to him.

'The conclusion you reached there is virtually identical to that in October 1968, isn't that so?'

'Yes.'

'There is not a hint from you of any added danger with blue asbestos anywhere in that report, is there?'

'No.'

'I've already taken you to your earlier safety officer reports, and they also say the same thing, don't they?'

'Yes.'

'So, for a matter that you thought was a point of principle and vital to the safety of the workforce at the factory, you simply said nothing, isn't that right?'

'In those reports, yes.'

'For the entire time you were employed at Henry King Industries, you mentioned not a word of the peculiar danger of blue asbestos, did you?'

'In the reports, that's correct. But that meeting with Kruger, Mathers and Frew took place. I'm not lying. It happened.'

'I see, so this meeting took place, did it?'

'Yes, it did. And I saw with my own eyes blue asbestos being used right up to 1969.'

'I see, but you made no mention of it in your reports, did you?'

'No.'

'You made it up, didn't you?'

'No!' Dymock replied belligerently.

'Yes, thank you, Mr Dymock, that will be all.'

There were no questions in re-examination. Sutton sat playing with his Mont Blanc. Viviana thought that if he'd focused on Lawson's questions, he may have asked whether any safe exposure level for crocidolite was in place in 1968 or 1969. He and Lucas should have known that there was no threshold limit value for crocidolite at the time – given its lethality, none could safely be set by any health authority. She knew this from talking to Dr Smith and reading the NHMRC documents he referred to in his statement. But she had been told to forget about using Dr Smith.

Russell Dymock left the courtroom.

She followed him out with Gary Shaw to thank him for giving evidence.

'You did a grand job, Russell, a grand job,' Shaw said, patting him on the back.

'It doesn't feel like it,' Dymock said.

'Don't you worry about it, Russell. You did very well. Who are they going to call to refute your evidence? No one is my guess. Put your mind at ease, Russell. You did a great thing today for all the victims of asbestos in this country. A great thing.' Shaw shook Dymock's hand vigorously. 'All the best, Russell, we'll let you know the outcome.'

Chapter 72

'Dymock was hopeless,' Sutton announced at lunch in his chambers. 'Utterly hopeless.'

'Lawson seemed to know we'd be calling him. How could that be?' Lucas asked.

'No idea.' They both turned to Viviana.

'Don't be ridiculous.' She glared at them.

'Lawson is either very good and knows every single Henry King discovered document back to front, or someone tipped him off,' persisted Lucas.

'Even for you, that's stupid,' Viviana said.

'If you don't mind, I have to think about our tactics and calling Dr Phillips. We can do without your antagonism, Viviana,' Sutton said. 'And don't tell Gary Shaw I said Dymock was hopeless. It was his idea.'

'I think he might have been able to deduce that himself, Geoffrey.'

'Look, I have to have some quiet time to think about whether I need to ask Dr Phillips anything extra.'

'Fine, I'll leave you to it.'

After lunch, Sutton called Dr George Phillips, the geologist. Viviana thought he was, at best, a lightweight. His report in James Henderson's case appeared identical to hundreds of others Viviana had seen. She had not bothered to read it.

Sutton started by tendering Phillips's report, without objection, on the question of breach of duty of care. He then asked Dr Phillips to provide oral evidence about the importance of Wagner's paper in 1960.

'Wagner's paper was epochal,' Phillips said.

'What was that?' Judge Byrnes asked.

'Epochal, your Honour, in highlighting the specific danger of blue asbestos. From that article alone, a reasonable asbestos products manufacturing company would have been aware that even slight or minimal exposure to blue asbestos could cause the fatal cancer called mesothelioma.'

Both Jeremy Lawson and Pat Sandaver objected to the additional evidence, but as it was mentioned obliquely in Phillips's 63-page report, Judge Byrnes allowed it. By the time Phillips had finished giving his evidence in chief, it was the afternoon of the second day of the hearing. Sutton had certainly done some work preparing Phillips, Viviana conceded. After he was finished, Viviana felt reasonably optimistic – for a moment.

'When were you first asked to provide an expert opinion in asbestos litigation, Dr Phillips?' Lawson commenced.

'I think it was in about 1989, Mr Lawson.'

Phillips was a slightly built, quiet, unimpressive man. He was the type of man Bruce Fraser assumed would have a low opinion of himself, only to be surprised to discover he was as egotistical, conceited and arrogant as anyone else. Looks and manner could be deceiving, Bruce thought. He leaned forward to hear what Lawson was going to ask Phillips next. He was keen for some sport.

'And was the request for that report made by Mr Gary Shaw from Shaw & Fletcher?'

'I object!' yelled Sutton.

'Yes, Mr Sutton. What is your objection?' asked Judge Byrnes.

'Relevance, your Honour. What has a 1989 report got to do with Mr Henderson's case.'

'I assume that Mr Lawson is setting out the groundwork for a subsequent submission on Dr Phillips's qualifications and expertise. Am I right, Mr Lawson?'

'Yes, your Honour, that is so.'

'Very well, you may proceed, but please remember I have taken out that short leash again for your cross-examination, Mr Lawson,' she cautioned.

'Thank you, your Honour. Would you mind answering the question, Dr Phillips?'

'Yes, it was for Gary Shaw.'

'Prior to the request for that report, you had never been asked by anyone to provide any advice or opinion about asbestos-related diseases. That is so, isn't it?'

'Yes, I think that's right. I may have had a number of other requests from law firms, but I think they followed this one.'

'Apart from requests for expert reports by lawyers, you had never been asked to provide any advice or express any opinion on asbestos-related diseases up to that point to any other person, that's correct, isn't it?'

'Yes, that's right.'

'What you did in 1989, then, for the first time in your life, was commence reading as much as you could of the literature on asbestos-related diseases, their prevention, various safety equipment that was available over the years and things of that nature, is that so?'

'Yes.'

'You had no specific knowledge about those matters and you had not developed any specific expertise over the years while a lecturer in geology, had you?'

'Well, I knew about dust in general and the basic safety techniques to bring dust down, but in relation to asbestos, you're right, Mr Lawson.'

'It is the case, is it not, that all of your expert knowledge about the dangers of asbestos has been obtained from reading articles and textbooks for the purpose of legal proceedings?'

'Yes.' Dr Phillips swallowed slowly. Bruce looked at him. Something bitter seemed to have caught in his throat. It was probably the gunk that could build up on the overactive vocal cords of a phoney, he thought.

Viviana, at the same time, realised that Phillips had been unmasked. It had been bound to happen sooner or later. Viviana hoped he'd worked out that it would be better not to fight.

Bruce, on the other hand, wanted to see some blood in the water.

'Now, Dr Phillips, you specifically refer to the Wagner article of 1960 as being a turning point, so to speak. I want to ask you about matters up to 1960, do you follow?'

'Yes.'

'Would you agree that, up until 1960, what was known, based upon your reading and research, was that asbestos could cause asbestosis in workers who were exposed to raw asbestos fibres day in, day out, over many years. Would you agree?'

'Yes, but it was known that asbestos could also cause lung cancer.'

'I'm getting to that, Dr Phillips, don't jump ahead, please.'

'Sorry.'

'Up to 1960, what was known about lung cancer and asbestos exposure was that lung cancer could be caused by asbestos exposure, but only if a worker had developed asbestosis. Would you agree?'

'Yes.'

'And up until Wagner's article, mesothelioma was not even known to be associated with asbestos exposure, isn't that right?'

'That's right.'

'Now, can we turn to Wagner's article of 1960? Based upon what you've already said in evidence, you would not have read that article when it was first available in the 1960s?'

'No.'

'That article reported on a series of cases of mesothelioma in South Africa, did it not?'

'Yes.'

'And you have told her Honour that a reasonable medical practitioner, safety officer or industrial hygienist reading that paper for the first time in the 1960s ought to have concluded that blue asbestos was extremely dangerous in that it caused this cancer called mesothelioma and that even slight exposure could be responsible. That is so, isn't it?'

'Yes.'

'And you also say that, after reading this article, Henry King Industries should have ceased using blue asbestos as soon as possible, is that so?'

'That is what I have said, Mr Lawson.'

'Well, Dr Phillips, when you studied this article, as a retired geologist, I assume you took note of what was said on page 1, that it was "A preliminary publication" and that the problem was still being investigated?'

'Yes, I noted that.'

'Did you read, Dr Phillips, that the inhabitants lived in an area where extensive open-cut mining of crocidolite took place?'

'Yes.'

'And that the mining, milling and bagging of the blue asbestos was a family affair with people living in very close proximity to their place of work?'

'Yes, I read that.'

'And you would have appreciated, after reading the description of the workplace, that the individuals who developed mesothelioma were likely to have had very significant exposure to asbestos every day?'

'That follows, yes.'

'The sorts of exposures involved were likely to be heavy daily exposure, wouldn't you agree?'

'Yes, but there were some cases where there must have been lighter exposure.'

'And what cases are you referring to, Dr Phillips?'

'Well, there was the case of a woman who worked in an asbestos warehouse for six years. That doesn't sound like heavy exposure to me. There were also cases involving housewives, servants, cattle herders, farmers and an accountant.'

'Yes, Dr Phillips, but without knowing precisely the history of asbestos exposure involved, you're unable to say whether it was heavy or not?'

'I agree.'

'For all a reader knows, those people had heavy daily exposure living in a home only yards from an asbestos mill.'

'That's possible. It's also possible that they had minimal exposure as a bystander.'

'But you cannot tell from reading the article, can you, doctor?'

'No, that's true.'

'And to do so is simply speculation and, I suggest, unscientific?'

'There is an element of speculation.'

'Do you say speculation is a valid scientific method?'

'No.'

Viviana's instinct had told her it was a mistake relying on Dymock and this man to prove exemplary damages. She felt that all the work she had done with Dr Smith and Mr Berendetti was going down the toilet. There was nothing she could do but watch as the disaster unfolded. She observed Sutton, waiting for an objection, but it never came. He seemed to have thrown in the towel.

'You are aware, Dr Phillips, of the monograph Biological Effects of Asbestos, published in 1965?'

'I am aware of it, yes.'

'This special issue containing the proceedings and reports of the conference of 1964 was published in December 1965 and first appeared in Australia in March 1966, isn't that right, Dr Phillips?'

'Well, I did not read it then, but I know it was published in December 1965, so I assume it wasn't available here until early 1966.'

'Anyone claiming to have read it in Australia in 1965 is probably making that up, wouldn't you agree?'

'Yes, or their memory is playing tricks on them.'

'This was the first time that the paper by Drs Newhouse and Thompson was also published, wasn't it?'

'I think that's right. It may also have been published in another journal at the same time, but I'm unsure about that.'

'It wasn't until the paper by Newhouse and Thompson that anyone could possibly have suspected that the risk of mesothelioma from exposure to crocidolite was much less than that required to induce asbestosis. That's the case, isn't it?'

'It was an important paper, yes.'

'And it was only after the publication of the Newhouse and Thompson study in 1965 that specialists in the field ought to have considered that exposure to blue asbestos needed to be cut back below the levels for white or brown asbestos?'

'Yes.'

'It was certainly not the case that immediate moves should have been put in place to take blue out of the product altogether?'

'It would have been reasonable to stop using blue, but I agree that it wasn't mandatory from what I've read.'

'And it certainly wasn't mandatory given that Wagner's article in 1960 was described as a "preliminary investigation", correct?'

'Correct.'

'You would agree, wouldn't you, Dr Phillips, that it wasn't until the very end of the 1960s that the scientific community generally accepted that mesothelioma could be caused by exposure to asbestos at much lower levels than were known to cause asbestosis and, even then, it was only in relation to blue asbestos?'

'Yes, I agree with that statement.'

'I see. So, that is what we now can accept as your view, Dr Phillips. Do you agree that it would have been highly unlikely that a safety officer or even a geologist, such as yourself, would have formed a different view in the 1960s?'

'I agree, it would have been unlikely at the time.'

'The awareness of the dangers of blue asbestos and mesothelioma was an area for specialist occupational physicians and the like, wasn't it?'

'Yes.'

'A mere safety officer without that sort of expertise or qualifications was unlikely to know more about the subject than an occupational physician, wouldn't you agree?'

'Yes, I think that's likely.'

'And if a company employed an occupational physician, you would have expected him to advise stopping blue at the end of the 1960s.'

'Yes, or earlier.'

'But if a company kept on using it until the end of the 1960s, that would have been reasonable?'

'Yes, although I think it should have stopped using it earlier, after Wagner's paper came out.'

'But you would agree, doctor, that in areas of medical science, things are rarely black and white; there is room for legitimate differences of opinion?'

'Sure.'

'And here, although you think blue asbestos should have been removed from products in 1965 or earlier, you accept, don't you, that it was reasonable to hold a contrary view?'

'Yes, I suppose.'

'And so it was reasonable to form the opinion that it was safe to keep using blue, so long as the exposure wasn't heavy, until the end of the 1960s.'

'I don't agree with that opinion.'

'I know you don't, doctor, but you accept that reasonable minds may differ and that others could quite reasonably recommend its use until the end of the 1960s so long as the exposure wasn't heavy?'

'Yes, I accept that.'

'Indeed, if an occupational physician recommended ceasing the use of blue asbestos in 1966 after the publication of Biological Effects of Asbestos, you'd regard that as good advice?'

'Yes, given that I now accept that the Wagner study in 1960 was preliminary.'

'That sort of advice by an occupational physician in 1966 would not have just been good, it would have been ahead of the game, so to speak?'

'Yes.'

'Exemplary, wouldn't you say?'

'Well, I suppose it would have been.'

'It's not supposition, Dr Phillips. It would certainly have been exemplary advice, correct?'

'Yes.' Phillips looked for help at the plaintiff's end of the bar table. Nobody returned the look.

'Thank you, Dr Phillips. I have no further questions.'

'No re-examination,' Sutton said.

'You may be excused, Dr Phillips,' the judge said. She peered down from her seat at Geoffrey Sutton. 'Do you wish to try another witness this afternoon, Mr Sutton, or is that it for the day?'

'We have arranged for Drs Haug and Freeman to give evidence tomorrow morning, your Honour, if that is convenient.'

'It is. Officer, adjourn the court.'

Outside in the hall, Viviana felt embarrassed by the Phillips debacle. 'Exemplary damages for exemplary advice!' she overheard Bruce Fraser say to someone on the phone.

She had to regain control of the matter. James and Jenny deserved better than this shemozzle. What could she do? She didn't want to serve Dr Smith's statement in such circumstances. The claim for punitive damages had to go. She had to convince Shaw to give it up.

Chapter 73

In Sutton's chambers, the morning after George Phillips gave his evidence, Viviana agreed with Sutton that the best strategy with Drs Haug and Freeman was to tender their reports and then turn them over to the defendants for cross-examination. She listened as Sutton 'worded them up' about the anticipated line of cross-examination.

'Jeremy Lawson, in particular, will endeavour to have you implicate the Scottish exposure as the cause of James Henderson's mesothelioma. Nothing to worry about,' he said. 'We all know that the Australian exposure was significant.'

'We do.'

In court, Viviana was not so sure they understood.

Lawson asked, 'So, in other words, Dr Haug, you cannot say to her Honour which of the two sources of asbestos exposure, Scotland or Australia, was the cause of Mr Henderson's mesothelioma?'

'Well, no. All I know is that asbestos is essentially the only known cause of mesothelioma. Mr Henderson has had significant asbestos exposure. That exposure was the cause of his mesothelioma. As to saying which period of exposure was responsible for the mesothelioma, I don't think anyone knows. I can say, however, as I have said in my report, that Mr Henderson had significant exposure in Australia and that it, if taken on its own, can be considered to be the cause of his mesothelioma.'

'But equally the Scottish exposure taken on its own could be the cause of Mr Henderson's mesothelioma?' Lawson persisted.

'Yes, that's what I've said.'

Pat Sandaver then cross-examined Dr Haug into the same position in relation to the Australian exposure: Dr Haug agreed that he couldn't say whether the Disaster Gorge, Riverwood factory or building product exposures were all responsible for James Henderson's mesothelioma or whether one in particular could be incriminated. Bruce was pleased that the V&L barrister finally did something useful. All this uncertainty helped the causation defence.

Dr Freeman gave similar evidence.

Viviana was worried. Sutton and Lucas, however, seemed unfazed. 'Didn't it make causation more difficult?' Viviana asked before the hearing resumed.

'No. As far as I'm concerned, and as far as I could gauge Judge Byrnes's view on the issue, we're on course to establish that the Australian exposures materially contributed to Henderson's mesothelioma. Don't you agree, Greg?'

'I do.'

Viviana thought otherwise. The exemplary damages claim was a basket case and now causation seemed unclear. She desperately wanted things to improve.

Sutton told her that he wanted to call his star witness, Professor Schaffer, last. 'I want to close the plaintiff's case with a bang,' he said. 'It's unlikely Lawson and Sandaver will lay a hand on him. It's even possible that the defendants will roll over and settle after he gives evidence. So, after Haug and Freeman, we'll call Tom Forgan.'

And now Dr Forgan was in the witness box. There was a chance the day could go from bad to worse, Viviana thought.

During his earlier conference with Forgan, Sutton had made it clear that he wanted to paint a picture of Dr Forgan being, by local standards, as well credentialled as Professor McGuinness in the field of epidemiology and biostatistics. He thus spent considerable time in examination-in-chief asking Dr Forgan to describe in painful detail everything on his CV. His curriculum vitae was undoubtedly impressive; the man himself less so. Viviana watched anxiously as he gave evidence. A tall, pale man with a silver goatee, Forgan had the habit of talking to his chin. This made him hard to hear and hard to take as a witness of authority. The frequency with which he said 'umm' didn't help.

After almost two hours of pulling-teeth evidence, Sutton eventually got to the critical issue. 'You have read through the transcript of Mr Henderson's evidence and read his affidavit. Does his evidence affect your opinion on causation in any way?'

'It doesn't, no. I remain umm of the view that Mr Henderson's Australian exposure was the cause of umm his mesothelioma.'

'And why is that, Dr Forgan?'

'Well, umm, Mr Henderson had the majority of his exposure to crocidolite in Australia. He may have had some exposure to blue asbestos in Scotland, but that's speculation. Even if he did, there's umm no doubt he had a lot more in Australia, both in the Riverwood factory run by Henry King and while at umm Disaster Gorge. Epidemiological studies have shown that the risk of developing mesothelioma is umm many times greater with exposure to crocidolite than umm to the other fibres. Therefore, even though he had heavy exposure in Scotland, his exposure to crocidolite in Australia meant that the risk of getting mesothelioma was umm highest in Australia.'

'Thank you, Dr Forgan.'

Jeremy Lawson was quick to his feet. Bruce knew that the barrister, unlike many of his colleagues, was prepared to tackle an expert witness in the expert's area of expertise. If you didn't, an expert could bamboozle the court with junk science.

'Dr Forgan, the aim of epidemiology is to identify associations between diseases and various factors, is that right?'

'Yes.'

'It does that by studying populations and identifying whether there is a statistically significant increased risk of an association between a disease and a particular factor, correct?'

'Yes.'

'From epidemiological studies on asbestos-exposed populations, you are able to ascertain which factors carry the greatest risk of the development of mesothelioma?'

'Umm, yes, that's correct. We can calculate the magnitude of the risk of developing mesothelioma from a number of factors, such as umm type of fibre, concentration of exposure, type of product, length of exposure, and umm other things.'

'Your opinion in this case is based on a number of studies about the risk of developing mesothelioma?'

'Umm, yes.'

'And those studies indicate that the risk of subsequently developing mesothelioma is highest for those exposed to crocidolite, is that so?'

'Yes.'

'So, your opinion is that Mr Henderson's exposure to crocidolite carried the greatest risk of his later developing mesothelioma?'

'Yes.'

'That exposure increased the risk that he would subsequently develop mesothelioma, is that what you're saying?'

'Umm, each of his exposures increased the risk that he would later get mesothelioma, but the risk was greatest for his exposure to crocidolite at Disaster Gorge and in Riverwood.'

'Tell me, Dr Forgan, does time since first exposure have any impact on the risk of a person later developing mesothelioma?'

'Umm, yes,' Forgan said to his chin. His answer was muffled by both his beard and the nutty, woollen tie he was wearing.

'Time since first exposure has a very strong effect on the risk of developing mesothelioma, doesn't it, Dr Forgan?' Bruce could see Lawson's eyes gouging into Forgan's skull like a trephine. The witness would not make eye contact with the barrister.

'Umm, yes.'

'You haven't mentioned time since first exposure in expressing your opinion to this court, have you?'

'No.'

'Why not?'

'I didn't think it was as important as Mr Henderson's exposure to blue asbestos.'

'It is the case, Dr Forgan, isn't it, that time since first exposure is the most important factor in quantifying the risk of a person subsequently developing mesothelioma?'

Forgan remained silent.

'That's true, isn't it, Dr Forgan?' Lawson demanded. 'Do I need to take you through the epidemiological studies on this issue, doctor, the very papers on which you rely?'

'I object, your Honour. My learned friend should let Dr Forgan answer the question,' Sutton complained.

'Yes, Mr Lawson, allow Dr Forgan the courtesy of answering your question without being badgered,' Judge Byrnes said. 'Dr Forgan, if you could answer Mr Lawson's question, please.'

Tom Forgan hesitated. He looked at the ceiling, down at his feet. You could almost hear his brain whirring. All eyes in the courtroom were upon him. He rested his bony elbows on the edge of the witness box and put both of his hands to his head like a monk in prayer.

'Umm, that is true,' he eventually admitted.

'You deliberately omitted to refer to the most important factor in determining the risk of developing mesothelioma, is that right?'

'I didn't refer to it.'

'No, Dr Forgan, you deliberately chose to ignore it, didn't you?'

'I didn't refer to it,' Forgan stubbornly repeated.

'Well, Dr Forgan, you didn't omit it by accident, surely. I mean, someone of your standing and intellect would surely not omit such an important piece of information?'

'Umm, I may have been a little preoccupied with the crocidolite and forgot to refer to time since first exposure.' Forgan seemed powerless to resist the bait to his ego offered by Lawson. This could only end badly for him, Viviana thought, and in a mired position on causation. Everything was unravelling.

'Oh, I see. It wasn't deliberate, but a simple slip. An unintentional error, is that what you're saying, Dr Forgan?'

'Umm, yes.' Viviana could see that some members of the audience were starting to smile.

'Very well. Let's now remedy that mistake. I would like you to look at the calculations in this document.' Lawson handed the tipstaff a copy of Professor McGuinness's calculations on aetiologic contribution. 'You'll see that the document is the supplementary report of Professor McGuinness.'

'Yes.'

'You agree that Professor McGuinness has made some computations based upon Mr Henderson's evidence on his exposure in Scotland and in Australia?'

'Yes.'

'And he has taken into account Mr Henderson's exposure to blue asbestos in Australia?'

'Yes, he has, although he's also said that he may have had exposure to crocidolite in Scotland.'

'Yes, but he's provided two calculations, hasn't he: one based on no crocidolite exposure in Scotland and another based on some crocidolite exposure in Scotland, but less than at Disaster Gorge and Riverwood, correct?'

'Yes.'

'And he has also taken into account time since first exposure, isn't that right?'

'Yes, he has,' Forgan mumbled.

'And the methodology he's used in calculating contribution to risk of developing mesothelioma is correct, isn't it?'

'Yes, the risk rises exponentially with time.'

'And you would agree, wouldn't you, Dr Forgan, now that you've had a chance to consider the impact of time since first exposure, that those calculations provide a reasonably accurate and scientific assessment of the risk of each period of exposure to the development of Mr Henderson's mesothelioma?'

'They are umm reasonable,' Forgan conceded.

'Thank you, Dr Forgan.'

Sutton put his hand over his mouth and turned to Lucas. 'Shit.'

'Re-examination, Mr Sutton?' the judge asked.

'No, your Honour, that will be all. May Dr Forgan be excused?'

'Yes.'

'What's next, Mr Sutton?'

'Professor Schaffer tomorrow morning, your Honour.'

'10.00am tomorrow, it is then.'

Chapter 74

Professor Schaffer had been warned by Sutton about what had happened to Dr Forgan. In fact, Gary Shaw had turned up in Sutton's chambers to reinforce the importance of his evidence. Viviana had kept her boss up to date with proceedings at the end of each day. She knew Sutton did the same, but suspected Shaw received two vastly different accounts. Underneath Shaw's customary bombast, there was likely to be some anxiety.

'Now, David, as you're well aware, your evidence is crucial to success in the case. Judge Byrnes respects your objectivity and scholarship, so we need to get this right.'

'Understood.'

'From what we've seen, it's important not to downplay the Scottish exposure.'

'It hasn't been going too well, is that the case?'

'No, not at all. It's going well. I think we simply need to embrace the evidence and use that to our advantage.'

'It's not an issue, Mr Shaw. My views on causation remain as expressed and reasoned in my report. I will explain that to the court.'

'Very well, I'll leave you alone. Over to you, Geoff.'

Professor Schaffer was well known to the Tribunal. Viviana noticed that Sutton didn't need to trouble the professor in outlining his qualifications to the judge. She readily accepted his expertise.

Sutton started by taking Schaffer through James Henderson's transcript of evidence. He accepted that the Scottish exposure was significant and contributory to the development of his mesothelioma. He stressed, however, that Mr Henderson had a long and significant exposure in Australia and that this also materially contributed to the development of his mesothelioma. At the conclusion of his evidence, Viviana breathed a sigh of relief. She heard Sutton do likewise. Finally, she thought, someone who said the right thing. Someone who looked and sounded like a real expert. She hoped that opinion would survive cross-examination.

'Professor Schaffer, you are a medical oncologist, correct?'

'Yes, Mr Lawson, I am.' Schaffer had a beautiful speaking voice. He was from a generation that enjoyed British grooming and manners and understated elegance. Viviana sat back, admiring the way his grey hair was parted precisely above the arch of his left eyebrow. He had a tanned, blemish-free face, a patrician nose and a masculine jaw. He looked immaculate in the witness box with his blue blazer and Egyptian-cotton shirt. A light shower of dandruff was the only flaw in his otherwise superb presentation.

'You haven't studied epidemiology, have you?'

'No, Mr Lawson, but I'm familiar with its concepts, having read and analysed many papers over the years.'

'Have you ever personally conducted any epidemiological study?'

'No, but I've been co-author of many studies published in peer-reviewed journals.'

'Have you studied biostatistics?'

'No.'

'Have you ever conducted any epidemiological study of an asbestos-exposed population?'

'No.'

'Have you conducted any scientific research into asbestos-related diseases?'

'As I said to your colleague earlier, Mr Lawson, I've read widely in the area and I am the co-author of the soon-to-be-published twelfth edition of the prestigious textbook The Treatment of Chest Malignancies. I wrote the chapter on mesothelioma.'

'Thank you, Professor, I look forward to reading it. Now, your opinion is based upon epidemiological studies of the association between asbestos exposure and mesothelioma, isn't that right, Professor Schaffer?'

'Yes, Mr Lawson.'

'And you say that Mr Henderson's exposure to asbestos in Australia materially contributed to the development of his mesothelioma?'

'Yes, that is my opinion. Each exposure materially contributed to the development of his mesothelioma.'

'It is the case, professor, that each exposure increases the risk of a person subsequently developing mesothelioma.'

'Yes.'

'I see. So, in essence, you say a material increase in risk is the same as a material contribution?'

'Yes, each exposure increases the risk. I like to consider that the cumulative increase in risk effectively means a cumulative contribution to the development of the mesothelioma.'

'And what is the basis of your opinion that each exposure actually contributes to the development of the mesothelioma?'

'It's a matter of commonsense, Mr Lawson. You're correct in saying that epidemiology tells us that each exposure increases the risk of the development of mesothelioma. Epidemiology cannot tell us that a particular exposure was, in fact, the cause of a mesothelioma. I cannot exclude any exposure to asbestos, so long as it occurred within the appropriate latency period, as a cause of the mesothelioma. If I cannot exclude it as a possibility and I know that the exposure has increased the risk of a person later developing mesothelioma, then I see no reasonable basis for ignoring it when talking about cause and effect.'

'So, what you're saying, professor, is that no one can say which exposure was the culprit. All that one can say is that each exposure increased the risk of developing mesothelioma. Because you can't exclude any exposure as a possible cause, you are personally inclined to say all are contributory. Is that a fair summary of your opinion?'

'Yes, Mr Lawson, that is a fair summary.'

'Nobody knows what triggers the onset of a mesothelioma, isn't that so, professor?'

'Yes, that is correct, Mr Lawson. There are various hypotheses about why mesothelial cells suddenly become cancerous, but nobody truly knows the reason.'

'Does each exposure to asbestos cause the mesothelial cells to become malignant?'

'Nobody knows, Mr Lawson, that's what I'm saying.'

'Some asbestos fibres inhaled by a person may have no effect while some other fibres may, in fact, have an effect and trigger the cancer, is that right?'

'Yes, that may be the case, but it is uncertain. Nobody can say.'

'Despite this uncertainty about whether an actual exposure has any effect at all, you are of the opinion that all exposures should be taken to have physically contributed to the development of Mr Henderson's mesothelioma, is that right?'

'Well, yes, Mr Lawson, as I said before. I hope that is clear.'

'Yes, very clear, Professor Schaffer. Your opinion amounts to no more than guess work, does it?'

'Really, Mr Lawson, that was uncalled for!' Judge Byrnes interjected. 'Professor Schaffer is a well-respected expert in this tribunal.'

'Yes, thank you, your Honour. But that is correct, isn't it, Professor Schaffer? Your opinion amounts to guess work as to whether one exposure contributed to the development of Mr Henderson's mesothelioma or not?'

'Mr Lawson, I do not engage in guess work. While I concede there are scientific uncertainties about the pathogenesis of mesothelioma, I refuse to accept that this is a matter of guess work.' Professor Schaffer answered with an appropriate level of indignation, Viviana thought.

'At the very least, however, Professor Schaffer, would you agree that your opinion on causation, to the effect that an increase in risk can be assumed to be a material contribution, is idiosyncratic?'

'Mr Lawson, as I have said a number of times, it is not a matter of my personal point of view, but a matter of commonsense. Because I cannot exclude any exposure as a possibility, I include them all. And that is on the basis that science indicates that all exposures cumulatively increase the risk of a person developing mesothelioma.'

Viviana enjoyed the exchange. Schaffer's manner was one of patiently dealing with a dim-witted, but likeable, schoolboy.

'Are you aware of Sir Richard Doll?'

'Yes, of course, Mr Lawson. He is one of the world's leading experts on asbestos disease epidemiology.'

'Julian Peto?'

'Yes.'

'Corbett McDonald?'

'Yes, another legend of asbestos disease research.'

'Dr Christopher Wagner?'

'Certainly.'

'They are all well-respected researchers in the field of asbestos disease epidemiology, aren't they, Professor Schaffer?'

'Yes, Mr Lawson, as I have said.'

'You are aware, Professor Schaffer, that they all have published widely in epidemiology, indicating there is a relationship between fibre type and the development of mesothelioma.'

'Yes, crocidolite and amosite are more hazardous than chrysotile.'

'And they have demonstrated also that the incidence or risk of mesothelioma is proportional to time since first exposure, haven't they?'

'They have.'

'In layman's terms, Professor Schaffer, this means early exposure confers greatest risk in the aetiology of mesothelioma, isn't that right?'

'Yes, that is what it means.'

'You accept, don't you, the accuracy of these scientific findings?'

'I do. The association between early exposure and risk of mesothelioma has well and truly been established.'

'The studies have demonstrated that the mesothelioma rate increases according to time since first exposure raised to a power of between three and four, isn't that right?'

'Yes, that relationship is sometimes referred to as "Peto's formula",' explained Professor Schaffer. 'It means that the risk of mesothelioma increases exponentially with time.'

'In this case, Mr Henderson's earliest exposure was for several years in Scotland, correct?'

'That is the evidence he gave.'

'It means, doesn't it, that the risk of his developing mesothelioma was greatest for the period in Scotland?'

'Yes, that is correct, although his crocidolite exposure in Australia had a significant effect.'

'Yes, Professor Schaffer, but the relationship with fibre type is not exponential, is it?'

'No, Mr Lawson, that is right. The relationship with time is by far and away the greatest predictor of mesothelioma.'

'You have read Professor McGuinness's calculations based upon the Peto formula, haven't you?'

'Yes, I've been provided with his reports. He is a well-respected researcher in this area, having co-authored a number of papers.'

'Do you consider his calculations to be accurate?'

'Yes.'

'Do you consider his calculations to be based on valid science?'

'Yes, as we have been over, Mr Lawson, the relationship has been validated across a number of studies.'

'Do you therefore accept, Professor Schaffer, that based on those calculations, there is about a seventy-five percent chance that Mr Henderson's mesothelioma was caused by his Scottish exposure?'

'We have been over this before, Mr Lawson. It doesn't matter whether you talk of chance or risk or incidence rate or whatever. If you say there is a seventy-five percent chance that the mesothelioma was caused by Scottish exposure, then you are ignoring the significant exposure in Australia. Although that is calculated at twenty-five percent, I do not think you can ignore it. It was still significant. I take the view that all exposures contributed to the mesothelioma. They all contributed, as we have gone over, to the risk of Mr Henderson later developing mesothelioma. Because science doesn't know precisely which exposure caused the mesothelioma, and we know all exposures increased the risk or added to the risk, then I think it only fair to say that all contributed to the mesothelioma.'

'Thank you, Professor Schaffer. You've made your position clear. I have no further questions.'

Chapter 75

As they sat in Jeremy Lawson's chambers at the end of the fourth day of the hearing, Bruce Fraser, Charlie Boustead and Paul Morahan felt as good as they had ever felt during the course of an asbestos trial. The plaintiff had abandoned the claim for punitive damages and made an offer to settle of $300,000 plus costs.

'Well, I think Shaw will be reluctant to pull that stunt again. Backfired magnificently,' Morahan said. 'It's time to shut the thing down, I think, and settle. We've weathered the backlash from TV reports and the headlines in the paper, and now there's silence. Gary Shaw rarely sits in the courtroom and Sutton's increasingly desperate to settle.'

'Not that you'd know. You weren't in court, I'm told,' Boustead observed.

'I've been keeping an eye on things. I've read the transcript,' Morahan protested.

Bruce Fraser smiled. He kept on smiling even when his boss glared at him.

'Can we get back to the topic,' Morahan said. 'The question is whether we should negotiate a settlement now that the plaintiff's offer is more realistic. We've achieved somewhat of a capitulation – I'm sure they'll come down even lower, maybe to $200,000.'

'The problem is legal fees,' Boustead said. 'They'll be quite high now that the hearing's been going for almost a week. I object to paying Shaw, Sutton and anyone else for bringing such a spurious claim. It encourages them to do it again.'

'True, Charlie, but it remains a good result for us to get them down so much on damages and to see the back of a punitive damages claim. What do you think, Jeremy?'

'I think we go to judgment. Let's not lose sight of what we're trying to achieve – a test case on causation. It's gratifying to be rid of exemplary damages, but that was a distraction. Professor McGuinness has already arrived—'

'Yep, he's champing at the bit to get into court. He's been holed up in the Sheraton for two days. I think he's getting sick of room service,' Bruce explained.

'Well, he did arrive early. Listen, Charlie, you've paid for him to come out here, why don't you get your money's worth? The plaintiff's experts have finished and he can be called on Monday or Tuesday after Parko. Sutton will ask for a lay day or will fill in the day on Friday tendering documents or a schedule of damages. McGuinness won't take more than a day. We're so close. Let's press on.'

'Yeah, I think that's the right thing to do, Jeremy,' Charlie Boustead concluded. 'Don't bother countering the plaintiff's offer. Tell 'em to shove it up their bums.'

'I'll ring Viviana Glosioli and advise her that my clear instructions are to reject the offer in those terms,' said Bruce.

He felt elated that his client was backing his strategy. Morahan was less sanguine. 'I don't like risks, Charlie. Litigation's all about managing risks. I've done this work for many years. I'm familiar with the issues and what some of our witnesses have to say. I think we should settle it. Who knows what the Court of Appeal will do? I don't trust them up there, even though most are Jacksons alumni. And that's where we'll inevitably end up.'

'Rest assured, your position's noted, Paul,' Charlie responded. 'But nothing ventured, nothing gained. Now, let's get this show on the road. I'm looking forward to it. I might even come to court to watch McGuinness.'

◆

After Bruce Fraser informed Viviana there would be no offers from the defendants, she called a crisis meeting in Sutton's chambers.

'I don't think we could have done any more,' Sutton said to Lucas, Viviana and Gary Shaw in his chambers. 'Forgan was a disaster, but even he supports the argument that James Henderson's Australian exposure materially contributed to his mesothelioma. All this nonsense about increased risk, not knowing which exposure was the cause of the mesothelioma, etc, is all irrelevant, in my opinion. We all know it's not a matter of scientific certainty, it's only a matter of commonsense. That's the law. And Schaffer said his opinion was based on commonsense.'

'I agree,' said Lucas.

'Of course, we'll win. It would have been nice to settle it, but a beautiful victory on Christmas Eve will be equally as sweet,' Shaw added.

'You've been quiet, Viviana. What do you think?' Sutton said as he took a sip from his teacup, the liquid glistening on his protuberant bottom lip.

'Viviana's confident as well, Geoff,' Shaw answered for her. 'Isn't that right, Viv?'

'I think Mr Henderson is at risk of losing,' she said, rage building within her. 'It all depends on whether a court accepts his Australian exposure made a material contribution to his mesothelioma.' She looked fiercely at the men in the room. 'If we'd kept the offers sensible, we wouldn't be in this place. We're now prepared to offer exactly what the defendants offered when we were down at Kiama to take James's evidence. We were too greedy.'

'Relax, Viv, we did the right thing by the client. The defendants were being stingy and unreasonable. Their view of the law is wrong. The Beaver will find for Mr Henderson, you mark my words.'

Viviana had little doubt about that herself. She was worried about the Court of Appeal. And thought the rest of the team should have been as well.

Chapter 76

Jeremy Lawson and Bruce Fraser spent most of the weekend following Professor Schaffer's cross-examination with Professor McGuinness, going over his evidence and preparing the closing submissions to put to Judge Byrnes. They both knew from experience that as soon as the defendants' cases were closed, Lawson would be asked to make his final address. In mesothelioma cases, counsel had to be prepared to do things on the run. Lawson had anticipated virtually all the turns of event in the trial. Bruce knew he didn't like surprises. He wasn't going to be presented with one in this case right at the end.

McGuinness told the two lawyers that he'd spent much of the time since his arrival in Sydney reading the transcripts of evidence of his counterparts.

'I don't think, John, you're going to be overly troubled by Sutton's cross-examination,' Lawson said. 'He'll basically try to bully you into admitting that Mr Henderson's Australian exposure materially contributed to his mesothelioma.' Lawson sat in a lounge chair in Professor McGuinness's hotel suite. Folders and papers were strewn across a coffee table and a larger table McGuinness had requested hotel staff bring to his room.

'I don't think our Mr Sutton will be too sophisticated in his attack on me.' McGuinness agreed, munching on a cracker. 'From the transcript I've read, he seems to be taking a fairly simplistic tack.' McGuinness briefly stood to brush some crumbs from his sky-blue shirt. His hair was flecked with grey. Just the right amount to look sage, rather than past it. Rather like Professor Schaffer, but without the studied facade, Bruce thought.

'I'm not sure how he'll go about it because I'm damned if I can think of a solution to his predicament,' Lawson said. 'As I read your reports, John, there's no question that exposure increases the risk of mesothelioma and that's all anyone can say.'

'Correct, Jeremy.' McGuinness had the engaging habit of smiling as he spoke. Despite the American accent, Bruce found McGuinness's speech captivating. He found himself nodding in agreement with McGuinness's opinions even when he didn't fully understand what he was saying. The friendly glitter in his eyes, the smile and his concise explication all tended to lure the listener in.

'Well, I guess we'll find out soon enough whether Mr Sutton can pull a rabbit out of a hat,' McGuinness went on. 'You know, in the States, blowhards like Sutton no longer exist. He's like a caricature of a barrister – something out of Victorian England.'

'I don't want you to get the wrong impression of Geoffrey Sutton, John,' Lawson was quick to respond. 'He's a highly successful barrister and he wouldn't have got to that position without some ability. I've seen him demolish witnesses. Don't give him an opening. He'll fish around for you to make an error and then go in hard when he thinks he has one. If he chances on a point to attack your credit he'll go straight in. So, watch out.'

'I'll be on guard, Jeremy, but I'm not worried.'

◆

The respiratory physician, Professor Herbert Parkinson, who'd examined James on behalf of Henry King Industries, was cross-examined on Monday morning, after his report was tendered to the court, by Gregory Lucas. Sutton told Viviana he had handed the baton to Lucas so he could concentrate on the preparation of his cross-examination of Professor McGuinness. The truth was fairly obvious to Viviana – he simply didn't want to do it.

As a junior barrister perennially accustomed to sitting next to senior counsel who did all the talking, Lucas was visibly apprehensive about his performance. He should have been. He was no match for the erudite Parkinson. Viviana almost felt embarrassed on his behalf. Lucas was one of the many barristers who considered it good practice to preface tough questions with 'I suggest to you' or 'I put it to you' when all that was required was plain English. To Viviana, such phrasing was code for 'I'm going to put a very important proposition to you, and if you agree with it, then my client is going to win his case.' A dullard could work it out.

The cross-examination didn't commence well. As Lucas stood up, his gown became trapped under the leg of his chair. The force propelling him quickly and keenly to his feet was met by an opposing and greater force which dragged him back down into his seat with a smack. He then took about a minute to unravel the tail of his robes from the wheel of his chair. Even Judge Byrnes was tittering by the time Lucas eventually stood to commence his cross-examination. It wasn't worth the wait. After an hour of very long questions, Lucas reached a crescendo of sorts.

'I put it to you, Professor Parkinson, that Mr Henderson's exposure in Australia materially contributed to his mesothelioma.'

'No, it did not.'

'I suggest to you that it did.'

'No, it did not.'

'I suggest to you that all Mr Henderson's exposures to asbestos caused his mesothelioma.'

'No, Mr Lucas, as we have been over before. All his exposures added to the risk that he may develop mesothelioma, but it is impossible to say whether one exposure or another actually physically caused his mesothelioma.'

'I suggest to you, Professor Parkinson, that you are confusing notions of scientific certainty with the legal test of causation on the balance of probabilities. What do you say to that?'

'I say to that, Mr Lucas, that you are confusing the concept of risk and physical cause and effect. And if you want to talk about the balance of probabilities, then, as I have demonstrated, the balance of probabilities suggests that the cause of Mr Henderson's mesothelioma was his exposure in Scotland. In fact, there is a seventy-five percent probability that that was the cause.'

'Well, Professor Parkinson, I put it to you that Mr Henderson's Australian exposure significantly contributed to his mesothelioma.'

Professor Parkinson looked up at Judge Byrnes inquiringly. Jeremy Lawson rose. 'I object. That question has been asked countless times by my learned friend. There is a limit, surely, your Honour!'

'Yes, Mr Lawson, I tend to agree. Mr Lucas, that question is rejected. You have already asked it.'

'Well, yes, in that case, your Honour, well ... yes. No further questions.'

Viviana could again sense her case going down the gurgler. She hoped Lucas would follow. Thankfully, there were no members of the Henderson family in court to witness the farce. Maybe Sutton could grab the impetus back from the defendants.

'I call Professor John McGuinness, your Honour,' Jeremy Lawson announced, after Professor Parkinson had been excused.

Professor McGuinness entered the courtroom, smiling warmly at Judge Byrnes. He was dressed in beige corduroy trousers, white shirt, Yale tie and tweed sports jacket. He appeared both earthy and refined. Prompted by Jeremy Lawson's questions, he explained his reasoning in simple terms, referring to medical articles as required to reinforce his points. Bruce could sense that even Judge Byrnes was being won over. He must be a fantastic lecturer, he thought. His performance in examination-in-chief was mesmerising.

◆

The next morning, when Geoffrey Sutton rose to tackle McGuinness, Viviana wondered how his, she hoped, carefully thought-out plan would go.

'You give evidence regularly in litigation in the United States, don't you, Professor McGuinness?' Sutton started his salvo.

'I'm not sure what you mean by "regularly", Mr Sutton. I do, however, testify in areas of my expertise in courts in the United States from time to time.'

'And it is the case, is it not, that the preponderance of the cases in which you testify are for defendants?' Viviana had received an email from a member of the American Trial Lawyers Association, suggesting 'everyone' knew Professor McGuinness was a defendant's man. Viviana thought it quite flimsy, but had passed it on to Sutton as he was the barrister and would be better able to evaluate its utility. He must have found it useful, she thought. He certainly gave the question the necessary forthright tone.

'No, that's not correct, Mr Sutton.' Professor McGuinness smiled. 'I make it a point of habit to accept offers to provide an opinion from both plaintiffs and defendants in equal share. I never depart from that practice. And, of course, my duty to the court is always to provide an objective, independent opinion.'

'Yes, but Professor McGuinness, you accept these offers to provide an opinion in return for payment of a considerable amount of money, don't you?' Sutton blundered on.

Lawson rose a little as if he were tempted to object, but sat back down again. Viviana understood why. McGuinness could look after himself. 'Yes, I do charge significant fees for my work. Just like you would, Mr Sutton, as a, how do they call it in Australia, silk?'

All in the courtroom laughed, including Judge Byrnes. Sutton puffed out his cheeks, reddening in the face. 'Right, well, Professor McGuinness, crocidolite is the most potent mesotheliomogenic fibre, isn't it?'

'Yes, I believe I've already said that in court today, Mr Sutton.'

'If you have a man with two separate periods of exposure, one of which is to crocidolite and the other not, then the exposure to crocidolite is far more likely than the other to have caused his mesothelioma, wouldn't you agree?'

'I assume, Mr Sutton, you mean with all other things being equal?'

'Yes, of course, professor.'

'Well, if that's the case, then you're talking about concurrent exposure because otherwise there can't be two separate periods of exposure at the same time. Are you referring to concurrent exposures?'

'No, yes, umm, ahh, no, I am not.'

'Very well, you are referring to sequential exposures in which case all things can't be the same between the two periods of exposure. One must have been earlier than the other. One period may have been to crocidolite and the other to amosite or chrysotile, but they can't be identical in all other facets. One must have come first. And the one that comes first, Mr Sutton, has a much greater probability of resulting in mesothelioma than the other. So, what are you asking me to assume in your hypothetical case?'

'Well, umm, I want you to assume that the first exposure was not to crocidolite, but the second exposure was to crocidolite. What is your view then?'

'Are you asking me to assume that the intensity of exposure is the same in both periods?'

'Yes, I am,' Sutton assured McGuinness, not sounding confident he should be providing such an assurance.

'Very well, and is the first exposure to amphibole asbestos, if not crocidolite? And is the exposure in both situations out of doors or in confined spaces?'

'Listen, professor, just answer the questions I'm asking you,' Sutton spluttered.

'I'm endeavouring to do that, Mr Sutton, but I'm unsure of the assumptions you're asking me to make,' McGuinness said in his friendly, measured manner.

'It's simple, professor. Two periods of exposure. Both of equal intensity. Both for the same number of years. One to crocidolite and the earlier period to a mixture of amosite and chrysotile. The first one indoors, the second period largely out of doors and not in confined spaces. Got it?'

'Got it, Mr Sutton. Just one further question. What products are we talking about? Are we talking about insulation products and lagging in the first period or something else? Are we talking about raw asbestos fibre in the second period or to asbestos fibre released from cutting or working with asbestos cement sheets, or something else?'

'I'll try to make it clear, professor. In the first period, the exposure is to insulation products and lagging. In the second period there is indoors exposure to raw blue asbestos followed by a short period of exposure to a mixture of all fibre types followed by a longer period of outdoors exposure to asbestos released from asbestos cement sheets while working as a builder. Do you follow?'

'Yes, I do, Mr Sutton. We now have four periods of exposure not two. What you are asking me to assume is essentially Mr Henderson's exposure to asbestos, is it not?'

'Well, that's not what I was trying to get at, but yes, assume that to be the case.' Sutton must have felt as though he was the one who'd been cross-examined into making a concession he didn't want to make, Viviana thought.

'Very well, then the answer to that question is as per my evidence earlier today and in my reports. The earlier period of exposure contributed the greatest risk to Mr Henderson's developing mesothelioma. On the balance of probabilities, the earlier period of exposure caused his mesothelioma. It had a seventy-five percent probability of causing it.'

'And the second exposure, or periods of exposure, in Australia, materially contributed to its development as well, didn't it professor?'

'No, Mr Sutton, it did not. It contributed to the risk that he may go on to develop it, but risk and actual physical cause are two different concepts.

Just because an exposure increased the chance or risk that something may happen in the future doesn't mean to say that it was the cause of that subsequent event. You see, Mr Sutton, medical science can't say whether a mesothelioma is caused by one or other or both exposures in your example. We don't know when a mesothelioma is triggered or why it is triggered. Who can say which risk materialised? All we know is that, from population studies, such as those in which I've been involved or in those I've referred to, the incidence rate of mesothelioma is proportional, in an exponential way, with time since first exposure. It's also proportional, but not exponentially, to the concentration of exposure, the fibre type to which a population is exposed, the type of products a population works with, and probably some genetic factors as well. The period of exposure earliest in time has the greatest chance of being the one that materialises or "comes home" to cause the mesothelioma.'

'Are you saying that Mr Henderson's exposure in Australia could not possibly have caused his mesothelioma?'

'No, I'm not saying that, Mr Sutton. I can't exclude it as a possible cause—'

'I see, professor, so you concede, do you, that Mr Henderson's Australian exposure could quite possibly be the cause of his mesothelioma?' Viviana wondered whether Sutton had spotted an opening.

'Of course, I concede that, Mr Sutton. Although, when one looks at my calculations of aetiologic contribution, the risk is far higher for the Scottish exposure, I accept that the Australian exposure increased Mr Henderson's risk of developing mesothelioma. It may quite possibly be the cause, but can I say that as a matter of probability? No, I cannot. And nor can any other expert, based upon the scientific studies that have been published to date on the subject. We do not know.'

Sutton appeared to have missed most of Professor McGuinness's explanation. He must have believed he had extracted a telling concession when the professor said, 'Of course, I concede that.' Viviana saw his shoulders relaxing. His frown disappeared. 'Thank you, Professor McGuinness.' He sat down, turning around to Viviana behind him with Gary Shaw. He nodded to them as if he had done his job. Viviana sat still and expressionless. He had not achieved a single thing.

After Professor McGuinness left the court, Judge Byrnes called on Jeremy Lawson to commence his closing address. Viviana expected him to ask for further time to prepare. She was dismayed when Lawson stood promptly, handed up a written outline of his submissions and commenced his address on the question of causation. Why couldn't she brief barristers like him?

Lawson was methodical and, Viviana knew, basically correct. Sandaver simply adopted Lawson's submissions. When it came to Sutton, he sounded like he'd already spent more than enough time on the case and didn't want to expend any further energy on it, particularly in the event that the plaintiff lost. He repeated in several different ways what he'd said in chambers to the members of James's legal team. He was flat. His tone was tired. He succeeded in closing the case with the faint, impressionless plop of a pebble into a pond. It was up to the judge to get James over the line.

Judge Byrnes thanked counsel for their assistance and advised them that she would deliver her judgment the next morning in light of Mr Henderson's critical condition.

◆

Later that evening, Jenny received a call from Viviana. The solicitor had updated her every afternoon or evening during the trial, describing how the evidence had gone, advising Jenny about how Shaw, Sutton and Lucas believed the case was going. She had carefully omitted to mention her own anxieties about the outcome or her opinions on the evidence. She needed to remain upbeat for her clients.

'Viviana, tell me what you genuinely think about the case.'

It was the one question she dreaded. 'Well, Jenny, it's not really for me to say. I'm not the one who's led the evidence in court or cross-examined the witnesses. That really is a matter for counsel.'

'Viviana, I trust your opinion. You know that. You've been sitting in court, listening to the evidence. You know what's been happening. Please tell me what you think.'

'Jenny, to tell you the absolute truth, I'm worried. Although I think Judge Byrnes will find in James's favour, I'm worried that the defendants will appeal the decision to the Court of Appeal.'

'An appeal? I don't know if James can hang on that long. He's very sick, you know, Viviana.' Jenny sounded distraught. 'I think he's holding on for the sake of the court case. He wants to know the decision before he dies. I wish he had something better to focus on, but that's all he has right now.'

'I'm sorry, Jenny, but you wanted to know what I thought. I think that's the reality. And I can't say what the Court of Appeal will do. The judges up there, well, they're not like Judge Byrnes.'

'I don't like the sound of that.'

'We'll see, Jenny. Let's cross that bridge when we get to it – if we get to it. Okay?'

'Okay, Viviana.' She put the phone down and turned to James.

His ears had pricked up when he heard the telephone ring and the mention of Viviana's name. He lay on the electric bed like a rag doll – crumpled into the bedclothes. Not much different in form from the pleats and folds in the sheets. His skin was yellow, drawn, almost translucent. His eyes were glassy blue marbles tucked deeply into the sockets of his face. Jenny sat down on the chair next to his bed. She stroked his arm. 'That was Viviana, dear. The judge will be deciding your case tomorrow.'

'At last,' came the sound of his voice, a rustling as soft and delicate as silk against her ear.

'Yes, James, it will all be over tomorrow. Viviana was very optimistic. She says the judge is likely to find in your favour.'

'I hope so.'

Chapter 77

On Wednesday 23 December 2002, the parties attended court to take judgment. Judge Byrnes read from her prepared manuscript. She appeared haggard, her eyes bleary. She doubtless had worked on the judgment most of the night, Bruce Fraser thought. Initially she spoke in a faltering fashion, gaining strength as she continued:

Saul Bellow once wrote, 'You don't know what you've got within you.' He may have been referring to other matters, and to events decades in the past, but his words are as apt today as they were then. They are particularly apt to the case of James Henderson. He never knew what he had within him. What he had inside him were asbestos fibres. Deadly asbestos fibres from the work he did to support his family; sitting there for years before causing cancer. Mr Henderson is now slowly suffocating to death due to a cancer known as mesothelioma. As it grows, he loses life. His family loses hope...

Bruce looked towards Jeremy Lawson. He raised an eyebrow. Why was a Catholic judge quoting a Jewish writer in an asbestos diseases trial?

Mr Henderson is a 67-year-old married man. He is a brave man, struggling to fight a horrible cancer that he knows will soon kill him. I heard Mr Henderson give evidence. He did so in a stoical, courageous manner. He is in a terrible state. I give this judgment ex tempore because of the urgency of the situation.

Mr Henderson worked for five years in the shipyards on the Clyde River in Glasgow before migrating to Australia. His work as a fitter and turner exposed him to high concentrations of amphibole asbestos from the lagging used to insulate ships. That exposure was frequently in confined spaces.

When he arrived in Australia, he worked in the Disaster Gorge mine and mill owned and operated by the second defendant, V&L Ltd. Although that exposure was for not quite two years, it was daily, heavy and exclusively to blue asbestos, known geologically as crocidolite. Studies of the workers at Disaster Gorge have proved 'Disaster Blue' to be one of the most potent inducers of mesothelioma on the planet.

Mr Henderson then worked for the first defendant, Henry King Industries Limited, at its Riverwood asbestos cement factory. Mr Henderson was employed in various capacities throughout the factory for about three years. He was exposed to blue, brown and white asbestos on a daily, heavy basis.

Mr Henderson finally worked as a builder, initially for a Mr Reginald Blaxland, and then on his own account, for thirty-two years. He regularly handled asbestos cement sheets made by the first defendant during that period. That exposure was much lighter than his previous exposures. It was intermittent, largely outdoors and to dust mainly made up of cement and silica rather than asbestos fibres. While there was some blue asbestos in the mix, most of the fibre to which Mr Henderson was exposed was white asbestos with a smaller proportion of brown.

Mr Henderson, as I said, gave his evidence truthfully and bravely. No serious attempt was made by counsel for the defendants to gainsay that evidence. I accept it in its entirety.

Breach of duty was not disputed by either defendant. Based on the expert evidence of Dr George Phillips tendered by the plaintiff, I find that both defendants breached their duties of care to Mr Henderson by not issuing warnings, supplying him with effective respiratory equipment or in taking any number of cheap, simple precautions to keep dust down.

The real issue in the case is causation. In that regard, I have heard the evidence of eminent local and international experts, who have each referred to numerous medical articles on the subject. Each of the experts did his very best to give open and honest evidence. I was impressed by them all...

Judge Byrnes proceeded to summarise the expert evidence. It took an hour. Bruce grew restless, impatient for the result. Just when it seemed that Judge Byrnes was steering her way towards a decision on causation, she changed tack and launched into a lengthy analysis of the law on the issue. Finally, she moved on to her decision:

As I have said earlier in these reasons, I was impressed by the objectivity and integrity of the experts called by the parties in the case. Professor McGuinness, in particular, was a most captivating and learned man. His evidence I found very helpful in explaining the epidemiological science underpinning much of what we currently know about mesothelioma.

At long last, Bruce thought, a judge in the ADT was going to find for a defendant at first instance. It had been worthwhile paying McGuinness's enormous fee in bringing him out to Australia. He started to feel something like pride, even joy, but then...

Unfortunately, I found Professor McGuinness's evidence to be largely irrelevant. The same can be said for the evidence of Professor Parkinson and, indeed, the defendants' submissions. It seems to me that the defendants have tried to elevate the common law test of causation to one demanding scientific certainty. While scientific rigour is to be applauded in certain areas, it has no place in a court of common law jurisdiction. Causation is a matter of simple commonsense. It need only be proved on a balance of probabilities rather than to the point of 100 percent scientific certainty.

I am satisfied that the plaintiff has proved that the defendants' breaches of duty materially contributed to his mesothelioma. Despite their frank acknowledgement of the uncertainties involved in this area of science, Drs Freeman, Haug, Forgan and Professor Schaffer steadfastly remained of the view that the plaintiff's exposure to asbestos in Australia materially contributed to his mesothelioma. That is all he had to prove. I am fortified in this opinion by the concessions made by Professor McGuinness in cross-examination. He, quite properly in my view, admitted that the Australian exposure could have been the cause of the plaintiff's mesothelioma. This frank admission provided credence to the plaintiff's case on causation which, as I have said before, was being advanced on a simple commonsense basis rather than the scientific certainty contended for by Professor McGuinness.'

Bruce regretted allowing himself some hope. He should have seen it coming, but, even so, Byrnes's superficial, unintellectual analysis was galling. In front of him at the bar table, Sutton and Lucas were already shaking hands and smiling. Lucas swung around towards Viviana Glosioli and Gary Shaw and gave them a fist pump behind the veil of his robes. Strangely, Viviana didn't seem overly happy.

I now turn to the question of quantum. Mr Henderson is a relatively young man. He has ... only ... been retired for a short time...

Judge Byrnes was visibly distressed. The words were slow to come as she fought back the tears. The lawyers looked up at her heaving chest below her wooden turret. The three reporters in the gallery rapidly jotted down notes. Over the next thirty emotional minutes, the judge spoke of James Henderson's pain and suffering, the great loss to his family, the tireless care provided to him by his wife Jenny and daughter Kate. Then it was all over.

There will be a verdict and judgment for the plaintiff in the sum of $473,000.00.

All rise!' the tipstaff intoned.

The judge departed for the seclusion of her chambers where, Bruce thought, she could reflect on her mistaken view of the law over a cup of tea. He packed up his books as Lucas, Sutton and Shaw whooped and backslapped each other. He glanced at Viviana. She stood like a black flamingo, observing impassively, waiting to take flight.

'This calls for a celebration!' Sutton shouted. 'Lunch at Rockpool! It's on me!'

The heat and fury of the trial vanished. James Henderson's lawyers noisily left the court. Bruce looked around the courtroom. The stacked and packed metal trolleys, remaining to be collected by paralegals, stood as characterless monuments to a battle now lost and won.

Chapter 78

Jenny rushed to James's bedside. 'You won, James! You won! That was Viviana. The judge delivered her judgment this morning – about five minutes ago – you've done it!' She kissed him on the cheeks, the lips, the forehead. She hugged him gingerly about the shoulders. James was half asleep and very weak, but he smiled as he kept his eyes closed. Lifting herself slightly above him in order to see him more clearly, Jenny noted his contented smile, and was happy. It was finally over. He could be at peace. He had been right to fight them. He had beaten them. She bent over again to hug him.

She stayed gently clasped to him until her worry about suffocating him pushed her away. Kate came in from hanging the bed linen on the clothesline as Jenny stood up. She saw her mother's face brimming with news. 'What is it, Mum?'

'Dad's won his case! That was the solicitor. He's won! I better ring Robert and Douglas.'

'Oh, that's fabulous news. That's fantastic, Dad,' Kate said, depositing the laundry basket on the kitchen bench, and walking over to her father to kiss him.

'What happens now?' she asked.

'I'm not sure. We just wait for the cheque, I think – \$473,000.'

'Wow! That's a lot. Isn't that more than Viviana told you she was expecting if Dad won?'

'Yes, I think so.'

'What about an appeal? Aren't they likely to—' Kate stopped abruptly as her mother shook her head and put a finger to her lips.

Jenny need not have been apprehensive. James had drifted off to sleep in a morphine haze.

Most of his days were now spent asleep or zonked out by the medication. He couldn't go to the toilet on his own anymore. He couldn't be showered, even with assistance. His feeble bag of bones could not support itself. Jenny sponged him every morning to make him comfortable. It took a great deal of ingenuity and effort to co-ordinate lifting James to change the sheets. He may have become less mobile, but his night sweats had not eased. They were worse.

His condition had deteriorated dramatically after he gave evidence. Within twenty-four hours, he'd become permanently bed bound. He asked for morphine every two hours. Jenny didn't know whether she should give him extra doses. She rang Dr Jimmy Yeong, the oncology registrar at Wollongong Hospital, who said that she could administer morphine every one to two hours. Jenny was nonetheless reluctant to give James more. She felt she was losing her husband to the oblivion the drug provided when she wanted him alert, talkative, even if it were only for a few days. Kate argued that her father wouldn't ask for morphine if he were not in pain. Jenny knew this was true. James was not the sort of man who complained about anything unless he had to. It hurt her to know that he was silently fighting a horrible pain. It was like some dreadful creature eating away at him from the inside.

He hardly ate anything. He sipped trivial amounts of the thin chicken broth Jenny prepared, some water, and that was about it. The community nurse, who visited daily, insisted James required admission to the palliative care unit at Wollongong Hospital. Jenny flatly refused to allow James to spend a single second away from home. Dr Yeong was brought in to mediate. After speaking with the consultant, Dr Pryde, he reluctantly agreed with Jenny so long as she and Kate believed they could manage. They assured him they could. But James developed pressure sores over his buttocks and heels. The visiting nurse was furious when she found out, but her anger was directed more at herself than Jenny and Kate. She shouldn't have been angry. By the time the ulcers developed, James had virtually no flesh between his sacrum, hips and the bed. A parchment-thin wrapping of skin was all that covered his bones. It split like paper, exposing the white bone and yellow cartilage beneath. The same outcome would have occurred in hospital. Dr Yeong prescribed antibiotics to ward off infection. Movement caused pain. As there was no longer any barrier between James's bones and the bacteria on surrounding surfaces, Dr Yeong was forced to increase James's morphine. An infection could not be avoided.

The morning after the judgment, James weakened further. He lapsed into unconsciousness. His breaths were feathery light. Jenny had to put her ear to his mouth to hear anything. She telephoned Dr Yeong. He told her it was not long now. Kate telephoned Robert and Douglas. They said they were on their way. Kate told them to hurry. And then the gurgling sound returned. At first, it was only a slight bubbling on inspiration. As time went by, it became audible while James inhaled and exhaled. It was a coarse, ugly noise. Jenny had been taught how to use the suction equipment, but when she tried to suck the awful sound away, James's face would contort in what she thought was pain. Within minutes of clearing his airway, the gurgling returned, vibrating through his chest, threatening to drown him in his own saliva.

Jenny and Kate sat either side of the bed. A haunting time with every moment full of anguish. Despair opening up in the expanding gloom of the room to fill the world. Jenny could see herself reflected in her daughter's face, could recognise the frank desolation staring back at her, and could feel it within herself – making her as one with James in his, their, pain. The nightmare interrupted only by the occasional mopping of the forehead, the smoothing of James's thin locks from his face, the sporadic flicker of movement of his eyes under their lids.

Robert and Douglas arrived together, having driven down in Robert's car. They strode through the door purposefully, as if they might be able to do something, to take control. The dismal scene before them shattered their resolve, sent them falling clumsily into chairs, which they drew close to their father's bed. They reached out to hold their mother's hands. She turned to them, exposing her raw, feverish emotions. The vigil continued.

Late in the afternoon, James let out a groan. His eyes remained closed. The family looked at his pale withered face, his brow twisted in unknowable horror. His stertorous breathing resumed its toil. Mucus trickled from the edges of the nasal prongs delivering oxygen into the choking cavity of his chest. James groaned again. His arms flexed slowly at his sides. Jenny stared at Kate in shock. Then James's hands lifted as if pulled by an unseen puppeteer; his eyes opened, staring sightlessly at the ceiling. Jenny gasped, cried out, 'James, I'm here, James!' She grabbed his hand and squeezed it tightly. 'I'm here. I'm here!' His eyes rolled back. Their light flared like a gas lantern just lit, then dimmed and went out. His arms weakened, and his left hand flopped down on the bed. But Jenny held firmly to his right. 'No, James, No! Don't go! Don't go! Don't go!' she wailed. 'Don't leave me!' His jaw slackened; his breathing stopped. He lay motionless, mouth agape, eyes fixed on eternity. Jenny fell forward onto his chest, her cheek against his. Douglas stood and put his arm around his mother. And they stayed like that, bawling, until Jenny was awakened from her trance by the icy touch of James's skin against hers.

◆

That day, Viviana Glosioli was served with a notice of appeal filed by Henry King Industries Limited. After she learned of James Henderson's death, she received a second notice of appeal – from V&L Ltd.

PART VIII

Chapter 79

The day after James died, it was Christmas. They all drove up to Robert's home for the day. Jenny stared like a zombie at her grandchildren as they giggled and ran in the yard, playing with their new toys and climbing all over Tess. Her general practitioner had prescribed sedatives. She refused to take them. She couldn't feel anything anyway. She sat numbly, fiddling with the plate of roast turkey and vegetables she had been served.

'Where's Grandpa?' Robert's son, Duigald, asked her. She looked into the toddler's inquisitive, sparkling blue eyes, his innocent face, the mop of wavy blond hair like his grandfather's. Her speechlessness unnerved him. He started to fidget. 'What's wrong, Grandma?' Jenny studied his concerned little face, watched him put his small hand on her knee. She dissolved, trembling, into tears. The sound built within her, growing up and out of the depths in which she had locked herself away for months. She doubled over in sorrow, then threw herself back against the chair, howling, trying to cover her face as Duigald ran away, crying in fear. Robert embraced her, drew her up into his arms. He led her down the hallway and into the spare bedroom. 'It will be okay, Mum,' he said.

By the new year, things had not improved. Jenny was not okay. Viviana had rung to explain that, as executrix of James's will, Jenny needed to take over the claim on behalf of his estate. She was reluctant to have anything to do with the legal proceedings. Indeed, she couldn't think of anything worse. The lawyers had given James a false victory. She felt he had been betrayed. With Viviana's help, however, she forced herself to be involved. She had to – for James's sake. He would have wanted to see it through to the end. He wouldn't have given up without a fight. Viviana also explained that there was a small risk that, if she lost the appeal, the defendants could seek to recover their legal costs from her. That could be as much as $250,000. 'I can't afford that. I'd have to sell the house,' she told Viviana.

'Jenny, I only mention it as a theoretical risk. It's extremely unlikely. I've never known a successful defendant try to recover costs from a losing plaintiff, particularly in circumstances like yours. The adverse publicity a corporate defendant would receive is security enough against an attempt to recover costs from a grieving widow. Can you imagine it? I really believe it'll be okay, so please don't worry about it.'

Viviana's explanation appeased Jenny to a degree. It sounded logical. Besides, the defendants had already lost. Viviana had reported that Geoffrey Sutton believed the defendants were up against it with their appeal.

'Jenny, I assure you everyone is doing, I'm doing, as much as we can to hold onto the hard-won victory. All you can do is wait. I'll keep you updated with any new developments.'

'Viviana, please tell me what you think. Of course, I'm interested in what the barristers say, but I very much want to hear your thoughts. I trust your instincts.'

'As I've mentioned before, I'm worried, Jenny. I'm afraid you could lose. Henry King's American expert witness was very impressive. I hope I'm wrong. I don't want to upset you.'

'Viviana, it's okay. When there are real problems to be faced, I want to know about them. I want you to tell me.'

'Okay, Jenny. I'll do my best.'

Jenny knew she was hopeless at waiting. Time with herself was her worst enemy. She couldn't tolerate the awful, slow torture of loneliness at

Kiama. It seemed cold even though it was the middle of summer. After a while, she closed up the house and moved up to Sydney with Tess to stay with Robert's family and then with Douglas and his wife. The hubbub of family life distracted her. As autumn and the hearing in the Court of Appeal approached, Jenny moved in with Kate and her partner, Rod.

They all tried to cajole her into several low-key outings, but she proved hard to shift. The weight of her melancholy increased, dragging behind her like a heavy iron ball. She had little motivation, picked at the meals provided for her, and struggled to fall asleep. She couldn't stop seeing James's waxy grey death mask and the unnatural lipless gape of his mouth. She hadn't been able to push it closed when he died. His face was there in front of her when she closed her eyes. It was there as a grim apparition when she opened them. It just wouldn't go away. She doubted her life would ever have meaning again.

Chapter 80

'No offence, Jeremy, but I think it would be prudent to brief a top QC to lead you in the appeal,' Paul Morahan said as he, Bruce Fraser, Jeremy Lawson and Charlie Boustead discussed tactics for the appeal in Lawson's chambers.

'What we need,' he continued, 'is a senior counsel who's a real heavy hitter. These are serious and important issues. We need the bench to see that.'

'Jeremy and I have toyed with the idea already,' Bruce said. 'We think it will cost too much and will erode much of Jeremy's preparation time in having to bring a QC up to speed. Jeremy already has mastery of the facts and knows the law inside out. We don't want to put our arguments at risk because the judges are distracted by an ill-prepared silk.'

Bruce also thought that because the appeal judges reputedly had towering intellects and minds like steel traps, they were more likely to be attracted to Lawson's unemotional, intellectual style. The Court of Appeal was a very busy and hard-working court, having to deal with many disgruntled litigants. Bruce wanted to make its job easier.

'Yeah, I tend to agree. Jeremy's the one to take us forward,' Boustead said.

'I hope you're right,' Morahan said. 'Because I'm not convinced.'

◆

'Can't we brief a recognised appellate advocate to lead Sutton?' Viviana asked at the regular Shaw & Fletcher asbestos team meeting.

'No, it's unnecessary,' Gary Shaw said. 'Geoffrey Sutton is, after all, a senior counsel. It would look absurd. He has run appeals before. He knows what he's doing.'

'He's not a specialist appellate silk, though. His appeals have been about damages, not causation.'

'Viviana, I understand your reasons for wanting a new leader, but it's not on. We'll go with Sutton. He's got us this far. He can take it all the way. It would be insulting to do otherwise.'

'Who cares if he's insulted?'

'I do. He's an important part of our asbestos business. I can't afford to get him offside.'

'I see.'

'I hope you do.'

She could. Viviana knew Shaw could not retain the services of a high-profile appellate barrister without paying for it. Sutton was briefed on a 'no win, no fee' basis. He would only get paid if they won. Shaw had already forked out a fortune on medical experts for the case; she knew he wasn't about to throw any more money at it by briefing a heavyweight QC. It was only about money. Sutton would have to do.

◆

Jenny didn't want to attend court, but Viviana convinced her to. The truth was Sutton had insisted Jenny attend because he thought the presence of the 'grieving widow' would garner some sentimental support for the case. What a silly ploy, Viviana thought. She did, however, as she was instructed.

The courtroom was on the eleventh floor of the Supreme Court building. The packed lift stopped at almost every floor on the way up. Jenny found herself pressed into a corner behind tall, black-robed figures wearing wigs; prim, emotionless women; and a few 'civilians' like her – wide-eyed and frightened. The lift opened onto a brightly lit, charmless foyer. As she moved along the equally sterile corridor, Jenny noticed courtrooms on either side. Groups of barristers and other suited men and women joked or argued animatedly outside the entrances. She felt alien. She should not have come. Thankfully, Kate had insisted on coming with her.

The courtroom itself was large and bright. It had high ceilings, an ornate coat of arms below where the judges sat, and rows of tables. Viviana spotted Jenny and Kate soon after they peered through the door. She motioned for them to sit in the front row of the seats reserved for onlookers. Geoffrey Sutton, Greg Lucas and Gary Shaw greeted her in turn. They wished her well. Jenny looked around the room. She recognised the same lawyers who had been present in her house when James gave his evidence. She felt uncomfortable at the memory.

Suddenly, an echoing thump sounded three times on the wooden door behind the judges' bench. 'All rise!' declared a man dressed in a military-style uniform. Jenny stood as three sombre men entered the courtroom, bowed, and sat down. She took Kate's hand as she heard her name being called: 'Matter number 23001, Henry King Industries Limited and V&L Ltd and Jennifer Henderson as executrix of the will of the late James Henderson!'

Jenny didn't know who the judges were. They wore wigs, but unlike those worn by the barristers. Theirs were more tightly curled, thicker, and with no pigtail at the back. She thought the judges added some colour to the courtroom with their vivid red robes. But as they started speaking, Jenny realised that was all the colour they would provide. The atmosphere was grim.

The middle judge spoke frequently. He seemed to Jenny to be the one in charge. He was thin, serious. The stiff, straight line of grey eyebrows projected from his brow like a windbreak. His big nose curved downwards as if pulled by invisible wires. Jenny thought he must not be a very happy man seeing how often he frowned. The judge to his left was similarly thin, and only marginally less severe looking. He had a larger head. Jenny wondered whether that meant he had a bigger brain. The third judge had a broad, ruddy-cheeked face dominated by thick black spectacles, like those worn by FBI agents. His eyes appeared unusually large through the lenses. She didn't see much hope in them.

As she was scrutinising these men, Jenny was again dismayed to hear her name mentioned. Geoffrey Sutton was on his feet gesturing at her and saying to the judges, 'Mrs Henderson, your Honours, is here today in court. Although it will no doubt be very distressing for her, having lost her husband, we considered it important for her to attend.' Sutton donned a mask of great solemnity.

The middle judge interrupted his act. 'Mr Sutton, we will have none of that emotional theatre in this court. Please turn to your arguments.'

'Yes, your Honour.'

Oh dear, Jenny thought. She tried to listen and understand the argument, but was lost within several sentences and spent the remainder of the morning sitting perplexed, worried and sad. The FBI judge interrogated Sutton as if he were a suspect on espionage charges. When the middle judge started his own inquisition, Jenny felt all was doomed.

At the luncheon adjournment, Viviana told her that she could go. 'I think I might, dear; I don't like those men up there. They seem very mean.'

'They are, I'm afraid. I'll let you know if anything happens. It might take two to three months for the decision.'

'Thank you, Viviana. I understand.'

She was glad to be out of that friendless place.

Chapter 81

In early May, Jenny decided it was time to return home. She didn't think it fair to impose on her children any longer. They had their own lives to live. She had to move on and face her home, James's home, alone. Early one Saturday, Robert drove her down to Kiama with Tess.

It was cold and blustery when they arrived. The grass was overgrown, and the mailbox was overflowing with advertising flyers, local papers and letters. Robert insisted on mowing the lawn and helping with the groceries before he departed. He even cut some wood for the fireplace, just in case the weather remained cold. He delayed leaving as long as he could. Jenny eventually had to push him out the door. 'I'll be fine. I've coped on my own before, you know, when your father was sick,' she said. 'I'll be all right, I promise. I've got Tess to watch over me.'

'Okay. I'll go, but ring me if you need anything, anything at all.'

'I will. Now, please, go.'

She watched him reverse out of the driveway, the headlights like beacons in the murky light of dusk. She waved as Robert turned the car into the street and continued waving until the car was lost to sight. A dark, lonely figure sweeping her arm from side to side in the shadow of the trees.

Jenny shivered as the swirling darkness closed around her and hurried in to the warmth of the house. It didn't look lived in. It was too neat, too ordered. After James died, the bed and other pieces of hospital equipment had been collected. Kate had cleaned the house. She was as obsessive as her mother about tidiness, although Jenny suspected the industry had a lot to do with distracting herself after her father's death. Jenny knew how therapeutic a good clean could be. She'd been doing it for weeks while James was ill.

Now that she was in her home alone, Jenny regretted the decision. The emptiness was oppressive. Tess looked up at her, waiting for action. There was nothing to give. She remembered the day when James was first diagnosed with mesothelioma. How she'd wandered the house, crazy with fear and depression. She could feel herself sinking again. She remembered being tossed in the cold foam of the surf, feeling as useless as waterlogged flotsam, a completely meaningless thing without her James. She was lost.

As the dark thoughts returned, Jenny panicked. She clutched at her clothes, pulling the neck of her jumper down to give herself air, to release the pressure. She felt faint. Her head was spinning, and she couldn't stop it. She crashed into the bedroom and onto the bed, breathing shallowly.

When Jenny opened her eyes, the ceiling light was blazing above her. She was exhausted. She must have blacked out. She didn't want her life to be governed by such uncontrollable panic. James would be disappointed in her. She forced herself to have a shower, feed Tess and make some pasta for dinner. After she'd washed up and dried the dishes, she sat on the verandah, rugged up in her dressing gown, listening to the waves and feeling the chill air on her skin. The lights from neighbouring houses twinkled and flared through her watery eyes. Were there couples chatting to each other? Were they entwined in bed, at peace in a warm embrace? How many were feeling the loving caresses of their husbands? She stayed outside until the cold made her nose run. She wanted her James back. She wanted to feel the warmth of his body beside her in bed.

◆

Jenny woke late and couldn't be bothered changing out of her pyjamas. She put on her dressing gown and made a cup of tea. She went downstairs and into the garden, damp clumps of wet grass adhering to her slippers. The shrubs needed a hard pruning. Some tree branches were hanging over the gutters. They would have to be cut back. The paint was peeling off the back door and the path to the beach was almost lost to weeds. She couldn't take Tess down there. So much to do, she thought. How can I possibly do it? I need him so much.

She went back inside, leaving a trail of grass behind her. The many useless tasks of life overwhelmed her. Panic again began to take hold, its tentacles stretching around her, squeezing the air from her lungs.

The telephone rang. Jenny grabbed at it as if it was a lifeline. 'Yes?' she puffed.

'Jenny, it's Viviana. Are you okay? You sound out of breath.'

'I had to run. I was outside. What is it?'

Viviana paused. 'Jenny.' She paused again.

'What is it, Viviana?'

Silence.

'It's bad, isn't it?'

'Yes, I'm afraid it is.

'What?'

'I'm terribly sorry, Jenny. We lost the appeal. The Court of Appeal has found for the defendants. I'm sorry.'

'Lost?'

'Yes.'

'I see. It's over then?'

'Well, we can seek special leave to appeal to the High Court,' Viviana explained.

'No. I want it to end. I can't do this anymore.' Jenny put the receiver down while Viviana was speaking. 'I'm sorry,' she said to the empty space around her.

Chapter 82

Viviana read the Court of Appeal's conclusions. She realised, seeing it in black and white, what she had always been worried about – a strict legalistic approach to causation.

It may be accepted that a material contribution is all that the plaintiff must prove on the balance of probabilities to succeed. But the law requires a plaintiff to be able to point, on a balance of probabilities, to the particular defendant or defendants who was or were negligent: it is not enough that he can say that one of them must have been and all of them may have been negligent. Proof of causation is often difficult for a plaintiff. The law recognises this difficulty. But the difficulty does not mean that basic legal principles are to be abandoned. Judge Byrnes ignored those principles. The law does not equate the situation where the defendant has materially increased the risk of injury with one where it has materially contributed to the injury. That is what Judge Byrnes did. This critical elision was at the heart of the error in her reasoning.

The medical evidence in this case rose no higher than establishing that, over the course of Mr Henderson's lifetime, a quantity of inhaled asbestos fibres remained in his lungs. One or more of those fibres eventually migrated to the lining around the lungs, known as the pleura, where they triggered the development of a mesothelioma. No expert could point to the mechanism by which the fibres triggered the mesothelioma. The fibres may lie dormant in a person's chest for decades before the cancer is triggered. This medical evidence is critical to proof of causation. It does not permit any conclusion as to which source of exposure triggered the cancer. It is not enough to say that the plaintiff suffered asbestos exposure from no other sources and therefore as it must have been one or more of the defendants in this case, they may all be treated as being vulnerable to a claim being made against them. Evidence that demonstrates that all exposures could be causative or that one exposure cannot be excluded as a possible cause (such as the so-called concession of Professor McGuinness) is no more than proof of a possibility. The law does not attach liability to a defendant if a plaintiff can only establish that the breach of duty possibly caused the injury.

The overwhelming evidence established that the greatest risk of Mr Henderson's developing mesothelioma was his exposure in Scotland. Even if it were permissible to equate risk to contribution, the evidence supports the finding that the Scottish exposure was more probably than not the cause of his mesothelioma. The evidence demonstrated a seventy-five percent probability that this exposure was the cause of his mesothelioma.

The plaintiff's expert evidence rises no higher than establishing that the defendants' exposure possibly contributed to Mr Henderson's mesothelioma. Drs Freeman and Haug were essentially concerned about Mr Henderson as their patient. They made no attempt to point to one or other of the exposures as being causative. Dr Forgan's evidence was marred by his error in excluding time since first exposure when considering which period of employment carried the highest risk of mesothelioma. It was a fatal flaw in his evidence and it ought not to have been ignored by Judge Byrnes. The evidence of Professor Schaffer provides no scientific or rational basis for converting an increase in risk to an actual cumulative effect and, hence, a material contribution. His physical effect theory amounted to no more than a personal opinion without foundation. The court was asked to accept his opinion simply because he is an eminent expert and what he said could be assumed to be the case. Professor Schaffer had no scientific basis for asking the court, in effect, to make this leap of faith. His conversion of a material increase in risk to a material contribution was not justified.

In truth, Mr Henderson could not point to any one of his exposures to asbestos or, indeed, all his exposure to asbestos and say that that exposure caused or contributed to his mesothelioma.

In the circumstances, the appeals by Henry King Industries Limited and V&L Ltd must succeed. The judgment against them should be set aside.

Viviana sat at her desk, sunk in gloom. Where to from here? Jenny didn't want to go any further. Who could blame her?

But something had to be done. It just didn't feel right that James should lose simply because medical science had not yet advanced sufficiently to provide a precise answer to the question of which fibre was responsible. It was like some type of perverse whodunnit and yet it wasn't a criminal case, where proof was required beyond reasonable doubt. One or both of the defendants had killed James – and now they could be getting away with it.

What could she do? The High Court? Even if Jenny agreed to that, Viviana could guess how that farce would play itself out. The High Court, more interested in constitutional law than asbestos victims, would refuse special leave to appeal on the basis that no point of principle arose. She would be sitting in the crowded courtroom with other hopefuls, listening to a stony-faced septuagenarian declare that the Court of Appeal had got it right. Hopes crushed just like that.

Buoyed by its triumph, Henry King Industries would ill-advisedly come after Jenny for its costs, threatening to sell her home from under her to make its point; to warn off all the other men and women who dared to think they had been harmed by its products.

Viviana could hardly bear to think of Bruce Fraser's boastful behaviour or his rise to the dizzying heights of partner. She knew she couldn't countenance a moment longer near Gary Shaw. Or at least no longer than it took to find a new job. James and Jenny Henderson had surely deserved better than the slack 'roll-your-arm-over' style of litigation they received. As much as it hurt, she had to admit to being part of that process. She had gone along with it. She despised herself for her involvement. But what could she do? The best thing might be to accept the umpire's decision and move on. Move on with her life.

PART IX

Chapter 83

'I refuse to accept that Jenny Henderson won't agree to seek special leave to appeal in the High Court,' Gary Shaw told Viviana from the doorway to her office. 'She's simply feeling overwrought. She'll come round in time.'

Viviana knew he was so confident in Jenny's changing her mind that he'd had the necessary appeal documents filed in the High Court registry, and served on the defendants. It was plainly unethical to do this without the client's instructions, but he was desperate. There were a lot of legal fees at stake.

'We have to persuade the woman to press on.'

'Why can't you simply respect her decision, Gary?'

'Because it's wrong, and you know it is.'

He was right, of course, although Viviana felt his reasons were less than noble. 'Give her a call, then, Gary.'

'This can't be done over the phone. There's no way Jenny Henderson is going to travel to Sydney to discuss the case in our offices. There's no choice but to drive down to Kiama to see her – with you.'

'No way.'

'Viviana, I've invested a considerable sum in this matter, and I'm not about to see it pissed up against a wall because some woman doesn't have the guts to fight on or because my reputedly hard-nosed associate's gone weak at the knees!'

'Jenny Henderson isn't going to budge if that's the way you're going to carry on.'

'So, you'll do it?'

'I will, but I'm driving separately.'

'No, we go together. It'll be an opportunity to discuss the case and our strategy both in dealing with Jenny Henderson and in the High Court proceedings.'

◆

Viviana was reluctant to travel with Shaw, but she finally agreed. She hoped he was serious about talking about the case because she was eager to share her opinion about how the High Court proceedings should be approached. She suspected Shaw was likely to have other motives for travelling together, the more obvious of which she did not wish to consider. It had taken appreciable tact and careful persuasion on her part to obtain Jenny's consent to the meeting. She knew success would entail even greater diplomacy. She and Shaw had to somehow work together.

Viviana had dwelled on the decision since it had been handed down. She tortured herself with feelings of guilt. She should never have allowed herself to be reassured by Shaw's platitudes or Sutton's baloney. How could she have fallen for it? How could she have fallen for Shaw? He was hideous. What the hell was wrong with her? She took a deep breath as they bypassed Wollongong, speeding south past the Dapto dogs racetrack.

'You're very quiet, Viviana,' Shaw remarked. 'I thought we were going to talk tactics.' He looked sideways at her over the top of his Serengeti shades. His fleshy bulk filled the leather bucket seat of his Maserati.

'I'm thinking,' Viviana replied.

'I hope it's about me,' Shaw said with a grin, turning again to look at her. He took his left paw off the steering wheel and moved it in the direction of Viviana's thigh, but quickly returned it as he saw Viviana's hand rise, ready to swoop down and whack it.

'Look, Viviana, we have to work together on this one, right?'

'Tell me something I don't know.'

'Fine. So let's make sure we're talking the same language with the client. It's a very tricky situation. Very delicate. I'll do the talking. All you need to do is back me up.'

'Mmm.'

'Right, that's settled then. You can't jump ship when there's still a chance of victory. I'm simply not going to let that happen.'

'You mean you're not going to allow her to drop the case when there's a chance you might still get paid?'

'Yeah, and what's wrong with that? Do you think we're an offshoot of the Red Cross? This is a business.'

'It's not only a business though, is it, Gary?'

'What do you mean?'

'We're professionals as well. We have duties, you know.'

'Well, how naive can you get? I should never have trusted you with this case. It was obviously beyond you.'

'Just watch the road, Gary.'

◆

Well after Shaw's capacity to endure the sphinx Viviana had become had collapsed, the Maserati arrived at the Henderson home in Kiama. Shaw cautiously manoeuvred the car down the overgrown driveway towards the path to the front door. He seemed no longer able to tolerate the tense confines and burst out of the door as if shot from a cannon.

'Hello, Mrs Henderson, good to see you,' he boomed.

'Good morning, Mr Shaw,' Jenny said.

Viviana, to her surprise, found herself moving forward to embrace Jenny. It was the first time she'd demonstrated any emotion to a client, perhaps to anyone outside her family. Jenny seemed to appreciate it.

'Hello, Jenny. I'm glad you let us come and speak to you.'

'That's okay, Viviana. I've been thinking about it a great deal.'

'Excellent, Mrs Henderson,' Gary Shaw added as he donned his suit coat.

'Please, come in. I'll put on the kettle.'

Jenny led them through the door. Inside, the air was musty, cold and unpleasant. Like death, Viviana thought. Upstairs on the verandah, Tess the dog sat hopefully, peering in through the sliding glass doors, eager to join in.

Jenny had a haggard, yet resolute demeanour, Viviana observed. It was unnerving. It caused Shaw to hesitate before he commenced his planned speech. When he began, he spoke oddly as if the membrane was peeling off the roof of his mouth from the too hot tea Jenny had served them. 'Mrs Henderson – Jenny – as you know, the result in the Court of Appeal was very disappointing. Very disappointing, indeed. We understand that you may feel very unhappy and negative towards any further litigation. That's to be expected after all you've been through. Many clients have felt like that. But these cases aren't all straightforward – yes, I remember assuring you that your husband's case was simple and straightforward – I haven't forgotten. I still maintain that view. Just because the Court of Appeal disagrees with Judge Byrnes doesn't make them right or the case more complicated. There are some pretty fundamental principles at stake here and we believe the High Court will set the record straight. I urge you to reconsider your position or, at least, the position Viviana tells me you have in relation to further litigation. I've discussed the Court of Appeal's judgment with Mr Sutton and Mr Lucas. They believe you have very good prospects of having the decision overturned by the High Court. If you stop now, then you'll never know. You'll never have the satisfaction of having this wrong righted. Jenny, sometimes you have to see these things through to the end. You know, until the proverbial fat lady makes an entrance. Ha! Ha! I gave a commitment to act for your husband to vindicate his rights. I give the same commitment to you today. You have to battle on, Jenny, you owe it to your husband. He would have liked—'

'Stop that!' Jenny commanded with whispered, forceful authority.

'I'm sorry, what—'

'Mr Shaw, I want you to stop talking.' Jenny held her mug in her hands. She needed to grip something, to steady herself. She had rarely spoken her mind. She shied away from confrontation, ran for the hills at the first sign of conflict. That had to change if she was to do what her heart was telling her. She fixed her green-blue eyes on the blubbery giant before her. 'Don't ever assume what my husband would have wanted.'

'I'm terribly sorry, Jenny, but—'

'You will call me Mrs Henderson, Mr Shaw.'

'Yes, certainly, Mrs Henderson, as I—'

'I don't like you, Mr Shaw. I don't want to talk to you anymore.'

Viviana sat marvelling at the spectacle. It was worth the hideous drive from Sydney.

'I can assure you, Mrs—'

'I asked you to be quiet. Please show me that courtesy in my own home! You, Mr Shaw, are a conman. You deceived my husband with your false promises. You and that QC of yours and his stupid lackey. I want nothing to do with you or them again. I've thought about this for many days. I accept that it's too late to find new lawyers to act for me. I accept that I need to still use your firm. And I'll continue to do so – on one condition.' Jenny was trembling. She wanted to be sick.

'Yes, and what is that condition?' Shaw asked.

'That I only deal with Viviana. She makes all the decisions and she uses barristers that she wants and not those dreadful men you foisted upon James.'

'Now, Mrs Henderson, that's—'

'That's what I want, Mr Shaw. Take it or leave it.'

Gary Shaw twisted in his chair and studied Viviana's face. She gave just enough away. 'I see,' he said with some bitterness. 'I get the picture.'

'I'm glad you do, Mr Shaw. I want to see this through to the very end for my husband. If I'm to do that, I have to do it with someone I can trust, and the only person I trust is Viviana.'

'Very well, Mrs Henderson, I accept your condition. I must, however, caution you against it. While you're free to decide your legal representation and to remove me from being personally involved in the case, I believe it would be foolhardy in the extreme to dump Mr Sutton and Mr Lucas from the case.'

'I've thought about that and I'm willing to take the risk. You may be impressed by them, but I'm not. Viviana will find me someone good.'

'I'm not so sure. Anyway, if that's your position, I guess I'll have to accept it.'

'It is my position, thank you.'

'Very well.' Shaw rose ponderously. 'Now that we've agreed to all that, I think we can go. Come on, Viviana.' Shaw peered down at his senior associate. She was smiling pleasantly. 'Are you coming?'

'No. I'll stay here, if that's okay with Jenny, and talk over a few things.'

'Yes, please stay, Viviana. I'll drive you to Sydney myself when you're ready. It's about time I saw some of my grandchildren again. It will do me good.'

'Right, I see. Good. Well, then, I'll go... No, don't get up, Mrs Henderson. I can find my own way out, thank you. Viviana, I expect a brief to go out by the end of the week – and please, someone who knows what he's doing.'

'Of course. Or a she for that matter.'

Shaw blundered down the corridor. Jenny laughed, with a mixture of relief and nervousness, as she heard footsteps on the stairs and Shaw slamming the front door. Soon afterwards came the roar of his car's preposterous engine, and a high-pitched whir as it reversed up the driveway.

'I've never done anything like that in my life, Viviana. I hope it's the right thing.'

Viviana leaned forward and clasped Jenny's hands. 'It's okay. You did the right thing. I'll do my best for you.'

'I know you will, dear. That's all I hope for. That's all James wanted.' She started crying. Viviana squeezed her hands to reassure her. There were no excuses now.

Chapter 84

Viviana walked Tess along the beach. She felt the salty breeze on her face and shook her hair out of its tight ties. It flew about her head as she pushed into the wind. What must people be thinking? A laughing woman walking barefoot on the sand, dressed in a smart black skirt and jacket.

Back at Jenny's house, she showered and put on somebody's spare pyjamas. She looked in the mirror. She felt naked without her makeup and dark, threatening wardrobe. Who is this person? she asked. She put on a jumper over the flannel pyjama top and went into the kitchen where Jenny was preparing dinner.

'Viviana, dear, you look so young, so pretty,' Jenny said.

Viviana blushed. She hated being vulnerable or, at least, feeling vulnerable.

'Come on, help me with the vegetables.'

Viviana was soon busy peeling potatoes and blanching broccoli. It brought back memories of her own family and the ease with which she moved in that environment.

They chatted for hours after dinner. Viviana learned all about the Henderson family – she knew every detail of James's work history, but she scarcely knew a thing about James Henderson as a man or the family that loved him so dearly. She told Jenny that she believed James should have settled for the sum first offered by the defendants. It was a good offer. She shouldn't have persuaded him to reject the offer and bat on.

'Viviana, you shouldn't think that way. Although I always wanted the legal proceedings over, James saw them as a point of principle. He wanted a judgment in his favour. It was the only way he believed he could be vindicated. You didn't influence him or make him do something he didn't want to do. And although I told you I wanted no more of this legal case, I knew deep down that would have been wrong. James would never have given up. He would have found a way through. I owe it to him.'

'I understand. You loved him. What else could you have done – what else can you do now?'

'I can give up. And if I did, I know he wouldn't hold it against me. After all, he spent most of his life protecting me from all sorts of stresses and worries. That was what he did. He would accept my decision to end this. He never held anything I did against me, Viviana, and I'm not perfect. I've done some things that were hurtful. I suppose we all do at some time. Things that hurt others, or even ourselves. It's very important to be able to forgive. James could, even if he demanded a lot from himself.'

'I understand, I think, what you're telling me, Jenny. I know it's not right to dwell on past mistakes.'

'It's true, dear. It does you no good in the end. You shouldn't, I shouldn't. Of course, it's easier said than done, but it's the truth.

'We all have choices, Viviana. James and I made our choices when we sailed from England in 1957. I made choices when I decided to marry him and follow him to New South Wales. My family told me I was throwing my life away by not marrying a doctor I knew from England. But they were my choices to make, not theirs or anybody else's. That's why James would forgive me if I chose not to go on with this case. He'd understand my reasons, my fears. Yet that's not the point. You see, Viviana, what he couldn't forgive is that these companies didn't give him any choice. They hid things from him. He wasn't given the chance to change his future, our future. He understood perfectly what it was like to make a bad decision and live with the consequences. That was something he could control. This wasn't. And that's why the case was a point of principle for him. That's ultimately why I've decided to fight on. To try to bring them to account for taking away James's ability to decide what was best for him. It's what's fair. They knew it was dangerous. They must have. I know in my heart I'm right.'

'You are right, Jenny. There was a cover-up. Someday, I hope it all comes out.'

Jenny looked sad.

'I'm sorry, Jenny, that doesn't help. I shouldn't have said it.'

'It's okay, Viviana. I know it's the truth. Sometimes, it's difficult to accept it.'

'I understand. You know though, if it gets too hard, you still can decide not to press on, despite what Gary Shaw thinks.'

'I appreciate that, dear. But not now. I can't give up. And Viviana, I fear it's not just about James.'

'What do you mean, Jenny?'

'These men, these faceless evil men, not only killed James – Viviana, they invaded our home. You know James would come home in his dusty overalls and give Robbie or Dougie or Kate a hug – throw them into the air and catch them. They loved that. Used to laugh hysterically. But it's not only that. Twelve Hibiscus Avenue, Bankstown, our family home. It was made of asbestos cement too. You see, Viviana, these people exposed my little children to their dust! What if something happens to them? What if they get what James contracted? I couldn't live with myself, Viviana. I couldn't.'

'I'm sure they'll be all right.'

'How can you be certain, Viviana? How can anyone?'

Chapter 85

Bruce Fraser pushed the pause button on his Dictaphone. There was no mistaking that pounding footfall. He turned the machine off and looked at the doorway to his office just as Paul Morahan came striding through like a small ent advancing on Isengard.

'Well, Fraser, you can put a hold on the celebrations for now: Shaw has filed a special leave application in the High Court.' He slapped the document down on the desk.

'It's not what I'd call a surprise, Paul. What choice did they have?' He glanced at the front page, noting that the application had been filed two days earlier. Why had Morahan delayed giving it to him?

'Well, Fraser, they could have accepted the result and not been such sore losers.'

'That wasn't going to happen, was it?'

Bruce gazed at Morahan with disdain. Ever since the win in the Henderson appeal, there had been talk in the office about fast-tracking him into partnership. Bruce knew Morahan would find that a very bitter pill to swallow, but he could hardly object when it was common knowledge that most of the Henry King Industries board were asking why Bruce wasn't already a partner.

'Of course, Shaw had no choice. You need to get on and get this High Court thing sorted. I don't have to tell you there's a great deal riding on it!'

'I understand how important it is for the client and this firm. I'll arrange a meeting with Jeremy Lawson this afternoon to discuss the special leave application.'

'Good.' Morahan hesitated for effect, then continued. 'You should know that V&L want to be represented by the same counsel – you know, a united front so to speak. We'll be briefing a silk to appease them.'

'No!'

'Yes!'

'But Lawson did a fantastic job in the appeal. He knows it back to front.'

Bruce could see Morahan was delighted at scoring a hit. Bruce knew he'd lose control of the case if he were compelled to brief a senior barrister to lead Lawson. He and Jeremy had got it this far. It was crazy to change tack now.

'He did an admirable job, Bruce, and everyone is very appreciative of his efforts. It's time, however, to have a serious heavy-hitter bring it home. We're in the High Court, Fraser, in case you didn't know. Anyhow, I put my recommendation to the chairman, Terry Abrahams, yesterday, when I met him, Charlie Boustead and the V&L team. All agreed with the suggestion. In fact, V&L refused to share the costs of representation if Lawson didn't have a leader.'

'Why didn't you tell me about the meeting?' Bruce now realised why Morahan hadn't given him the special leave application earlier.

'You were busy. I didn't want to interrupt.'

'This is a bad decision, Paul. A very bad decision.'

'It's too late to change it now. One day, if you become partner, you'll understand the importance of risk minimisation and protecting the firm's reputation in difficult situations. We can't allow such a big case to depend on the abilities of junior counsel. We'd have no leg to stand on if the client sued us in negligence – it can't criticise us when we've briefed eminent senior counsel.'

'That's pathetic.'

'But the correct decision, nonetheless. I must say I'm rather surprised at your reaction, Bruce. You see, this is the time when one's judgment is called into question. It takes years of practice in litigation to develop a sound judgment. It's what our clients expect from us when the stakes are high. It's the one trait that distinguishes partners at this firm from more junior legal staff. Do you follow?

'Now, Bruce, my judgment is that we need to brief Daniel Bolton on this one. Two of Australia's biggest companies agree with my judgment.' Morahan rested his knuckles on Bruce's desk as if he were a silver-backed gorilla. 'Do you disagree?'

Bruce was on the brink of self-immolation, but he held it together. He refused to give Morahan the pleasure of a reaction. He stared out through the glass office walls to the secretarial bays beyond like a pale, freckled Easter Island sentinel. 'No,' he said.

Morahan paused a moment, then strode out of the office, no doubt feeling very pleased with himself.

'Janice, get me a coffee, please,' Bruce asked his PA as he got up and walked to her cubicle.

'Anything wrong?' she asked.

'Everything,' he said.

Chapter 86

Viviana was thinking about what Jenny had said to her. This case was not only about James Henderson. There were many more families, thousands of victims of asbestos exposure out there. Shaw & Fletcher received hundreds of inquiries from grieving relatives every year. James's case was of general importance and something the High Court should be interested in.

Viviana saw how serious the situation would become for all these people if the Henderson decision became the leading authority on causation. It was critical the High Court overruled it – but on what basis? There had to be a solution. She would think of it, she had to. If she couldn't, then she had to find someone who could. That brought her back to the conundrum she'd been wrestling with for the past hour – who to brief?

She trawled through the Bar Directory again, searching for a name to jump off the page at her. She hardly knew any of the listed barristers. The only ones she'd heard of were those her firm briefed, their opponents and the high-flyers who did all the High Court appeals – the silks whose names were littered throughout the Commonwealth Law Reports: Daniel Bolton QC, Robert Christopherson QC, Stephen Duchesny QC, Roy Williams SC, or Daffyd Robertson SC. She didn't want any of those. She would never be able to get them interested in a 'no win, no fee' brief. Gary Shaw wouldn't fund someone else when Sutton would do it 'on spec'.

What she needed was someone at least as smart as Jeremy Lawson, who knew the law (or was willing to come to grips with it), but who wasn't fixated on the legal fine print. Someone who could step outside and see the big picture. She knew she could riffle through the Bar Directory for days and never find the answer.

Then she had a thought – who would the big firms use if they had to argue that something was unfair? That was surely what it was about: fairness. Jenny had said so, and she was dead right. The Court of Appeal's judgment was plainly unfair to all but the large defendant corporations, who'd got rich on the labour of men like James Henderson. The top-tier law firms would naturally brief one of their own: an honours graduate, someone who'd briefly worked in their offices before going on to Oxford for a Bachelor of Civil Law, a year as an associate to a High Court judge, before finally being 'called' to the Bar. They would likely use someone who worked in administrative law because that branch of the law was all about questions of fairness and private rights. She would need to read a few administrative law decisions, identify some names, ask some of her university friends who worked in those skyscrapers in Phillip Street and Martin Place. She would find the right man for the job. And it had to be a man because that was how she would maximise the chances of any argument being heard.

◆

Viviana was convinced she had her man, a senior junior barrister called Oliver Capper. An old friend at Falk, Maguire & Tsikleas had told her he was the leading junior in the field of administrative law. He acted for all her firm's council, club and association clients. He knew how to twist the facts and torture the law to fit a client's needs. A quick check in the law reports confirmed his appearances in many cases, including many High Court cases.

Viviana's friend told her that Capper had once applied to be silk and was rejected. The rejection was ostensibly on the basis that he needed 'another spell in the pasture', but, according to her friend, it was, in truth, due to his having given one of the silks on the selection committee a frightful hiding years earlier. The silk involved was never briefed by the particular law firm again. He lost a substantial source of income, and never forgot that case. When it came to decide Oliver Capper's application, he couldn't avoid his professional jealousy and personal vindictiveness guiding his decision.

Aghast at the snub and its obvious source, Capper never applied for senior counsel again, and refused to appear with senior counsel in any of his cases. Viviana heard that he was unpopular with his colleagues, but very popular with solicitors and clients. They were interested in having the job done rather than in the political niceties of the Bar. Capper had a huge practice. The Bar Council begged him to apply again for silk. His continued practice as a junior barrister was an embarrassment to the organisation.

When her friend described this history to her, Viviana immediately thought he would be perfect. She rang his chambers and asked to speak to him.

Viviana expected Capper to sound terse, harsh, or even dismissive. Instead, she was surprised to hear a pleasant voice at the end of the line.

'Oliver Capper.'

'Hello, Mr Capper, my name is Viviana Glosioli. I'm a senior associate at Shaw & Fletcher. I wonder whether you'd be prepared to accept a brief from me in an asbestos diseases case in the High Court.'

'Please, Oliver is fine. Asbestos case, you say?'

'Yes. I know you don't do dust, but—'

'I'd be happy to have a look at it. I assume, since you're from Shaw & Fletcher, that you act for the plaintiff?'

'Yes.'

'And what's it about?'

'Causation.'

'I suppose you're going to ask me to do it 'on spec', aren't you?'

'Well, yes. Everyone's been doing it on a 'no win, no fee' basis from the start.'

'And why change now.'

'Well, the client can't afford to pay her legal costs as they're incurred.'

'I understand.'

'Does that mean you'll accept the brief?'

'Viviana, you do understand I haven't been involved in a personal injury matter for years?'

'I assumed that was the case.'

'I see. Why me, then?'

'Well, Oliver, this is an important case, and I'm looking to brief someone from left field, so to speak. I hope you're not offended.'

'I'm flattered actually. And you have previously briefed?'

'Geoffrey Sutton and Greg Lucas.'

'And you want to change?'

Viviana thought she could hear Capper chortling to himself.

'Yes.'

'You know you're probably asking me to accept a brief against solicitors who frequently brief me?'

'Yes.'

'Right. Here's what I'll do. Send me the brief and I'll have a look at it. I'll then appoint a time to confer with you. I'll let you know then if I accept the retainer. That should be some time in the next two weeks.'

'Okay. I'll send it over this afternoon.'

'Very good. I look forward to receiving it.'

Viviana had mixed emotions when she put the phone down. Part of her was thrilled with the thought of trying something new. The other part screamed that she was mad as a hatter for briefing a stranger to personal injury law. Shaw would have a fit.

◆

Two weeks after her initial phone call, Viviana met with Capper in his chambers. Unlike Sutton and Lucas, Capper didn't work out of the Selborne-Wentworth bunker in Phillip Street. Viviana had never briefed a barrister in outlying chambers. She'd assumed that the best ones were all in Selborne or Wentworth.

Capper's chambers, Street Chambers, were on the sixtieth floor of Macquarie Tower in King Street. As she entered the foyer and saw the artwork, furnishings and the panoramic view of Sydney Harbour, she dismissed all notions that barristers in outlying chambers were second best.

Oliver Capper didn't look second best either. A tall man of about forty-five with dark hair that was in need of a trim, he came out to the foyer to introduce himself and collect her. Another change from Sutton who always had his secretary act as his usher. Viviana could feel Capper's obsidian-dark eyes examining her. The lines on his face spoke of humour, sadness, energy and wit. He was an attractive man when he smiled, Viviana thought. An intelligent man when he spoke. His friendly greeting lasted just longer than was comfortable. Did he find her amusing? Did he find her attractive? She should have worn something else, something less, well, black. In any event, she thought, as she followed him to his room, it wasn't as though Capper was Mr Colourful. He wore graphite trousers, a crisp white shirt, black cufflinks and a patterned silk tie, the blue of which was so dark it could have passed for pitch.

Capper's chambers had none of the knick-knacks, studied clutter or antique furniture of Geoffrey Sutton's. It was a large, light, sparse room. Capper worked at a smooth, honey-toned desk adjacent to the window from which he could see Sydney Heads, the Royal Botanical Gardens, Woolloomooloo and the Coca Cola sign on the hill at Kings Cross. All his briefs were hidden behind cabinet doors. The only things before him were the Henderson brief and a notebook. Viviana saw several bullet points and red and blue writing scrawled on the paper. From the edge of the folder containing the briefed documents poked numerous iridescent Post-it tabs. Viviana was reassured – Capper had read the brief. That was novel.

Capper didn't offer refreshments or have his 'girl' come around and bring out the bone-china cups. He got straight into it.

'Viviana, I've read the material and I'm happy to accept a retainer on a conditional fee basis.'

Viviana sighed.

Capper smiled. 'You seem relieved.'

She reddened. 'I'm sorry. I am. I'm very relieved.' She laughed and felt very self-conscious.

'Now that problem's out of the way, let's talk about the case.'

Viviana opened her pad to take notes.

'I think the appeal to the High Court has merit. Not because the Court of Appeal got it wrong, but because they never considered an important aspect to the common law principles of negligence and causation.'

Viviana stopped writing to look up.

'The Court of Appeal judges were correct when they said proof of a possibility or proof of an increased risk or chance did not amount to proof of causation. The law requires proof of a probability, not a possibility. But saying the plaintiff only established a material increase in his risk of developing mesothelioma was not the end of the matter. They still had to decide whether that was a fair or just outcome having regard to the reasons there's a tort called negligence in the first place – what purpose it serves to society, and any policy considerations that may be relevant.'

Viviana was transfixed. Capper was explaining what her gut told her to be true. It was what she'd been trying to formulate in her own mind. For the first time in her career, she believed she was working with someone on her own wavelength; someone she could work with as part of a team.

'Now, the Court of Appeal might say, and with some justification, that they did not look at this issue because they weren't taken to it – with all due respect to previous counsel—'

'Oh, don't give them any respect, Oliver, they don't deserve it.'

'Okay, then I won't. They did a crap job. Don't you dare tell anyone I said that.'

'I won't.'

'Good. Now, when I say crap, I mean industrial strength crap. Total crap, in other words ... but again, you didn't hear that from me.'

'Of course not. You heard it from me.'

'I think the Court of Appeal judges should have looked at the issue more closely themselves. You can't just leave it to counsel. Now, we'll have to amend the special leave application and draft a notice of appeal – they're rubbish. Missed the point completely.'

Viviana was nodding.

'Good, I can do that by the end of the week. The special leave application is listed in four weeks. That should be plenty of time to prepare the submissions so long as the defendants don't make nuisances of themselves, objecting to the amendments. Do you know who they've briefed yet?'

'The defendants are being jointly represented by Daniel Bolton QC with Jeremy Lawson.'

'I see. They've wheeled in the big guns. I'm not sure Bolton will do a better job than Jeremy Lawson, though. He's a bloody good barrister. We were at Stewarts Dann together for a few years before coming to the Bar.'

'Isn't Daniel Bolton meant to be the best appellate barrister in the country?'

'Yes, or one of them. But he relies too much on his juniors, spreads himself too thinly. My guess is he'll hinder rather than help their case. He costs a bomb and looks and sounds the part, but I reckon money would be better spent elsewhere.'

'I hope you're right. My boss nearly had a coronary when he heard Bolton was being briefed. Actually, I wish he had had one. It's going to happen one day.'

'You don't like where you work?'

'No.'

'Because?'

'I'd rather not say.'

'Fair enough.'

Viviana stared down at her notes without reading anything.

'Okay, let's get back to the case,' Capper said. 'Viviana, I need you to start assembling bundles of authorities. We have to investigate this point across the common law countries. Some cases will be from Canada, some even from South Africa. Okay?'

'Yes.'

'Here's the current list.' Capper handed a sheet of paper to Viviana, who reached to take it. The tips of their fingers touched with the exchange. It was plain he had already done significant work on the case. That was an unusual approach to preparation based upon what Viviana had seen of the efforts of Sutton and Lucas. She now had to tell Shaw.

Chapter 87

'Who the hell is Oliver Capper?' Gary Shaw asked.

'A very experienced, very good barrister,' Viviana replied.

'Never heard of him. Does he do personal injury?'

'No.'

Shaw shook as if a depth charge had exploded in his bowels, waves of vibrating pinguidity surging up his body into his jowls. 'What the hell! You can't be serious! I want this guy off the case!'

'No! I have Jenny Henderson's instructions to retain him. She agrees he'll be perfect.'

'You two are demented. And who's leading him?'

'No one.'

'This is a gee-up, surely. No silk and the defendants have got Daniel Fucking Bolton, his Lordship!'

'I'm serious.'

'When this goes pear-shaped, and it will, you are out on your arse, Viviana! And don't expect my insurance to cover you when that ungrateful Henderson woman sues you for incompetence. You're on your own! You got that?'

'I've got it, Gary. Loud and clear.'

'If it weren't for your pathetic pact with Mrs Henderson, you'd be gone already and we'd be doing it my way. If she didn't agree, I'd probably dump her as a client as well, but I'm not so sure the Legal Services Commissioner would see the reasonableness of that move.'

'You can't sack a client! Not at this stage.'

'I know, I know, didn't I just say that?' He glared at her. 'Oliver Capper – what a joke!'

Shaw had moved into Viviana's office and stood over her desk. She stared back at him, the smell of his odious cologne washing over her like steam in a sauna. The impasse ended when Shaw's secretary came in to advise him that Geoffrey Sutton was on the phone.

'What does he want? He's probably heard the good news too. Jesus!' Shaw stomped out of the office. Viviana hoped that would be his last input into the case.

Chapter 88

Viviana rang Jenny to explain the special leave application and when it was to be heard. 'It's like a mini-hearing. It only lasts about twenty minutes. Only two or three judges hear it. Basically, if they like our arguments, then they grant leave. If they do, we all traipse down to Canberra so that the whole of the High Court can hear what we say.'

'I see, so it could all be over this Friday with the special leave application?'

'That's right, Jenny. It could be all over. But Oliver thinks they'll give us leave to appeal.'

'I hope that's right. I've been given those sorts of reassurances before, you know, dear.'

'I know you have, Jenny,' Viviana said, embarrassed at the thought of Sutton and Lucas. 'Oliver is different. I really believe he knows what he's doing. I think his arguments make sense. And I'm not just saying that to make you feel less worried. I agree with them.'

'I know you're not, Viviana. Fingers crossed. Do I have to be there?'

'No, unless of course you want to. You're welcome to attend, but it's so short it's not worth it. If – I mean when – we win, you'll probably want to be in Canberra for that.'

'Okay, dear, I won't come. You make sure you ring as soon as you get the result. I won't be able to do a thing until I know.'

◆

Friday came. Viviana walked to Oliver Capper's chambers and then to the High Court building in Sydney. The court was in the same building as the Court of Appeal, a khaki-coloured bunker. Viviana hoped it would not bring the same bad luck.

Up on the twenty-third floor, the corridor was packed with barristers, solicitors and nervous clients. There were nine applications for special leave that morning. They were third on the list. Viviana and Capper entered the court and found seats near the front. Capper looked well-prepared and in command. Neither of them knew which judges would be hearing the applications. There were only two associates organising papers and books on the bench, so Viviana assumed there would only be two judges. As they spoke quietly about who the judges might be, Viviana saw Jeremy Lawson walk by with an older, very handsome barrister. Capper followed her gaze to the two men.

'Daniel Bolton,' he said.

Viviana examined the legendary silk. She knew he was in his sixties, although his straight spine, impeccable robes and tanned skin had her thinking he was younger. His face was still taut around the jaw. His lips were those of a cherub, his voice, when he greeted Capper, crisp and charming. 'His Lordship', that's what they call him,' Capper murmured after Bolton turned back to his junior.

'He's not English, is he?' Viviana queried.

'No. Spent some time at Oxford studying the classics, and came back with that voice. He's worked hard at his image.'

'All rise!'

Viviana stood and turned to the judges' bench at the front of the courtroom. A door at the rear opened, and two older men entered. They were dressed almost completely in black, but did not wear wigs. Viviana could barely tell them apart, although when she looked closely she realised one was bald and the other had the illusion of baldness – his pate was sprayed with a thin layer of grey hair, very much like instant grass on a freeway siding. Capper leaned towards her and whispered, 'Bald one's Gibson; the other's Farrow.'

'Please be seated!'

'The Papuan Porky Punster Pty Limited and Gags Ahoy Pty Limited and Another!'

Viviana suppressed a giggle as the barristers announced their appearances and began their arguments in the first special leave application. The two judges interrupted frequently. Neither barrister could develop any momentum with his argument. Viviana had difficulty ascertaining the nature of the dispute. It sounded like a copyright case about balloons. As each barrister reached ten minutes of argument, a light was turned on in front of him as a warning that it was time to finish. It was a brutal, cut-throat process. At the end, special leave was refused.

The second application was also unsuccessful. And then it was their turn.

'Jennifer Henderson and Henry King Industries Limited and Another!'

Viviana sat rigid. Capper moved forward to the bar table. 'May it please the court, I appear for the applicant.'

'Yes, Mr Capper.'

'May it please the court, I appear with my learned friend, Mr Lawson, for both of the respondents.'

'Thank you, Mr Bolton,' said the judge Capper had identified as Justice Gibson. 'Mr Bolton, we think it best if you begin.'

Viviana wondered whether this was a good or bad thing. Oliver Capper gave nothing away. He gazed up at the bench serenely.

'Delighted, your Honour.' Bolton rose to his feet again. From behind, his poise and the sheen of his robes gave him the look of a sleek panther. He exuded a nonchalant power. He commenced purring and the whole court stopped to listen. If he had a tail, it would have been flicking side-to-side, threatening action.

'Your Honours, what you have before you is an attempt, and without doubt an interesting, clever and courageous attempt, to attack the orthodox conception of the law of causation in this country, which has been analysed and defined repeatedly by this court and requires no further elucidation in what is nothing more than an instance of their Honours in the Court of Appeal stating and applying principles as well worn as any in this country to indisputable facts, so that we say there is no issue of general importance or any grave injustice for your Honours to consider or rectify through a grant of special leave and proceeding to a full airing by the court, as if, your Honours, the tragic circumstances of the case warrant a departure from sound legal principles...'

Viviana listened to Bolton, spellbound by his voice and demeanour. But the more she listened, the more her mind drifted. It was impossible to concentrate on what he was actually saying. His voice had her lulled, floating, wandering over white sands, sailing up into the clouds on the faintest of zephyrs ... his voice humming in the background ... coming in and out of focus...

Viviana snapped back to attention and turned around. The entire audience seemed bewitched by Bolton's speech. She wondered, though, whether anyone understood what he was saying or were simply pretending to understand. His locutions made comprehension difficult. She couldn't tell whether he was still in his first long sentence or whether his studied pauses marked the beginning of something new. All she could make out was an argument that it was unfair to depart from orthodox legal principles. Viviana thought that could have been said in a simple one-liner. But who was she to judge? By the attentive look on the faces of the judges, they seemed to understand what Bolton was saying, and did not interrupt, as they had in the previous cases. She wished they would because the grandiloquent passages made her brain hurt. The red light came on, and still he spoke. Viviana was concerned that Bolton was eating into Oliver's time to address the bench. He wouldn't have time to respond. She started panicking. Should Oliver object? Why wouldn't Bolton stop?

'Thank you, Mr Bolton,' Justice Gibson eventually said. He then turned to Capper. 'Mr Capper.'

Oliver Capper stood. 'Thank you, your Honour.'

'Mr Capper, we have one concern with your argument.'

'Yes, your Honour.'

Viviana's anxiety spiked. They didn't like the argument! Poor Jenny.

'What you seem to be suggesting is that an exception be granted to mesothelioma sufferers from a strict application of causation principles. Have we paraphrased your arguments accurately?'

'Yes, your Honour. I contend that an exceptional and less demanding test of causation should apply in the circumstances of this case and similar cases.'

'I see. On what basis?' asked Justice Farrow. 'If we are to consider taking such a step, then it would need to be based on principle, not whim.'

'I accept that, your Honour. In my submission, it's a step that would be based on principle.'

'Would you care to explain?'

'Certainly, your Honour. The starting position is, of course, what Mr Bolton has stated already – that it's not enough to show that a defendant's wrongful conduct increased the risk of injury being suffered or that it may have caused it. It must be proved on a balance of probabilities that the defendant's conduct did, in fact, cause the injury. In other words, that the injury would not have occurred absent the defendant's conduct. Here, your Honours, the consensus of expert evidence essentially establishes that the state of medical science about the mechanism by which asbestos fibres cause mesothelioma does not enable Mr Henderson, who was exposed to asbestos both in Scotland and Australia, to satisfy the settled test of causation. All the evidence proves that each exposure to asbestos cumulatively increases the risk of mesothelioma occurring. Several further propositions can be added.

'First, Mr Henderson's mesothelioma was only caused by asbestos. No other candidate has been suggested.

'Second, each defendant, in essence, admitted it had a duty to protect Mr Henderson against the risk of injury in the form of mesothelioma.

'Third, they both admit they failed in their duty to protect Mr Henderson.

'Fourth, the very risk they were obliged to protect him against occurred.

'Fifth, if Mr Henderson was only exposed to asbestos from one source, there would be no question that that tortfeasor would be liable. It is said, however, that because there are two tortfeasors and more than one source of exposure, Mr Henderson cannot win because he can't prove what is, in effect, scientifically incapable of proof. He is effectively less well protected where his rights have been infringed by two or more wrongdoers rather than one. What this means is that it is apparently reasonable and just for these defendants to be derelict in their duty to Mr Henderson and expose him to a lethal dust, but not to be liable because he cannot prove precisely which one did it. Equally, one could add that they cannot prove the Scottish exposure did it rather than the exposures they are responsible for.

'I submit that the mechanical approach to causation advanced by my learned friend must be questioned in cases like the one before your Honours. The purpose of tort law, particularly negligence, is to allocate responsibility for injury and loss. It is about correcting wrongful conduct. Victims should not be left without remedy where defendants have engaged in wrongful conduct. Questions of causation, your Honours, cannot be answered in a legal vacuum. They must be answered in context having regard to the purpose sought to be achieved by the common law tort of negligence. Policy considerations and those of fairness and justice require that defendants, who are usually insured, compensate a victim who suffers an injury the risk of which they created and were obliged to protect against.'

Capper sat down.

'Thank you, Mr Capper,' Justice Gibson said. 'We don't require anything further from you, Mr Bolton.' Daniel Bolton nodded courteously from his chair. The two judges whispered to each other. Then Justice Gibson turned back to the bar table. 'There will be a grant of special leave in this case. We will take recess.'

'All rise!'

◆

Outside the courtroom, Viviana could barely contain her excitement. She congratulated Capper and then found a relatively quiet corner in the corridor to ring Jenny.

'Jenny, it's Viviana,' she whispered. 'Guess what? We won! We're going to Canberra!'

'Really? Another chance! That's great news, Viviana. Thank you so much.'

'Don't thank me. You need to thank Oliver. He was amazing. Anyway, I've got to go. I'm not meant to be using my phone here.'

'Okay, dear, you go. Say thank you to Oliver. I knew I could trust you.'

Chapter 89

'Well, that worked, didn't it, bringing in his Lordship. Superb judgment, I'd say.'

'Settle down, Fraser. Special leave doesn't mean they'll win the appeal. It had nothing to do with Bolton. Those judges have to show some compassion. After all, there are many asbestos cases out there – it's an important issue. They'll down the plaintiff after a full hearing.' Morahan sounded as if he was trying to convince himself rather than placate Bruce.

'I'm bloody worried,' Charlie Boustead said. 'I can smell trouble. Where did they dredge this Capper fellow up from? He was bloody good – and I don't like that.'

'Charlie, I've instructed our admin law people never to brief him again,' Morahan confided.

'What the ... is that all you can think of doing?'

'It's a start.'

'This isn't a game, you know.'

'Of course not. And as you might recall, Charlie, I advised against this whole course when they dropped the punitive damages claim and offered us $300,000. I said settle.'

'Don't remind me, Morahan.'

Bruce didn't like the turn of events. Morahan was telling everyone he had been right. What had he said during the trial? That he had done this for years and knew what he was doing. That was a joke. This, however, was bad. All Bolton had been able to argue was that the strict application of causation law inevitably led to judgment for the defendants. Capper had agreed but argued that sometimes hard cases called for a flexible approach out of fairness. Since when did fairness have anything to do with it? No one could have predicted this line of argument.

'Look, I think we should try to settle before we have the full hearing,' Charlie Boustead said.

'That would be admitting defeat,' complained Bruce. He'd had a lengthy meeting with Jeremy Lawson on his own after the special leave application. Lawson remained firmly of the view that a proper, principled approach to the question of causation favoured the defendants. He didn't think the full High Court would come at the 'bleeding heart' approach put forward by Oliver Capper. Bruce tended to agree.

'I've told you what Jeremy thinks,' Bruce said. 'The chances of losing are remote. It would open the floodgates to more and more claims.'

'Bruce, you've done a pearler of a job so far. So has Jeremy, but even a slim chance of losing isn't something I like facing, especially when they start bending the rules on causation. We can buy out the risk by settling. That'll leave us with the Court of Appeal's judgment as a binding precedent in this state.'

'That's a good idea, Charlie,' added Morahan. 'Really good.'

'Yeah, thanks. I do have a working brain up there somewhere, you know.'

'But people will know the truth,' argued Bruce. 'The decision in the Court of Appeal is already tarnished.'

'Maybe, but it's still a binding decision until overturned. I don't want to let that happen. I can tell you neither does V&L. And we smashed them on exemplary damages with Dymock, as you remember. No, Bruce, that's the decision. You can get on the blower and get Glosioli to accept. You can start at $300,000 and go as far as $500,000.'

'That much?'

'Yes. I want this finished.'

◆

Viviana could not believe it – $300,000 plus costs. She had won, or Jenny had won, thanks to Oliver's cleverness. They were pitiful, the defendants. When it got a trifle hot, they gave up. She shook her head in disbelief as she telephoned Jenny.

'Hello, dear. You sound flustered. What's happened? Is anything wrong?'

'No, nothing's wrong, Jenny. I've got some good news. The defendants want to settle. They've offered you $300,000 plus costs. From the sound of Bruce Fraser's voice, I reckon they'll go higher. You've won, Jenny! They've given up!'

'That's good, Viviana.' She paused at the other end of the line. 'Does that mean they agree the Court of Appeal got it wrong? Do they agree that James should have won?'

'Well, in effect, that's what they're saying, although they can't agree in black and white that the decision was wrong. They can't consent to it being overturned or for judgment to be entered in your favour. Only the High Court can do that.'

'I see. So, James will still go down as having lost?'

'On paper, yes. But Jenny, they wouldn't agree to pay anything if they thought they were right. By paying money to you, they're admitting that they did the wrong thing by James. They admit that you and James were right.'

'I'm not interested.'

'Jenny?' Viviana had figured Jenny would be the last person to want to keep running the case.

'I'm not interested in settling. For anything. I want the High Court to decide.'

'Jenny, are you serious? This is what we've been fighting for.'

'No, it isn't, Viviana. It's what some of the lawyers have been fighting for. It wasn't what James was fighting for. It's not why I decided to keep going. He deserves more...' Her voice faded.

'Jenny? Are you all right? Jenny?'

'I won't do it!'

'Okay. I understand. It's okay. I'll tell them. I'm sorry. I should have known.' Viviana heard muffled sobbing. She could picture Jenny covering the mouthpiece with her hand, trying desperately to regain her composure. 'It's fine, Jenny. Don't worry. I'm sorry I upset you. I'll let them know straightaway. All right?'

After a pause, Jenny answered. 'Thank you, Viviana. I'd like you to tell them, please that I'm not interested in any offer they care to make unless they admit they were wrong and killed my husband.'

'I will, Jenny. I'll do it now. I'm sorry.'

Viviana hung up and rang Bruce Fraser.

'Rejected? Are you winding me up? No? I can make another offer, Viviana, you know?' Bruce said.

'I wouldn't bother, Bruce. My client's instructions are clear. She will not settle. She wants this final day in court in Canberra.'

'If that's what she wants, then I guess we'll see you in court. Cheers, Viviana.'

Viviana thought he sounded pleased that it wasn't going to settle.

She knew one person who'd be most unhappy if he knew his client had rejected a generous offer of compromise. Viviana decided never to tell Gary Shaw. While he was bound to find out at some time, she wasn't going to hasten that moment. Shaw had popped his head into her office after the special leave application to utter an oily 'Well done'. That was as good as his good side got. She didn't wish to see the other, apoplectic side of her employer again.

Chapter 90

The day before the High Court hearing, Douglas came down to Kiama to pick Jenny up and drive her to Canberra. It was April 2004, almost two years since James's diagnosis. She had told Douglas not to worry, but he insisted.

Jenny was quiet during the car trip to Canberra. While she was interested in stories of the grandchildren, she could mostly only concentrate on one thing, willing herself to remain calm. Douglas stopped talking after a while.

They had a Thai takeaway meal before retiring early. Jenny doubted she'd be able to sleep because the fears had returned. Every appeal brought them back. Memories of James, loneliness, her failings, her outrage. They left her exhausted and defeated. This was the last time she would be put through it. She prayed it would be worth it.

In the morning, Jenny woke early and went for a walk in the brisk, dry morning air. To her surprise, she'd slept soundly. She'd had to prod her memory to work out where she was and why. When the realisation kicked in, it triggered a nervous gush of acid from her stomach. She hoped the walk would ease the nausea. It helped, but didn't prevent a growing dread, and the same foreboding she'd felt on the day of the Court of Appeal hearing. By the time she had showered, eaten and dressed, she was a nervous wreck. So much for her resolve.

'Come on, Mum, it'll be okay. Just try to breathe. It helps, you know.'

Douglas hugged his mother. She was shaking. He wiped away the tears on her cheeks. 'We really have to go.' She nodded gamely and he led her gently out the door.

Outside the High Court, Jenny was thrilled to see her other children. 'What are you doing here?' she asked as if annoyed, while embracing them in turn.

'Are you kidding? We weren't going to miss this,' Kate said.

'Yeah, it's not every day your mother's in the High Court, you know,' Robert added.

'Why didn't you tell me they were coming, Dougie?'

'Because you would have objected to any fuss being made and your anxiety levels would have gone through the roof.'

Jenny smiled ruefully. 'Well, now I'm ready for just about anything. Let's head inside.' Her words were strong, but her voice trembled.

She wasn't sure what to make of the High Court. The building was a concrete and glass cubic structure and from the outside she imagined it to be a cold, insensitive place. Inside, however, the ceilings soared. A warm, bright light shone over panels of caramel-coloured wood, interspersed with ripples of concrete.

Viviana and Oliver Capper were waiting, seated on a black leather sofa. Viviana introduced Jenny to Oliver and apologised for having to rush off to prepare a few last-minute things for the hearing. There was not a hint of black in her clothing.

The family moved slowly into the courtroom. It was massive, like a small auditorium, Jenny thought. One end was dominated by a bench of the same caramel wood she'd seen outside. Behind the bench were seven burgundy-upholstered high-backed chairs. And behind them was a row of mobile bookshelves and several more modest chairs. Below the judges' bench was the winged expanse of the bar table. Jenny saw Jeremy Lawson sitting there with an older, distinguished-looking man, who turned and smiled pleasantly at her when he heard the family approaching.

They took seats as close to the bar table as possible, behind where they thought Oliver Capper would sit. There were two trolleys nearby, both of which were burdened with leather-bound books. Behind Lawson and his companion sat a huddle of dark-suited men and women, some of whom Jenny thought she'd seen before. Yes, she definitely remembered the earnest-faced, red-haired fellow with glasses. He'd been at the house when James gave evidence before Judge Byrnes.

Soon after they'd settled themselves, Viviana and Oliver Capper swept past along the burgundy carpet. Capper nodded to the two other barristers and sat down. Viviana sat in the row behind the barristers.

Before long, the judges' support staff entered, young men and women with bright but pale faces, busying themselves with papers and books, binders and notepads, hurrying between the bench and their own stations, ensuring all was in order, the chairs were straight, the glasses of water full and the parties ready.

When the court officer boomed the familiar 'All rise!' the seven High Court judges walked into the court, bowed and took their seats. Jenny didn't think they looked as mean as the Court of Appeal judges. Perhaps it was because they weren't wearing wigs or because three were women. They were unsmiling, but not uncaring in manner, she thought, directing their associates about with murmuring efficiency, readying themselves for the arguments, surveying the audience with interest. The judge in the centre was a wrinkled, austere-looking man of Jenny's vintage. He had a piercing, searching gaze. When he trained it on Jenny for a few seconds, she experienced a disquiet so profound she almost rushed out of the court for air. She began to doubt her initial assessment of this group that would decide James's legacy. They were serious. This was no place for sentimentality.

Viviana turned to smile at her, and Jenny managed a wan smile in return. She hoped she could get through this.

◆

Viviana had dreamed of one day being in the High Court and here she was. She tried to curb her excitement, to focus. This was the pinnacle of the profession. If only her parents were here to see her in this magnificent courtroom. But as soon as she turned to Jenny and her family in the seats behind her, she quickly stopped thinking of herself. Jenny appeared in a daze of worry, and generally looked afraid.

As Oliver developed his argument, Viviana started worrying too. None of the judges asked him any questions. Was their case so preposterous, the judges couldn't be bothered? That couldn't be right; two of them had granted special leave to appeal. She watched their faces as Oliver spoke, trying to spot a reaction that could tell her how he was going.

For a long time, Oliver went on unimpeded, which allowed him to talk smoothly, deliberately. Behind Viviana, Jenny tried to focus on what he was saying. She understood some of it but lost the thread when he referred to decided cases or quoted excerpts from law reports. She heard the repeated refrain of 'fairness'. At one stage, he read from a judgment saying something about 'The law stinking in the very nostrils of the public.' It sounded an odd thing to say. Some of the judges chuckled at this reference. Jenny didn't know whether that was a good or bad thing.

And then the questions started. One after the other, they were served at Oliver. He dug them up into the air and batted them back with force, as if he were on a volleyball court. He let none go to ground without a response.

Viviana was impressed. She turned again to Jenny with her family. Jenny seemed more settled, though she held Kate's hand tightly. One exchange, however, troubled Viviana. The bald judge, Justice Gibson, peered down at Oliver, blinking and squinting near-sightedly, like a mole. 'What you are asking, Mr Capper, is for this court to overrule decades of settled law just because some say the result for people like Mr Henderson would otherwise be too harsh. That seems a very flimsy basis to change the law.' The comment prompted a wave of sage nods among the people sitting behind the defendants' counsel. Two of the other judges also appeared to agree with the statement.

'Not so much overrule, your Honour, as adapt or extend,' Oliver Capper replied without pause. 'The approach for which we contend is consistent with the decisions of the House of Lords in Bonnington Castings v Wardlaw, and McGhee v National Coal Board. It is consistent with the reasons of Justice McHugh in this court in Chappel v Hart, and it is consistent with the object of the tort we are discussing, and the policy or social purpose it seeks to reflect. In the circumstances of this case, a material increase in risk should equate to a material contribution.'

Viviana again checked on Jenny. Perhaps Jenny shouldn't have come.

'But what about the evidence of Professor Schaffer, Mr Capper? He seems to say that each exposure constituted a material contribution rather than a material increase in risk?' asked one of the female judges.

'He does, your Honour, but I cannot with any conviction support his theories on this aspect of the case. Analysed carefully, his evidence is simply, like all the other experts, that each exposure increases the risk of developing mesothelioma. He says that he likes to think of that as a material contribution, but I don't consider there to be a proper foundation to his extrapolation. That is merely his personal opinion.'

'I must say, that is a brave concession, Mr Capper, in light of all the other issues in the case,' the Chief Justice said.

'And a proper concession, in my view,' added the bald judge.

Jenny didn't like the tone of the bald judge's comments. She couldn't imagine that any 'concession' no matter how 'brave' could be a good thing for the case. Kate squeezed her hand and looked anxiously at her. Had Oliver Capper made an awful mistake? Was he no better than Geoffrey Sutton?

The opposing barrister was soon on his feet. He was a very polished performer, Jenny thought. But he used too many fancy words for her liking. As with Capper, the bench gave him a lengthy, uninterrupted opportunity to articulate his clients' case. When the questions came, they seemed fewer and less pointed. The barrister was able to use each question as an opportunity to give Oliver Capper's arguments a polite put-down.

Shortly after the lunch break, it was over. The Chief Justice thanked the barristers for their helpful submissions and announced that the court would reserve its decision. The next minute, Jenny was in the foyer with her family, waiting for some final words from Oliver and Viviana. She was numb. It had been a rollercoaster of emotions and she was spent.

'What did you think?' Robert asked.

'Don't know.'

'Good, I think.'

'Not sure what to believe. Didn't like the bald one, I can say that much,' Kate said.

'No, neither did I,' Jenny agreed. 'I didn't like his questions. I don't think he liked Oliver's arguments. But what would I know?'

'Don't be so quick to judge, Mum,' Douglas reassured her. 'No pun intended. But I wouldn't be so sure he hated Oliver's arguments. He might have loved them and only sounded negative to fool the other side into thinking he was being fair.'

'Didn't sound like that to me,' said Robert.

'Here they come.' Jenny moved aside to allow Viviana and Oliver into their ring. 'Well done, Oliver. Thank you so much,' she said with an effort.

'My pleasure, Jenny.'

'I think it went very well, Jenny,' Viviana said.

'I'm not sure about that, Viviana.' Oliver corrected her. 'It went as well as expected. They listened to the argument. They asked all the questions I thought they would. All we can do now is wait.'

'What was that bit about a "brave concession", Oliver?' Douglas asked. It was what everyone wished to know.

'Really, Douglas! Don't be so rude,' Jenny scolded him as if her son were still ten years old. Viviana grimaced like an infant with wind. She thought it had been a weak point in his submissions.

'Look, Mum, I need to know.'

'It's okay, Jenny. It's a fair question,' Oliver replied. 'Douglas, I gave a great deal of consideration to the evidence of our experts in the Asbestos Diseases Tribunal. Judge Byrnes accepted Professor Schaffer's material contribution theory, but the Court of Appeal rejected it out of hand. I think they were right to do so. It made our case look weak to try to convince the High Court that Schaffer's opinion had merit and that he was the only expert who'd got it right. That didn't ring true. All the experts were eminent scientists. It was unlikely that only one had stumbled on the truth. What Professor Schaffer was saying was his personal or idiosyncratic view; it wasn't backed up by science. All the other experts said exposure increased the risk of getting mesothelioma. We'll only win if the High Court thinks a material increase in risk is enough to prove causation in these types of cases. It's why they granted special leave to appeal. So, I made the forensic decision to concede Professor Schaffer only talked about increases in risks, not increases in contributions. I know it may not have sounded like it, but the judges probably appreciated my doing that.'

'I understand,' Douglas said, still frowning.

'Yes, I see now what you're saying,' Jenny said, also frowning.

As they continued to discuss the proceedings, the defendants' team sauntered past. The stylish QC at the head nodded with impeccable good grace and timing as he led them through the revolving glass doors. Bruce Fraser and Jeremy Lawson acknowledged Jenny. The others looked ahead. A thick-set, surly man at the rear grumbled, 'Let's get a bloody drink, I need one after that.'

PART X

Chapter 91

Viviana had warned Jenny that the High Court would take many months to deliver its judgment. 'It might not be until 2005,' Viviana said. Jenny didn't believe her. Why would it take that long? The arguments in court had lasted less than a day.

The seasons changed. Warmth returned to Kiama. The gloom of winter lifted. Jenny felt less oppressed. She never enjoyed days when the clouds hung so low that she thought she would suffocate. It reminded her of England.

She started to do chores around the house. She spent more time outside, bringing the garden back under control. The children visited several times for working bees. The house was painted, gutters cleared, and branches lopped. By the end of spring, Jenny had the property closer to the standard she thought James would have demanded of himself.

She sat on a garden chair in the sunshine with a cup of tea, feeling very pleased with her efforts. Tess sat at her feet, occasionally looking up at her and briefly wagging her tail. Jenny half expected James to come around the corner with some shears or a rake, or pushing the mower, beaming at her with that kind, handsome, honest face of his. 'A cup of tea? Just what I need, Jen,' he would have said, wiping the sweat from his forehead, putting his hat on the back of the chair and washing his hands with the garden hose coiled neatly by the tap.

She missed James almost every day. On some days, the loneliness was like a virus she couldn't shake. It made her ache all over. But life was gradually becoming more bearable. The secret was keeping busy and allowing time to do the rest.

As spring flowed into summer, she became increasingly restless. Why were the judges taking so long? She telephoned Viviana for news, but she knew that she would be the first person contacted when the decision was made. She asked Viviana whether it was a good or bad sign that the court was taking so long. Viviana said it could be either.

Every time Jenny heard the telephone ring, she thought it was Viviana. Her heart would race and her head pound. Then, when she answered and heard the voice of the plumber or the neighbour, she chided herself for being so foolish. She needed to stop panicking every time she heard the phone. She told herself to take a deep breath and then move at a normal pace to answer it. The technique never worked.

Early in December, a heatwave hit Kiama. It was too hot to go on the beach, so Jenny stayed indoors or sat on the verandah to catch what passed as an afternoon breeze. She had to rise early to water the plants. It was sticky and stifling by mid-morning. She didn't normally mind the heat, but this was something different. The temperature was several degrees above the limit of her tolerance. The only positive twist she could put on it was that it wouldn't last. She expected a cool change from the southeast any day. It took its time coming. And when it did, the wind came howling in over the sea, chopping it up into a moiling green and white soup, dragging in from the ocean clouds shaped like the muscular shoulders of a brute. The weather bureau issued gale warnings and the rain bucketed down, heavier than anything she had seen in her life. She watched it all on centre stage, through the windows looking out onto her verandah and beyond.

Douglas telephoned on the morning of the second day of storms to check she hadn't been washed away.

'No, everything seems to be holding up down here,' she assured him. 'No leaks, nothing broken. Just a lot of leaves and twigs on the grass and the verandah.'

'Righto. Well, ring if there's any problem. I might come down to help when it clears.'

'No need.'

'I'll come anyway.'

She accepted the feebleness of her pretending not to require help, but she hated to think she was a burden to her family. The charade had become almost a standing joke.

The telephone rang again. 'Yes, Dougie, what did you forget to tell me?'

'Hello, Jenny, it's Viviana.' Jenny started. Her chest heaved; her throat tightened. She couldn't speak. She knew what was coming. It would be horrible.

'Jenny?'

She swallowed a couple of times. Her mouth felt dry. 'Yes, Viviana, I'm here,' she croaked.

'Are you all right?'

'Yes, fine.'

'Well, Jenny, I have something to tell you.'

'Yes, what is it, dear?'

There was a long pause. Then, 'You won!'

'Viviana! Oh my God, we won!'

'Yes, the decision came down this morning. I didn't want to tell you yesterday that it was being delivered today because I knew you'd get too worried.'

'No, I wouldn't have ... but is it true? I can't believe it! We won!'

'Yes, I haven't read it all yet because it's hot off the press, and very long. But it's a 4:3 decision. Four of the judges agreed with Oliver's arguments and three didn't. And guess what? Justice Gibson, you know, the bald judge, he found in your favour – as well as Chief Justice Lobergeiger,

Justice Farrow and Justice Kleinschmidt, one of the women judges.'

'Oh, Viviana. I don't know what to say. Please thank Oliver for me. And, of course, I thank you very much as well. Thank you so much.'

'I will. I'll pass it on to Ollie. And thank you, Jenny, for allowing me to be your solicitor. It was an honour.'

'Any time. You've been great, Viviana. More than great – brilliant!'

'Let's not take it too far, Jenny. Anyway, I've got to call a few others and read the decision. I'll see you soon.'

After she pushed the 'end' button on her mobile phone, Viviana went into the nearby cafe, 'QC's', to have a coffee and read the judgment. As she turned the pages, she was amazed at how closely the majority judges had followed Oliver's submissions. She had no doubt that James would have felt chuffed at being the man at the heart of such an important decision. She knew also that Jenny's elation would quickly turn to sadness at the thought of James not being alive to hear he had won.

Viviana felt strangely distant from the emotion and conflict the case had produced in her – in everyone. She had no desire to gloat. Poor Bruce, she thought, he'd still become a partner one day. Maybe not at Jacksons. She had a new job to look for herself. She read on, smiling. The majority had written a joint judgment. It was worth re-reading the concluding passages:

In determining the question of causation, it is necessary first to determine whether a defendant's breach of duty was the cause, in fact, of the plaintiff's injury. Put simply, this is a factual question as to whether, in the absence of the defendant's negligence, the injury would have been sustained. This must be satisfied by a plaintiff on the balance of probabilities. Regardless of the answer to the first question on factual causation, it is also always necessary to determine whether it is appropriate for the scope of the defendant's liability to extend to the harm caused to the plaintiff and whether responsibility for the harm should be imposed on the defendant.

Questions of causation are not answered in a legal vacuum, but, rather, they are answered according to the purpose for which the questions are asked and the rule by which responsibility is being attributed. It is not possible to give a commonsense answer to the question of causation unless one understands the purpose and scope of the rule of law being considered. Put another way, the question of causation should be answered in the context of apportioning or allocating responsibility. That purpose, in relation to negligence, is the assignment of liability to one person to pay damages to another rather than in engaging in philosophical or scientific debate, still less casuistry. By allocating responsibility in an individual case, a court sets the standards of conduct that may be expected of other persons in positions analogous to the defendant. This calls for a normative decision whether a defendant ought to be held liable to pay damages for the harm suffered. That normative question involves a decision based on policy considerations. Such considerations, here, should reflect a fundamental purpose of the law as a matter of policy that dangerous, potentially lethal substances like asbestos should not be allowed to be present in such appalling quantities in the workplace.

In the circumstances, we consider that the plaintiff should succeed on policy grounds. Such a result reflects the nature of the correlative rights and duties of an employee and an employer, an employee's right to a safe work environment, and an employer's obligation to ensure that such an environment is created. It also applies to a manufacturer and a user of dangerous products. To find against the plaintiff would not reflect the reasonable expectations of the public in contemporary society. To leave the worker without a remedy, as the normal approach to causation would indicate, would render the duty of the employer useless in the cases where it may be needed most. The function of the law is to enable rights to be vindicated and to provide remedies when duties have been breached. Unless this is done, the duty is a hollow one, stripped of all practical force and content. The same applies to the obligation of a manufacturer to a consumer or user of a product.

The crux of the defendants' argument is that, if the plaintiff's argument is upheld, then an employer or manufacturer may be held liable for damage it has not caused. The risk is greater when not all employers responsible for exposing a plaintiff to asbestos are before the court. This is always likely to be so given the long latency of the disease of mesothelioma and the likelihood that some defendants potentially liable will have gone out of business or disappeared or be resident overseas and unable to be traced. The defendants argue that it would be unjust to impose liability on a party who has not been shown, using orthodox causation principles, to have caused the damage complained of on the balance of probabilities. On the other hand, there is a strong policy argument in favour of compensating those who have suffered grave harm, at the hands of their employers who owe them a duty to protect them against that very harm and fail to do so, when the harm can only have been caused by breach of that duty and when science does not permit the victim accurately to attribute, as between several employers, the precise responsibility for the harm he has suffered. We consider that such injustice as may be involved in imposing liability on a duty-breaking employer in these circumstances is heavily outweighed by the injustice of denying redress to a victim. Otherwise, if a defendant could point to exposure outside of its workplace, then it would obtain a complete immunity against suit for mesothelioma because a plaintiff would never be able to prove precisely which exposure caused his disease. We consider that employers should be liable for an injury squarely within the risk which they created and that they and not the plaintiff should suffer the consequence of the impossibility of proving which exposure or exposures were causative. In the circumstances of this case, and similar cases, a material increase in risk is sufficient for the purpose of causation at law and may be accepted as satisfying the requirement of a sufficient causal link. We again consider this reasoning to be applicable to manufacturers of dangerous goods like asbestos cement.

We leave for another day the question whether a defendant held to be so liable obtains any discount for the aliquot increase in risk caused by exposure to asbestos by defendants not sued by the plaintiff.

Chapter 92

On the weekend after the High Court handed down its judgment, Viviana and Oliver paid a 'surprise' visit to Jenny. It may have been a surprise to Jenny, but it had been carefully planned with her children as a celebration of the victory. Robert told Jenny he was coming down to help clean up the debris from the recent storms. Jenny expected him and his wife, but not the whole tribe and certainly not her lawyers. If anything, she expected more reporters. The day after the decision, she had been on the front page of The Telegraph:

WIDOW WINS IN HIGH COURT
An exclusive by Bruce Graham

Kiama woman, Jenny Henderson, won a landmark decision in the High Court on behalf of her late husband, James, who was exposed to asbestos by Henry King Industries and V&L decades ago. Her lawyer, Mr Gary Shaw (see photo), said the decision was the most important in this country in relation to causation and would help hundreds of asbestos victims receive compensation in the future.

The story proceeded to talk about Shaw & Fletcher rather than Jenny's case. It was accompanied by a photograph of Gary Shaw in front of some law books. There was also a small, blurred photograph of Belinda

Byrnes in ceremonial robes. Under the photo was the caption 'Judge Byrnes – got it right.'

In the days that followed the decision, Jenny became somewhat of a celebrity in Kiama. People congratulated her when she walked along the beach, said 'Well done' at the shops and dropped friendly notes in the letterbox. She was the subject of a small article in the local paper, The Kiama Kourier, which, at her request, included one of her favourite photographs of James, the one with his foot up on the tyre of a flatbed truck.

◆

Robert and his family were the first to arrive on Saturday morning. Jenny had barely had time to say hello to them when Douglas and Kate appeared in line down the driveway.

'What's this?' Jenny asked Robert. 'What have you been doing behind my back?'

'Nothing much. Well, maybe a little,' he said, grinning.

'Hi, Mum,' Douglas said. 'Congratulations!' His daughter, Harriet, rushed up to her grandmother and jumped into her arms. 'Hello, Grandma,' she said, runny nose and dribbling mouth wrapped up in Jenny's skirt.

'Hello, my dear, what a surprise seeing you here today!' She released the child slowly and blotted the damp patch with her handkerchief.

'Daddy says you're having a party.'

'Does he? It certainly looks like it, doesn't it?'

'There's another car, Grandma,' she said, pointing to a black Mercedes cornering sedately into the driveway.

'What's going on?' Jenny demanded of her children.

'It's a surprise party to celebrate your victory – to celebrate Dad's victory,' Kate said, giving her mother a hug.

'That's very kind of you, but how many are coming? Any more and they'll be backed up the road blocking the traffic. And who's that in the Mercedes?' Jenny screwed up her eyes, trying to penetrate the dazzling reflection from the windscreen. 'It's not … it is!' she exclaimed. At the top of the drive, Viviana waved as she and Oliver stepped out of the car.

'Hello!' Viviana shouted to Jenny. Oliver opened the boot and soon he and Viviana were carrying bottles of wine and a hamper of food towards her.

'What do you think you're doing here?'

'Surprised, Jenny?'

'Yes.'

'Well, your son, here, thought it would be a good idea if we came down to see you and celebrate the big win.' She glanced towards Robert to identify the guilty party. 'But if you'd like us to go, then that's fine too.'

'No, you can definitely stay.' Jenny laughed as they embraced.

She then stepped back to evaluate her solicitor. There was less makeup. Her hair was tied behind her neck, loose enough to allow it to fall forwards at the sides to frame her radiant face. She wore a summer dress, patterned with blue, mauve, pink and white flowers, nipped in at the waist. No stockings. White, slightly raised sandals. Oliver, beside her, watched Jenny's inspection with amusement. She appeared satisfied. 'Viviana, you look so...'

'Happy?' Viviana volunteered.

'Yes, that too. I was going to say "different".'

'Different and happy. I'll accept that. So long as you don't mean I look weird or something like that.'

'Of course not, dear. It's simply that I've never seen you in a dress like that before.'

'Well, it's not appropriate for court or conferences with clients, is it? I don't get an opportunity to wear nice dresses much.'

'More's the pity. You look fantastic, dear. I hope you get to wear outfits like this more often.'

'I guess I will be, Jenny. Now that I've resigned from Shaw & Fletcher.'

'Really? Good for you. What are you going to be doing?'

'Well, Ollie's encouraging me to go to the Bar, but I'm not so sure. I'll think about it.'

'I'm sure Oliver will look after you.'

'Naturally,' Oliver said, smiling at her.

Douglas soon had the barbecue going and the meat cooking. Viviana helped Jenny unpack the hamper in the kitchen. Kate bustled around with a platter of hors d'oeuvres. It soon became clear that Douglas had inherited something from his father – an unwavering ability to burn sausages and overcook the steak.

The burned offerings consumed, Robert filled the champagne flutes he'd brought down from Sydney. He poured lemonade into the children's plastic cups. When they were all full, he raised his glass to the gathering. 'Here's to Mum and Dad for their victory in the High Court and to Viviana and Oliver for their hard work in making it all possible!'

'Hear, hear!'

'To Mum and Dad!'

'Thanks, Viviana!'

'Well done, Oliver!'

'Mum, do you want to say anything?' Robert asked.

'Yes, I do, Robbie. First of all, thank you for this wonderful surprise. It really was unnecessary. Viviana and Oliver know already how grateful I am for their efforts in making this possible. But thank you, again!' She lifted her flute to them, glinting shards of light refracting through the glass. 'When this whole thing started, I was very reluctant for James and me to get involved with the law. I urged James to leave it alone. And as you know, I came very close to throwing in the towel. I'm happy I decided to fight on. James would have wanted me to do that. He would never have given up.' Jenny's lips began to quiver. Her voice wobbled, her words fragmented. Douglas, standing nearby, reached out and held her hand. 'James was my whole life. He gave me so many years of happiness. I loved him ... I love him with all my heart. This victory is for my James, my dear James.' Jenny lowered her head and sobbed.

Douglas moved closer and held her. 'To Dad!' he proposed. 'To James!'

Everyone raised their glasses again. Most of the children, having finished their lemonade, lifted empty plastic cups, looking around for guidance from their parents. Silence fell on the group as Jenny wept quietly into the embrace of her son.

'If I may, I'd like to say a few things,' Oliver Capper said, breaking the tension.

'Sure, Oliver. Go ahead.'

'Thanks. I want to say that this has been the most important case in my career. I would like to thank Viviana for giving me this opportunity and Jenny for having the courage to take it on. I know this decision will help many other victims to obtain justice against those companies that exposed them to asbestos dust. Jenny, many people will forever be in your debt, and your husband's debt. You should never forget that.'

Jenny raised her head and smiled at Oliver. 'Thank you,' she said softly. She dabbed her eyes and blew her nose.

'You okay, Mum?' Douglas asked.

'Yes, I'll be fine, dear.' She looked at her guests watching her and laughed. 'I'm okay, everyone. Don't look so worried. But if it's okay, I might go for a short walk on the beach. I need a bit of a break.'

'Do you want one of us to go with you?'

'No, it's fine. Tess will come with me.' At the sound of her name, the dog emerged from under the table where she'd been scrounging for scraps. 'You all stay here. I'll be back in half an hour or so. I'm not used to having a lot of people around. Come on, Tess.' She walked down the stairs and along the path to the beach, Tess bounding ahead.

After she removed her sandals, Jenny found the dry sand at the top of the beach too hot to walk on. She tiptoed as quickly as she could to the darker sand closer to the water's edge, then slowed into a comfortable stride, her small feet leaving imprints that were quickly erased by the advancing ripples. In front of her, a seagull scuttled away from Tess with businesslike haste, while further up the beach, another dog barked at a stick floating in the sea, uncertain whether to dash in to retrieve it. A young couple sat on a colourful turquoise towel above the high-tide line, gazing at the waves through stylish sunglasses, their wet hair swept back, their arms about each other's shoulders. Two young lovers, wrapped up in each other.

Jenny knew that feeling. She had experienced it many times with James. She had lost him, but not those memories. They would never leave her. She could draw on them whenever she wished. He would always be with her.

She could still picture him at her side, walking along this stretch of sand. What was he saying? Where was he skipping off to? Bedraggled, happy, alive from a dip in the ocean. She could sense his vigorous, vital energy just as truly as she felt the wind blowing grains of sand about her shins, and the cool lap of the water on her feet. If she squinted and peered into the haze, she could convince herself his lithe body was walking up ahead in his frayed navy trunks, waving enthusiastically for her to catch up so he could show her something interesting, ensuring she didn't miss out on seeing what he'd discovered, on being with him at every important moment.

'Jen, look at this! Look at this shell!' He pointed to a brown-and-pink cowrie, smooth, uncracked, the size of her fist. 'It's wonderful, James,' she said. 'A real beauty.'

'Just like you, Jen,' he said, grinning like an adolescent remembering his first kiss.

She let his voice echo within her. His glowing face filled her mind as she turned and headed back home. They'd be starting to worry about her. 'Come on, Tess, old girl, back we go!'

Where the beach poked a tongue of sand into the brush to form a path to the house, Douglas and his children were waiting for her. She waved to them, hand up as high as possible to make sure they saw her. 'Here I am!' she yelled. 'Here I am!'

And then pain. 'Aahh!' She quickly pulled her arm down and stopped, doubling over, holding her chest. Douglas and the children ran to her. 'What's wrong, Mum?' he asked.

She straightened, the pain easing. 'I think I've torn a muscle waving. How silly. I really am getting old!'

'You sure you're okay?'

'Of course. It's gone now. Well, almost. I suppose it's pretty easy to do things like this when you get to my age.'

'Okay, then. Coffee and tea are about to be served. Easy kids,' he said as his children hugged Jenny, preventing her from moving, 'Grandma's very precious.'

◆

The adults were sitting around the table on the deck, but most of the children were in the garden, kicking and throwing a beach ball, laughing and yelling and turning somersaults on the lawn. 'Hello, Grandma!' they shouted when Jenny reappeared on the balcony.

'Hello, dears!' she called, waving back at them.

'It's certainly a beautiful day. You're very lucky living down here,' said Viviana.

'It's what James and I planned for. We thought it was a magical spot as soon as we saw it,' Jenny said, sitting down next to Robert. 'Of course, there are a lot more people here now than when we first came down for a family camping holiday.'

Jenny leaned back in her chair, cradling her cup of tea. She could feel James near her. As if he'd accompanied her back from the beach. She closed her eyes, imagining the two of them sitting silently together, enjoying the breeze through the trees and the wash and crash of the ocean. Emerging from her reverie, she smiled warmly at the faces of her family and friends, reassuring them. 'I'm okay, don't look so concerned. It's been an emotional day. I was just remembering all the wonderful times I had here with James. And now I plan to have many more, even though I dearly wish he was here to share them.'

They smiled and sipped from their cups, relieved that Jenny had regained a spark of happiness.

Robert's youngest child, wee James, burst onto the deck, covered in grass and sweat. 'Grandma, Grandma! Can we play with the sprinkler?'

'Yes, can we, Grandma?' little Stephanie joined in.

'Of course, you can.'

'Jamie, you're getting grass all over Grandma,' Robert reproached his son.

'Don't worry. It'll brush off.'

'Let's go, Grandma.' James reached out and grabbed Jenny's hand. Stephanie grabbed the other one. Together they tugged and pulled her to her feet.

'Aahh!' The pain came back, piercing right through her, and halting her in her tracks. Stephanie immediately let go, but James, oblivious, kept on pulling and nearly dragged her over in his excitement.

'James! Let go!' shouted Robert.

When he saw his grandmother hunched over, her face contorted, her hands clutching her chest, James started crying. His mother quickly scooped him up and tried to hush him.

'What is it, Mum?' Kate asked. She and Douglas rushed around to Jenny's side of the table.

Robert put his arms out gingerly to support her. 'Mum, what's wrong? Should I call the doctor? Are you okay?'

Jenny looked up, frightened, her face ashen. Everyone could see her fear. It burst out at them. They looked at her aghast as the children continued to wail.

With a shudder, Jenny inhaled deeply, trying to stop the panic. A sharp, lacerating pain at the bottom of her ribcage took her breath away. In a heartbeat, she knew what it was. She recalled how James had described it as broken glass in his chest. Yes, that was what it was like, she thought. It was as if shards of glass were scratching the inside of her chest, tearing it, making it raw, making it bleed.

The panic rose like a wave before her. Rearing up, a rolling black wall, coming straight at her. She was soon going to be under. This time, she knew she would be taken. There would be no escape, crawling up the sand to firmer ground. There was no point in even trying. It was going to take her.

And she was scared. She had seen what it could do.

Viviana, her eyes welling with tears, looked at Jenny. She saw the terror. She understood what was happening. She knew what had suddenly started inside the chest of her friend.

References

1. *Fairchild v Glenhaven Funeral Services Ltd* [2003] 1 AC 32.
2. *Barker v Corus (UK) plc* [2006] UKHL 20.
3. *Baldwin (EM) & Son Pty Ltd v Plane* [1999] Aust Torts Rep 81-499.
4. *Bendix Mintex Pty Ltd v Barnes* (1997) 42 NSWLR 307.
5. *Chappel v Hart* (1998) 195 CLR 232.
6. *Environment Agency (Formerly National Rivers Authority) v Empress Car Co (Abertillery) Ltd* [1999] 2 AC 22.
7. *Wallaby Grip (BAE) Pty Ltd v MacLeay Area Health Service* (1998) 17 NSWCCR 355.
8. *Wintle v Conaust (Vic) Pty Ltd* [1989] VR 951.
9. *Hunter v John Meagher & Bryce Clover t/as Meagher & Clover* DDT No 41 of 1990. Transcript pages 211–340.
10. ERA Mereweather & CW Price, 'Report on Effects of Asbestos Dust on the Lungs and Dust Suppression in the Asbestos Industry' (1930) HM Stationery Office.
11. Waldemar C Dreessen et al, 'A Study of Asbestosis in the Asbestos Textile Industry' (1938) United States Government Printing Office.
12. Cecil G Roberts & Harry M Whaite, Studies in Industrial Hygiene No. 24. 'A Survey of Dust Exposure and Lung Disease in the Asbestos-Cement Industry in New South Wales' (1956) New South Wales Department of Health.
13. Wagner JC et al, 'Diffuse pleural mesothelioma and asbestos exposure in the North Western Cape Province', *British Journal of Industrial Medicine* (1960) 17: 260–271.
14. McNulty JC, 'Malignant pleural mesothelioma in an asbestos worker', *Medical Journal of Australia* (1962) 953-4.

15. Muriel Newhouse & Hilda Thompson, 'Mesothelioma of pleura and peritoneum following exposure to asbestos in the London area', *British Journal of Industrial Medicine* (1965) 22: 261–6.

16. Harold E Whipple (ed), 'Biological effects of asbestos', *Annals of the New York Academy of Sciences* (1965) 132: 1–766.

17. Newhouse, ML & Berry, G, 'Predictions of mortality from mesothelial tumours in asbestos factory workers', *British Journal of Industrial Medicine* (1976) 33: 147–51.

18. Berry, G, 'Prediction of mesothelioma, lung cancer, and asbestosis in former Wittenoom asbestos workers', *British Journal of Industrial Medicine* (1991) 48: 793–802.

19. Morgan RW, 'Whodunnit: Liability for mesothelioma cases', *Journal of Occupational Medicine* (1991) 33: 956–7.

20. Peto, J, Seidman H, Selikoff IJ, 'Mesothelioma mortality in asbestos workers: implications for models of carcinogenesis and risk assessment', *British Journal of Industrial Medicine* (1982) 45: 12435.

21. Doll, R, 'Mortality from lung cancer in asbestos workers', *British Journal of Industrial Medicine* (1955) 12: 81-6.

22. Seidman H, Selikoff IJ, Gelb SK, 'Mortality experience of amosite asbestos factory workers: dose-response relationships 5 to 40 years after onset of short-term work exposure', *American Journal of Industrial Medicine* (1986) 10: 479–514.

23. Hammond EC, Selikoff IJ, Seidman H, 'Asbestos exposure, cigarette smoking, and death rates', *Annals of the New York Academy of Sciences* (1979) 330: 473–90.

24. National Health and Medical Research Council, 'Code for the Handling of Asbestos by Small Users' (June 1978) Reprinted from the report of the 85th session of the council, Australian Government Publishing Service, Canberra.

25. NHMRC, 'Health Hazards Associated with the use of Asbestos in the Construction Industry' (1979) Australian Government Printing Office, Canberra.

Acknowledgments

I would like to thank the many men and women who have fought for justice for themselves and their friends, families and colleagues over many years as victims of asbestos exposure. They have only been able to achieve justice through the dedication, commitment and advocacy of plaintiff lawyers many of whom I have worked with or against over the years. It is relentless and stressful work. It is also a privilege to be allowed into another person's life or home and to observe first-hand the real trauma they are put through in the medical system and during litigation.

I would never have been able to see for myself the ordeal these people go through or to understand what was known about asbestos and the diseases it can cause without the opportunity I was given when I changed careers from medicine to law. I particularly wish to thank Mark Knight and the lawyers I worked with at Arthur Robinson & Hedderwicks (now Allens> <Linklaters), Peter Hobday and Maryjane Crabtree.

I would also like to thank my master, Tom Wodak, for imparting (or trying to impart) his considerable wisdom and common sense when I became a barrister.

This work could not have been written without all the experiences I have had as a lawyer. I thank everyone I have opposed or worked with or appeared before in giving me such a rich experience.

Finally, I wish to thank my wife, Helen, and my children for the personal sacrifices they have made to ensure my career prospered. I am always in your debt.